ORACLES OF DELPHI KEEP

THE CURSE OF DEADMAN'S FOREST

VICTORIA LAURIE

A YEARLING BOOK

Text copyright © 2010 by Victoria Laurie
Cover art copyright © 2010 by Antonio Javier Caparo
All rights reserved. Published in the United States by Yearling, an imprint of Random House Children's Books, a division of Random House, Inc., New York. Originally published in hardcover by Delacorte Press, an imprint of Random House Children's Books, New York, in 2010.

Yearling and the jumping horse design are registered trademarks of Random House, Inc.

Visit us on the Web! www.randomhouse.com/kids
Educators and librarians, for a variety of teaching tools, visit us at www.randomhouse.com/teachers

The Library of Congress has cataloged the hardcover edition of this work as follows:
Laurie, Victoria.
The curse of Deadman's Forest / Victoria Laurie. — 1st ed.
p. cm. — (Oracles of Delphi Keep)
Summary: According to prophecy, a trip through the magical portal near the Dover, England, orphanage where Ian and Theo live will bring them to the third Oracle, a child with extraordinary healing powers to help defeat a great evil, but it will also lead to Ian's death.
ISBN 978-0-385-73573-5 (hc) — ISBN 978-0-385-90562-6 (glb)
ISBN 978-0-375-89649-1 (ebook)
[1. Oracles—Fiction. 2. Prophecies—Fiction. 3. Orphans—Fiction. 4. Brothers and sisters—Fiction. 5. Space and time—Fiction. 6. Dover (England)—History—20th century—Fiction. 7. Great Britain—History—1936–1945—Fiction.] I. Title.
PZ7.L372792 Cu 2010   [Fic]—dc22   2010008424

ISBN 978-0-440-42259-4 (pbk.)

Printed in the United States of America
10 9 8 7 6 5 4 3 2 1
First Yearling Edition 2011

For my grandparents,
Carl and Ruth Laurie

THE CRONE

City of Phoenicia 1331 BC

The great Phoenician Oracle Laodamia stood, pensive and troubled, on the terrace overlooking her garden. It was a warm summer night, but a shiver snaked its way down her spine.

She'd had another nightmare, the same nightmare, in fact, that had haunted her for weeks. And try as she might, she could not escape the terrible jumble of images that always began with four beautiful maidens being lured belowground by the underworld god Demogorgon, then ended with a massive conflict involving machinery and weaponry too fantastic to believe.

One thing was certain: if these visions of war and destruction were a portrait of the future—as Laodamia suspected they were—mankind was most assuredly doomed.

But what her role in all this was, Laodamia could not fathom. Even though she'd spent many a night worrying and wondering how she could possibly prevent what she knew was to come, the answers always eluded her. And that night was no different. The soft breeze and soothing flower scents wafting up from her garden brought her no new clarity. With a heavy sigh, she turned to go back to her bed, but as she was about to walk away from her terrace, a movement in the shadows caused her to jump.

"Do not be alarmed," called a voice from her garden.

"Who's there?" demanded the Oracle.

A shadowy hooded figure hobbled forward to stand in the faint light of the moon just below her balcony. "I mean you no harm," said the stranger. "I'm just an old crone begging the great Oracle for a brief audience."

Suspicious at first, Laodamia squinted at the intruder, but when the figure pulled back her hood and lifted her face for inspection, the Oracle could see she really was just an old woman. "Come back in the morning," Laodamia said gently. "I will have some bread and wine to share with you, old one, and then I will look into your future."

She had spoken with kindness, so Laodamia was shocked when the crone began to laugh softly. "It is not *my* future that concerns me, Oracle," she said. "It is yours."

A cold prickle curled along Laodamia's skin and for a moment she did not respond. Instead, she used her intuitive powers to assess the woman below. She knew immediately that the old woman meant her no harm, but she also had the sense that even given this late hour, she should grant the woman an audience. "Very well," she said at last. "I will come to you on that bench." The Oracle pointed to a beautifully carved stone chaise placed in the center of her magnificent garden.

Laodamia lit a lantern and carried it with her to meet the crone, who was patiently waiting on the bench when she arrived. The light cast eerie shadows in the wrinkles of the stranger's face. She appeared ancient and Laodamia couldn't help staring at her. The crone chuckled again, as if reading the Oracle's thoughts. Laodamia quickly dropped her eyes to her lap and apologized. "Forgive me, old one, but your face suggests a very long life."

This seemed to delight the crone. "Yes," she said, her voice raspy and dry with age. "I have lived far longer than I should have. And I shall not soon die, Oracle, which is even sadder still."

Laodamia regarded the woman again, puzzled by such a statement, but as it was the middle of the night and she was weary, she thought it best to get to the heart of the matter. "How may I assist you?" she asked.

The crone studied the Oracle for a long moment before speaking, and when she did, her voice was soft as a whisper. "I know of what you dream," she said.

Laodamia was startled by the statement and quickly dismissed it. She'd told no one what she'd been dreaming for the past month. Even though many of her attendants had sensed her fatigue and unease, she'd always covered it by suggesting that she was worn out from all the festivities surrounding her upcoming wedding. She attempted to cover yet again in front of the old crone. "I've been dreaming of my beloved," she said coyly. "Surely you've heard the talk of our impending marriage?"

The crone's face registered disappointment. "Do you

take me for a fool, Oracle?" she asked pointedly. Laodamia's eyes widened. She was shocked by the impoliteness of the question, but before she could answer, the crone added, "I know where your dreams begin, in a cave with four maidens. I also know that your dreams end in a war that will decide the fate of man."

Laodamia gasped and her hand fluttered to her chest. "How could you know that?" she demanded. "I've told no one!"

The crone's smile returned. "I know what I know. But your role has not yet been revealed to you, has it, Oracle?"

Laodamia sat speechless next to the crone. It was as if the old woman were again reading her mind.

The crone took her silence for confirmation and chuckled. "I am here to reveal your part. It begins with a gift."

Laodamia recovered her voice. "A gift?"

Instead of answering her directly, the crone reached into the folds of her cloak and withdrew a small crystal. The lantern's light caught the stone, and small rainbows of color shimmered and bounced off it as the old woman cupped it in her gnarled hand and held it out to the Oracle. "Take this," she said without further explanation.

Laodamia looked closely at the beautiful object the woman was offering her. "Oh, but I couldn't, old one," she protested. "The gem appears far too precious for you to part with so easily. Surely you could trade it for food and lodging for yourself?" she suggested, noting the poor woman's ragged clothing and thin appearance.

4

The crone ignored the suggestion and placed the crystal into Laodamia's palm. "It is yours for the time being," she said. "And I've a feeling this gem will come back to me one day. An orphaned child of immense importance will return it to me when the hour of need is great. But for now, it is yours to use, then give away as you see fit."

Laodamia stared with wonder at the beautiful gem in her palm. "Exactly how am I to use this?"

Again the crone ignored the Oracle's question and instead got to her feet and began to shuffle away. "I must be off to see about my daughter."

"Your daughter?" asked Laodamia, and in that moment her intuitive powers detected a great sadness from the crone and she had a vision of a burial. "I'm so sorry for your loss, old one," she said gently.

The crone stopped moving and regarded Laodamia over her shoulder. The glint in her eyes held a mixture of emotions, from guilt to sadness to resignation, but the old woman did not comment further. Instead, she merely nodded and began to shuffle away again.

"Wait!" called Laodamia, getting up and moving toward the crone. "May I at least offer you a soft bed and a meal in the morning?"

But the crone waved her hand dismissively and continued on her mission.

Laodamia tried one last time to engage the old woman. "May I at least know the name of the one who has offered me such kindness?" she asked.

At this the crone paused and turned to look back at the

Oracle. "It is of no consequence," she said. "And I shall not bother you again. Use the crystal, Oracle. It will help direct you in your purpose." And with that, the crone disappeared into the shadows of the night.

Laodamia blinked in surprise. She'd been watching the crone one moment, and in the next the old woman had completely vanished.

Mystified by the encounter, the Oracle returned to the bench and sat down to study the crystal the old woman had given her. The gem was warm, and as she held it close to the lantern, she could see the smallest sliver of pink at its core. Laodamia could identify nearly every mineral known to man but she'd never come across one quite like this.

She was, however, adept at pulling out the energy of a crystal and discovering its secrets, so with little hesitation, she eased her awareness into the stone, seeking the treasures it might hold.

The next thing she knew, she was being roughly shaken. Laodamia blinked as sunlight sparkled through her half-closed lids. "Mia?" said a familiar voice, filled with concern. "Mia, please talk to me."

With effort Laodamia tried to wake herself from an unconscious state that felt much deeper than sleep. After a moment she stared up at her beloved in confusion. "Iyoclease?" she said. "What are you doing here?"

"By Zeus!" whispered Iyoclease, hugging her close. "I came the moment your servant told me you were found in the garden and they could not rouse you. I've been calling to you for many minutes, trying to bring you out of your trance."

Laodamia pushed away from him a bit and looked up in astonishment. "What's happened?" she asked as he lifted her carefully to carry her inside.

"You tell me," he said, his face gentle and kind.

"We found you lying by the bench," explained someone walking next to Iyoclease. Laodamia looked over and was relieved to see one of her most faithful apprentices, Adria.

And suddenly, it all came back to her in a flood. When she saw the position of the sun, Laodamia realized she'd been in some sort of trance since the night before, and remembered the things she'd seen during that time.

As Iyoclease laid her gently on her bed and smoothed back her hair, she knew with an absolute certainty what she must do. The crone had been right; the crystal had indeed clarified her role. "Iyoclease," she said urgently while he placed several pillows under her head.

"Shhh, my love," he whispered. "I've sent for one of the healers. You should rest until she comes."

"No!" she protested, gripping his arm. He looked at her in alarm but made no move to pull away. "Please," she begged him. "I do not need a healer. I need parchment and my stylus. I have a prophecy that must be recorded." The Oracle was afraid she might forget some of the messages that had come through her encounter with the crystal, and she was desperate to write them down.

"Mia," Iyoclease said gently, sitting down next to her. "This is no time for prophecy writing."

But Laodamia was insistent and eventually the writing materials were brought to her. Before she began to recount her terrible visions and the mission she was about to embark upon, however, she reached out to her betrothed and placed the crystal into his palm. "Here," she whispered to him. "Take it."

He looked at the pretty stone, with its unusual heat, and asked, "Is this some new charm to keep me safe?"

Laodamia shook her head, recalling the visions that had come to her and the gemstone's important role in them. "No, my love. It is for your sister. You must have Adria make it into a sturdy necklace for her to wear."

Iyoclease laughed. "Mia," he said, "if you are thinking of giving it to Pelopia, Selyena will surely fight her for it. Perhaps I should cut it in half so neither feels slighted?"

Laodamia clutched at Iyoclease's chest in horror. "No! Iyoclease, you must let no harm come to this gem. And it is to be given to your youngest sister, Jacinda."

Iyoclease appeared unsettled by his betrothed's urgent request. "Mia," he said in a soothing tone, "Jacinda would lose it. She's far too young to entrust with something so obviously precious to you."

But Laodamia merely shook her head and insisted that he give it to Jacinda to care for. "It must go to her and no other," she said, knowing that for the gem to fall into another's hand would irrevocably alter the future. "Promise me you will see to it that she alone receives it and instruct her that she must wear it always?"

"Of course," he said, wrapping her hand in his. "Yes, my

love, I will do as you ask. But tell me why it must go to my baby sister of all people."

"She is the only soul who can deliver it to the Guardian," Laodamia said, already reaching for the stylus and blank parchment on her bed.

"The Guardian?" Iyoclease repeated.

"Yes," said Laodamia. "I've seen it in my visions. Jacinda will entrust it to the Guardian, who will in turn give it to the One."

Iyoclease's face clearly showed his confusion. "And who is this One, Mia?"

"The greatest Oracle who will ever live, and the only one who can save mankind."

Iyoclease continued to look at her with concern. "I thought *you* were the greatest Oracle who ever lived."

But Laodamia simply shook her head. "No," she said, her voice barely more than a whisper as she considered the raw power she'd felt from the One in her visions. "There is a gentle but profoundly intuitive soul, yet to be born, with far greater powers than I have. One who will be called upon to save the world from an unspeakable evil. But first I must write about the Guardian," she mused.

"The Guardian?" Iyoclease asked again.

Laodamia nodded distractedly. "Yes," she said. "Only the Guardian can protect the One long enough to gather the others. They will all be needed, you see. And I must write to tell the Guardian and the One how and where to find each of the others."

"Are you quite sure you wouldn't rather rest?" her betrothed asked.

Laodamia smiled at him, caught once more by the beauty of his face and his vivid blue eyes. "Yes, my love, I'm sure."

Iyoclease got up from the bed and regarded her. "Is there anything else that I can do for you before I go, Mia?"

Laodamia looked up from the first words she was already writing on the parchment. "Yes, please," she said earnestly. "You may find a man named Phaios. You will discover him in the market, selling small trinkets. There is a sundial that he has recently acquired. He is about to discover that the dial does not work and will be anxious to be rid of it. I must have that dial, Iyoclease."

He smiled at her and leaned in to kiss her on the forehead. "Then you shall have it," he assured her, and off he went to find his betrothed her treasure.

THE DIAL

Dover, England, July 1939

I an Wigby sat deep in thought at the top of the stone steps of a creepy old tower in his home at Delphi Keep. The keep was an orphanage located in the village of Dover, England, that had the supreme good fortune of having the kindly Earl of Kent as its patron. Downstairs, Ian could hear the chatter, giggles, and roughhousing that were commonplace within such a large orphanage. But that day he wasn't in the mood for fun and games, because he was far more interested in the small bronze sundial he was turning over and over in his hand.

Ian knew that at first glance, this ancient relic hardly seemed worth a second look, unless one considered that it had been discovered in a silver box buried deep in a cave in Morocco amid the largest pile of treasure Ian had ever seen. But what was even *more* remarkable was that the silver box containing the sundial had been intended for Ian all along, bequeathed to him three thousand years earlier by the most powerful Oracle ever to have come out of ancient Greece. Laodamia of Phoenicia had a special quest for Ian and his surrogate sister, Theo, that involved nothing less than saving the world from a tragic and rather abrupt end.

Ian had already become quite familiar with some of Laodamia's other prophecies, which foretold of a time when mankind would be brought to the edge of its own destruction by a massive military conflict involving all the great powers of the world. This war would cost millions and millions of souls their very lives, and this massive devastation would nurture, feed, and make ever more powerful the vile underworld god, Demogorgon.

Ian knew the ancient legend of Demogorgon, which held that he had long before been imprisoned in the underworld by his jealous siblings, and ever since, the evil deity had been plotting his revenge.

Ian was also painfully aware that Demogorgon had set the seeds of his escape thousands of years before Ian's birth, during the time of the Druids, when the underworld god had lured four innocent maidens deep belowground and returned them some months later all heavy with child. One demigod had been born to each of the maidens, who were said to have perished giving birth to their beastly children.

But Demogorgon's offspring had survived and even thrived, and legend further held that all were bound by blood to serve their evil father in his quest for escape. To that end, Demogorgon had bequeathed each of his children command over one of the four elements: To his son, Magus, Demogorgon had given the power of fire. His three daughters, Caphiera, Atroposa, and Lachestia, ruled water, air, and earth in turn.

Over the many millennia since their birth, the four demigods had grown into powerful sorcerers. And according to *everything* Ian had read about them, they were a despicable and deadly lot indeed.

Laodamia's prophecies had also revealed that in return for their loyalty and servitude, Demogorgon had promised his offspring that once he was free, he would strengthen their powers a hundredfold, and each would receive one quarter of the world to rule over as he or she saw fit. Ian knew that if that happened, so volatile were the sorcerers that no living creature would survive their rule for long.

And yet, in the midst of all this doom and gloom, there was hope. According to Laodamia, one thing could stand against the combined forces of Magus, Caphiera, Atroposa, and Lachestia; a group of seven orphans, each imbued with a unique and powerful metaphysical gift, could form a united front and defeat the demigods, thus keeping Demogorgon imprisoned for eternity. The trick, Ian knew, was locating all of these special children in time.

This was the heart of the quest Laodamia had set out for Ian some three thousand years earlier. And the young man of nearly fourteen still found it astonishing to be at the center of such an important mission, which he'd never wanted but could hardly turn down, even though the thought of failure and the resulting consequences terrified him.

Still, he had found some encouragement in the rhyming prophecies and magical items Laodamia had left for him in her small treasure boxes, which she'd hidden in various places all about the world. He knew that the Oracle had left him one box for each orphan he was supposed to find, but the boxes weren't together and finding them was nearly as difficult as locating the orphans.

The first box Ian had discovered quite by accident a year earlier in his own village of Dover. It had contained an aged replica of the handwritten map he'd drawn and kept under his pillow, detailing the many tunnels that ran below his home and Castle Dover. It was an exact copy, with the notable exception that it indicated where a magical portal was located near Castle Dover.

The first box had also yielded a prophecy from Laodamia, which had revealed their overall mission and suggested that Theo was the first of seven special orphans, or Oracles. Additionally, the prophecy had instructed them to find the second box and the next Oracle by going through the portal.

It took Ian and his companions a bit to figure out how to use the portal, but eventually they had discovered themselves through it and, to their immense surprise, in the quite foreign land of Morocco. After a harrowing adventure, the group had eventually returned with the second Oracle, a young boy named Jaaved, and two other very special gifts meant to aid him on his quests. Around his neck Ian wore a piece of the Star of Lixus—an enchanted five-point opal that gave its bearer command over any language ever spoken. And in his hand was the rather unassuming sundial made of tarnished bronze. Ian was not fooled by the casual nature of the relic. He knew that it held a magical secret, and when one considered who had sent it and for what purpose, well, it was easy to see why the sundial was likely to be quite extraordinary indeed.

But he still couldn't fathom what he was supposed to do with it. He knew it was important. Laodamia's riddle—also found in the box, next to the dial—told him so. But what magical power it held, he had yet to discover.

And this frustrated Ian no end, because try as he might to figure it out, the sundial didn't appear to work. Whenever Ian held it up to a source of light, like the sun or a lamp, no shadow formed across the face of the dial; instead, its surface remained unaffected, which, as far as he knew, defied the laws of physics.

So it was with a scowl that Ian stared at the small bronze relic in his hand, wondering how to unlock its secrets, when the door at the bottom of the steps opened wide and someone from below called, "Ian? You up there, mate?"

Ian started. "Yeah, Carl. I'm up here."

"Oy, Theo! I found him!" Ian heard his best friend say.

This was followed by a flurry of footfalls as three children rushed up the stairs. "We were wondering where you'd gone off to," Carl said as he reached the landing and promptly came over to sit down next to Ian.

"I told you he'd be up here," Theo said with a smug smile. Ian grinned back. There was no hiding from Theo.

"Trying to work the dial again?" asked Jaaved, the boy they'd brought back from Morocco. He'd settled in very nicely at the orphanage.

"Yeah, but it's no use." Ian scowled. "I can't get it to cast a shadow."

Theo crouched down in front of Ian, her eyes alight with mischief. "So leave it and come with us to the shore!"

Ian couldn't help smiling at her. "The shore, eh?" He knew she'd had enough of caverns and tunnels on their dark adventure the year before. Lately, she'd preferred the wide-open space of the shore.

"Yes!" Theo replied. "It's a lovely day and Madam Dimbleby gave us permission to walk down to the water as long as all our morning chores are done. Jaaved's even promised to find me a trinket." Jaaved was very sensitive to minerals and crystals, and since he'd made the keep his home, he'd returned from the shore on more than one occasion with a lost ring or a pocket watch—once even a diamond broach.

Ian glanced over his shoulder out the window at the beautiful summer day and was strongly tempted to say yes. His eyes moved back to the sundial, however, and he sighed. "I'd like that, Theo, but I think I'll stick with this for now and try to work out the prophecy."

Theo pouted. "I've told you over and over, Ian: Laodamia's riddle won't produce a single clue until the time is right."

"Yes," Ian agreed, knowing that his remarkably intuitive sister was likely correct. "But still, I rather think I'm close to working parts of her prophecy out. I just need a bit more time to sort it through."

Theo sighed and stood up. "Very well," she said. "Come

along, Jaaved. Let's get to the shore while the weather is still pleasant. I've a feeling the wind's going to pick up later."

Ian looked askance at her, surprised she'd been rude enough to leave out mention of Carl. "You're taking Carl along, too, aren't you?" he suggested gently.

Theo was already walking back down the steps. Over her shoulder she said, "No. He'd rather stay here with you. Right, Carl?"

Ian glanced at his friend, who smiled sheepishly. "She's right," Carl said. "Besides, that'll give me a chance to finish the fortress." He indicated the oblong square of old desks, chairs, and blankets that made up their pretend castle. They'd been working on it here and there the past few weeks—or rather, Carl had been working on it while Ian attempted to figure out the dial and the prophecy.

"We'll see you at dinner," Jaaved said, following Theo down the steps and leaving the boys alone.

"You sure you wouldn't rather go to the shore?" Ian asked Carl.

"Naw, mate," Carl said with a wave of his hand. "I've seen enough of the sea to last me a lifetime."

Ian knew that Carl was referring to his time spent in the port town of Plymouth, where he'd been in a miserable orphanage until the earl discovered him and brought him to Delphi Keep nearly a year before.

"Right," said Ian, secretly happy for the company as he got up and moved to the window. "I'll get back to working this out, then." When he'd settled himself in the light from the window, he held the dial up, looking for any hint of a shadow.

Carl joined him by the window and both boys peered down hopefully. "It's the oddest thing, isn't it?" Carl asked. "I mean, how is it that a shadow won't form?"

Ian stared at the face of the dial in his palm, perplexed. "I've no idea."

"And Laodamia's not much help with it either, is she?" Carl remarked.

Ian set the sundial on the windowsill and fished around inside his shirt pocket, then pulled up the translated prophecy from the silver box they'd discovered in Morocco. He studied it a moment before reciting it out loud, hoping that this time he might find the answers to the riddles it contained.

> "The first of you shall be the last
> As time reminds you of the past
> Wait until the summer's heat
> Wakes the serpent from its sleep
> It strikes at those within your halls
> While you are all confined by laws
> Venom sends them all to bed
> While two of yours could soon be dead
> To the portal you must go
> As seeds of hope within you grow
> To find the Healer on your own
> You must venture past the bone
> Hold your hand within the ray
> And let the dial point the way

It will guide you to the curse
Find the meaning in this verse
Curse is kept by ancient crone
Whose past entwines within your own
Crone can make your quest secure
But heart of crone is never sure
Ancient one guards bane of earth
To whom her ties began at birth
Magus comes for sister kin
When fever lights the palest skin
Find the crone within the trees
She will bring you to your knees
Do not argue, pay the price!
Choice will grip you like a vise
Put your faith in Theo's sight
You will find your sister right
Once the healer has been named
Loam of ground no longer tamed
Unleashing wrath from ancient stone
Hear the earth below you moan
Fly away, back to your cave
Those you leave cannot be saved
Search for box within the mist
Past comes forward with a twist
Do not linger past the time
When you hear the sound of chime
Leave more questions to the fog
Lest you sink within the bog
Seeker, Seer, Healer true

Members gather to your crew
Find the next, there's four to come
Each will give one part of sum
Will you win or will you lose?
It will lie in who you choose."

"Have you noticed that she starts and ends both of her prophecies the same way?" Carl asked, referring to the first line and the last three lines of each of the two prophecies they'd discovered within the treasure boxes. Carl pointed to the text in Ian's hands. " 'The first of you shall be the last,' and then this bit, 'Each will give one part of sum. Will you win or will you lose? It will lie in who you choose.' " Carl studied the scroll over Ian's shoulder before he added, "I think in the beginning she must be talking about Theo. You know, how she's the first Oracle? She's the Seer, don't you agree?"

Ian nodded. "Most definitely. But I'm not certain what Laodamia means when she says she'll be the last too."

Carl scratched his head. "Well, we know we'll need to gather all six Oracles besides Theo before we're strong enough to face Demogorgon's crew. And we also know that along with Theo, we have Jaaved—our Seeker—so once we have this Healer person, we'll only need four more before we're ready."

Ian looked up thoughtfully at Carl. "Exactly," he agreed.

Carl squinted at the tight script of their schoolmaster, Thatcher Goodwyn. Their schoolmaster had helped translate the prophecy with their friend, the ancient Greek expert Professor Nutley. "I think the part we should be most concerned about are those lines that say a serpent will enter the keep and attempt to kill two of us."

For the past several months, especially since the weather had turned warm again, Ian, Carl, and the keep's grounds-keeper, Landis, had conducted regular inspections of the grounds, looking for any snakes that could present even a remote threat to the keep. But their searches had been futile, as they'd done little more than turn up a harmless garden snake or two. "I'd wager it's an adder," said Carl smartly, pointing to the line mentioning the serpent. "They're quite poisonous, you know."

But Ian wasn't as certain. He knew about adders, but they were reputed to be shy of humans, and he'd never heard of one biting more than one person at a time. He also knew from the book he'd read on native reptiles of Britain that the adder's venom was typically not poisonous enough to kill a person. The more common reaction was swelling and discomfort around the bite mark.

Ian had the distinct feeling that Laodamia meant something far more deadly would enter the keep during the height of the summer, but he felt he would not know what that was until they all encountered it.

That was why he was so intent on discovering how the sundial worked. He believed that if he could simply unlock its secret, he might be able to bypass all that nasty serpent business.

Still, it appeared that there were far greater dangers in store for him even after the serpent appeared. A terrible curse and an old crone awaited them through the portal.

Laodamia's prophecy suggested that Ian had met this old crone before, but he could not remember ever meeting anyone who fit her description.

As Ian continued to gaze down at the prophecy, he realized that Carl was still reading over his shoulder, and when Ian caught his friend's eye, Carl blushed slightly. "Sorry," he said, stepping back with a sigh. "I'm afraid I can't make sense of any of it. Serpents, fevers, curses, crones, and this bit: 'Loam of ground no longer tamed.' . . . What does that even *mean?*"

Ian had a theory, but he'd not had the courage to voice it until Carl asked. "I think she's talking about Lachestia," he whispered.

Carl stared at him with wide unblinking eyes, and the quiet of the tower room seemed to settle about them eerily. "You think she's talking about Magus's sister?" he said in a hushed tone.

Ian nodded. "She's the sorceress of earth, remember?"

"Oh, I remember, mate. I also remember the professor telling us she's the most dangerous of that awful lot. But I thought he told us she'd been killed three thousand years ago."

Professor Nutley had managed to uproot a few legends about the four sorcerers of the terrible underworld god, Demogorgon. Magus and Caphiera they'd already had the great displeasure of meeting, but the other two, Atroposa and Lachestia, remained a bit of a mystery. Atroposa was the sorceress of air, and she appeared to be the least terrible of the four demigod siblings. But Lachestia was said to be the most deadly creature that had ever roamed the ancient world. Legend suggested her capable of causing destruction on a massive scale. But a story that had emerged from a forgotten reference text in the professor's library suggested that after destroying a series of villages in eastern Europe, Lachestia had vanished into the heart of a cursed forest and was never seen again.

It was widely accepted that the sorceress had perished, but Ian felt strongly that the legend was wrong. He had a deep nagging suspicion that Lachestia was merely lying in wait for the perfect opportunity to rain down havoc again, and as the newspapers were widely reporting the increasing tensions of Europe these days, Ian was filled with dread that her reemergence would be quite soon indeed.

"Naw, mate," Ian said to his friend. "I don't think Lachestia's dead. I think she's just waiting for the right time to show herself." To prove his point, he quoted the prophecy. " 'Loam of ground no longer tamed, unleashing wrath from ancient stone. Hear the earth below you moan.' I believe Laodamia's got to be telling us about Lachestia."

"So who's the crone? And what's that bit about a curse she holds?" Carl wondered.

Ian shook his head. "I've no idea," he admitted. "But we should be able to discover her by using this." Ian lifted the sundial again, holding it up to the sunlight. "If I can figure out how to work this, we should have our answers."

Carl sighed and turned to his pretend fortress again.

"Good luck," he said. "I'll be fiddling with this in the meantime."

"Yeah, all right," Ian muttered, squinting at the sundial and willing its shadow to appear.

After a bit Carl broke the silence. "Ian, have you seen that plank of wood I rescued from Landis's woodpile? I thought it'd be a good piece to fit over this open section here."

Ian glanced up distractedly. "Plank?" he repeated.

"Yeah," said Carl. "You remember? I brought it up here last Saturday."

Ian did remember Carl struggling with a large section of wood up the stone staircase, but he couldn't recall where Carl had set it among all the other clutter. "Sorry," he said with a shrug. "I've no idea, mate."

Carl scrunched up his face and stared at the piles of wood and blankets, scratching his head again. "Where did I put it?" he mused to himself.

Ian looked down again to continue examining the sundial only to gasp when he realized that the face of the dial had changed dramatically from just a few moments before. The surface was no longer dull and tarnished but reflected brightly as if it'd just received a thorough polishing. And more astonishing, it appeared to be working; there was a distinct triangular shadow on it. "Carl!" he shouted. "Come have a look!"

His friend hurried over. "What?" he asked, and Ian pointed to the small relic in his hand. Carl gasped too. "Lookit that, it's got a shadow!"

"It just happened," Ian said, his hand trembling slightly with excitement.

"What'd you do to it?"

Ian tore his eyes away from the sundial and blinked up at his friend. "Nothing," he admitted. "I mean, nothing I can think of."

"Take it out of the sunlight and see what happens," Carl suggested.

Ian hesitated; he didn't want to risk doing anything that might cause the shadow to disappear, but quickly realized he couldn't hold it in the sunlight forever. So, taking a leap of faith, he moved it into the shade, and to both boys' surprise, the shadow remained on the surface of the sundial. "Gaw blimey!" Carl said, his voice filled with delight. "Would you look at that?"

"It's working!" Ian replied excitedly while he moved the sundial even deeper into the shade with no effect on its surface. "I don't know how, but it's working!"

And for a while both boys stared at the dial's face, waiting for the shadow to fade, but after several minutes it was clear that the thin strip of darkness was there to stay.

Soon the delight of their discovery waned and Carl said, "Well, I'm going back to the fort. Give us a shout if you figure out what it's pointing to." And he turned away.

But something Carl said was like a trigger in Ian's mind and he thought back through what had happened right before the shadow had appeared. Carl had been asking about the plank of wood; Ian had told him he didn't know where it was; then, when he'd looked back down, he'd seen the thin strip of shadow, which seemed to be pointing like a compass's arrow across the room. Ian's head snapped up and he looked over at the pile of spare wood covered by one of the moth-eaten blankets the boys had pinched from the cellar. Ian realized suddenly that the finger of the shadow seemed to be pointing directly at that pile of wood!

"Carl!" Ian said, his voice edged with excitement. "Check under that blanket and see if your plank of wood is there, would you?"

Carl looked at him oddly but moved away from another pile he'd been fishing through and lifted the blanket. There, right on top, was the long plank of wood he'd been searching for. "*There* it is!" he said triumphantly, pulling it out.

But Ian was already staring in amazement back down at the sundial's surface. The shadow had faded the moment Carl had lifted the blanket, and the surface of the relic returned to its dull, tarnished appearance. "Crikey!" he exclaimed. "I've got it! Carl, I've got how it works!"

Carl hurried over to him again and looked at the dull face of the dial. "Uh-oh," he said. "Your shadow's gone, mate. Sorry."

"No, you don't understand," Ian said, bouncing on the balls of his feet. "Ask me where something is and I'll show you how it works."

"Like what?" Carl asked, obviously confused.

Ian turned in a circle, looking for anything he could suggest, when his eyes lit on something across the room. "The treasure boxes," he whispered.

"All right," Carl agreed. "Ian, where did you put your treasure boxes?"

Immediately, the dial's shiny surface returned and a shadow appeared across the face, pointing directly at a long stone bench by the stairs on the far side of the tower. Carl gasped, his head pivoting from the shadow to the bench. "Ian! It's pointing right at your hiding spot!" Carl was the only other person besides Theo who knew Ian's secret hiding place.

Both boys hurried to the other side of the room, and Ian held the dial out so that they could see what happened the moment Ian lifted the loose plank that hid his treasure boxes. The instant his hand touched the silver top of the first box, the shadow disappeared.

"Remarkable," Ian whispered, in complete awe of the magical instrument in his hands.

"Bloomin' *brilliant!*" Carl said enthusiastically. "Let's make it a bit more challenging, though, shall we?"

Ian nodded, delighted that he'd finally managed to work out the secret of the sundial. "Where's Theo?" he asked, and immediately the sundial's shadow pointed right behind him. Ian turned and he and Carl looked out the far window, which gave a lovely view of the English Channel. The boys both knew that the shore where Jaaved and Theo had gone was in that very direction.

Carl laughed and slapped his knee. "Smashing!" he gushed.

Ian smiled happily while he looked from the dial to the

window, and was about to agree with Carl when something on the distant horizon caught his eye. From the window Ian could see all the way across the channel to France, and something large appeared to materialize just offshore.

Ian squinted and moved toward the window. "Ask it something else!" Carl urged, still bubbling with excitement.

"Hang on," Ian said, distracted by the shape, which he could see was zigzagging over the water. "Carl?" he said as a chill crept over him.

"Yeah, mate?"

"Do you still have those field glasses handy?" On a recent trip to London, Carl had purchased a set of binoculars, and he usually had them on hand for spying on the other orphans outside in the yard.

"Of course," he said. "Why don't you ask the dial where they are?"

Ian glanced down, and sure enough, the dial was pointing behind him, toward the fort. But Ian was more concerned with something else at the moment and he had the eeriest, most unsettling feeling. Something large and cone-like was zigzagging back and forth across the horizon. It appeared to be just off the shore of Calais, and he couldn't be sure, but it also appeared to be getting bigger. "Can you hand them to me, please?"

Carl paused, then came to stand next to him and pointed out the window. "Ian," he gasped. "What's *that?*"

"I can't tell," Ian murmured. "That's why I need the field glasses."

Carl hurried to the fort and rooted around under the

blankets and planks of wood. Ian knew the moment Carl found the field glasses, because the shadow on the dial disappeared. "Here you are," Carl said, giving them to Ian in exchange for the dial.

Ian focused the field glasses, searching the water for the dark shape. A moment later he had it within his sight and sucked in a breath, nearly dropping the field glasses in shock. "It's a cyclone!"

"Let me see!" Carl said, and Ian gave him the binoculars. "I don't believe it!" Carl said as he caught sight of the funnel cloud moving at an alarming rate across the sea. "I've heard of waterspouts before but I've never actually seen one!"

Ian wasn't really listening to his friend, because at that moment he realized that the funnel cloud was quickly traversing the English Channel, and its course—although slightly sporadic—put Dover right in its path.

"Carl," Ian said, a sudden panic making his hands shake, "give me the sundial again, would you?"

Carl lowered the lenses and handed over the dial. "Here," he said.

Ian wasn't sure if the question he had in mind would work, but he had to try. "Where will the cyclone strike?"

A thick shadow appeared across the face of the dial, pointing directly in front of them and marking the place that the relic had earlier identified as Theo's location. "Theo!" Ian shouted, and whirled around in panic, then dashed toward the stairs.

"It's heading straight for the shore!" Carl gasped from behind him. "We've got to warn her and Jaaved!"

29

Ian reached the landing and launched himself down the stone staircase several steps at a time, mindless of his own safety. There was terror in his heart as he imagined Theo and Jaaved caught within the cyclone's funnel and whirled out to sea.

He reached the door in full panic and pulled the handle, but the door refused to open. It was stuck fast. Ian hit the door with his fist in frustration. "Not again!" he shouted. "You hateful spook! Let me out!"

It was well known by all the children at the keep that the east tower was haunted by a rather unruly ghost who enjoyed trapping wayward children who ventured up to this tower by locking the door from the outside. The ghost didn't typically bother Ian and Carl, but at that moment, the cantankerous spirit's prank was the last thing they needed.

Carl was beside Ian in a moment. "Don't tell me it won't open!"

"It's that stupid ghost!" Ian growled as he pulled with all his might on the door. "We've no time for this! I order you to open this door immediately!"

Carl joined him by pleading with the ghost. "It's a matter of life and death! Stop playing pranks and let us out!"

But the door held fast and Ian could only think about the cyclone swirling ever closer to their shores and how little time they had to reach Theo and Jaaved.

"Let me try," Carl insisted as Ian strained again and again on the handle.

Ian backed away, his arms shaking from his effort, and he watched his much thinner companion pull the knob.

"Maybe there's something in the tower we can use to pry it open," Ian said in desperation, and he didn't wait for Carl to agree with him but ran back up the steps to look about for anything they might use.

But as he crested the landing, he stopped short when he saw that the cyclone was much closer to their shoreline, and he had a sinking sensation when he thought about how quickly it was bearing down on the area where Theo and Jaaved were. Ian knew that the path down to the shore was long, steep, and totally exposed to the sea, so even if Theo and Jaaved saw the waterspout in time to run, they'd be hard-pressed to make it to safety in time.

"How can I get to Theo?" Ian cried, and just as he said this, something sparkled on the floor. Ian glanced down and realized, to his surprise, that in his mad dash to the staircase, he'd dropped the sundial on the ground. As he bent to pick it up, his eyes strayed to the shadow that had just formed on its surface. The thin gray line pointed to his left, toward the bench where he kept his treasures.

From down the stairs Carl called, "Ian! The door still won't open! Bring something to whack the hinge with!"

But Ian was hardly listening. He had immediately recognized that the rhetorical question he'd asked was being answered by the sundial, and his eyes moved frantically to the bench again. Without hesitating a moment longer, he snatched the dial off the floor and raced to the bench. The dial's shadow became thicker the closer he got to it—almost as if it were pointing down. Quickly as he could, Ian began pulling the slats out of the bench, thinking perhaps the dial was pointing to one of them, but the shadow didn't change as he tugged each slat up and set it to the side. "What?" he asked, frustrated when his efforts revealed nothing. "What are you pointing to?" The shadow began to pulse, as if sending him an urgent message. At that moment he heard a scream from two floors below, and he knew that one of the other children had caught a glimpse of the cyclone.

Carl had clearly heard it too, because he shouted up to Ian, "They've seen it too! Oy! Help us out of here! We're trapped in the tower room!" Carl pounded on the door, but to no avail. No one heard them with all the shouting and thundering of footfalls echoing about the keep.

Meanwhile, Ian was desperate to discover what the dial wanted him to find in the bench. He tugged hard on the very last slat, ready to give up and head back down the stairs to help Carl with the door, when, suddenly, there was a loud groan, and to his amazement a small section at the bottom of the bench fell away, exposing a dusty metal ladder leading down into darkness.

For the briefest moment Ian was so stunned that all he could do was stare, and then Carl's banging brought him to his senses again and he shouted to his friend. "Carl! Come quickly! I've found a way out!"

Without waiting for him, Ian put the sundial into his pocket and stepped into the bench, lowering himself to the top rung of the ladder. He dug into his other pocket, pulled out his pocket torch, and switched it on, thankful that he'd had the foresight to change the batteries recently. "Carl!" he shouted again when his friend continued to pound on the door below. "Quit the door and come up here, *now*!"

Carl ran up the stairs only to stand frozen, staring at Ian, whose head was barely visible from the lip of the bench. "Crikey!" Carl said at last. "What's that, then? A secret passageway?"

"Yes!" Ian replied impatiently, and gave one last glance toward the window. "I asked the sundial how we could get to Theo and it pointed to the bench. Now hurry along, we've no time to waste!"

Ian and Carl got to the business of rushing down the ladder, which was slippery with dust and grime. Before stepping into the bench, Carl clicked on his own torch, and Ian was grateful for the extra light. As he climbed down, Ian wondered how old the iron rungs were, as they did not appear to have rusted much over time. Then again, the atmosphere appeared quite dry within the narrow space where the ladder had been secured. He just hoped the rungs were secure all the way to the bottom.

"How far down do you think it goes?" Carl asked from a few rungs up.

Ian angled his torch awkwardly in his fingers while holding fast to the iron bars, trying to peer down into the darkness. "I've no idea," he said, moving as quickly as he dared down the ladder. "But I suspect it goes to the main floor."

Ian soon discovered that he'd guessed wrong. The ladder extended well past the main floor, all the way belowground to a cavern that ran under the cellar of the keep. He knew this because at one point there was a crack in the stone the ladder was attached to, and his light pointed into the cellar itself while the rungs continued down another five meters or so.

Finally, the boys were able to stop their descent and put their feet firmly on the ground of the cavern. "Gaw!" Carl said, pointing his torch about the large enclosure, which had a tunnel leading out from it. "Would you look at *this?*"

Ian, however, was impatient to get to Theo. Shining his light on the surface of the dial, he saw that the shadow pointed straight ahead to the tunnel. "No time for ogling," he snapped, grabbing Carl's collar. "We've got to reach the shore ahead of the cyclone!"

The two boys dashed into the stone corridor as fast as their legs could carry them. The tunnel led them in a straight line but the grade of the floor gradually dropped them lower and lower. Ian could feel that they were running downhill and only hoped that the sundial was correctly navigating them to Theo and Jaaved.

They'd gone only a few hundred meters when they passed a fork in the path, and Ian paused impatiently while flashing the beam on the dial's surface to make sure they were still on course. To his relief, the shadow pointed straight ahead, and Ian put his faith in it and dashed on.

The farther they traveled, the damper the air became, and Ian began to make out the briny scent of the ocean.

"It's leading us straight to the channel!" Carl said, and as if to confirm this, there was a noise that sounded like the pounding of waves onto the shore.

But then they heard something else and Ian's heart sank. It was a scream that sounded as if it came from a long way off, and he would have recognized that voice anywhere. "Theo!" he shouted, his heart racing with the terrible thought that they'd be too late, and he urged his legs to move faster still.

Carl kept pace with him—he was the only boy in all of Dover who could, in fact—and together they rushed through the tunnel, straight toward a small pinpoint of light not far off.

Struggling for air, Ian could see that a hundred meters ahead was the mouth of a cave, opening directly onto the sea. He could make out daylight and the sound of surf mingled with something much more ominous. It was like nothing Ian had ever heard before, like a train and a great howling wind mixed together. And just above that noise he distinctly heard Theo's terrified scream.

Gritting his teeth and putting every ounce of energy he had into his final sprint, he reached the end of the tunnel, which deposited him and Carl directly into the back of a very large cave overlooking the shore some ten meters below.

The boys dashed into the heart of the cave only to stop short. In front of them was a huge swirling mass of black wind that all but blocked out the sun. It was so powerful that the current coming off it immediately knocked both of them off their feet. Sand and shells vaulted through the air around them, peppering the walls of the cavern with loud thwacks, and water pelted Ian so hard it felt as if he were being hit with rocks.

"Theo!" Ian shouted, struggling to his feet. He had to hold his arm over his eyes to protect them from the wind, water, and debris. He struggled to remain standing while straining his ears for Theo's voice, but nothing came to him save the roar of the cyclone bearing down on them. *"Theeeeeeoooo!"* he shouted again, panic welling within his chest when he could not see or hear her.

Ian was forced to turn his face away from the brunt of the wind, and saw that Carl had also managed to gain his footing and was hugging the wall of the cavern, making his way toward the ledge. "I hear her!" he called to Ian.

Seeing his friend have an easier time of it against the wall, Ian staggered to the side of the cavern as well, moving as quickly as he could against the elements. The cave was growing very dark while the cyclone thundered closer and closer to the shoreline, blocking out the daylight, and as Ian reached Carl's side, he heard a faint scream and knew it was Theo. "She's just outside the cave!" Ian shouted, crawling past Carl to the edge, where he was forced to get down on his hands and knees lest the wind knock him off his feet again. *"Ian!"* he heard faintly from just below. *"Help us!"*

Ian had to pull himself along the lip while he tried to locate her exact position. He could see the short shoreline about twenty feet below, and beyond that the swirling ocean, which had been churned a dark brown by the driving force of the cyclone. To Ian's horror, the terrible storm was now a mere five hundred meters offshore.

At the rate it was moving, he knew he had less than a

minute or two to get Theo and Jaaved to safety, or they'd all be doomed.

Squinting as sand and sea pelted his skin, Ian shouted to Theo, still attempting to locate her in the chaos. To his relief she called back more clearly. "There!" Carl said from beside him, pointing down and to the left. "On that ledge!"

Ian followed Carl's finger with his eyes and gasped when he saw Theo and Jaaved flattened against the cliff face. His heart panged when he took in her terrified face and the closeness of the cyclone's funnel; he had to help her as quickly as he could. He took off his belt and looped the end through the buckle, then wrapped the small noose around his wrist, pulling it tight. He then offered the other end to Carl. "I'm going to lower myself down," he shouted above the roar of the wind. "Take this and don't let me fall off the face of the cliff!"

"Hang on!" Carl said, gripping Ian's arm before he could shinny over the side. "You'll need more length than that." Carl too quickly removed his belt and connected it to Ian's. He then tightly gripped the end and braced his feet against a rock. "Off with you, then!" he said when he was ready.

Ian wasted no time lowering himself over the ledge, holding tightly to the part of the belt wrapped round his wrist while finding handholds in the soft limestone with his other hand. As he worked his way closer to Theo, his grip slipped from the rock before his feet found purchase, and he knew he would have fallen straight off the cliff onto the shore below if the wind hadn't pushed him back toward the rock and if Carl hadn't pulled tightly on the other end of the belt.

Somehow, Ian managed to hug the rock and carry on until he felt hands grip his legs. He looked down to see Theo's pale face near his knees. "Climb up!" he shouted to her. "I've got a firm hold here! Climb up and get into the cave!"

Theo's light blond hair whipped around her. She hesitated only a moment, then, with Jaaved's help, crawled up the rock, gripping Ian tightly, and managed to make the ledge. Once she was secure, Jaaved hurried up as well, and Ian would have breathed a sigh of relief if the cyclone hadn't started to pull him away from the rock.

Struggling to cling to the limestone with one hand while he held the belt in his other, he could hear Theo, Jaaved, and Carl all urging him to climb back up to the ledge, but every time he moved, the whirling wind that had pinned him to the rock before attempted to pull him away from the cliff's face. "Come on, mate!" Carl demanded. "Just climb!"

Ian knew he had little choice but to take the chance, and he tried reaching up with one hand to pull himself along, but the moment he let go of the rock, the wind lifted him away and he lost his grip altogether.

For a frightful moment he dangled in midair, perpendicular to the shore, and all he could see was the enormous black wall of the cyclone. Convinced he was about to breathe his last, Ian closed his eyes, but suddenly, Carl, Theo, and Jaaved gave a tremendous heave to the belt and it was just enough to pull him back into the rock face.

The cyclone, however, continued to try to pull him away, and to make matters worse, the wind threw rocks,

38

sand, and other debris so forcefully at him that he looked down to see that his exposed skin had started to bleed from dozens of small cuts.

"Hurry!" Carl shouted, and Ian felt like he was the rope in a terrible game of tug-of-war, one half of him being pulled toward the encroaching cyclone, the other being pulled back toward the cave.

And throughout those awful seconds, Ian felt he could do little to help. Worse still, he could feel his wrist begin to slip in the loop of belt around it. Try as he might to hold on, his grip was loosening.

It was with tremendous effort that he reached with his other hand and gripped the belt tightly, just as his friends all gave one final tug, and like a cork from a bottle, he was released from the vortex of wind and went tumbling back into the cavern.

He barely had time to collect his wits before Carl gripped him by the shoulder and pushed him across the chalky floor. "We've got to make it back into the tunnel before the cyclone sucks us out of the cave!"

His friend had shouted directly into his ear, but the noise from the cyclone nearly drowned the words out. Ian took one quick frantic look about him, saw Theo nearby, and grabbed her hand tightly while shouting at Carl to hold on to Jaaved. Making for the tunnel at the back of the cave, the foursome had to dodge large rocks, driftwood, and other debris as it rained down all around them and rammed the walls and ceiling.

The ground began to shake and Ian realized that the

cyclone was just about to collide with the 350-foot face of the cliff. With supreme effort he half dragged, half threw Theo into the mouth of the tunnel before reaching behind him to grip Carl and Jaaved and tug them through the narrow entrance as well, everyone tumbling forward in a tangle of arms, torsos, and legs.

The moment they were in the confined space of the tunnel, Ian felt a fraction of relief from the suction of the wind, and he wasted no time pulling himself and Theo to their feet. "Run for it!" he shouted to Carl and Jaaved, and the four dashed deeper into the tunnel. Gripping Theo's hand tightly, Ian had gone no farther than twenty meters when he felt the full impact of the cyclone hitting the cliff's face. It slammed into the rock with such force that it knocked all four of them to the ground again.

The noise of the impact was tremendous, like the sound of ten locomotives all colliding at once. It was certainly the loudest sound Ian had ever heard, and he threw himself over Theo, trying desperately to protect her. He could feel her screaming beneath him, but her terror was completely drowned out by the collision of the cyclone and the rock.

For long terrifying seconds the walls and floor of the tunnel shook, fragments of rock rained down on them from the ceiling, and dust filled the air with suffocating swiftness.

Ian held tightly to Theo, praying desperately for a miracle—quite certain that the tunnel would not withstand the forces being exerted upon it.

And then, in an instant, everything stopped.

BLACK, COLD, AND TERRIBLE

Magus the Black stood with two of his three siblings on the shore of Calais, staring out at the distant British coastline as the last threads of the cyclone evaporated. He looked first at his sister, Caphiera the Cold, whose eyes were hidden behind dark sunglasses, while she peered through the lens of a long silver spyglass. Magus was unsure how she could see anything through the sunglasses, they were so dark, but he dared not question her, lest the recent fragile peace between them be ruined. He couldn't help noticing when Caphiera's gruesome smile spread wide, exposing her sharply pointed teeth, just before she lowered the instrument. "She's done it," she announced triumphantly.

The edge of Magus's long cloak rippled with small flames as he turned to stare at his other sibling, Atroposa the Terrible.

He'd spent much of the past year wasting his time and energy fighting with Caphiera, until their sire had stepped in and brokered a truce. The underworld god had then ordered them to work together to find Atroposa, suggesting they would need the sorceress of air to complete their mission.

While Caphiera had searched west, Magus had looked east, and he'd finally located the sorceress in the wind-ravaged steppes of Tibet. Even though his discovery of and renewed alliance with Atroposa would surely bring them one step closer to fulfilling their plans, Magus regretted having to bring her into the fold.

He had no love for any of his three sisters, but Atroposa he disliked most of all. She could fan the flames of his temper like no one else. He could never quite pinpoint what specifically about her drove him to distraction, especially since it seemed *everything* about her set him on edge.

Even now as he regarded her, perched on the edge of a rock overlooking the sea—her attention still focused on the spot where the cyclone had struck—she irritated him immensely.

She was an eerie creature for certain: from her ashen skin, which lent her a ghostly countenance, to the lidless slate-colored eyes, set deep within a bony skull, that stared out hauntingly. Her nose was slight but crooked, and wafer-thin gray lips pulled pensively over a double row of pointy teeth. The rest of her was a flurry of constant movement. Her tattered clothing, which barely covered her reed-thin limbs, rippled and swirled about her while white, nearly translucent tendrils whipped and danced wildly about her frightening visage.

But her voice was perhaps her most disquieting feature. When she spoke, it was exactly like the moan of a haunting wind at the peak of a terrible storm. The sound was sure to beckon one's worst nightmare, and few were those who could tolerate it for long without being driven completely mad.

And although Magus was not likely to be rendered insane, he still detested every word she spoke, even when it was to tell him some good news for a change.

"It is done," Atroposa announced. "The One is dead."

Magus eyed the distant shore and frowned skeptically. Nearly a year earlier, the sorcerer had attempted several times to kill the young Oracle Laodamia had named the most important of them all—and every attempt had failed. Somehow, each time Magus was sure the child would not live to take another breath, she and her companions escaped him.

So he stood there, eyeing the distant coastline, unconvinced, and called to his she-beast. "Medea!"

The great hellhound approached him cautiously, careful to avoid getting too close to Caphiera the Cold.

Magus studied his hellhound with a small measure of sympathy, but they would need Caphiera's help to get across the channel and verify that the girl was in fact dead. "Sister," said Magus as politely as he could. "Might you assist us?"

Caphiera's blue lips smiled devilishly. "Of course, Brother," she said, waving her hand across the water. Instantly, a thick bridge of solid ice formed in front of Magus, extending as far as the eye could see. Magus presumed it went all the way to Dover.

His hellhound took a tentative step onto the bridge when Magus gripped the beast's furry neck, halting it. "Wait!" he commanded, sneering in irritation at Caphiera. "Remove the trap you've set in the middle," he spat, knowing her dislike of his pets all too well. It would be just like her to create an open section midway across the channel so that his favorite beast would fall through and drown.

Caphiera chuckled wickedly and snapped her fingers.

"And the spikes."

Caphiera stopped laughing, her face registering irritation, but snapped her fingers again.

"And the—"

"It's perfectly safe!" she insisted with two final snaps. "Now send your mutt across, Magus, or settle for Atroposa's word."

"Go," Magus said quietly, pointing to the distant shoreline. "Bring me back evidence that the child either lives or has perished, but tread carefully, Medea."

The hellhound raised her nose, sniffed the wind, and, with a swiftness that defied her size, raced forward onto the icy bridge.

Some time later, and much to Magus's relief, his beast returned unharmed, carrying one small shoe, which she dropped at her master's feet.

Magus bent to pick it up and his black eyes smoldered. "The girl is dead?" he asked the beast, still doubting it could have been that easy.

The hellhound gave a rough shake of her head, adding a

growl as her hackles rose. Magus turned angrily to Atroposa. "You have failed!" he snapped. "Medea has confirmed the girl lives."

"Impossible!" the sorceress howled. "Your pet is wrong! No mortal could have escaped my wrath!"

Beside them Caphiera the Cold began to cackle, her laugh like giant icebergs grating against each another. "It seems that all your plans for slaying this child end in failure, my brother."

Even though Atroposa had sent the cyclone, the idea had been Magus's, so Caphiera's words made him bristle. Thin streams of smoke trailed out of his nostrils, curling about the sides of his head like ram's horns. "Careful, Sister," he cautioned.

But Caphiera was hardly put off by his warning. "You know the prophecy you stole from that dim-witted archeologist in Greece as well as I do, Magus," she sneered. "You waste time here when Laodamia has already given you the answer to your dilemma. The great Oracle herself has described exactly how to go about destroying the One."

Magus's eyes simmered with anger while his frosty sister recited, " 'A time of grave danger shall come when the sorceress of earth shall arise from her stony tomb to take the life of the Guardian. And with the Guardian's demise, the One shall quickly fall, for none alive can stall this fate. If the Guardian perishes and the One falls before the time of gathering is complete, no hope can be given to the way of man.' Do you not remember?"

"I remember," Magus growled, irritated.

"We must leave the task of slaying this child to our other sister, I'm afraid," said Caphiera with a tsk.

"But that would require *finding* Lachestia," whined Atroposa with a shudder. "No one has seen her in over three millennia."

Caphiera nodded, folding her long bony arms across her chest. "Yes, but find her we must, dear Sister. The prophecy requires it."

"Do we have to?" Atroposa moaned. "Caphiera, you *know* what she's like."

Magus fully understood his sister's dread. Lachestia was unquestionably the most temperamental and unpredictable of all Demogorgon's children. In times past, Lachestia had sought to kill each of her siblings at least once, but she'd shown a particular malice toward Atroposa, who'd barely escaped their last few encounters with her life. Lachestia could be relentless in her malevolent pursuits, not to mention that Magus was certain she was quite mad. Lachestia was lethal, not just to her enemies, but to everyone she came in contact with—her siblings included. That made this pesky business of obtaining her cooperation to fulfill the prophecy all the more problematic.

"We've little choice, Atroposa. We must locate Lachestia, convince her to join us, and employ her to find and kill this Guardian," Caphiera insisted.

Atroposa's bony face looked miserable. "I don't think it wise for me to attend the search for her."

Embers flared at the edge of Magus's cloak. Leave it to his

simpering sister to try to wiggle her way out of an unpleasant duty. He looked at Caphiera, who stared coolly at the sorceress of air. Magus nearly smiled. He'd let Caphiera put Atroposa in her place.

But what Caphiera said was, "Of course *you* cannot search for her, dear Sister. Lachestia would surely kill you the moment she spotted you."

At first Magus was angry that Caphiera was allowing Atroposa to bow out, but the more he thought about it, the better he felt about leaving her behind. She would annoy him no end along the journey, anyway. He was resigned to traveling only with Caphiera when she turned her wicked face to him and announced, "Magus should go alone."

"*What?*" he roared.

Caphiera toyed with her spyglass, a knowing smile tugging at the corner of her blue lips. "You're the only one Lachestia likes," she said simply.

"Lachestia likes *no* one!" Magus spat back.

Caphiera tapped her finger against her chin thoughtfully. "Yes," she conceded. "You might be right on that, Magus, but she clearly dislikes you the least of all of us. I'm certain that if you find her and act quickly enough, you might convince her to help us before she does you great bodily harm."

"Oh, yes!" Atroposa said quickly. "Magus should go alone!"

Magus's temper began to flare again when he realized his sisters were joining forces against him. "You cannot expect me to locate Lachestia on my own!" he shouted. "No one has seen or heard from the sorceress in over three thousand years!"

Caphiera appeared unfazed by her brother's outburst; she calmly placed the spyglass within the folds of her fur-trimmed cloak and said, "Now there, I might offer some assistance. I have heard of a seer who has told of our sister's return. Word has reached me that the Witch of Versailles has been having visions, Brother. She might know where our dear Lachestia resides. I believe *you* should be the one to go to the witch and see if she will aid you in discovering our long-lost Lachestia."

Magus scowled and shook his head angrily. Leave it to Caphiera to send him on such a dangerous quest alone. He searched for an argument to get him out of the errand. "The prophecy is incomplete, Caphiera. We cannot be certain that if Lachestia kills the Guardian, it will be enough to destroy the One. Do you not remember that several lines of the prophecy are missing? What good would it do to awaken Lachestia if all she will do is kill the Guardian and not the One?"

Caphiera's blue lips pursed into a pronounced pout. "Oh, I remember that several lines are lost to us, Magus," she snarled. "And I ask you: whose fault is that?"

"Our brother's," replied Atroposa promptly. Magus smoldered where he stood, quickly realizing he would not win this argument. Granted, he *had* set the fire that had killed the archeologist who'd discovered the original prophecy, and that fire *had* resulted in the loss of the last few lines of the scroll, but he hardly thought it fair that that should be held against him. After all, they'd have nothing if not for his efforts. He was about to say as much when Atroposa added, "You should have been more careful, Brother. Who knows how important those lost lines are? It's your fault we must guess at how to dispose of the One."

"Exactly," said Caphiera, smiling gruesomely at her sister. "Which is why *he* should be the one to find Lachestia and entice her to join our quest. Once our wayward sister has been so directed, I'm certain she will handle the killing of two mortal children with ease, and then we can carry on with our plans unhindered by Laodamia's pesky prophecies."

Magus's cloak rippled with flames again and his eyes narrowed dangerously while he glared at his sister and fought to control his temper.

"Yes, Magus should be the one to find Lachestia," Atroposa eagerly agreed again. "It is only fair, since he ruined the prophecy in the first place."

Caphiera crossed her arms and stared at her brother contemptuously. "Shall we put it to a vote?" she asked.

Magus spat into the water near his feet, and his spittle hissed when it hit the sea. Caphiera had tricked him into this, and he knew that if she and Atroposa went before Demogorgon and told him of their suggestion, his sire would certainly order him to find and free his sister on his own. And Magus had also heard the rumors about the Witch of Versailles's visions, but he'd ignored them, because Lachestia's unpredictability made her a danger to him as much as anyone else.

Still, if those few lines from the scroll he'd stolen from

the burning tent of that archeologist were correct, and the Guardian's death was the key to bringing down the One, then what choice did he have but to engage Lachestia in his plans? The dilemma was how to control the sorceress of earth once he rediscovered her. Past experience had proved that it would require a delicate touch, and Magus doubted that either of his other two sisters was up to the task.

There was the possibility that after three thousand years, Lachestia had gained some lucidity. Perhaps once the One and her Guardian were dealt with, he could convince Lachestia to join him in a secret alliance against Caphiera and Atroposa. When their sire escaped and the world was theirs, it would be less bounty to split between siblings, after all.

"There is no need for a vote," he said finally. "I shall visit the Witch of Versailles and find Lachestia on my own."

Caphiera smiled triumphantly. "Of course you will, *dear* brother," she said. "Meanwhile, Atroposa and I shall retire to my fortress, as it is far too hot this time of year for me to be of any further service to you." Turning to her sister, Caphiera said, "Come, dear, you look winded. Let's get you to the mountain pass, where you can rest in cool comfort." And with that the two sorceresses left Magus to smolder moodily and stare out to sea.

SECRET PASSAGES

I an rolled over onto his back and lay in the cool darkness for several long moments, his hand still gripping Theo's arm tightly.

"You all right?" she whispered.

"Yes," he said, sitting up and coughing from the dust still swirling around them. "That was a close one, though."

"Too close," agreed Carl, and Ian noticed that his voice came from about five feet away.

"Is Jaaved all right?" Ian asked.

"Fine, thank you," said Jaaved, and Ian was surprised to hear him just behind Theo.

"It's pitch-dark in here," Theo said. "Shouldn't we be able to see some daylight?"

"I think the entrance to the tunnel caved in," Carl moaned, and Ian heard him shuffling around in the dark. "Hang on," he added, and then a light switched on and they could faintly make each other out.

Ian smiled gratefully at his friend, glad at least Carl had

had the good sense to hang on to his torch. "I lost mine in the cavern," he admitted.

"No worries, mate," Carl said good-naturedly. "One's all we need, really." Carl then got to his feet and attempted to wipe some soot off his trousers.

Ian glanced back at Theo, seeing for the first time that she'd lost her shoes. "What happened to your shoes?"

Theo blushed. "They slipped off when I was climbing up the rock," she explained, accepting Ian's hand. They both got to their feet. "What tunnel is this, do you think?"

Ian's face brightened when he realized she knew nothing about what he'd discovered just before rushing to rescue her. "Oh, Theo, you won't believe it! This tunnel leads right up to the tower room at the keep!"

Theo blinked. "It what?"

"We saw the cyclone from the window in the tower," Carl explained. "And Ian pulled up the slats in the bench and a trapdoor opened to a ladder that led down to this tunnel."

Theo's eyes widened. "Incredible!" she said.

"It is, isn't it?" Ian agreed. "I'd no idea there was a tunnel leading directly to the keep, but it makes sense, doesn't it?" The land spreading out from Castle Dover and the keep was riddled with tunnels and hidden caverns. Some of these were natural, and some were man-made. Most of the latter were dug out by either the local population, who feared invasion from the sea, or the men in service to the many earls of Kent who'd held the land—providing each earl with an escape route should the keep or the castle ever be besieged.

"That might make sense, Ian, but I still find it hard to

believe there was a hidden stairway within the keep that we never knew about," Theo said.

"Well, then, perhaps it should remain a secret," Ian suggested, staring meaningfully at his three companions. Ian was worried that if the adults learned of the escape route, they'd order it blocked up.

"Might come in handy at some point to have a way out of the keep without anyone knowing about it," Carl agreed.

"But the exit is blocked," Jaaved said, gesturing to the large pile of rubble behind them.

"We can work on clearing that out later," Carl said with confidence.

"Yes," Theo agreed, and Ian noticed that her hand had moved up to clutch the crystal pendant she wore around her neck. "That might be wise."

Ian studied her. "Theo?" he asked.

"Yes?"

"Did you get a feeling about the cyclone before you went to the shore?" Theo's ability to predict the weather was uncanny, and Ian was privately wondering why she hadn't mentioned any ill feelings she might have had earlier. The only thing she'd said was that the day might grow windy, but she'd hardly looked concerned when she'd said it.

To his surprise, Theo appeared quite troubled. "I had no idea we'd be hit by a cyclone," she whispered.

"What's that?" Carl asked, leaning in.

Theo cleared her throat and spoke more clearly this time. "I didn't know. I felt no warning at all. In fact, it was Jaaved who first noticed something wrong."

Ian looked at Jaaved, who nodded. "Her crystal was pulsing red," he explained.

Ian remembered that it was Jaaved's grandfather who had told them about the magic of Theo's crystal and explained how it would be able to alert her to evil by flashing red in times of grave danger.

"Until Jaaved mentioned that something was amiss, I'd no idea, Ian."

"We saw the cyclone right after the pendant gave us warning," Jaaved explained. "And by then, it was halfway across the channel and making its way directly to us."

Theo nodded. "We knew we'd never get up the road in time, so Jaaved suggested we find shelter in one of the caves along the shore, and at first we took refuge in one of the lower caves, but the wind whipped the pebbles from the shore at us and we knew we couldn't stay so close to the ground. That's when we decided to attempt a climb up to a higher cave, but the cyclone reached us much sooner than we thought it would. It was almost as if it had a will of its own—like it aimed itself directly at us."

A dark and terrible thought entered Ian's mind. What if the cyclone hadn't been just a freakish weather occurrence—but a product of more sinister forces at work?

He nearly voiced his opinion out loud, but one look at Theo's troubled face and he decided she'd had enough to worry about for the day. "Well, you're safe now," he told her, forcing a smile. But Theo hardly looked reassured.

"Ian," she said softly. "Do you think that cyclone could have been the work of Atroposa?"

"Atroposa?" Carl asked. "You mean the daughter of Demogorgon?"

Theo nodded. "She's the sorceress of air, you know. A cyclone would have been well within her powers to create."

Jaaved also appeared troubled. "It did follow us up the shore when we made for higher ground, Ian," he said. "And I don't really know how to explain it, but it felt sinister, as if it were a thing of dark magic."

Carl ran a hand through his hair. "Crikey," he said. "If one of them can create something like that—what chance does Theo stand against them?"

"That's it," Ian said firmly, fearing for her safety. "You're never leaving the keep again."

But Theo glared at him with firm determination. "Don't be daft," she told him. "Of course I'm leaving the keep. Remember Laodamia's prophecy? We're scheduled to go through the portal soon enough."

"I don't know how you'll accomplish that, Theo," Carl said. "The earl's locked it up tight. No one can get past that iron gate without his permission and he's certainly not going to let you go through the portal again."

Shortly after they'd returned from their journey to Morocco, the earl had thrown an enormous padlock around the bars of the gate at the entrance of the tunnel leading to the portal. The earl had also gone as far as to expressly forbid the children to go near it, for their own safety.

But Theo crossed her arms and looked stubbornly up at Ian, as if daring him to agree with Carl. Ian decided not to argue the point with her and attempted to change the subject. "Come along," he said, waving for his friends to follow. "We'd best get back to the keep before anyone realizes we're missing."

But when they made their way to within ten meters of the ladder leading to the tower, they came to another barrier. A huge stone slab that had been set into the wall had fallen across the tunnel, dropping a good portion of the roof on top of it. Ian approached the slab and inspected it. "Blast it!" he groaned, surveying the huge pile of rubble heaped on the slab all the way to the ceiling, which effectively cut them off from the secret entrance to the keep.

"Would you look at that?" said Carl, and for a moment, Ian thought he was talking about the cave-in, but then he realized that Carl was actually referring to the slab.

"Look at what?" Ian asked.

"This stone," Carl said. "Does it look familiar?"

At first Ian had no idea what Carl was talking about, but when he looked closer, he saw something on its surface that he recognized. Small angular letters ran down the flat side of the slab. "It's a standing stone!" he gasped, utterly surprised to find one of the huge stones down there in the tunnel.

Ian and the others were very familiar with the stones; they'd been educated by Professor Nutley, who was something of an expert. Used for various religious purposes in Druid times, the stones were typically massive and used to mark an area of sacred ground.

In fact, the entrance to the magical portal a stone's throw away from Castle Dover was hidden under three standing stones, and Ian strongly suspected that those monoliths held a bit of magic in them as well.

Carl nodded. "The question is, why is this stone down *here* of all places?"

"To protect the keep," Theo said, reaching out to touch the slab.

Ian's brow furrowed. "What do you mean, to protect the keep?"

Theo smiled patiently at him. "Don't you think it's curious that none of Demogorgon's brood have ever raided the keep, Ian? I mean, we've seen Magus's hellhounds and that awful couple the Van Schufts, but neither Magus nor Caphiera has ever set foot on the keep's grounds.

"Lady Arbuthnot and I have long suspected that the keep itself must be protected by some form of magic, something that keeps the likes of Magus and Caphiera out. And if this tunnel leads directly up to the heart of the keep, then there must be some magic associated with the standing stone." Stepping closer to the slab, Theo ran her hand along the lettering tattooed into the hard rock. "I believe that these markings invoke some sort of protection which radiates upward and protects the keep."

"But the entrance to the portal has those same standing stones and markings, and Caphiera had no trouble coming down there, now, did she?" Carl argued.

Theo sighed. "Yes, that *is* a valid point, Carl. And I said the same to Lady Arbuthnot, but then she pointed out that when we returned through the portal last year, only a few hours had passed on this side of the portal, and both Caphiera and her icy deathtrap had completely vanished, as if all that ice had never even existed. Lady Arbuthnot thinks, and I agree, that the sorceress was unable to remain in the portal tunnel because of the magic of those stones. And that is why, since then, neither she nor any of her siblings has returned to destroy it."

Ian thought about Theo's logic, and it did make a great deal of sense to him. "She's right, you know," he said to Carl, who still looked a bit doubtful. "If I were Magus or Caphiera, the first thing I'd do is destroy that portal if I could. It's at the heart of all of Laodamia's prophecies so far and it seems to be the gateway to finding the rest of the Oracles. Magus has to know that, so the fact that he hasn't attempted to reduce it to rubble says that it must be protected somehow."

"Along with the keep," Theo said, and Ian watched her lean forward and place a gentle hand on Carl's wrist, moving the torch along the walls and revealing half a dozen more standing stones set at even spaces into both sides of the tunnel wall, beginning about ten meters back. All the stones were arched and marked with the same angular lettering, indicating they were set there on purpose. Ian marveled at the engineering required to set such large and heavy stones deep into an underground tunnel. He was surprised that none of them had noticed the stones until they'd come across the one blocking their exit.

"Yeah, well, a lot of good that protection is doing us now," Carl grumbled as Theo let go of his arm and he turned back to the cave-in. He then ducked low and shone his torch under the belly of the stone slab, pulling out a few smaller rocks so that he could get a better look. "It's blocked all the way to the other side," he announced.

Ian squatted down next to Carl and peered into the shadows. Under the slant of the slab he could see nothing but small rocks and debris. "We'll have to clear it out," he said. He didn't know how far back the cave-in went, but the exit behind them at the cavern looked far more challenging to clear.

"What about that fork we passed?" Jaaved suggested while Ian and Carl looked glumly at the mess in front of them.

The boys turned to Jaaved. "Yeah," Carl said, his face brightening. "We could try heading back that way and see if it leads to a way out!"

"Whichever way we decide, we'll need to be sure of it," cautioned Theo. "I don't expect your torch to last more than an hour or so, Carl."

Ian looked nervously at Carl's torch, and the light did seem a bit dimmer. Then he had an idea and he pulled the sundial from his trouser pocket, grateful that it hadn't been lost in the powerful storm. Placing it in his palm with the twelve o'clock marker pointing toward his fingers, he lowered it into the torch beam and asked, "Sundial, which way is the quickest out of here?"

Immediately, a shadow formed across the dial's surface, pointing to the six o'clock position. "Good heavens!" Theo exclaimed when she realized what had just happened. "Ian! You've discovered how to work it!"

Ian smiled proudly. "Carl and I came across the answer

right before we spotted the cyclone. That's how we knew about the secret passage leading down here, in fact. The dial works very much like a compass. You just need to ask it where something is, and a shadow will form, pointing in the direction of whatever you're trying to find."

"Well, let's not spend our time talking about it here," Jaaved warned. "We should wait to do that when we're aboveground and use what torchlight we have left now."

Ian nodded and waved his friends back down the tunnel. "Very well. We'll go where it's telling us."

It turned out that Jaaved's suggestion to take the fork was right after all. The sundial's shadow changed once they reached it, indicating that they should follow the new direction, and to their immense relief, they soon discovered they were in an alternate tunnel, which led to another—much shorter—iron ladder. Ian stood at the base of it and stared up at what looked like a trapdoor. "I wonder where we are?" he mused just as Carl's torch blinked noticeably.

"Let's not wait to find out, Ian. My torch is nearly out."

Ian backed away from the ladder and motioned for Theo to go first. "After you," he said politely.

Theo eyed him in alarm. "I'll go last," she said, and even in the dim light, Ian thought he could see her blushing. He then realized that poor Theo was wearing a skirt, and that she might be worried about maintaining a sense of modesty.

"Of course," he said quickly, hoping no one else noticed. "Carl, Jaaved, why don't you two go and see if you can get that trapdoor open? Theo and I will be up in a bit."

"All right, then," Carl said agreeably, handing Ian the small torch, which Ian shined up the ladder so that they could see where they were going, and before long the two boys were at the top, shoving on the trapdoor. "We've done it!" Carl called when they'd pushed their way through.

Ian looked at Theo and smiled in reassurance. "I'll go up slowly. If you think you might slip, grab hold of my trousers, all right?"

Theo nodded and they went up the ladder together. Soon enough they too were through the door and had climbed into a small wooden shack filled with all sorts of gardening tools. "Where are we?" Theo wondered.

Carl grinned knowingly. "We've come up in the gardener's shack at the edge of the earl's hedge maze. Jaaved's already had a look around." Carl motioned over his shoulder at Jaaved, who was nodding enthusiastically.

"It's true," the young Moroccan said. "We're within Castle Dover's walls, right next to the maze."

Ian was surprised they'd found their way underground to the earl's backyard. "I never would have imagined we'd end up all the way over here." The earl's castle was a full kilometer away from the keep.

Theo distracted him from puzzling out the route when she tugged on his sleeve and said, "We should get back to the keep."

Immediately, she had his full attention, especially in light of what had happened to them that afternoon. "What is it? Is it another cyclone? Can you sense it this time?"

Theo smiled at him, as if she was amused by his alarm.

"No, it's nothing like that. But I do believe it's nearly time for tea, and if we're not back home by four o'clock, the headmistresses will be worried."

"Oh," he said, relieved. "All right, let's hurry, then, but remember, this tunnel and where it leads shall remain our little secret." Carl, Jaaved, and Theo all nodded and Ian led the way out of the shack and back toward the keep, using a shortcut through the garden gate that he knew well.

When Ian and the others finally walked up Delphi Keep's long drive a bit later, they saw a large group of children; both headmistresses; Landis, the groundskeeper; and several other men, including their two schoolmasters, on the steps of the keep. To Ian's surprise everyone appeared terribly upset. Madam Dimbleby, in fact, looked just short of hysterical. "Oh, my children!" they heard her wail. "They're lost! Lost forever!"

Ian, Carl, Theo, and Jaaved all stopped in their tracks to look at each other in alarm before dashing toward the group. "Perhaps they found shelter in time, Maggie," Ian heard Madam Scargill say as she patted her cousin on the back.

But Madam Dimbleby was inconsolable. "Gone!" she wailed. *"Gone!"*

Carl was the first of them to reach the large crowd, and Ian overheard him asking a girl named Angela, "Who's gone?"

"Ach!" Angela screamed when she noticed Carl next to her. This was quickly followed by a gasp from the collection of children and adults as everyone turned with large eyes to stare at the foursome who'd just arrived within their midst.

"They're *alive!*" someone shouted, and then everyone began talking at once.

Ian was immediately pulled into Madam Dimbleby's tight embrace, and she sniffled into his hair. *"Where have you been?"* she demanded.

But Ian was having difficulty breathing, squished so close to the headmistress that he found he couldn't speak. Next to him he heard Theo say, "We were at the shore, ma'am."

Madam Dimbleby then released Ian, much to his relief. Wiping away her tears, she said, "But the cyclone!"

"We found shelter along the cliffs," Carl said quickly. When Madam Dimbleby's eyes studied his dust-covered clothing, he added, "We found our way to a cave where we were able to get out of the wind, but the cliffs shook so hard, I'm afraid we got a bit dusty."

At that moment Thatcher Goodwyn, their schoolmaster, stepped forward and Ian noticed right away that the man was clutching one of Theo's shoes. "Thank heavens," he said, dropping to one knee to look closely at her. "I felt certain the beast had swallowed you whole!"

There was another collective gasp from Ian and his companions. "The beast?" he asked.

Thatcher looked over his shoulder at his twin brother, Perry, who nodded grimly and explained, "While we were searching for you along the beach, we came across the most astonishing thing: a bridge made of solid ice leading from the shore all the way out to sea. A most unnatural occurrence, which was why we were immediately suspicious of it."

"Caphiera's doing!" Theo said, her eyes opening wide.

"Yes," Thatcher agreed. "It could only be Caphiera."

"But I thought you said something about the beast," Carl reminded them.

Again, Perry exchanged a meaningful look with his brother. "As we moved away from the ice bridge to continue our search for you, we saw Magus's beast bolt out of a nearby cave with a girl's shoe in its mouth. We were caught completely unprepared, you see. Neither of us had thought to bring our rifles, and we were forced to retreat as the beast made its way onto the ice and ran back across the channel."

"Is the ice bridge still there?" Ian asked. He worried that the beast might come back once it realized Theo was still alive.

"The ice began to melt in earnest the moment the beast was out of sight," Thatcher told him. "I've no doubt it's long gone by now."

Theo shivered next to Ian and he reached an arm around her shoulders. "There, there, Theo," he said. "That nasty creature only managed to nick one of your shoes."

"It's not that, Ian," she told him softly. "It's that now we have proof that Magus, Caphiera, and Atroposa are all working together. I fear we're in terrible danger."

"Atroposa?" repeated Perry, and his eyes lit with understanding. He turned to look out to sea. "Oh, my," he said. "The cyclone! Yes, that must have been the work of the sorceress of air!"

Madam Dimbleby had been wringing her hands the whole time they'd been talking, and her face visibly paled when the discussion turned to Magus, Caphiera, and Atroposa. "We'll have to alert the earl immediately!"

"Leave it to me," Thatcher volunteered, getting to his feet and motioning for his brother to follow him.

"We should also inform Professor Nutley," Perry suggested as the two began to walk quickly down the drive.

Thatcher called over his shoulder to the headmistresses, "We'll be back this evening. Please ensure the children remain inside the keep until our return."

Madam Dimbleby nodded dully, and Madam Scargill waved her hands at the large crowd still hovering about the front steps. "You heard your schoolmasters," she said to all the children. "Let us move along inside and see to supper."

The dishes from their evening meal had just been cleared when the sound of a motorcar crunching along the gravel reached Ian's ears. He hurried to the door and pulled it open to find the professor, his schoolmasters, and the earl approaching the front steps.

"Good evening, Ian," said the earl kindly.

"My lord," Ian replied, feeling a wave of warmth for the man who was his patriarch.

"I'm very glad to see you safe," said the earl as he stopped in front of Ian and laid a gentle hand on his shoulder.

"Thank you, my lord." Ian then greeted Professor Nutley, Thatcher, and Perry while the earl said his hellos to the headmistresses and the other children.

Once the greetings and salutations had been seen to, the earl called all the adults and Ian, Theo, Carl, and Jaaved to a closed meeting in the headmistresses' private study. "Best not to worry the other children with our discussion," Ian heard the earl say to Madam Dimbleby.

When everyone was comfortably seated in the study, the earl began. "I have spoken at length with Masters Goodwyn about today's events, and while I am very glad to see the four of you safe, I am most troubled by the power of the forces against us. Professor Nutley has suggested to me that he would like to offer a plan to help keep you out of harm's way, so I shall turn this discussion over to him."

The professor nodded formally to the earl and cleared his throat. "I consulted with a few of my scientist friends this afternoon when word reached me of the waterspout off the coast, and they confirm our suspicions—barometric readings and the mild weather conditions over the channel could not possibly have supported a waterspout of the size and strength as struck the cliffs earlier today. Therefore, with the other evidence noted by Thatcher and Perry of the ice bridge running straight from Calais and the appearance of the beast, we must conclude that at least three of the four offspring of Demogorgon have now combined forces and are working against us."

The professor seemed to pause for dramatic effect, but Ian was aware that everyone in the room had already concluded as much, so the poor old man was left looking slightly disappointed by the lack of reaction from the faces staring intently at him. He cleared his throat again and continued. "Dover is not safe," he announced. "As long as Magus, Caphiera, and now Atroposa know that Theo resides at the keep, I fear another attack is imminent, and I'm quite convinced that that will put all the children here in grave danger."

Madam Dimbleby's hand moved to cover her heart, and Madam Scargill frowned more deeply than usual. "What are we to do, Professor?" Theo asked meekly.

"Why, my dear girl," the professor said with a twinkle in his eye, "we must go to Spain!"

The room fell into a stunned silence. Ian was the first to break it when he repeated, "Spain? Why would we go there, Professor?"

In response the professor reached into his blazer pocket and extracted a folded piece of paper. "I have in my possession a letter from Señora Latisha Castillo," he said. Ian's brow furrowed. He was quite certain he'd never heard the name. "Latisha," the professor explained, "is the younger sister and only surviving heir of my former colleague Sir Donovan Barnaby."

"Sir Barnaby?" Thatcher said. "Wasn't that the archeologist chap who was with you in Greece and unearthed some of Laodamia's scrolls?"

"It was indeed, Master Goodwyn," replied the professor. "And as you also know, Barnaby was killed some years ago while on a return trip to Greece when the tent he was sleeping in caught fire, poor fellow."

"And you've recently been in touch with his sister?" Ian asked, anxious for the professor to tell them why he wanted them to go to Spain.

The professor seemed to remember the letter in his hand

and got back to it. "Barnaby used to talk very affectionately of his sister years ago when we shared stories around the camp-fire in Greece. And I'd quite forgotten about Latisha until last year, when I came across some of my old friend's notes.

"It took several months to locate her—she's moved to Spain and married a banker, you see—but eventually, I tracked her to Madrid and began correspondence. And it was all rather ordinary until this letter arrived and Latisha mentioned that she had kept many of Barnaby's diaries. In fact, she even has the one recovered from the fire, which he wrote in the very night he died." The professor then stared meaningfully around the group. But Ian had no clue why the old man considered that significant, and he could tell that no one else in the room did either. He was about to ask when Carl beat him to it.

"Pardon me, sir," said Carl timidly. "But I don't under-stand what that's got to do with anything going on here."

The professor looked surprised. "Why, my young Master Lawrence!" he said. "It's got *everything* to do with what's happened here! You see, Barnaby kept a journal to record the events and discoveries he'd found on each of his arche-ological digs.

"And the reason this particular journal is so important is because right before Barnaby died, he uncovered a lengthy scroll hidden underneath the marble flooring of Laodamia's villa. That scroll was thought lost, completely destroyed by the fire in Barnaby's tent, you see, but his sister has revealed to me that my good friend actually managed to copy down much of the scroll in his last diary before he was taken from us!"

"But I still don't understand what that's got to do with Magus, Caphiera, and Atroposa showing up again," Carl admitted, scratching his head.

The professor's eyes were bright as he looked at Carl and replied, "Laodamia's scroll was hidden in such a fashion that I believe she must have been certain it would never be found. It was not with the other scrolls, nor was it tucked away in one of her silver boxes for Ian and Theo to find. Whatever prophecy she recorded on that particular piece of parchment must have been too important to allow anyone else to see, yet also too important to destroy. It is my firm belief that the only thing Laodamia could hold so vital would have to do with all of this. At the very least, we must embark to Spain and discover the truth of it. And, might I add, if we were able to do so in secret, we might remove Theo from the threats that surround her at this time."

Ian felt goose pimples line his arms. Deep in his bones he had a feeling that the contents of that scroll could change everything. They had to get to Barnaby's diary.

"The professor is right," Theo said, and Ian saw immediately that she was fiddling with her crystal and held a faraway look in her eyes. "The content of the scroll is important to us. It reveals something . . . something I feel we must know."

The professor's chest puffed out in a way that suggested he was rather proud of himself. "You see?" he said, pointing at her. "Even our own little Oracle agrees."

But one glance at the schoolmasters and the headmistresses told Ian they at least still held some doubt. He knew that the decision would rest with the earl. When all heads turned to him, the earl surprised them by asking the professor a question. "Professor Nutley," he began, "am I correct in saying that there is a fourth offspring of Demogorgon that was not accounted for by today's events?"

"Yes, my lord. Lachestia the Wicked, sorceress of earth, has not appeared to have contributed to the chaos of earlier. But that could be because the last legend that supports her existence suggests that she vanished over three thousand years ago, and she is presumed to have perished within a cursed forest."

"Wish the rest of that mingy lot would all vanish in a cursed forest," Carl muttered. Ian smiled. He couldn't agree more.

The earl sighed heavily and a deep frown settled onto his face. "Perhaps you are right, then, Professor. The keep does not appear to be the safest location for our four special children. Perhaps a sojourn in Spain would allow them some respite from all this trouble."

But Madam Dimbleby protested. "Professor Nutley, with all due respect, the newspapers still report pockets of trouble in Spain. Don't you think it's a dangerous environment for children?"

Ian knew from reading the papers, which often cluttered the earl's library, that she was referring to the newly ended civil war that had devastated Spain for several years.

"Not at all," said the professor. "The conflict ended months ago, Madam. And I can assure you that Madrid is quite safe. I firmly believe the best thing to do would be to escort the four children out of Dover. Besides, they're on summer holiday at present, and a trip to Spain would be an excellent educational opportunity for them."

"Can't you simply request the diary from Señora Castillo?" asked Madam Scargill.

"I have," said the professor. "But her husband recently passed away, I'm afraid, and the poor woman is quite starved for company. She would much rather we come to visit, you see, and she is insisting that Barnaby's diary is far too precious a memento for her to part with. She has graciously invited me and anyone else who would like to join me for the journey. If we leave within the next day or so, we'll not be away longer than a fortnight, which I believe will be just enough time for things to settle down here."

Ian gave the earl a long and hopeful look. He very much wanted to go to Spain, as he'd never been there before.

The earl pulled at his red beard thoughtfully. "Very well, Professor," he said. "We shall go to Spain and visit with the good Lady Castillo."

"You're going along as well, my lord?" asked Madam Scargill in surprise.

The earl nodded. "I have never been to Madrid," he confessed. "And that is the one city I've always longed to explore. Of course, I shall also feel better about the safety of the children if I'm there to protect them."

Across the room, Jaaved announced, "If you please, my lord, I'd like your permission to stay here."

The earl looked at the boy curiously, but Ian understood. Ever since they'd come through the portal, Jaaved had repeatedly told them how uneasy he felt about leaving Dover.

When Ian and Carl escorted Theo to Lady Arbuthnot's in London, Jaaved never wanted to go with them, and the only time the younger boy had willingly ventured beyond the outskirts of the village was when Carl was in hospital. Ian thought it likely that the Moroccan orphan couldn't quite believe the good fortune the keep had provided him. For the first time in his life, Jaaved had a secure home and an education and was surrounded by people who loved him. Ian thought that perhaps Jaaved was afraid to step beyond the borders, lest he discover that it had all been a dream after all.

The earl eyed Theo, as if asking her whether Jaaved would be safe enough if he stayed behind. Theo nodded after a moment and the earl said, "Very well, Jaaved. But I shall request that you not travel beyond the walls of the keep."

"I promise," Jaaved said, looking relieved.

"We'll just need to pack a few things," Perry announced, as if it were already decided that the schoolmasters would go along.

The earl looked kindly at Perry and Thatcher and said, "About that . . ."

"Yes?" they asked together while Ian's eyes darted to the earl. It almost sounded like he was working up to tell them they weren't invited.

"I wonder if I could ask you to stay behind on this journey, so that you might be of some service to me here in England."

The twins flushed at the same time, making them look more alike than usual, and Ian felt uncomfortable witnessing their embarrassment. "Why, of course, my lord," Thatcher said quickly. "We're always willing to be of service to you in any way we can."

The earl then told the men about an orphanage in Cornwall that he'd been sending a fair amount of money to. The orphanage was rumored to be in desperate need of repair and quite overpopulated. The earl needed an envoy to go and ensure that the money he'd donated was being put to good use, and that more beds were being made available to the children housed there.

"It shouldn't take longer than a fortnight," he told the schoolmasters. "And Cornwall's a lovely town. You'll rather enjoy it, I'm sure."

The schoolmasters were quick to agree and take up the charge. Once that was settled, the earl got to the business of protecting the other inhabitants of the keep. "I'll hire some men from the village to patrol the grounds, day and night. And I must insist that the children stay on the keep's property for the time being, unless accompanied by Landis or one of my men." Looking at Ian, Theo, Carl, and the professor, the earl announced, "We'll be off the day after tomorrow," which settled the matter for good. The earl got to his feet then. "Thank you, Maggie and Gertrude. I'll not keep you a moment longer, as I'm sure you have quite a few tired heads to put to bed."

It was the headmistresses' turn to blush, and Ian saw Madam Dimbleby's eyes move quickly to the clock, which indicated that it was well past the youngest orphan's bedtime. "Yes, of course!" she said, slightly flustered. "We must get the wee ones to bed at once."

The earl gave a slight bow and opened the door to the study, allowing them all to leave. Ian could hardly contain his excitement but realized almost immediately that he needed to wipe the broad smile from his face when he saw the way the other orphans were looking at them as they exited.

He knew that none of the other children would trade places with either him or Theo, especially given the day's harrowing events, but all the children at the keep were aware of the special treatment Ian, Theo, Carl, and Jaaved were afforded—especially by the earl. He knew to them it looked like favoritism, and he had to concede that perhaps there was a little truth to that.

So he made a conscious choice to keep his features neutral while he moved through the crowd on his way to his room. But he couldn't help overhearing the muttered frustrations of many of the children nearby when Carl announced that he, Ian, and Theo would be going to Spain. Ian pulled Carl by the arm and coaxed him to the stairs. "What're they all miffed about?" whispered Carl as they moved away from the others.

"Pay it no attention," Theo said softly as she came up next to them. "But we'd best keep talk of going to Spain to ourselves until we actually leave."

Carl looked dejected. "I thought they'd be happy for us," he said moodily.

"Theo's right, Carl," Ian told his injured friend. "And I think we should keep all our plans as private as possible from now on. You never know who might be listening."

"I quite agree," Theo said smartly. "After all, we've no

idea how the sorcerers knew Jaaved and I were at the shore today. I think it best if we tell no one what we're up to. That way, we can be certain to escape to Spain without anyone being the wiser."

Carl lifted his chin and regarded Theo. "You think there might be a spy working for Demogorgon's lot?"

Theo sighed and paused on her way up the stairs to gaze at them both soberly. "My intuition is insisting that we should be careful, Carl," she whispered. "Very, *very* careful about what we tell anyone from now on."

Ian couldn't help looking suspiciously back down the stairs at all the children he'd shared his home with the whole of his life. He hated the niggling feeling of mistrust forming in the pit of his stomach.

Several hours later a figure clad all in black hurried away from Castle Dover and through the seaside village to a waiting motorcar. The door to the auto opened and the figure climbed inside, then closed the door quickly before speaking to the driver. "They leave the day after tomorrow," she said.

"Where?" asked the driver.

"To Spain."

"Spain?"

"Yes. To Madrid."

"What is it they seek in Spain?"

"The earl's maidservant didn't know. All she could say for certain was that the earl's plans had changed at the last minute, and that he intends to take the children with him on the journey."

The driver was silent for a long time. "Master will insist we find out why they are going there."

"Yes, my thoughts exactly."

"We have friends in Madrid," he said after a pause. "But I would not trust them to uncover this information alone, and I cannot go. I received a telegram from the master earlier this evening. He needs my assistance in Versailles. I must depart for France immediately."

"I can go alone, Dieter," volunteered the passenger.

Again the driver was silent while he contemplated that. "Very well," he said, relenting. "Follow them, Hylda. Once you arrive in Madrid, make contact with our Spanish comrades and enlist their help to discover why the children are journeying there."

"Of course," she replied with a wickedly sly smile she reserved only for her husband.

"And if you gain the opportunity . . . ," he added, allowing his voice to trail off.

"Kill them?" she asked coyly, stroking his cheek.

"Yes," he confirmed. "And have no doubt, *liebling*, if you do, our master will be most pleased." And then he leaned in to give her a kiss. "Most pleased indeed," he whispered again before starting the car and driving off.

A DARK MEETING

Magus the Black sat across from the Witch of Versailles and was already irritated by the woman's nervous manner. Since he and Dieter had entered her dirty and cluttered flat, he'd been unimpressed, and he had already made up his mind to kill her for wasting his time.

He watched her with disdain while she hovered over her crystal ball, waving her shaking fingers and muttering under her breath. He'd asked the woman only one question, "Where is my sister, Lachestia?" and for the past several minutes, she'd been mumbling incoherently, delaying her answer.

Magus looked over his shoulder at Dieter, who only shook his head contemptuously and frowned as the woman muttered on and on under her breath.

Magus turned back to the witch, his eyes smoldering with impatience. He knew she could sense the evil that wafted off him, but it had made the woman almost too petrified to help him, and he was quickly becoming tired of it.

He allowed her only a few more moments before he slammed his fist onto the tabletop, causing sparks to fly out from the impact. "Speak, woman!" he shouted at her.

The witch was so startled that she reeled backward and nearly toppled out of her chair, but Magus's outburst seemed to shake some sense into her, and the ugly middle-aged woman gasped, "She resides in a grave!"

Magus's sneer turned sinister. "If you are telling me that my sister is dead, then we are finished here." The sorcerer knew that his sister lived. Her passing would most definitely have been noted by his father when her spirit was received in the underworld.

"I did not say she was dead," the witch added in a rush. "I meant to say that she resides underground."

Magus tapped his fingers on the tabletop, and each tap left a black smudge in the wood. "Where?" he asked after a long silence.

The witch wiped a strand of stringy gray hair out of her eyes and focused on her crystal ball again. "She is imprisoned by stones," she said to him. "Deep within a forest bound by a powerful curse. Within the earth that surrounds her are the bones of dead men, too numerous to count."

Magus's fingers ceased their tapping. "Where?" he repeated, and this time his tone was deadly.

The witch closed her eyes to concentrate. "East," she whispered. "Just the other side of Germany. You will find your sister at the German/Polish border on the edge of a village . . . called . . ." The witch's voice trailed off for a moment as she concentrated. "Lubieszyn!"

Magus leaned back in his chair and crossed his arms, considering what the witch had told him. He was well aware of the legend regarding the last sighting of Lachestia. He recalled the time, some three thousand years earlier, when word had reached him that the sorceress had destroyed a series of villages during her personal raid on the lands east of the Rhine River, and that she had entered a forest rumored to be cursed and was never seen again. He suspected that the legend might be true, especially as the witch had just unwittingly revealed a significant clue.

Only his Druid ancestors had power over the likes of Magus and his sisters. In the early days, after Magus and his siblings had destroyed their own village, the elders of all the Druid tribes had gathered and focused their mortal yet considerable magic to create powerful structures capable of imprisoning the demigods.

These structures were made of standing stones—huge monoliths positioned in a ring and inscribed with ancient magical symbols that could slowly drain all the power right out of any of Demogorgon's offspring. It would take many thousands of years to eventually render Magus and his sisters completely powerless and send them to the underworld to greet their father—unless the stone tasted a drop of their blood; then their demise would speed along quite rapidly. But no living person knew that besides Magus and his sisters.

Still, the threat of the stones was enough to cause him to avoid places like Stonehenge and Grimspound—and Delphi Keep, for that matter.

He could often feel the power of the standing stones he knew must be buried somewhere underneath the structure that housed those cursed children, because he could never make it within half a kilometer of the keep before feeling his powers weaken. And that wretched portal was protected as well, by another series of stones, which covered the entrance.

So if the Witch of Versailles was right, and his sister Lachestia had ventured unwittingly into a forest with a ring of hidden standing stones, then she could very well have been entrapped by them.

While Magus was thinking on this, he noticed the witch eyeing him cautiously. She seemed to want to say more, but again looked too frightened to speak. "*What?*" he snapped when she remained mute.

The witch shivered with fright, but she still managed to answer the sorcerer. "The forest that imprisons your sister is cursed, Sir Magus. If you enter the wood, I fear you too will be trapped."

"What power fuels this curse?" he pressed, testing her.

"An ancient one," whispered the witch. "Set in stone."

Magus smiled and decided not to kill the witch after all. "I'm also looking for some children," he said casually. "A boy named Ian and his sister, Theo. I mean to find them at their most vulnerable and destroy them. Can you divine when and where I might have an opportunity to carry out my desire?"

The witch looked doubtfully back into her crystal ball. She gulped and eyed the sorcerer nervously again. "They are well protected," she said. "There are many who gather round these children to ensure their safety."

Magus nodded, understanding fully.

"At this time, Sir Magus, I cannot discover the moment when they will be made vulnerable to you, but I shall keep looking if you'd like."

Magus reached into the folds of his cloak and pulled out a large gold coin, which he tossed at the witch. She caught it easily. "I'd like that very much, witch. Very much indeed."

MADRID

Ian, Carl, and Theo sat lazily on the train, all three of them looking absently out the window at the scenery flashing by. It had changed little on their progression south through France and Spain.

They passed farm after farm and had certainly seen enough grapevines to last a lifetime. The only thing that seemed to change was the steadily increasing temperature. It was hot and muggy inside the train, and Ian pulled at his damp shirt and looked longingly out the open window, which gave at least a little relief from the hot summer day.

Beside him Theo squirmed and murmured something, and Ian realized she was asleep. Carl had also dozed off and Ian was just thinking about doing the same when Theo's murmurs became more agitated. He put a gentle hand on her shoulder and she brushed him off angrily. "Theo," he said into her ear. "You're dreaming."

Theo gasped and bolted awake. "No!" she shouted,

and blinked rapidly while she looked about in a wide-eyed panic.

"What's happening?" Carl grumbled from the opposite side of their box compartment.

"Theo's had a bad dream." Ian placed his hand on her arm. "You all right?"

Theo's breathing was ragged. "I've had the most awful nightmare."

"Theo?" said a voice, and they all looked up to see the earl staring at them from the open door of the compartment, his face concerned.

"I'm fine, my lord," she said quickly, but Ian noticed that she reached up to clutch the crystal at her neck. "Just a bad dream."

The earl smiled but the concern never left his eyes. "Well, I'm quite relieved to see you're all right. We're coming into Madrid in a bit. Might be prudent to look lively and gather your belongings together."

"Yes, my lord," they all said, and for the first time in the two long days their journey had taken them, Ian felt an intense excitement build in the center of his chest.

"I hope we get something to eat soon," Carl complained.

"I'll just be glad to be off this train," Ian told him while reaching up for his satchel just above their heads. "I feel like we've been boxed in for ages."

Carl suddenly pointed out the window and exclaimed, "Oy! Look over there! We're coming into the city!"

All three of them eagerly leaned forward and stared out the window as the first signs of Madrid came into view.

Ian could hardly believe his eyes when the teeming capital of Spain unveiled itself in quick flashes of majestic cathedrals, gilded statues, beautiful old stone buildings, and more modern architecture.

In some respects, Madrid reminded him very much of London; in other ways, it held fiercely to its own unique personality, and he could not wait to set off and explore it.

Finally, the conductor made the announcement that they were coming into the Madrid station, and the three orphans gathered up their belongings. When the train slowed to a stop, Ian heard snatches of conversation coming from some of the other passengers and he smiled, because he could understand them all perfectly, thanks to the small pouch he wore round his neck and the tiny piece of magical opal tucked inside.

Standing beside him, Carl must have been thinking the same thing, because he said, "Lucky for us Jaaved gave us each a piece of the Star, eh, mate?"

Ian nodded and was about to turn to answer his friend when he felt someone staring at him. He looked up to see a woman with black hair quickly turn her face away. Ian would have thought nothing of it if he hadn't noticed a man a few paces away looking from the woman to Ian and back again.

The stranger held his attention mostly because he appeared to be the most physically powerful person Ian had ever seen. He had dark olive skin, black curly hair, and a well-trimmed beard. His physique was nothing short of intimidating as he all but towered over the other passengers, with his huge broad shoulders, and arms thick with corded muscle. The man also carried himself with the confidence and alertness of a warrior.

His attire was fairly simple: he wore a white linen shirt, black trousers, and shiny leather boots. His sleeves were rolled up to reveal his strong arms, and around each of his wrists was a beautiful bronze cuff. The stranger's face was square, broad, and handsome. His intense eyes suggested a keenness of mind. He stared without blinking at Ian, as if he were daring the boy to say something.

Embarrassed, Ian nodded, and the stranger nodded back, but Ian's primary attention quickly returned to the woman he'd caught staring at them. Her face was still turned away, and he thought he might have imagined her interest in him.

He didn't have time to consider these two longer, because the doors to the train opened, and people began to shuffle forward. Ian stayed back with Carl and Theo as the woman exited quickly, followed closely but discreetly by the powerful man with the bronze cuffs.

The earl found them and encouraged them to exit as well. "Children!" he called from several people back. "Wait for us out on the platform."

Ian nodded and held firmly to Theo's hand while he moved into the aisle and shuffled along with all the other passengers to the exit. They squirmed their way off the train, and once on the platform, they waited for the other members of their party. The earl came first, followed by the professor, who appeared stiff and sore from the long journey.

Ian gave a cursory look around for the man with the cuffs, but he and the woman were nowhere to be seen.

"Do we all have our luggage?" asked the earl when he and the professor joined them.

"Yes, my lord," they all answered.

"Very well," said the earl. "Let's see about acquiring a taxi, shall we?"

The earl led the way through the crowd to the street, where cars and people bustled about, and he waved his hand for a car. All the taxicabs passing them were full, but then Ian spotted a rather run-down cab parked just a few meters away, and noticed the woman with the dark hair talking urgently to the driver.

Ian looked for the man with the bronze cuffs again and found him nearby, pretending to read a newspaper.

Ian wondered what sort of relationship the pair had when, to his surprise, the woman handed the taxi driver several bills before darting quickly away. Ian thought it quite curious that she'd paid the driver without getting into the motorcar. He would have thought on it longer, but at that moment he realized the driver was waving to him. "You there!" the man called.

Ian's eyes opened wide with surprise. "Me?" he called back.

"Yes!" said the man, moving forward with a broad, friendly smile. "Do you need a taxicab today?"

The earl had stopped trying to hail the many cabs whizzing past and turned his attention to Ian. "Master Wigby," he said softly but sharply. "Remember to be careful not to give your language skills away!"

Ian quickly tore his eyes from the approaching taxi

driver. "I'm terribly sorry, my lord," he whispered. The earl had warned the children about wearing their pieces of the Star, as he thought their adeptness with the native Spanish spoken around them might call attention to them, but Ian, Theo, and Carl had all been reluctant to comply.

The earl laid a gentle hand on his shoulder. "Very well, lad, tell me what he's saying, but in a whisper, if you please."

"He wants to know if we'd like a taxi."

"Oh, how convenient," said the earl, already picking up his bags and preparing to walk toward the man waving them over to his car.

"Wait," Ian said, catching the earl by the sleeve.

"What is it, lad?" asked the earl.

Ian looked around him. Something didn't feel quite right, especially when he realized he'd lost sight of not only the woman with the black hair, but the man with the bronze cuffs too.

Unfortunately, Ian had no time to express his concern, because the taxi driver had reached them and was already lifting the earl's bags for him. "You want taxi?" he asked enthusiastically, his voice heavy with an accent, which was the only way Ian was able to determine he was now speaking English.

"That's exactly what we'd like, my good man," said the professor, leaning heavily on his walking stick as he set off for the taxi. Before Ian could say another word, Carl and Theo had picked up their satchels and were following the professor to the motorcar.

"Is everything all right, Master Wigby?" said the earl,

obviously still waiting for Ian to reveal what he'd wanted to tell him. But the driver was still standing in front of them, nodding eagerly as he pointed to his taxi.

"You come. I will take you, no?"

"Er . . . ," Ian said. "Everything's fine, my lord. Just a bit tired from the journey, I suppose."

"Well, then," the earl said, tipping his hat to the driver as they began to walk toward the waiting motorcar. "Let us make haste to our final destination, shall we?"

Ian had little choice but to hurry along to the taxi, where the professor was already waving the slip of paper with Señora Castillo's address on it at the driver. "We'd like to go here," the professor insisted when the driver finished putting their bags into the boot of the car.

"Yes, yes," the driver assured them after looking at the address and smiling broadly. Ian found his smile and good nature quite disarming. "We go now, yes?"

"Yes, my good chap," the earl said, and promptly got into the front seat of the taxi.

Ian squished into the back with Theo, Carl, and the professor and soon they were off.

"You all right?" Theo whispered beside him when she caught Ian craning his neck to stare out the back window. He was still looking for the two strangers from the train.

"Fine," he murmured, turning around again. He didn't want to alarm Theo, especially when what he'd seen had probably been nothing but a coincidence of events out of context.

The trip to Señora Castillo's house was long, as the heavy midafternoon traffic slowed their progress, but finally they seemed to clear the thickest part of the congestion, and long stretches of roadway paved with beautiful, lush green fields came into view. Soon afterward they entered a long private drive, which ended in a large three-story home.

Once the taxi came to rest in front of the double mahogany doors, Ian and his friends bounded out, anxious to do something other than sit. The driver was just as friendly at the end of their trip and helped them unload their bags, then tipped his hat when the earl paid him. Everyone hurried to claim their luggage, but before they had a chance to knock on the door, it opened and a short portly woman with red-apple cheeks and a kind smile was standing there, gazing happily at them. "At last you're here!" she said with a small clap.

Ian hoped this was Señora Castillo, because he liked her immediately. The professor waddled forward and pulled off his hat, bobbing his head in earnest. "My apologies for being frightfully tardy, Señora Castillo. The train was late leaving Toulouse yesterday and that put us off schedule, I'm afraid."

The elder woman tsked. "Pesky trains," she said while the professor dipped his head to kiss her hand politely. Ian hid a smile when she blushed and fanned her delighted face. It seemed the señora was so happy to see her brother's friend that she almost forgot the rest of the group was there.

Belatedly, the professor realized the others were standing about awkwardly and he hurried to make their acquaintances. "May I introduce you all to Señora Latisha Castillo, the gentle sister of my dear friend and esteemed colleague Sir Donovan Barnaby."

At the mention of her brother, Señora Castillo's smile faded just a bit. But as they all went forward to introduce themselves, her bright spirits returned and she welcomed them with a boisterous wave into her home. As they'd agreed before they'd left the keep, the earl was introduced as Mr. Nutley—the professor's nephew—and Ian, Carl, and Theo were presented as the earl's children, which Ian decided wasn't far off the mark. "Come, come!" she sang, ushering them into her foyer.

Ian observed that even though the señora's house was grand, there weren't any servants about to collect their satchels and hats. But he soon discovered why when Señora Castillo flushed with embarrassment and hastily asked them to leave their bags near the stairs. "I'm terribly sorry to find myself short staffed for your visit. My manservant resigned nearly a fortnight ago, and I haven't had the courage or the energy to interview for a replacement. Hiring qualified servants can be so taxing in Spain—especially for a foreigner. My husband, Ernesto, used to handle such things, you see. Since his passing, I've lost the gardener, the manservant, and my driver! I find the process of looking after the staff and this home quite overwhelming at times."

The earl was quick to put Señora Castillo at ease. "Please do not worry over it, señora. We are perfectly capable of tending to our own things."

Señora Castillo smiled gratefully. "At least I've managed to keep the cook," she told them with a laugh.

And it was then that Ian was struck by the most delicious smell.

Carl—who was a true fan of all things delicious—whispered, "Gaw, blimey! I can't wait to taste whatever *that* is!"

"Carl," said Theo sternly, "remember your manners!"

Carl blushed and Ian ducked his chin to hide his smile. Although she was three years his and Carl's junior, there was no doubt that Theo would be the first to reach adulthood. In fact, Ian often wondered if she hadn't got there already.

Fortunately, no one else appeared to have heard their exchange, because Señora Castillo was talking with great haste, telling them all about how long it had been since she'd had visitors from her own country. "The last person to spend a holiday with me here in Madrid was my dear mother, but she's passed now some ten years. And during this whole frightful time since the war began, it's no wonder everyone's kept away.

"So I shall take it as a hopeful sign that you were willing to come all this way, Professor Nutley, to spend some time in this beautiful city and look over Donovan's old diaries."

"We're most grateful for your hospitality, Señora Castillo," said the professor with a slight bow, which made their host blush again.

From just behind the flushing woman, there appeared a pencil-thin and very severe-looking servant in a long black dress and white starched apron. "Lunch will be ready very soon, señora," she announced.

"Thank you, Carmina."

Carl nudged Ian discreetly and whispered, "I can't wait to tuck into that meal."

Señora Castillo's eyes immediately opened wide and she

91

stared at Carl in shock. "Did the lad just speak Spanish?" she asked.

The earl was quick to place a hand on Carl's shoulder and answer, "Oh, no, señora, I'm afraid none of us speak Spanish, and other than their native English, my children speak only a bit of French, which, as you know, at times might sound quite similar. They were practicing their lessons, in fact, on the train, and I believe Carl was merely demonstrating what a quick study he is."

Ian could sense the stiff posture of Carl standing beside him. "Bonjour, madame," he said meekly.

Señora Castillo laughed merrily. "What a charming young man!" she exclaimed. "And might I also say what handsome children you have?" She eyed each of them in turn and pointed to Ian and Theo. "These two look very much alike, but this young man must favor his mother, am I right?" Ian wanted to laugh when she singled out poor Carl again.

The earl, however, seemed to notice Carl's discomfort. "Yes, my second son does indeed resemble his mother, who was quite beautiful, as you can well imagine."

Carl let out a breath he'd obviously been holding and looked up gratefully at the earl, but Señora Castillo clasped her hand to her heart and looked at the earl in earnest. "Did you say 'was,' Mr. Nutley?"

The earl nodded gravely. "Yes, I'm afraid so."

"Oh, my!" exclaimed their hostess. "I hadn't realized the children's mother had passed away. Such a tragedy!"

Ian shifted uncomfortably. He knew that it was important to lend a few facts about themselves to Señora Castillo in order not to appear too secretive, but all this emphasis on their mothers being dead unsettled him. *Was* his mother dead? he wondered. He'd likely never know for certain.

The earl nodded again and the señora clasped his hand for a moment before her face suddenly flashed into a brilliant smile. "All this melancholy talk simply won't do after you've all endured such a long journey. Come along into the dining room, if you please, and we'll enjoy an authentic Spanish lunch and talk of happier things."

It seemed to Ian that he and Carl weren't the only ones looking forward to tasting whatever dish had that amazing smell, because everyone hurried after their hostess into the dining room.

Once they were seated, Señora Castillo's cook served them steaming plates of the best-tasting seafood stew Ian had ever had in his life. While he ate, he made sure to hold his tongue, lest someone say something in Spanish and cause him to slip. He settled for listening to the conversation the adults were having.

He learned that Señora Castillo's husband had passed away only the year before. She claimed that he had kept her in Spain through the war. "I couldn't leave my beloved Ernesto," she said. "And he was far too sick to travel for many years before he died. No, in the end it was better that he remained here, surrounded by his books, his art, and his people. I do miss him, though," she added sadly, her eyes misting. "As I said, no one comes round to visit an old lady in mourning anymore."

The table fell silent and Ian was sure no one knew what to say. But Theo surprised him when she reached out and took hold of the woman's hand. "You'll be all right," she assured the widow. "And I expect you'll soon visit your homeland, Señora Castillo. I've a mind to say that in just a short time, you'll want to come back to England again."

Señora Castillo's face registered some surprise. "As a matter of fact, my dear young miss, I received a letter from a cherished friend this very morning asking if I might want to join her for a visit! How uncanny that you should mention it to me this afternoon!"

Theo smiled knowingly. "I believe you should accept the proposal, ma'am."

Señora Castillo continued to look at her with some surprise, and the professor steered the conversation back to the reason they'd traveled so far. "I'm anxious to look at Donovan's journals, Señora Castillo. Have you by chance located them among his things?"

"Oh, yes, Professor," she said, pulling her attention away from Theo to beam at him. "Donovan was quite the prolific writer, you know. He was always scribbling in his journals. Even as a boy he wanted to capture the essence of his life by chronicling everything that happened to him. Such a shame he was with us for so brief a time. I'm sure he would have had the most wonderfully adventurous life."

"From what I've heard," said the earl in a kindly voice, "your brother's life was already rich with adventure, Señora

94

Castillo. I should also be most interested to read his journals."

Señora Castillo nodded at him enthusiastically. "Yes, yes," she said. "However, I must warn you that many of his later journal entries are nearly illegible. Donovan had the most dreadful penmanship, I'm afraid. I should think you'll find deciphering his scribbles to be a task requiring patience and a keen mind."

Ian watched the professor beam at Señora Castillo. "I'm sure I'm up for the challenge," he said.

By this time Carmina was gathering up the dishes, and Ian couldn't help noticing she was eying them all a bit warily. Theo was also keeping close watch on the servant, and the moment the cook went out of the room again, Theo leaned in and whispered, "I don't like her."

He would have whispered back that he agreed, but Señora Castillo was getting to her feet and encouraging her guests to do the same. "I should think you all must be quite exhausted from your long journey and in need of rest. If you will all follow me, I will take you upstairs to your rooms and allow you time to refresh yourselves."

They took hold of their luggage and trooped up the stairs behind Señora Castillo, and Ian was delighted with the warmth and spaciousness of the house. As he crested the landing, he saw that it fed into a corridor with several doors. "The boys will be in here," the widow announced, opening the first door on the left and revealing a good-sized room painted robin's-egg blue with a twin bed on each side of the window.

Ian and Carl thanked Señora Castillo, who patted them each on the back before leading the rest of the party farther down the hallway.

While the others were being shown to their quarters, Ian made quick business of unpacking his suitcase. It took him no time at all, as he'd brought only two spare pairs of trousers and three extra shirts. He opened one drawer in the bureau, thinking Carl could take the other, but as he turned around to tell Carl this, he discovered his friend curled up on the far bed, snoring softly.

Ian shook his head. All Carl ever seemed to need after a large meal was a nice long nap.

A giggle from behind told him that Theo found it as funny as he did. He turned to face her and held a finger to his lips, although he was smiling too. "I think he's set a new record," he whispered. "We only came upstairs a few minutes ago."

"Are you tired?" Theo asked, coming to sit on Ian's bed.

"No, not really."

"Care for a card game?" she suggested. Ian smiled again and sat down opposite her on the bed. They kept their voices to a whisper so as not to disturb anyone taking an afternoon nap, which, judging from the sound of the snores coming to them from the hallway, included the professor and the earl.

Not long into their card game, Ian heard a soft knock on a door somewhere outside the open window. He and Theo both looked curiously first at each other, then at the window to peer outside.

Right below them stood a man at the back door of the house. Ian couldn't see his face, but there was something familiar about the man's cap. A moment later the door was opened and Carmina's voice carried up to them. "Yes?" she demanded.

"Good day," said the man. "I was here earlier. I delivered your guests from the train station."

"Oh?" said Carmina. Ian realized that the man below was, in fact, their taxi driver. He wondered the same thing Carmina asked. "Did they leave some baggage behind in your taxi?"

The man removed his hat and began fingering it nervously. "No," he said, his voice noticeably quieter. "And if I could please ask you to speak somewhere privately? The news I have to share I would not want overheard."

Ian caught his breath. Whatever this man had to say, Ian was now quite certain he must work to hear it.

To his relief, Carmina didn't move away with the cab driver but remained standing right under their window. "You may speak freely, sir. My employer is taking her afternoon nap, and she is a woman who sleeps deeply."

The driver continued to fiddle with his hat nervously. "I am more worried that your guests might overhear."

Carmina made a derisive sound. "The English travelers?" she asked. "They speak only English and a bit of French, I'm told."

At this the driver stopped playing with his hat and tucked it under his arm. "Ah," he said. "That is very good."

"Now tell me what you want or I will ask you to leave,"

Carmina snapped, and Ian was glad she was being so insistent, because he was just as impatient to hear what the driver had to say.

"There is some interest in your guests," the man confessed, and Ian felt a tickle of fear creep through him. "I have a patron who would very much like to know who it is they are visiting, and why."

Carmina stepped out onto the back steps and took a package of cigarettes and a lighter from her apron pocket. She offered a cigarette to the driver, who declined; then she lit her own and said, "How much would your patron pay for this information?"

Beside Ian, Theo sucked in a small breath, and Ian held a finger over his lips.

"She would be willing to pay handsomely," the man assured the cook, and he then reached into his blazer pocket and pulled out a few bills.

Carmina snatched the money right out of the driver's hand and said, "They come here to pay a visit to the widow Castillo. The old man is interested in some diary kept by the widow's brother, who died many years ago. I am told the English intend to stay a week or so to sort through the journal."

The taxi driver nodded enthusiastically. "I believe my patron would like to see this diary. Do you think you might be able to secure it for me?"

Carmina looked about nervously, and both Theo and Ian pulled their heads in from the window, lest either one of the pair below look up. "I believe that can be arranged," they heard her say. "For double what you have just given me."

"Of course," the driver said easily.

"The visitors are taking a siesta right now, and later tonight, after I have cooked them a nice hearty meal, they will surely wish to turn in immediately. I can also ensure that their sleep is sound enough that they will not overhear my securing the diary and delivering it to you. Where should I meet you?"

"I will have my lorry parked on the road behind those woods," said the driver. Ian inched his nose above the sill to peek out at the woods set behind the back garden.

"Make sure you have the money," Carmina reminded him curtly. "Now go before the widow wakes and sees you."

A moment later they heard the closing of the back door, followed by the quick footfalls of the driver hurrying down the dirt path to the woods.

Ian's heart was racing and he and Theo stared at each other with stunned expressions. "This is terrible!" Theo whispered.

Ian nodded dully, too surprised to speak for a long moment. He thought back to the woman from the train who'd been quick to turn away the moment he'd looked at her, and how later he'd seen her hand some bills to their taxi driver but hadn't got into the taxicab. He was convinced that she was a spy for one of the sorcerers, but what her true identity was, he had no idea. He also had the thought again that she and the man with the bronze cuffs could be working together.

"We've got to alert the earl," Ian finally said, getting up to move quickly to the door, but as he walked across the wood planks, they creaked loudly and he stopped, afraid Carmina might hear him and realize they were awake.

Theo seemed to be reading his mind, because she whispered, "We'll have to wait."

Ian turned back and tiptoed to the bed. "Yes," he agreed.

Much later that evening, after supper, when Señora Castillo had finally retired to bed, Ian whispered to the earl that he had a most urgent matter to discuss with all of them. They made their way to the widow's library, where Carl— who'd been told all about the treachery the moment he'd awakened from his afternoon nap—stood guard at the door, keeping a watchful eye out for Carmina.

"This is most distressing," said the professor after Ian recounted what he and Theo had overheard. "Most distressing indeed!"

"Professor," the earl asked, "has Señora Castillo given you her brother's journal yet?"

The professor nodded. "Yes," he said, pulling a singed leather-bound book from his blazer pocket. "She gave it to me just before dinner. But, my lord, I've only had a brief moment to look through it. Barnaby was a meticulous scribe, you see, and he made an exact replica of the last of the Oracle's scroll. There's a fair degree of smoke damage to the text. My eyes aren't what they once were; deciphering his scribbles will be rather slow going, I'm afraid."

"How long would it take you to translate the prophecy?" the earl pressed.

The professor wrinkled his nose and flipped carefully through several of the well-worn pages. "It won't be an easy translation," he admitted, adjusting his bifocals and squinting at the paper. "But I should think I'd make it through in a few days . . . a week at the longest."

The earl sighed heavily. "I'm terribly worried that's several days too long, Professor," he said softly. "Now that we know someone is indeed spying on us and wants that journal, I think it best to keep our visit here as short as possible. How much can you decipher by tomorrow evening?"

The professor's bushy white eyebrows rose. "I hardly think I could make it through a quarter of the text in that span, my lord."

"And you're certain Señora Castillo will not allow us to borrow the journal for a few weeks even if we promise to send it to her the moment we've finished with it?"

The professor shook his head ruefully. "Quite certain, my lord. She was insistent that I not leave this house with the journal. It records the last words and thoughts of her beloved brother and she's terribly afraid of losing it or having it further damaged."

"Pardon me," said Ian as a thought occurred to him, "but, Professor Nutley, might it be more prudent to make a copy of the prophecy and decipher it back home in England?"

Both the earl and the professor looked at him in surprise before the earl said, "Brilliant idea, lad!"

The professor nodded agreeably. "Yes, of course! I could have this copied word for word in a day, and if I start on it this evening, we might just be able to take our leave by sundown tomorrow."

"Excellent," said the earl with a satisfied smile. "Between now and then, professor, do not let that diary out of your sight."

"Does anyone know why the journal is so important to someone other than ourselves?" Theo asked, her hand at the crystal about her neck.

The professor opened to the middle of the book and squinted at the writing. "I can only think that our enemies would find it worthy of stealing, my lord, because it is obviously important to us. If it does contain a copy of Laodamia's last prophecy, well, then I should think it vital to our cause."

The earl looked gravely at the professor. "Then I urge you to make great haste in copying it. I will go into the city at daybreak to arrange passage back to England, but we mustn't tell Señora Castillo of our plans. If her cook truly is working as a spy, we cannot risk our hostess letting it slip that we plan to make our escape next evening."

"Very well," said the professor.

Just then, Carl turned away from the door and whispered urgently, "Carmina's coming!"

The earl pointed Carl to a chair across from him and quickly removed several chess pieces to make it appear as if he and Carl were in the middle of a game. Ian took the hint and dashed over to snag a novel from the bookshelves before sitting down next to Theo on the sofa. He opened the book just as Carmina entered the library without knocking.

"Good evening," she said with a thick Spanish accent

while carrying a tray loaded with steaming glasses of milk. "I have come to give you all a cap for the night."

Ian realized she meant the word "nightcap," and he eyed the tray of milk suspiciously. The earl smiled easily but made no move to take one of the glasses. "Thank you, Carmina, but I believe I shall have to pass on the milk, as it often upsets my sensitive stomach, and I don't recommend that the children have anything more than water so close to their bedtime."

Carmina's stern lips pressed together. "But it will help them for sleep time," she said.

The professor also smiled easily at her. "I'm afraid I too will pass on the milk, though it was most kind of you to pour us each a glass."

Carmina looked truly frustrated, and her eyes moved to Ian, Theo, and Carl.

"No, thank you," Theo said politely.

"No, thank you," Ian repeated, forcing himself to smile.

"Oh, can't I have some?" Carl whined before making a small yelping noise. Ian could have sworn he'd seen the earl's foot come down right on Carl's toes. "Um . . . but now that I think about it," he amended, "maybe my father's right and I've had enough milk for one day."

Carmina seemed to linger in the doorway, as if she were suddenly suspicious of them all. "You are sure?" she asked one last time. "Milk will put you right to sleep."

There was something quite eerie about the way she was trying to push a glass of milk on them, and Ian was certain she was up to something. The earl must have sensed it too, because his smile widened and he said, "That is, again, most kind of you, Carmina, but I don't believe any one of us will have difficulty sleeping tonight. And please, do not stay up late on our account. I can assure you we will be most content this evening. You may take your leave of us now."

Ian had to marvel at the earl, because although his smile was wide and friendly, his eyes and tone left no room for further argument. Carmina's lips then pressed together so tightly that they all but disappeared before she gave one curt nod and left the room.

Once she had gone, everyone held perfectly still for several moments before Ian got up quietly and tiptoed toward the door. He could see the cook walking slowly away, as if she was hoping to catch a bit of conversation. When she was finally out of earshot, Ian turned back to the group. "She's gone."

The earl let out a sigh of relief but cautioned the group. "We must be very careful for the next twenty-four hours. We don't want to rouse any suspicions, lest we put the dear Señora Castillo in any sort of danger."

"Do you think she might be in harm's way, my lord?" the professor asked.

But it was Theo who answered him. "Yes, Professor, I believe we're all in a bit of danger now."

"We must warn her," the professor declared, his face set deep with worry.

But the earl shook his head sadly. "We cannot risk it, my friend. If our delightful hostess believes our story, then she will have no choice but to dismiss Carmina, and given the loss of the rest of her staff, that would surely put her in a terrible state, with no one left to look after her. How will she manage? And do not forget that Carmina isn't working alone. If this taxi driver and his patron come round here after we're gone, I believe the señora would do well to remain blissfully ignorant of our suspicions."

The professor leaned back in his chair with a tired sigh. "Of course you're right, my lord," he said softly before getting wearily to his feet. "And in light of these most distressing circumstances, I shall now cease to dally down here, and find my way upstairs to begin copying the prophecy immediately."

The others got up as well and everyone headed off to bed most somberly. Ian saw Theo to her room, which was right next to his and Carl's. "Keep your door locked," he advised her. He hated that she was forced to take a room of her own, without protection.

"Of course," she told him. "And you be careful as well."

He smiled and ruffled her hair. "Don't worry about me," he said softly. "I can look after myself."

Theo arched her eyebrow skeptically but she merely said her goodnights and shut the door. Ian waited until he heard the lock click, then headed back to his room, noting that the professor and the earl were whispering quietly in the hallway just outside the professor's room.

Ian felt better knowing that the earl was looking out for them. His patron caught his eye just as he was about to turn back to his room. "Sleep tight, lad," he said softly. "We'll be off by tomorrow evening."

Ian nodded and joined Carl in their assigned bedchamber. His friend appeared distraught. "I don't like this business one bit," Carl said.

Ian yawned tiredly. "I know, mate," he agreed.

"I think we should keep watch on the hallway," Carl suggested.

Ian was surprised. The idea of posting a guard hadn't occurred to him, but now that Carl mentioned it, it seemed like a good one. "Might be a long night for us," he warned.

"I'm up for it," Carl said, and Ian remembered the nap Carl had taken that afternoon, which Ian well knew did not guarantee Carl would manage to stay awake during his watch. His friend had a reputation for requiring more than his fair share of sleep.

"You sure?" Ian asked, trying to gauge his friend's fatigue.

Carl pumped his head enthusiastically. "Of course!"

"Very well. If you see Carmina creeping about the hallway, looking for the journal, go out of the room and act like you're heading to the loo. That'll give her pause about sneaking around tonight, at least."

"Which will give the professor long enough to copy the journal," Carl said before eyeing Ian, who was swaying on his feet with fatigue. "Why don't I take the first watch?" he suggested.

Ian smiled gratefully. "That'd be smashing, thanks." Then he hurried into his nightshirt while Carl wrapped himself snugly in a blanket and took his pillow over to the door, which he opened just a crack before sitting down on the cushion to peer out into the hallway.

After setting the sundial on the small side table under the window, Ian climbed wearily into bed and turned off the lamp, whispering to Carl, "Wake me in a few hours, and I'll take the next watch till dawn."

The last thing Ian saw before sleep claimed him was his friend peeking intently out the slight crack in the door.

Several hours later Ian awoke with a start. Something he couldn't quite place had alerted him, and as he sat up in bed and squinted into the darkness, he heard two things that alarmed him. The first was the subtle snoring of Carl, fast asleep on the floor. The other was the creaking of floorboards just outside their room.

Quick as a flash, Ian dashed out of bed and over to Carl, who was curled up in a ball next to the door. Scowling, Ian leaned over his friend and peered through the crack just as a dark shape moved slowly past. It appeared someone was attempting to move quietly down the hallway.

Ian considered opening the door and confronting the person, but some eerie feeling deep in his bones told him to wait. So he settled for inching the door open enough to poke his head out, and squinted into the darkness.

Lit by the moonlight coming in the front window was the thin figure of Carmina, descending the staircase. And in her hand Ian could just make out a small leather book.

For one brief moment he was so stunned that he forgot himself and gasped. Carmina paused on the staircase and began to turn around, but Ian quickly pulled his head back. He crouched, frozen, until after a few seconds, he could hear the soft creaking of floorboards again as the cook continued to make her way down the stairs.

Without thinking, Ian flew into action. He hurried over to his clothes and grabbed his trousers and shoes and hastily pulled them on. In his rush to get dressed, he must have kicked Carl, who woke with a start. "Ow!" the boy moaned, disconcerted and testy. "What's happening?"

"You fell asleep!" Ian hissed. "Carmina has the journal! I'm going after her!" And with that he pulled open the door and tiptoed quickly down the stairs, pausing only briefly to figure out which way the cook had gone.

He heard a door creak open in the kitchen. Ian did not hesitate to move toward the noise, and he arrived just in time to see Carmina disappear through the back door.

Ian crept stealthily to the window over the sink and took a peek outside. The maid was heading to the left, down the pathway that cut through the garden. Ian waited until she was well away from the house before following her outside.

Keeping low to the ground, he trailed the maid as she walked quickly out of the garden, through the small patch of woods, and to the road that ran behind the house. Ian was grateful for the moonlight making her silhouette clearly visible, and continued for several hundred meters before he stopped abruptly because he realized Carmina had stopped. She stood out in the open, and next to her, parked on the dirt road, was a pickup lorry with its lights off but the engine running.

Ian darted behind a nearby tree and peeked out just in time to see the cook walk straight to the cab of the lorry and hand over the journal. Ian could hear muffled words exchanged but wasn't certain what might have been said before the driver handed several bills to her.

Behind him, he heard someone shout in alarm and he knew that Carl had likely alerted people within the house. Glancing quickly back, Ian could just make out lights coming on in the upstairs windows of the home, but when he looked again at the lorry, Carmina was already running quickly back toward the house. Meanwhile, the driver revved the engine and the lorry roared to life; then the engine sputtered and coughed and died almost immediately. The driver frantically attempted to turn it over, and Ian listened with a hammering heart as it whinnied and whined to no effect.

Carmina flew past Ian's hiding place on her way back to the house, and just as she passed him, Ian made a split-second decision. He sprang from his crouched position and ran as fast as he could toward the back of the lorry, making it to the rear just as the engine finally caught. Ian latched on to the lorry frame and swung his leg over the lip, tumbling into the bed. The old thing sputtered and jolted forward and Ian had to lie down flat or risk falling out of the lorry as it began to move down the road. He'd barely had time to collect himself when something landed right next to him in the bed, and Ian almost cried out in alarm before he realized that Carl was lying in a heap beside him, wearing a huge grin. "What are you *doing?*" Ian demanded.

"Same thing as you, mate!" Carl said, still wearing the grin. "I saw you climb in here, and I couldn't very well let you go off alone, now could I?"

Ian then realized what a foolish thing they'd done and how much trouble they were likely in. "Where's the earl?" Ian asked, close to Carl's ear. He motioned his friend over to the corner of the lorry bed, well out of the driver's line of vision.

"Back at the house," Carl told him. "I woke the professor, who'd fallen asleep at his desk. The journal and the copy he'd been making were both gone, so I asked him to fetch the earl while I ran after you."

"I don't know where we're going," Ian admitted while the dark countryside whizzed past them.

"You don't?" Carl said, and Ian suspected that it was starting to dawn on Carl how much danger they could both be in. "The earl will find us," Carl added after a few moments, but Ian could hear the doubt in his voice. "The important thing is to get the diary back."

"Yeah," Ian said. "Any ideas on how we'll do that?"

"I thought *you'd* have a plan."

"Naw, mate," Ian said. "I didn't think past jumping into the lorry."

"Uh-oh," Carl murmured.

Ian had to agree. They were in way over their heads. The best they could hope for was that the earl had somehow managed to follow them, but as Ian scanned the dark road behind them, he knew that wasn't likely. "All right," he said after a bit, "Let's put our heads together and think of what to do when this lorry finally stops."

For the next several kilometers, the boys talked through plans, none of which seemed very appealing, until they finally settled on simply waiting to see where the driver took them and assessing what to do then.

THE SECRET KEEPER

The lorry eventually stopped as the first rays of dawn began to turn the dark sky a murky purple. Ian sat up just a bit from his crouched position and took a look about. They seemed to have parked next to a large stadium and the heavy scent of livestock was in the air. "Gaw!" Carl whispered next to him, waving his hand in front of his nose. "What's that smell?"

But Ian was prevented from responding by the sound of a motorcar approaching the front of the lorry. When he lifted his head just a bit more to see it, he had to squint into the headlights. For a moment he thought the car might pass, but it came to a stop just in front of their lorry. Ian noted that both engines continued to run. Worried that the headlights might illuminate him, he ducked back down in the bed and waited with Carl to listen to what happened next.

The boys didn't have to wait long. Almost immediately they heard a door open, then shut, and footfalls clicked on the cobblestone as someone approached. "You have the journal?" a woman asked, her tongue rolling thickly over the words. Her voice sounded very familiar to Ian.

"You have the money?" the driver responded.

"Of course. But I want to see the journal first."

Ian and Carl sat as still as possible. They heard some rustling sounds before, "There, you've seen it. Now hand over the money."

The woman did not respond. Instead, her feet clicked away again; then another car door opened and closed before she came back to the lorry. "It is all here in my satchel," she said, her voice sinister and uncomfortably familiar. Ian knew it, but from where? "Now, give me the journal and I shall think about paying you."

"*Think* about paying me?" the driver repeated, as if he couldn't believe she would have the nerve to withhold his funds.

"The journal!" the woman snapped. "Give it to me!"

But the driver must have thought better about handing over the diary, because he replied, "I think I should keep it until you give me the money." And then the boys heard something make a distinctly metallic clicking sound and Ian could almost sense the tension in the air ratcheting up several notches. "Hand over the money," said the taxi driver. "Now."

The woman seemed to hesitate but then she spat, "You *dare* pull a gun on me, peasant?"

"Give me the money," the man repeated, his voice lethal.

Again the woman seemed to hesitate. "I will hunt you down and kill you," she vowed. Ian felt something heavy thump into the back of the lorry right next to him. He looked over and, to his horror, realized the woman had just thrown the satchel into the bed.

"You may try," he told her. "But you will not live long enough to succeed."

Again the woman spoke, but this time her voice was softer, almost soothing, and the things she told the driver sent the most frightful shiver up Ian's spine. "Yes," she cooed, ignoring his threats. "I shall enjoy killing you, Antolin. But not before I cut the throats of your wife and son."

The man audibly gasped, but he seemed to recover himself quickly. "A lucky guess, Frau Van Schuft. You do not know my family."

Ian's eyes met Carl's in the dim light. Carl's face reflected all the shock Ian felt. They were both quite familiar with Frau Van Schuft and her evil master. "It was not a guess, *peasant*," she taunted. "Your wife, Lera, and your son, Renaldo. They are in the flat just a few streets over, no?"

"I could kill you now, woman!" the man growled.

"Yes, you could," she said with a small sigh, as if she didn't have a care in the world. "But that would displease my associates—who are right now waiting for me—which would condemn your family to certain death. And you should also know that my associates would not stop at murdering your son and his mother . . . no, they would vent their fury on every member of your family. Your two brothers and your aging mother and father. Your parents are on the other side of the city, correct? They have a lovely little home, Antolin. I especially love the small garden in the back, where your mother keeps her chickens. And my loyal associates would make sure to leave you for last so that you could feel the full measure of their revenge. Perhaps they would even make you watch."

Ian's mouth had gone dry. Frau Van Schuft spoke as if she were talking about something as casual as the weather. Finally, the man who had taken the journal from Carmina spat on the ground and said, "If I give you the journal, you must promise to leave me and my family alone!"

"Give me the journal, Antolin, and I'll consider it."

There was another long pause as the taxi driver must have been thinking about the mess he'd got himself into, and when several seconds ticked by with no more sound, Ian couldn't resist taking a peek to see what was happening. With great care he lifted his head just a fraction and peered over the lip of the lorry. He could see the driver sticking his head out the window, staring angrily at Frau Van Schuft— who, Ian noticed, had taken great care to disguise herself, changing her long platinum blond hair to a short black bob.

Unfortunately, Frau Van Schuft must have sensed that someone was staring at her, because to Ian's horror, her head snapped in his direction and their eyes met. For a fraction of a second, no one moved. Frau Van Schuft snarled and reached forward to grab at him, but the driver of the lorry must have got spooked, because he hit the gas and sped down the street.

Ian lurched forward to grab the side of the lorry bed as the driver began to turn the wheel sharply; then he saw something whiz out of the cab and land with a small thwack on the pavement. He realized in that instant that it must be the journal.

Without thinking it through, Ian grabbed Carl roughly by the collar and lifted him to his knees. "We've got to jump!"

Carl responded immediately by lunging toward the side of the lorry, grabbing hold, and launching himself out of the bed. Ian jumped right after him and landed with a hard thud on the ground before rolling over and over on the pavement. "Ow!" Carl moaned from a few paces away. "That hurt!"

Ian crawled to Carl's side, his shins aching from the fall. "We've got to get the journal!"

"Go, mate!" Carl said, rubbing his ankle. "Hurry, before Van Schuft gets to it!"

Ian pushed off the ground and limped as fast as he could back to where he thought the journal had landed. In the distance he could hear the sound of someone running toward him and he knew it had to be that dreadful woman. Desperately, he searched the ground for the diary, and with a rush of relief he spotted it near a gutter, but at that very moment, a small gust of wind lifted the cover of the book, and the paper the professor had been copying the scroll onto flittered from between the pages and blew into the gutter. Ian gasped when he realized that hours of the professor's work had just been lost—but there was nothing he could do. As fast as he could, he darted to the mouth of the gutter and grabbed the journal, then turned to run back to Carl.

Behind him Frau Van Schuft yelled, "You there! Stop!"

Ian ignored her and dashed to Carl's side. His friend was attempting to stand. "Did you get it?" Carl asked.

"Yes, mate, can you walk?"

Carl took one small wobbly step just as something that

116

sounded like a car backfiring echoed loudly behind them. In the same instant, something smacked into the wall of the building next to them hard enough to send a spray of grit and bits of brick into the air. "She's shooting at us!" Ian yelled, grabbing Carl's sleeve and pulling him along the edge of the long building.

Carl limped beside him, not uttering a single word of complaint about his injury while the boys looked about for a place to hide. Behind them Ian could hear footfalls approaching, and when he risked a glance back, he saw Frau Van Schuft closing in, her arm raised and, just as he'd suspected, a gun in her hand. "Hurry!" Ian shouted as another BANG sounded and more brick splintered off the wall nearby.

The boys ducked sideways into an alley and were nearly hit by a motorcar turning the corner. The driver honked at them and Ian pulled Carl flat against the wall of the narrow alley, dropping the journal.

To his dismay, he quickly realized that the car had run over the diary and torn the cover and several of the pages right off. "The journal!" he cried after the car passed.

Another loud BANG sounded from the end of the alley, and something hot grazed the top of Ian's left ear. The pain was immediate and intense and he dropped to his knees, clasping the side of his head.

"We've got to run!" Carl shouted, trying to lift Ian to his feet.

Ian squinted against the pain and reached forward to grab the diary. Several more pages came loose, and it was as if the bound volume wanted to disintegrate in his hands. He desperately clutched at the papers nearby but he had to leave the front cover and the few pages attached to it while he staggered to his feet and hurried to get away from Frau Van Schuft, who was quickly closing in on him.

"I'll kill you both!" she shouted, and Ian felt certain she would make good on her threat.

"This way!" Carl called as he ducked down a two-lane street with a good deal of traffic already flowing in the early morning.

Ian realized that Carl assumed Frau Van Schuft would not fire her gun with so many people and cars about. He could only hope that his friend was right.

"We've got to cross the street!" Carl insisted, and to Ian's horror, his friend darted right into the middle of traffic. Cars screeched, horns blared, and Ian's heart felt like it would burst out of his chest. "*Carl!*" he shouted.

Miraculously, Carl managed to dart forward just before a large bus skidded past the spot where he'd just been standing. A few more car horns and angry fist wavings later, his young friend made it safely to the other side. Turning around, Carl motioned for Ian to follow.

Ian clutched the pages of the journal to his chest as he tried to find a hole in the flow of traffic so that he might cross as well, but just as he was about to dash to the middle of the road, he was grabbed roughly by the collar and dragged backward. "Let me go!" he shouted, reaching back with one hand to try to free himself.

Above him Frau Van Schuft's face was contorted in fury, and Ian found her surprisingly strong. Her grip on his shirt was ironclad and she pulled him with hard yanks into the doorway of a closed shop. There she pinned him against the hard wood and shoved her gun into the middle of his belly. "Well!" she crowed triumphantly. "You are not the One we've been looking for, Ian Wigby, but I'm told your death will assure us a victory all the same."

Ian closed his eyes and clenched his stomach muscles, bracing for the horrible pain he knew would follow, when instead of a BANG, he heard a muffled whump and the hand gripping him fell away.

Stunned, Ian opened his eyes to find Frau Van Schuft piled in a heap at his feet and the man with the bronze cuffs hovering over him. "Are you hurt?" the stranger demanded, a thick exotic accent coating his words.

Ian was too stunned to speak, but his hand drifted up to his ear, which he belatedly realized was bleeding. The large man in front of him squinted at him before placing his hand on Ian's head and tilting it to one side to inspect the wound. "You've lost the top of your ear, lad," he said. "But you're not likely to die from it."

Ian still found speech difficult, especially since Frau Van Schuft began to moan softly at his feet. The stranger eyed her menacingly, and Ian realized that his rescuer was reaching for a long knife tucked into his belt. "No!" he said, gripping the man's hand. "Don't kill her!"

The stranger eyed him skeptically, and Ian had the distinct feeling he was being measured up. Behind them was a series of car honks and screeching brakes and Ian knew that Carl was attempting another mad dash across the street.

His rescuer whirled around just as Carl cleared the last of the traffic and dashed forward with a crazed and angry look. "Leave him be!" he yelled while he approached at a run, and Ian realized Carl meant to barrel right into the man in front of him.

Ian stepped over Frau Van Schuft and blocked Carl's path. "Stop!" he said. "Carl, this man saved me!"

Carl barely managed to collect himself before bumping into Ian. Frau Van Schuft moaned again and her eyes fluttered when she made a feeble attempt to sit up. Quicker than Ian thought possible, the man with the bronze cuffs bent and struck her on the side of the neck with one hard blow. Frau Van Schuft wilted into unconsciousness again and while Ian and Carl stood in stunned silence, the man eyed the street suspiciously and commanded, "Follow me!"

Without another word he then turned and hurried off down the street.

Ian and Carl did not hesitate; they followed dutifully. Carl limped beside Ian while Ian still clung to the pages of the diary he had. With relief he could see that he'd managed to retain much of the diary and he could only hope that what he held to his chest was the section the professor had been working to translate.

The stranger led them through a dizzying array of streets and alleyways until they finally came to a small café brightly lit by the morning sunlight now warming up the day. Their savior motioned for them to sit at one of the tables, and told Ian, "I will be back momentarily. Do not leave until we've had a chance to talk."

Carl and Ian took their seats and Ian could feel a few patrons staring at him. He looked down at himself and realized with a bit of embarrassment that he was still wearing his nightshirt, which was stained with small dots of red. "Your ear's bleeding," Carl said helpfully.

Ian sighed. "I know, Carl."

A moment later the stranger returned and offered Ian a white washcloth and a large bowl of warm water. "Clean yourself up, lad," the stranger instructed.

Ian gingerly dabbed the cloth on his wound, wincing at the sting it caused. "It's just a nick in the top of your ear," Carl told him, trying to be helpful again.

"Thanks," Ian muttered as he dabbed at the blood on his cheek, neck, and nightshirt.

While Ian cleaned himself up, the stranger looked at them curiously. "Tell me," he said casually. "Why would Frau Van Schuft be so interested in you two?"

Ian looked at Carl, wondering how much they should reveal to this stranger, but Carl was distracted by a large tray of breakfast rolls sitting nearby. As if he had not heard the man, Carl turned to him and asked, "Do you think they'll take a few pence here in exchange for a roll?"

The stranger smiled brightly at Carl, his black eyes twinkling, and for a moment he looked so much like another older man they'd once known, Jaaved's grandfather Jifaar, that Ian felt a pang in his heart. "I suspect they'll take your pence, boy, but as they would prefer their own pesetas, of which I have plenty, why not allow me to purchase your breakfast?"

"That'd be smashing, thank you!" Carl said, again eyeing

the tray of breakfast rolls. "I'd like that one near the top, if you please. It's a bit fatter than the others."

Their savior chuckled softly and waved a hand at the waiter coming toward them. He ordered them each a cup of hot chocolate and a breakfast roll, allowing Carl to select his roll of choice from the tray. Once their breakfast had been served and Ian had had a chance to clean himself up, he thought perhaps the stranger had forgotten his original question.

The man sipped his café con leche casually and smiled at him over the rim. Ian smiled back and set the journal to the side of his hot chocolate so that he could take up his break-fast roll and bite into the delicious bread.

He closed his eyes for a moment, savoring the sweet honey taste, but when he opened them, he found that the stranger had taken the journal right out from under his nose and was carefully turning the pages.

"Give that back!" Ian snapped, then realized how rude he sounded to the very man who had saved his life. "Er, what I mean is, that journal is private, sir, and if you please, I'd very much like it back."

The man was looking at him with amusement. "I'm sure you do," he said evasively. "But what I want to know is, what is it about this journal that Frau Van Schuft finds so interesting?"

Ian gulped. He wasn't sure what the connection be-tween this kind stranger and Frau Van Schuft was yet, and he was afraid of giving out too much information before he knew more about what this man was after. "I've no idea what that vile woman wants with our journal."

Ian could tell immediately that the man sitting across from him didn't believe him for a second. "I see," said the stranger after a long moment, and to Ian's dismay, the man then pulled the page up close to read it.

"I told you that's private!" Ian snapped again, and he heard Carl suck in a breath of surprise next to him. Ian didn't care that he was being rude this time. He was afraid the man wouldn't give him back the journal and he knew that the professor needed to finish copying it.

But the man ignored his tone completely. He turned the pages casually, skimming their contents, and then in an instant of recognition, the man's eyes bulged and he gasped, "By Zeus!"

Ian blinked, thinking that was a very odd thing to say.

"By Zeus?" Carl repeated, obviously thinking the same thing Ian had. "Pardon me, sir, but might you be from Greece?"

The stranger across from them looked up at Carl, shock appearing on his face. "You can understand what I'm saying?" he asked, and Ian noticed belatedly that the man's thick accent had vanished. Obviously the stranger had switched from English to his native tongue—whatever that might be.

Ian cleared his throat loudly, trying to warn Carl, but his friend hadn't caught on, and said casually, "Yes, sir. You're speaking quite plainly, after all."

It was then that the stranger seemed to notice the small pouch tied to a cord around Carl's neck, and one glance at

Ian's collar revealed an identical necklace. "Your name," he demanded, swiveling his head back to Carl.

Carl seemed taken aback by the man's intensity, but he said, "Carl Lawson, sir."

This seemed to puzzle the stranger for a moment but he soon fixed his eyes on Ian and asked, "And you? What is your name?"

Ian thought about lying; he was growing increasingly worried about the man's reaction to the journal and to them. But while his mind raced to come up with a false name to offer the man, Carl said, "His name's Ian Wigby, sir."

The stranger gasped, his hand flying to his mouth as he stared wide-eyed at Ian, who could have kicked Carl. "Perhaps we'd better find our way back to our patron," Ian suggested calmly, and he began to rise from his seat.

"No!" the stranger said loudly, and both Ian and Carl scooted back in their chairs. "Wait," added the man in a much calmer tone. "Just a moment of your time, if you please."

Ian hesitated and noticed that Carl looked ready to dash away. "We're very grateful to you, sir, but we don't want any more trouble this morning." Ian discreetly eyed the journal lying on the table in front of the stranger. He couldn't judge if he'd have a shot at grabbing it and escaping.

The man sitting across from him seemed to realize that the boys were close to running, and he clearly worked to soften his features and offered Ian the journal. "Here," he said, giving it to him. "But promise me you will keep this out of the hands of Frau Van Schuft."

Ian took the journal warily, wondering if the stranger

was trying to lure him into a trap. "Who *are* you?" Ian asked once he'd tucked the diary securely into his waistband.

The man did not answer for the longest time. Instead, he continued to look at Ian in wonder, and to Ian's surprise, the stranger even seemed to be on the verge of tears. "I am someone who never thought I'd actually meet the likes of you, Ian Wigby," he finally whispered. "I am the Secret Keeper, and I thought the time for your arrival was perhaps lost or set far into the future. But what I am most concerned about is that you are so far away from the very place that can keep you safe. Why have you come to Spain?"

"We came for the journal," Ian said, hoping he could trust the man. "But might I ask how it is you know about me, and why you've been following Frau Van Schuft, and for that matter, why do you call yourself the Secret Keeper?"

"Yeah," said Carl. "What secrets are you keeping?"

The stranger gave them both a sad smile, as if he carried some tremendous burden. "I've known about you, Ian, from well before you were born. I've been following Frau Van Schuft because she is the servant of my enemy, and I have chosen to keep my enemies always in sight. To answer your final question, lads, I am the keeper of secrets so important that the fate of the world rests upon my shoulders, secrets from the past that I am bound by oath to carry into the future, and my journey has been both tragic and dangerous, but by that same oath I must carry on. And although I am tempted to alter the Fates and divulge all that I know here and now, Laodamia has strictly warned me against using such tactics."

Ian blinked. He had absolutely no idea what this man was talking about. But at the mention of Laodamia, he asked, "You know about the great Oracle of Delphi?"

The stranger nodded. "She is the one who bound me, lad. And she is also the one who first told me about *you*."

Carl held up his hand. "Wait a moment," he said. "How could *she* have told you anything? She died three thousand years ago!"

But the man ignored Carl's question and continued. "I am meant to hide what only you can find, Ian. I keep your secrets, you see. Yours and Laodamia's." Ian stared at him with no small amount of wonder. He felt he knew this man, even though he was fairly certain they had never met. Still, if he could just think about it for a few more moments, he might be able to figure out who this man was, but the stranger sat back with a sigh and said, "I would tell you more, lad, but I cannot reveal too much. It would alter your destiny. I will say only that I am relieved the Star has been found and your quest has finally begun. May Zeus himself guide you, Theo, and the others so that your mission can succeed."

Ian's jaw fell open. This man knew about Theo, their quest, *and* the Star of Lixus? But how could he know? How could he possibly know about their quest in Morocco, unless . . . Ian's heart began to hammer as an idea entered his mind. "You've been to Morocco," he said.

The stranger said not a word, but his eyes revealed the truth.

"You know what we found in that cave," Ian added, and again he was able to read the truth in the man's eyes. "And the only way you could know that is if you were the one to place the Star in the cavern for us to find!"

Carl gasped beside him and his head pivoted back and forth between Ian and the stranger. "What?"

Ian turned to Carl. "Don't you see, mate?" he said excitedly. "He's got to be the one who's been hiding the trea—" But the rest of Ian's sentence was cut off as the man placed a hand over Ian's mouth and shook his own head vigorously.

"Do not say one more word," he cautioned, looking about suspiciously.

Ian stared at him wide-eyed and Carl didn't seem to know what to do. He'd even left his breakfast roll only partially eaten. Finally, Ian nodded. He would be quiet. The stranger let him go and sat back in his chair again. "You must get back to England," he advised. "Spain is not safe for you." And then the man reached into his shirt pocket and retrieved a pen and a small piece of paper. He scribbled something onto the paper, folded it carefully several times, and handed it to Ian before his gaze darted to the street and his eyes narrowed angrily. "Now go!" he said as Ian held the folded paper and stared up at him in confusion.

"Sorry?" Ian said.

"There is a man on the corner over there who is an associate of Frau Van Schuft. She will be searching the streets for you, lad, and she will comb this city until she finds you unless you make haste." The man said all this in a whisper before reaching into his trouser pocket and pulling out several coins. He handed these to Carl, then turned back to Ian, closing his own palm around Ian's hand holding the message. "Read that later and it will explain much. For now, you and your companion must hurry out of the city and make haste in your journey back to your homeland. I will delay Van Schuft and her associates as long as possible." And with that, the man laid several more coins on the table and darted away.

Carl stood blinking dumbly after their benefactor, then at the coins in his hands. "What're we supposed to buy?" he asked Ian.

"I believe we're to take a taxi back to Señora Castillo's," Ian said, motioning for Carl to follow him out of the café.

Carl grabbed the rest of his breakfast roll and hurried after Ian. "But we don't even know where she lives," he complained.

"I do," Ian said, remembering the street name from the signpost next to Señora Castillo's house. He also remembered the address from the brass plate near the door. "Come on," he said once they'd made it to the sidewalk. "Let's get farther away from the café before we worry about nabbing a taxicab."

Hailing a taxi proved quite difficult for the two boys, as no driver seemed willing to stop and pick up two dirt-stained lads who looked very much worse for wear. "That's the sixth taxi to pass us by!" Carl whined. "At this rate we'll never get back."

"Perhaps we can find one that's already parked and show the driver that we've got money to pay him," Ian suggested.

"I suppose it's worth a try." Carl shrugged, and the boys began to walk along the now bustling streets, searching out a parked cab. They'd gone only three blocks when Ian was sure he heard his name being called. He picked his head up and looked about, but through the throng of people, he couldn't make out a familiar face. "Did you hear that?" Carl asked, looking about too.

"I thought I heard someone call my name," Ian said.

"Carl! Ian!" they both heard more clearly, and Ian would have sworn it was Theo's voice.

"Where is she?" he asked as he swiveled his head to and fro.

"There!" Carl said suddenly, pointing across the street to a blond head bobbing up and down through the pedestrian traffic.

"Theo!" Ian shouted, and nearly darted right into traffic in his haste to reach her.

Carl grabbed his arm just in time, which Ian thought ironic, given Carl's earlier dash into oncoming traffic, and the boys waited impatiently for the cars to clear. By the time they made it across, they could see that the earl was hurrying after Theo, and just behind him was the professor. "How did you find us?" Ian asked after hugging Theo.

She proudly held out the small sundial. "With this, of course," she sang.

Ian laughed with relief. Theo was a very clever girl and he was quite relieved she'd thought of using the dial to find them. But his good humor was short lived when he took in

129

the expressions of the earl and the professor. "I say," said the professor, eyeing the boys reproachfully. "You've put us through quite a fright this morning!"

"Sorry, sir," they mumbled in unison as Ian cast his eyes to the pavement.

"Ian, are you injured?" the earl asked with concern.

Ian touched the top of his swollen ear. "Just a nick," he assured the earl. "And Carl twisted his ankle a bit."

"It's fine, really," Carl said. "Just a bit stiff is all."

The earl bent to inspect Ian's ear, his eyes pinched with a mixture of worry and anger. He then bent to feel Carl's ankle before standing again. "Very well. You'll both recover from your injuries."

"We're most sorry to have caused you any upset," Ian added, wanting more than anything to remove that disapproving look from the earl's face.

Beside him Carl nodded vigorously. "Yes, most sorry," he agreed. "But we did manage to get Sir Barnaby's diary back."

The professor's bushy white eyebrows shot up in surprise. "Did you really?"

"Well, some of it was lost, I'm afraid," Ian admitted. "But we were able to retain most of it." Ian reached into his waistband for the journal. As he pulled it out, he dropped the folded piece of paper the stranger had handed him.

"What's that?" Theo asked as he bent to pick it up.

Ian took a big breath before he explained. "Carmina gave the diary to Antolin, the taxi driver who switched his motorcar for a lorry when he came to Señora Castillo's to get the diary. Carl and I managed to stow away in the back

130

of the lorry, and he drove us to the city, where we discovered that Antolin was working for none other than Frau Van Schuft! But she and he got into an argument and it all went terribly wrong. Antolin ended up tossing the journal out the window and we had to jump out of the lorry to get it before Frau Van Schuft could. Then she cornered me in a doorway and nearly shot me, but a mysterious man who calls himself the Secret Keeper saved me, but more about him later. The thing of it is, the Secret Keeper wrote something down on this paper, which he said would explain a few things."

"I say, you lads have had quite the morning!" said the professor, looking rather amazed by Ian's tale. "And I shall want to hear more about this mysterious stranger who helped you, but might I ask, what does your note say?"

"Dunno," Ian admitted. "I haven't had a chance to look at it till now."

The professor held out his hand and Ian obliged by letting him have the paper. The old man carefully unfolded it and gasped yet again when he took note of what was written there.

"What's it say, Professor?" Carl asked.

The professor looked up at Ian with large eyes, then over at the earl, his expression stunned. "It's written in ancient Greek," he explained. "And it says, 'Young boy Wigby, come this way.' "

THE TIES THAT BIND

Caphiera the Cold paced back and forth impatiently in front of the hearth she rarely used. Periodically she would scowl at the fire now filling her ice fortress with wretched heat and foul-smelling smoke. Her sister Atroposa stood nearby, fueling the embers with the soft wind that was ever present with the sorceress.

"*Must* you fan the flames?" Caphiera spat, irritated, even though she knew full well Atroposa could still the air around her about as easily as Caphiera could warm it.

Atroposa turned her hollow eyes to her sister, her hair whipping round her head with increasing velocity. "Must *you* be so impatient?"

Caphiera snarled at Atroposa and glared hard at her. The effect was disappointing. Atroposa seemed to be the only creature on earth capable of returning Caphiera's gaze without turning into solid ice. "My fortress is melting!" Caphiera grumbled, returning to her pacing.

Atroposa did not reply; instead, she turned back to peer intently into the embers, searching for the first sign of their father, which came very shortly thereafter. "He is here," she announced a moment later in her mournful voice, and sure enough, there came a horrific ripping sound and out from the hearth poured soot, smoke, and a sulfuric smell so offensive that Caphiera took a step back.

She recovered herself quickly, however, and forced her blue lips into a smile. "Welcome, Sire," she said, bowing low.

Her sister also bowed demurely, her ragged clothing sweeping in tatters along the icy floor.

"Daughters," said the voice, the sound like giant boulders grinding together. "What news have you to share?"

"Magus has gone east, Sire, in search of our beloved sister."

Smoke billowed from the hearth as the great underworld god considered that. "And have you killed the orphans?" he said at last.

Neither Caphiera nor Atroposa spoke at first, but finally, the sorceress of wind confessed, "We were not successful, Sire. I sent a most terrible cyclone after them, but they managed to evade it in the end."

The embers in the fireplace exploded in a shower of sparks that sizzled and hissed as they bounced about the ice floor and off the frozen walls. Caphiera winced when one ember hit her beautiful silver coat and burned a hole right through it. She was so irritated that for a moment she did not notice the sucking noises coming from the other side of the room. The sorceress of ice looked up belatedly to see something she had never witnessed before in all her life.

For the first time since Atroposa had donned clothing of any kind, it fell limply about her, and her long translucent hair hung still and lifeless. More worrisome was that she appeared to be choking. Atroposa's hands clutched at her neck, and her mouth opened and closed as she gasped for air. Her hollow eyes stared in shock at Caphiera as she sank first to her knees, then to a crumpled heap on the floor, where she began to twitch and convulse.

Caphiera turned to the hearth and addressed her father. "Sire," she began carefully, "I know my sister has undoubtedly disappointed you, but might I suggest that her skills may yet be useful to our cause?"

Heat erupted all along Caphiera's skin and she recoiled from the hearth. "You *dare* question *me*?" Demogorgon roared.

"No!" Caphiera gasped, sinking to her knees like her sister while a searing heat crept along every inch of her body. "Of course not, Sire! It's simply that we might both be of service to you as our cause advances!"

In the next instant both Caphiera and Atroposa were released from the underworld god's torturous wrath and the pair lay sprawled on the cold floor, Caphiera's coat and hair smoking and Atroposa gasping for breath. "There is a mission," said their sire into the silence that followed. "One that I cannot spare your brother for."

"Anything." Atroposa coughed, the sound even more hollow than usual. "Send us on any mission you choose, Sire!"

"There are rumors that the Secret Keeper lives."

"Adrastus?" said Caphiera, attempting to put out a small flame at the hem of her coat. "Surely no mortal could live so many centuries."

"And yet the rumors continue to reach me that he is alive and well," Demogorgon insisted. "You two must discover the truth of this talk. And if the Secret Keeper is yet alive, force him to reveal the location of the rest of Laodamia's treasures. The One cannot fulfill the prophecy without the boxes."

"As you wish," said Caphiera, bowing her head low and hoping the visit from her father was at an end.

"We will not fail you again," promised her sister.

"If you do," warned Demogorgon, "it will be the last thing you two *ever* do." And with that there was another horrible ripping sound and the remaining embers in the hearth flared before dying out completely.

Caphiera wasted no time getting up and staggering outside, where she flung off her ruined coat and lay down in the snow. Her skin sizzled against the cold flakes as she worked to bury herself in a nearby snowdrift. It was a long time before she felt well enough to sit up.

When at last she regained her feet, she saw Atroposa standing high on a nearby ledge, her hollow eyes staring into the face of a fierce northern wind, which whipped her hair and tattered clothing, rejuvenating the sorceress. Of all her siblings, Caphiera had always felt a certain kinship with Atroposa, but Caphiera vowed that should something go wrong along the way of this newest quest, she would make sure Atroposa would be left solely to blame.

OCÉANNE

Ian stared at the bit of paper and the writing on it as he sat in the cab speeding along to Señora Castillo's. His memory drifted back to the first time he'd seen those lines and squiggles, on a cavern wall near his home in Dover.

The script was identical to the writing on the wall, and he knew of only one other place where that sentence had been written—Morocco.

"But who was he, do you think?" asked Carl, and Ian realized that his friend was having an intense discussion with the professor and the earl.

The professor sighed heavily. "I've no idea, my young Master Lawson, but I'm very curious to find out."

"I know who he was," said Ian quietly, and immediately all eyes in the back of the motorcar turned to him.

"Who?" asked Theo.

"General Adrastus of Lixus," said Ian, absolutely convinced it was the very Phoenician general who had hidden a vast treasure that included the Star of Lixus for Ian to find in the foothills of the Atlas Mountains. A year earlier, before things had gone terribly wrong in Morocco, the professor had first told him the story of the famed general and how he'd hidden his treasure somewhere near the ancient city of Lixus before it was invaded by the Carthaginians. Ian, Theo, and Jaaved had discovered the treasure in a cave at the foot of the Atlas Mountains, and on the wall leading to the trove had been a message identical to the one scribbled on the paper in his hand. "He knew about Laodamia," Ian told them. "In fact, he claimed to have met her."

The professor made a derisive sound. "Met Laodamia? Poppycock! The Oracle died a full thousand years before the general was even born."

But beside him Theo gasped, "The portal! Remember last year—we were in Morocco for nearly ten days, but in Dover only a few hours had passed. I'd wager that if the man's claims are true, he could have used the portal to go back in time to Phoenicia and meet Laodamia."

The professor scowled. "That would be a pretty trick indeed, Miss Fields," he said. "To be able to connect three worlds spanning so many millennia seems quite extraordinary indeed."

But Ian was convinced they were on the right track. "He also knew about the Star, Professor," he explained. "He knew that we had recovered it without us having to tell him, and he even knew how it worked. Only someone with firsthand experience would know about its power."

"He knew about the Star of Lixus?" the earl asked, his eyes intent.

Ian nodded enthusiastically.

"But I thought that General Adrastus was lost at sea when he was chased out of Lixus by the Carthaginians," Carl said.

Ian, however, was not to be dissuaded from his convictions. "Don't you remember, Carl, what the man said to us about keeping secrets? Secrets of the past *and* the future. He *had* to be talking about the prophecies! We also know that Adrastus himself hid the Star, which was found *with* Laodamia's treasure box. How did he get them if not from her? And the writing on the wall back in Dover—Professor, you were the one to date it to an ancient Greek script roughly two thousand years old, correct?"

The professor crossed his arms and sighed deeply. "Yes," he said, as if giving in grudgingly to Ian's notion.

"Which would have been during the time that Adrastus ruled over Lixus." He stared at all the doubtful expressions, wanting very much to convince the group. "All the clues point to one man. It was the general," Ian repeated. "I simply know it."

"But how could it be, Ian?" Carl asked him reasonably. "He'd have to be immortal to have lived so long."

"He could have used the portal a second time," Ian replied. "Just like we did. I suspect that he discovered the portal sometime during his reign in Lixus. Perhaps he even stumbled into it unwittingly and found himself in Phoenicia, where he visited with Laodamia. He told us over breakfast that the Oracle had bound him by oath, so he must have received the boxes, then gone back through to hide the Star

139

and one of the treasure boxes, then used the portal again to leave me the second box back in Dover—or the first box, whichever way you look at it."

"I believe Ian may have a point," said Theo. "Adrastus could very easily have gone through the portal more than once."

But the professor didn't seem willing to jump to any conclusions just yet. "It would have to be an extraordinary coincidence," the old man said. "That entrance to the portal in Morocco was well hidden, after all. And it would have required that the passage be open when Adrastus was ready to travel through it. And might I also remind you, that time was only compressed by ten days on our venture. You are suggesting a three-thousand-year span overall, Ian. That would have to be an astonishing leap through time."

"But it does explain the writing on the cavern wall back in Dover," Ian said, "and the fact that two of the silver treasure boxes were found exactly where the message he left us told us to look."

"But assuming Adrastus did in fact come through the portal and, even more remarkably, assuming the general did arrive in our time, what would Adrastus be doing in Spain, of all places?" argued the professor. "If anything, I should think he would attempt to stay close to the portal or, at the very least, go back to Greece."

That made Ian pause, but Carl said, "He was keeping close watch on Frau Van Schuft, sir. He said he needed to keep his enemies close, remember, Ian?"

Ian nodded. "Yes, and he seemed to think we were all in

terrible danger. He said that we'd best make haste getting back to England."

The earl turned in the front seat to address Ian, but something else seemed to catch his eye and his face showed alarm as he peered out the rear window. "We're being followed," he said gravely. Ian began to turn around to look out the back as well but the earl stopped him. "Don't," he warned. Then he said to the driver, "Take us to trains?"

If the situation hadn't been so dire, Ian would have smirked at the earl's attempt at Spanish, but the driver understood him perfectly and nodded before turning at the next intersection.

The earl then pulled out his billfold and removed several bills before addressing the professor. "Here is enough money to book you all passage to Toulouse. Go to this address," he added after handing the professor the pound notes and taking out a pen and a scrap of paper, which he scribbled on quickly. "That is the home of a family friend. He will keep you safe until I am able to join you."

"Where will you be, my lord?" the professor asked, and Ian noticed that the old man's hand shook slightly when he took the paper.

"I'll be collecting our things and giving our apologies to Señora Castillo. I will explain to her that we have recovered Ian and Carl, along with her brother's journal, but that the diary was severely damaged in the attempt to collect it, and you will be doing your best to repair and restore it before returning it to her. I shall also try to convince her that she might be in jeopardy herself now that Frau Van Schuft is

141

aware of the journal and how much we are willing to risk to keep it. I will then ask Señora Castillo to come back to England with me as my personal guest. If all is successful, she and I will join you within a day or two."

"But what if they follow us?" Carl whispered, his face a bit pale.

The earl smiled confidently at Carl. "Not to worry, lad," he said. "I have a plan."

With Ian acting as translator, the earl was able to direct the driver through a series of right and left turns around the train station until they managed to lose the car tailing them long enough for Ian, Carl, Theo, and the professor to hurry out of the taxi and duck into a nearby alley. They hid in the shadows and watched as their cab pulled back into traffic, and not long afterward, the car that had been following them roared down the street in hot pursuit.

The moment it passed, the professor took Theo's hand and said, "Let us hurry along and do as the earl instructed."

They made it to the station without incident and the professor was able to book them passage on a train leaving thirty minutes later. Still, they all waited impatiently in a small nook near the platform, where they were hidden from most of the pedestrian traffic. There they stayed out of sight while watching the large clock mounted on the wall tick down to the time for boarding.

While they waited, Ian's gaze darted back and forth between the clock and the midmorning crowd milling about. He managed to tuck his long shirt into his trousers so as to

142

be a bit less conspicuous, but still he knew he was drawing some stares. "I almost brought you a shirt," Theo whispered contritely. "I had this most pressing thought before we left the house this morning in search of you to bring along some of your clothes, but I talked myself out of it in the end, because I couldn't imagine why you would need a shirt when you were coming right back to Señora Castillo's."

"It's all right, Theo," Ian said gently. "And perhaps it's a good lesson for you to trust your visions from now on, eh?"

Theo appeared chagrined. "You're starting to sound like Lady Arbuthnot." Ian laughed and ruffled her hair.

Carl then nudged him in the ribs. "Time to board, mates."

The professor held them back until most of the passengers had already loaded the train. He suggested it was best to wait and see who got on before they made their escape.

When a voice over the loudspeaker announced the final boarding for Toulouse, the four of them hurried onto the train just before the doors closed. Theo led them directly to a berth with four seats together and Ian immediately opened the window of the stuffy compartment before sitting down.

No one could relax until the train began to chug away from the station, and even then Ian found himself keeping a wary eye on any passenger who happened by their seats. But when the train finally left Madrid and began to traverse the Spanish countryside, both the professor and Carl propped themselves against the window and drifted off to sleep. Theo, however, fidgeted nervously across from Ian long after the train had passed out of the city.

Ian's gaze fell on her small satchel and he asked, "Do you have your playing cards with you? We could work through a few of your exercises."

Theo brightened immediately. "Yes!" she said, reaching in and pulling out a set of cards. "You'll help me practice?" she asked, referring to the game Lady Arbuthnot had created to help Theo strengthen her intuition.

"Of course," he said, happy that he'd found something to take her mind off their harrowing morning.

Theo handed him the cards. "Do you remember how to arrange them?"

Ian knew well by now how to set up the cards to challenge Theo's powers of sight and he was continually amazed at how accurate she was. "Certainly," he said, holding the cards up to eye level and sorting through them.

The game was simple, really; all he needed to do was arrange four cards in a row. Three of the cards were to have the same color, either red or black. The fourth card, however, had to be the opposite color, and it was Theo's job to pick out which card within the set of four was different from the others.

If she selected the wrong card, it went to Ian, and the cards continued to go to him until she selected the right one. If she selected the right card immediately, the entire row went to her.

After several minutes, Ian had all the cards arranged in groups of four. He held up the first four for her to make a selection, but before she even had a chance to pick, he said, "Wait a minute, you're wearing your crystal. Off with it."

Theo rolled her eyes but did as he asked and removed her necklace, then placed it into Ian's palm for safekeeping. He held up the cards again and watched her gaze intensely at his hand. After only a moment she reached forward and tapped the card on the far right. "That one," she said confidently.

"Are you *sure?*" Ian asked.

Theo laughed. "Hand them over, Ian."

Ian shook his head ruefully and gave her all four cards. "You're nearly too good for this game."

They played three more hands—all of which went to Theo—before Ian decided to make it more challenging. "Let's say that I'll only give you the hand if you can tell me which card is different and what suit it is."

"Very well," Theo agreed, rubbing her hands together eagerly. "Let's start with the cards you've got there." Reaching forward, she tapped the second from the left and said, "That one is a spade."

Ian's jaw fell open. In his hand he held two diamonds and a heart. He almost gave up the cards immediately but couldn't help asking, "What suit do you think the other three are?"

Theo's eyes narrowed as she concentrated. "I'd say those two are diamonds, but that last one I'm not sure of."

Ian looked at the card that puzzled her. It was the queen of hearts and he wasn't surprised that it confused her, as it was a richly decorated card. He noticed that the face cards were often the most frustrating for her. He flipped it over so that she could see, and she nodded as if she'd known it all along. "I can always tell when you've put a face card into the mix," she said.

Ian and Theo played all afternoon, interrupting their game only when the sandwich cart came round. Ian looked at the few pence in his hand and realized he had enough for only two sandwiches. He thought about waking up Carl and sharing his sandwich with him, but when he shook his friend's shoulder, Carl slapped at his hand and rolled over, so Ian shrugged and ate the entire sandwich.

He and Theo took up their game again and did not stop until Carl began to wake up from his long nap. By that time, Theo had mastered with 100 percent accuracy which card was a different suit, and she was even going as far as to tell Ian the number on each card in his hand.

As he held up the last round and looked to his right, where only two cards lay, and Theo's lap, where the other forty-six were collected, he had to smile when she smartly pointed to the remaining cards and announced, "Two of spades, four of clubs, five of diamonds, and six of spades!"

Ian gave over the hand, laughing admiringly.

"Gaw blimey!" said Carl, and Ian realized he was fully awake and watching them intently. "She's become really good at that, Ian!"

"That she has," he agreed, beaming at her before handing her back the crystal necklace.

Theo took the crystal and ducked her chin demurely, but Ian could tell she was immensely pleased with herself. "You'll have to ask Lady Arbuthnot for another game," said Ian. "You've mastered this one."

At that moment the conductor announced that they were pulling into Toulouse, and Ian was amazed that the time had passed so quickly. He'd been having so much fun with Theo that he hadn't realized how far they'd traveled.

The boys attempted to rouse the professor, who was softly snoring in his corner seat, but he seemed set on continuing his slumber. They finally managed to wake him up enough to get through to him. "Professor! We're coming into Toulouse!" Carl practically had to shout in the old man's ear.

The professor batted a hand at him. "I can hear you," he snapped, blinking his bloodshot eyes. "I'm not deaf yet, lad."

"Sorry," mumbled Carl.

Shortly thereafter the train squealed to a stop and Ian and the rest of his party rose and waited their turn to exit. He made sure to help the professor down the steps onto the platform, because even though Ian knew that the old man wasn't deaf, he was fully aware Professor Nutley was none too spry.

On reaching the platform, he and the others were immensely surprised when a gentleman of impeccable dress and handsome appearance stepped forward, tipped his hat, and addressed them. "Good afternoon," he said. "I am Monsieur Lafitte. My dear friend the Earl of Kent addressed an urgent telegram to my home this morning, begging me to offer safe harbor to a party coming here on the afternoon train. Would you by chance be the party my dear friend the earl spoke of?"

Professor Nutley nodded and extended his hand. "Very pleased to make your acquaintance, Monsieur Lafitte. I am

Professor Phineas Nutley and these children are the earl's wards."

The gentleman smiled and nodded to Ian, Theo, and Carl. "Might I suggest a short walk to my motorcar and a warm meal and cool drink at my home?"

The professor wiped his brow, which was creased with fatigue. "That would be most welcome," he said gratefully. "Most welcome indeed."

Monsieur Lafitte led the way to his motorcar, where a chauffeur assisted them by opening the doors and even helping the professor inside. Once they were under way, the professor said, "Might I inquire as to how you know the earl, monsieur?"

Lafitte smiled easily. "Hastings and I go way back," he said, and Ian noted that the man spoke English with only a tiny hint of a French accent. "Our mothers were the closest of friends, actually. And you may have noticed from my English that I was raised in England. My father was French, but his work required him to reside in England. When I was a young lad, we owned a home in London where the Arbuthnots were our neighbors, until my father passed.

"I was twenty-one when I inherited the Lafitte family vineyards here in France. We have two holdings here in the south, and one more near Rouen in the north. When my father was alive, he was more interested in commerce than wine making, but I'd always had a special affection for the trade, which was what brought me back to France after my father's funeral."

The professor was nodding, as if he'd heard the story

before. "I see," he said. "And you and the earl have remained close all these years?"

"Oh, yes," said Lafitte. "But I should hardly think Hastings feels as fond of me as I do him."

"Pardon?" asked the professor.

Lafitte laughed, as if there was some inside joke to what he'd just said. "Hastings introduced me to my wife, you see."

"Ah," said the professor, but Ian was still puzzled by the comment.

The mystery was soon cleared up when the gentleman added, "Of course, at the time of our introduction, Hastings was quite smitten with her. Unfortunately for him, my wife's heart turned in a different direction."

"Toward you," Carl said boldly.

Lafitte winked at Carl. "Indeed."

There was a bit of an uncomfortable silence after that; it seemed no one knew quite what to say. As long as Ian had known the earl, he'd never seen or heard of any sort of romantic interest the earl might have and it suddenly dawned on him that it was quite odd for a man of the earl's age and standing never to have married.

"Here we are," Lafitte announced into the silence as the motorcar made a right turn onto a private drive.

"My word," whispered Theo as she gazed at the grand chateaux at the end of the stretch of road. "What a lovely home!"

"Thank you, young miss," said Lafitte. "I believe you shall be most comfortably looked after until the earl arrives to escort you back to England."

149

"Did his telegram say when he might be along, sir?" Ian asked. He was terribly worried about the earl's being left behind in Spain.

"He assured me that he would be along on the last train out of Madrid. And that will put him in Toulouse no later than midnight."

Theo sat back in her seat with a sigh when the car pulled to a stop. "Thank heavens," she said as the chauffeur opened her door.

They all trooped out onto the driveway and waited for their host to lead them into the stately home. Monsieur Lafitte motioned them to a set of stairs leading to the front door, and Ian had a moment to take in the impressive yellow stucco structure with white shutters, flowering ivy, and a clay-tiled roof.

He could clearly see that the small castle was built in the shape of a horseshoe, with two tall towers flanking the main entrance.

"It's quite lovely, isn't it?" Theo whispered beside him.

Ian nodded. The place appealed to him immensely.

Once inside, they were met by one of the loveliest women Ian had ever laid eyes on. She was tall for a lady, nearly level with her husband, with a beautiful willowy figure, rich brown hair, large gray-blue eyes, and a delicate nose. She smiled at them each in turn, and Ian felt his insides flip over when her angelic gaze settled on him.

"Allow me to introduce my wife," said their host, "Madame Jasmine Lafitte."

"Good afternoon," she said in a smooth, husky voice,

adding a small curtsy, and Ian was so transfixed by her beauty that he almost forgot to bow in return.

Beside him Theo stifled a giggle. "Goodness, Ian," she whispered. "Try not to fall over, will you?"

Ian realized he'd bent over so low that it must look like he had a stomachache. He immediately straightened up and felt his cheeks flush. "How do you do?" he said belatedly.

Madame Lafitte smiled sweetly at him and turned round to wave at someone behind her. "And this is our daughter, Océanne."

Ian reluctantly tore his gaze away from the beautiful woman in front of him only to suck in his breath as he laid eyes on an even lovelier creature. Tall like her mother, with the same gray-blue eyes and facial bone structure, Océanne favored her father with her auburn hair and alabaster skin. "Hello, how do you do?" she said shyly, and Ian felt all the blood drain right out of his head when her own rich voice reached his ears.

"You all right?" he heard Theo whisper. Ian blinked hard, turning slightly to assure her he was fine, when he noticed she wasn't talking to him, but to Carl, who was swooning on his feet. "Carl," Theo said as the boy's knees seemed to wobble. *"Carl!"*

But it was too late. Carl's eyes rolled straight up into his head and he tilted backward. Monsieur Lafitte reached out in the nick of time and barely spared Carl's head from hitting the marble floor.

"Oh, the poor boy!" cried Madame Lafitte. "Is he unwell?"

"I believe it's because he hasn't eaten," Theo said,

crouching down beside Carl and looking up at Ian as if asking him when Carl had eaten last.

Ian tried to think back to when he'd seen Carl eat, and realized with alarm that his last meal had been the breakfast roll they'd shared with the general. "He only had a bit of bread this morning," he admitted.

"Oh, that won't do," said Monsieur Lafitte as he gently laid Carl down on the floor. "He's far too thin to eat so little."

"Margot!" called Madame Lafitte, and a maidservant rushed to her side. "Quickly, gather some pillows and a blanket for the lad until he comes round, and then we'll need to get some nourishment into him immediately."

The maidservant rushed off to do her mistress's bidding and Ian watched with concern until he noticed that Océanne had also knelt down next to Theo and her mother and was holding Carl's hand while wiping his brow. "Poor thing," she said with a tsk.

Ian felt a knot of jealousy form in the pit of his stomach. He'd had only half a breakfast roll and a small sandwich and you didn't seem him fainting at the first sign of a pretty girl.

Carl began showing signs of consciousness again. His hand gripped Océanne's and his eyes fluttered. "I think he's waking up," Océanne said just as the maid arrived with a pillow and blanket.

"What's happened?" Carl moaned as he tried to sit up.

Monsieur Lafitte placed a hand on Carl's chest to ease him back down. "There, there," he said, tucking the pillow under his head. "Lie still for a moment, lad."

"How'd I get down here?" Carl asked, his eyes now focused and staring at them in confusion.

"You fainted in front of everyone," Ian said bluntly, and tried not to notice when Theo gave him a reproachful glare.

"You've gone the whole day without a meal," Theo said gently. "Ian and I had a nibble from the sandwich cart on the train, but you and the professor were asleep when the cart came past, and we thought it best not to disturb you. I'm so terribly sorry, Carl. I should have insisted we wake you up for a bite to eat."

Carl blinked rapidly, as if he was trying hard to take in Theo's rushed explanation. "S'alright, Theo," he said, and this time he did sit up. "I'm fine, thank you all," he added as everyone seemed to crowd closer to him.

"Yes, well, if you feel up to it, come with us to the dining hall, young man," said Monsieur Lafitte, helping Carl to his feet.

By now Carl was looking rather sheepish and Ian felt a small pang of guilt for speaking so harshly to his friend. At least, he felt bad until he saw Océanne hold out her arm and say, "Lean on me, Carl. I'll walk you to the table."

Carl blushed and took her arm. "Thank you," he said. "And might I say, that's a lovely ribbon you're wearing."

The knot in Ian's stomach expanded and he could feel himself settle into a foul mood. "What's the matter?" Theo whispered as they were led directly to the dining hall.

"He's making a show of it all, don't you think?" Ian snapped irritably, pointing to Carl, who was walking ahead of them with Océanne.

"No," Theo said. "I think he's being quite good about it. After all, he fainted right in front of a group of strangers. I'd be horribly embarrassed if that happened to me."

Ian knew she was right, but still, he couldn't resist feeling angry with his friend as Carl continued to command Océanne's attentions. Ian was drawn to the girl in a way he couldn't quite describe. She was the most beautiful girl he'd ever laid eyes on, and he desperately wanted her to look at him the way she was fondly eyeing Carl.

The Lafittes' servants were already laying out several dishes filled to the brim with delicious-smelling food and Ian heard his stomach grumble. He stood back politely and waited for the adults to take their seats, noticing how Monsieur Lafitte pulled out the chair for his wife. Taking his cue from their host, Ian rushed to offer the same cordiality to Océanne. She smiled brightly at him and he felt his heart skip a beat.

Carl took the seat on the left of Océanne, and Ian was quick to take the right. Theo sat next to him and he noticed that she was struggling to hide a fit of giggles. "What?" he asked her innocently.

"Nothing," she said, ducking her chin.

Ian scowled at her and waited for his dinner to be served while he struggled to come up with something witty to say to Océanne. At Monsieur Lafitte's request, the professor was describing to their hosts the challenging time they'd had in the short day and a half they'd spent in Spain.

When he got to the point in his story when he admitted to falling asleep while attempting to copy the journal of his former colleague, and being shaken awake by Carl, Océanne turned to Carl and asked, "What happened next?"

Carl said, "Well, I followed Ian, who'd dashed out after Carmina. The cook had stolen the journal and she gave it over to a man in a lorry waiting on a nearby road. When I saw Ian sneak into the back of the lorry, I couldn't very well let him go it alone, so I jumped in after him."

"How very brave of you!" Océanne said.

Carl blushed and Ian ground his teeth together. "That?" Carl said. "Oh, that was nothing! You should have seen me dodge a bus in heavy traffic a bit later. Ian and I had to run for our lives when a wicked woman with a gun started shooting at us!"

Ian snorted derisively. "Sheer luck you weren't killed," he said bitterly, hearing the mockery in his own voice but unable to stop it. "And a load of good it did you! You had to cross right back through that traffic, didn't you? Lucky for me a passing stranger was nearby. I'd have been done for if I'd relied on you, Carl."

"Ian!" Theo whispered harshly, but he ignored her.

"Did you say that a woman was shooting at you?" gasped Madame Lafitte, her hand moving to cover her heart. "How dreadful!"

"The boys did have a rather perilous time of it," the professor commented, obviously enjoying all the attention they were receiving from the Lafittes. "A very evil woman named Frau Van Schuft was after the journal and seemed determined to have it at any cost. She even shot at Ian and nicked him in the ear!"

Ian moved his hand to his ear when he noticed the shocked stares of everyone around him. "It only stings a little," he said.

"I'll treat that with some salt water after you've eaten, Ian," Madame Lafitte promised.

"What happened next?" Océanne eagerly asked the professor.

The professor smiled and said, "Our brave lads managed to leap from the lorry, snatch back the journal, and attempt an escape. But Frau Van Schuft gave chase and corralled the boys on the streets of Madrid. If a very brave stranger hadn't intervened, I daresay, they might not have survived the incident!"

To Ian's immense frustration, Océanne looked at Carl with renewed adoration, and Ian simmered in his seat, pushing his food around, his appetite having all but left him. He said nothing more the rest of the evening unless directly asked, and all Theo's efforts to pull him out of his foul mood were in vain.

Shortly after their evening meal, Madame Lafitte tended to Ian's ear, making a point of assuring him that it wasn't serious. A bit later, dessert was served in the parlor; then, when Ian and Theo began to yawn, it was suggested by the Lafittes that they allow their guests to retire, as the day had obviously been quite long for them. More inquiries were made into Carl's well-being, and he reassured them over and over again that now that he'd had a bite to eat, he felt very well indeed.

They were led upstairs and shown to their rooms. To

Ian's irritation, he noted that he and Carl were to share a room again. Carl seemed oblivious to Ian's current state of discord and talked incessantly about how pretty Océanne was and how delightfully nice as well. It wasn't until Ian rolled over and snapped, "Would you please shut up, Carl? I'm trying to sleep!" that the room fell silent, although the air grew heavy with discontent.

Exhausted though he was, Ian struggled to fall asleep. He knew he'd been both unfair and unkind to Carl, but he felt that his friend should have at least noticed that Ian was attracted to Océanne too, and not made such a show of her obvious preference for him.

Ian awoke several times that night, tossing and turning as his thoughts churned as well. His black mood carried over to the morning, and when at last he gave up his effort to get some much-needed rest, he sat up in bed and glared hard at the sleeping boy across the room, quite convinced by now that Carl was not half the friend he pretended to be.

Silently, Ian put on his trousers, noting with a snarl that it was no wonder Océanne hadn't paid him the slightest attention—he was still dressed in his dirty and bloodstained nightshirt, for heaven's sake!

With a heavy sigh he left the room and made his way downstairs, only to stop short as the front door opened and in walked the Earl of Kent. Ian's mood immediately brightened. "My lord!" he called, and hurried down the last few steps. "You've come!"

"Good morning, Ian," the earl said cordially. "Yes, I've

made it at last. And my journey here was not without incident, I'm afraid."

"What happened?" Ian asked, but at that moment Monsieur Lafitte came through the door as well. "My butler will show you to your room directly, Hastings, as I'm sure you'd appreciate the opportunity to freshen up."

"That would be marvelous, thank you, Leopold," said the earl kindly.

"Hastings!" called a voice from down the hall, and both the earl and Ian looked up as Madame Lafitte rushed toward them, her arms outstretched and the most delighted smile on her face.

But Ian was shocked that the earl seemed to stiffen as she drew near, and when the lady leaned in to throw her arms about him, the earl pulled away. "Madame," the earl said cordially with a small bow. Ian noticed that the earl's eyes never met hers. "It is a pleasure to make your acquaintance again. I trust you've been well?"

Madame Lafitte seemed equally surprised by the rebuff, but she recovered herself quickly. "Yes, Hastings," she said, her hands fluttering at her collar as if she was suddenly nervous. "And you?"

"I've been well," the earl said, his posture rigid and his speech a bit clipped.

There was an awkward sort of silence that followed, and Ian caught a look that passed between the Lafittes, as if they were disappointed but not surprised by the earl's behavior. Even Ian knew that the earl was acting most unusually and he couldn't for the life of him understand why the earl would treat someone as nice as Madame Lafitte so frostily.

The earl seemed to be aware of the uncomfortable silence, so he quickly bowed to his hostess before excusing himself to the room the Lafittes' butler was ready to show him.

Ian moved out of the way so that the earl and the servant could climb the stairs, and as the earl passed, he whispered, "Come with me, lad."

Ian followed dutifully all the way up to the third story, where the butler opened a set of double doors to reveal a large suite, painted a warm shade of apricot, with gold crown molding and a beautiful fresco adorning the ceiling. The butler offered to unpack for the earl, but was declined, and after the man had bowed himself out of the room, the earl turned wearily to the bed, sat down, and said, "I was unable to convince Señora Castillo to come along with me."

"Do you still believe she's in danger because of us?" Ian asked, feeling the weight of responsibility that must be resting on the earl's shoulders.

"I do," said the earl. "It was all I could do to convince her to question Carmina, who turned hateful the moment she was accused of stealing the journal. She actually attempted to turn the blame on you and Carl, suggesting the two of you took it in the night while the professor slept, and then you lads invented some outlandish story to cover your thievery."

"But that's a lie!" Ian said, outraged by the accusation.

"Yes, Ian," said the earl, his eyes heavy with fatigue.

159

"And if it weren't for my title and the truth of who we all are, which I felt compelled to reveal to our hostess in light of the events, I should think Carmina's accusations most convincing to Señora Castillo. I have given my word to return her brother's diary to her, but I am worried about the consequences of doing that."

"Why, my lord?" asked Ian, wondering what consequences could result from returning the diary to its rightful owner.

"Because of what the prophecy within its pages might reveal. If Magus's spies are now aware of the journal and are also aware that it contains a copy of Laodamia's last prophecy, I should think they would stop at nothing to obtain it."

"There is reason to be concerned," said a voice from the doorway, and Ian was startled to see the professor up and about so early. When they both looked at him in surprise, the professor added, "I heard you'd arrived, my lord, and thought it best to talk with you as soon as possible."

"Of course, Professor," the earl said, waving him into the room. "Tell us what you've discovered."

Ian noticed that the professor was carrying the tattered remains of the journal. "I had thought to simply begin copying the text within again and translate it later, but sadly, there is very little left of Barnaby's notes."

Ian felt a pang of guilt. "The motorcar that ran over it made a terrible wreck of it, sir," he said by way of explanation.

"It did indeed," the professor agreed with a tired sigh. "Still, there is some of the prophecy left, and I've managed to translate it."

"So quickly?" asked the earl.

The professor frowned. "That's how little of it remains, I'm afraid." Ian stared at the floor. He felt terribly responsible for the diary's condition. "I'm assuming Laodamia's last prophecy does concern the children?" the earl said.

"Yes," said the professor, but he said nothing more. Ian looked up from the floor and saw that the old man seemed to be struggling with a decision. The professor looked gravely at Ian, and it was as though he wasn't sure if he should comment further. Finally, however, the professor gave another sigh and said, "The text talks about you specifically, Ian."

"It does?" Ian was surprised but knew he shouldn't be. Most of Laodamia's prophecies mentioned him.

The professor shuffled over to a nearby chair and sat down. He adjusted his glasses and carefully opened a folded piece of paper. "Yes, but first I must suggest that although you are mentioned, I do not believe that this prophecy was meant to be seen by you."

Ian's eyes widened. How could Laodamia not want him to see a prophecy that mentioned him specifically? After all, she'd written her other prophecies directly to him. "What makes you think she wouldn't want me to see it, Professor?"

"It is written in the traditional Phoenician script, my boy. Not like any of the other prophecies that Laodamia left for you in her silver treasure boxes. And after reading what's left of this one, I believe I know why."

Ian didn't know what to say, but his heart began to hammer. He knew there was some terrible prediction contained within that journal, and he could only imagine what it might be. Still, he found he didn't have the courage to ask about it.

But the earl did. "Tell us what the Oracle said, Professor. Please."

Professor Nutley took a deep breath and began to read the text. " 'The salvation for all mankind shall rest with the Guardian when the Eye of Zeus passes from the Guardian to the One. The One shall be an Oracle of unparalleled ability, with gifts like no other. The Guardian shall protect the One at the time of greatest peril, during the gathering, and upon the completion of the gathering of the seven. The One shall then draw upon the power of the other six Oracles destined for battle. These seven United will stand for the cause, to form a mighty alliance against the dreaded four.' "

The earl eyed Ian, the man's posture slumped slightly, as if he carried a great burden. "Wasn't it you who recovered Theo's crystal, the eye of Zeus, from the wreckage of the keep last year?"

Ian nodded gravely. "Yes, my lord."

The earl and the professor shared a look. "I am convinced that Theo is the One that Laodamia speaks of," the professor said.

"Then we should assume that Ian is the Guardian," said the earl. With a soft smile for Ian, he added, "He's been her protector from the moment she entered my keep."

Ian felt his cheeks heat under the earl's gaze. "The gathering of the six Oracles, we already know that's part of the quest Laodamia's set out for us. And Theo must be the seventh that will draw on the energy of the other six, which

162

makes perfect sense really, because Laodamia tells us in both of her prophecies that Theo is the first and the last of the Oracles. We've already acquired one of the other six and that's Jaaved, our Seeker."

"Yes," the professor agreed. "And it is also obvious that the dreaded four she speaks of are Magus, Caphiera, Atroposa, and Lachestia."

"Is that all she says?" the earl asked, and Ian knew from the professor's face that there was more.

The professor sighed again and gave a reluctant shake of his head. "No, my lord, there is more and I must warn you that this next bit is terribly troubling."

"What does it say?" Ian asked, even though a part of him was sure he didn't want to know.

Again the professor appeared reluctant to speak; he scowled down at his translation and took a moment before he read from it again. " 'There can be only one event that will throw the United off their path and doom the fate of man: a time of grave danger shall come when the sorceress of earth shall arise from her stony tomb to take the life of the Guardian. And with the Guardian's demise, the One shall quickly fall, for none alive can stall this fate. If the Guardian perishes and the One falls before the time of gathering is complete, no hope can be given to the way of man.' "

After the professor finished speaking, there was a gasp from the hall, and everyone turned to see Theo standing as still as a statue in the doorway, her face pale and her large green eyes brimming with moisture. "No!" she cried hoarsely, then flew across the room to hug Ian fiercely.

163

Ian was so taken aback that he barely knew what to do. He settled for patting her head gently and telling her not to cry. He hadn't even had a moment to process what the professor had said.

The earl, however, appeared to have understood it perfectly. "But, professor," he said, "the prophecy from the last box . . ." His voice trailed off just as Ian remembered six cryptic lines:

> *Once the Healer has been named*
> *Loam of ground no longer tamed*
> *Unleashing wrath from ancient stone*
> *Hear the earth below you moan*
> *Fly away, back to your cave*
> *Those you leave cannot be saved*

And Ian suddenly wondered if perhaps he was the one who might get left behind on their next quest. Theo seemed to be thinking the same thing, because she mumbled, "I won't let her take you, Ian. On our next quest, to find the Healer, I won't let Lachestia take you!"

Ian hugged Theo tightly, and tried to calm his own fears. "There, there," he said gently. "No one's going to do me in, Theo. We'll just have to make sure we avoid the sorceress when we go in search of the Healer."

But Theo looked up at him with such haunted eyes that he knew her gift of sight was telling her that might prove itself impossible. "I sense a great danger, Ian," she whispered. "I've seen that your path in particular comes so close to death that I cannot determine if you will come back through the portal alive."

Ian's heart felt as if it had fallen straight down to his toes. "That settles it, then, doesn't it?" the earl said, his voice firm.

"Settles what, my lord?" the professor asked.

"If Laodamia thinks that the children might not survive their next trip through the portal, then they shall not pass at all."

Theo snapped her head in the earl's direction, and Ian could clearly see the conflict on her face. "But, my lord! We *must* go through the portal. We have no choice but to add the Healer to our group! The Healer is essential to the six Laodamia has tasked us with gathering!"

But the earl's mind was made up. "No," he said firmly. "I shall not risk it. We will find another way."

"But the prophecy!" the professor cried, getting up from his chair to move closer to them. "My lord, if the children are not allowed to assemble what Laodamia calls the United, we are all most certainly doomed!"

The earl's brow lowered, and Ian saw a glint of anger in his eye, which was quite unusual for him. "I will not throw Ian's life away so easily, Professor Nutley!" the earl snapped. "And I shall not risk an encounter with this sorceress! We will find a way to fulfill this prophecy without sending the children back through the portal."

"But how, my lord?" Ian asked. "How can we possibly find the Healer without following the prophecy?"

The earl sighed heavily and sat back down on the

bed. He turned slightly and pulled a folded letter from his jacket. After opening it to read a few lines to himself, he said, "I cannot be certain, Ian, but there may yet be a solution."

The professor's mouth opened, and it looked as if he were going to continue to argue the point, but the earl held up his hand, ending their discussion. "Let us not talk any further about this until I've had an opportunity to investigate a few recent developments, all right?"

Ian noticed that both Theo and the professor looked rather doubtful, but they nodded in agreement all the same.

"Thank you," the earl said with a relieved smile. "Is there any more to this prophecy from Sir Barnaby's journal, Professor?"

The professor blinked, as if he'd forgotten all about the diary. "Yes, my lord, there is one small section that remains, and I must admit that it is most extraordinary, given Ian's encounter with the man who came to his rescue yesterday, and his conviction that he met none other than our Phoenician General Adrastus. Laodamia writes, 'I am awaiting the general from Lixus. To him shall go my treasure boxes, to be placed in the most secret of locations all around the world. He shall be the Keeper. The Keeper of my secrets. The Keeper of all our destinies.' "

"I was right!" Ian exclaimed. "Adrastus lives!"

But the professor still held some doubt. "Ian," he said soberly, "this does not clearly state that you were right and the general has somehow managed to live for two thousand years; this merely indicates that you were right in that Adrastus hid both the Star of Lixus and the second silver box for you. From the note you were handed by the stranger who saved you yesterday, it does appear that he also hid the first box in Dover for you to find, however, it does not *prove* that he is Adrastus."

"But he said he was the Secret Keeper!" Ian insisted. "He said almost exactly what Laodamia says. That he was the keeper of secrets and my destiny, and that's why he couldn't tell me any more, because he was afraid it might alter my fate."

Still, the professor appeared skeptical. "It would have to be an extraordinary occurrence, lad," he said.

"Yes, well, the portal is a rather extraordinary thing, don't you agree?" Ian argued.

The professor broke into a grin. "Point taken," he said with a chuckle.

The earl got up from the edge of the bed and moved to his satchel. He opened it and took out several articles of clothing, then handed these to Ian. "My clothes!" Ian exclaimed, happy to see a proper shirt for a change.

"In order to make a hasty retreat I'm afraid I had to leave all the extra satchels behind, Ian, but I did manage to get most of your clothes." The earl then reached into his bag again and came up with another pile—this he handed to Theo, who took it gratefully—and a final set, which he also gave to Ian. "See that Carl receives these, would you?"

Ian scowled. He was still a bit miffed with Carl this

morning. The earl must have noticed Ian's frown, because when Ian looked up at him, the earl had arched one eyebrow. "Is there a problem, lad?"

Ian was quick to shake his head. "No, my lord," he said, anxious not to involve the earl in his petty squabbles. The earl seemed satisfied but Theo regarded Ian in a way that told him she knew exactly what Ian was upset about.

"Very well," the earl said with a sigh. "If you will all go on and enjoy your morning, I will attempt to steal a quick nap before seeing to our continued travel arrangements."

Theo took Ian by the hand. "Come, let's have some breakfast, shall we?"

Theo waited outside Ian's door while he changed into a fresh shirt and trousers. He was grateful that Carl wasn't in their room, and he settled for tossing his friend's clothes onto the bed. Carl would find them easily enough.

After Ian had changed, he and Theo made their way down the stairs, and as they stepped onto the marble flooring of the front hall, they heard laughing coming from the dining hall.

Curious, they went to investigate, and Ian stopped short when he saw that Océanne was giggling merrily at Carl, who was attempting to balance a spoon on the end of his nose.

Beside Ian, Theo began to laugh as well, and that irritated Ian all the more. Océanne looked up as they entered, and clapped her hands. "There you are!" she said happily. "And you're just in time. Breakfast is about to be served."

Turning back to Carl with a humorous grin, she added, "I've made sure there's more than enough for seconds."

Carl's spoon clanked onto his plate and he smiled happily. "Brilliant!" he exclaimed, rubbing his stomach. Then he added, "And might I say that is a very nice jumper you're wearing, Océanne."

For a split second there was a strange quiet that enveloped the room as Theo and Océanne looked at each other in astonishment before both girls dissolved into a fit of giggles. "What?" Carl asked innocently, his cheeks turning red. He seemed to understand that the girls were laughing at him, but clearly had no idea why, so he turned to Ian and asked, "Mate, you'd agree, wouldn't you? Doesn't Océanne's jumper look nice?"

Océanne's beautiful gray-blue eyes turned to Ian expectantly, and for a moment he found himself unable to speak. And that was quite unfortunate, because both Theo and Océanne seemed to think that even more humorous.

Ian felt his own cheeks heat up and he turned on his heel and began to walk away. "Ian!" Theo called after him, but he did not turn back. "Where are you going?"

"I've lost my appetite," he said angrily, and felt just a little bit better when the giggling from both girls ceased abruptly.

"Aw, come on, mate!" Carl called to him as he walked out of the dining hall. "They were only having a laugh, after all."

But Ian was far too upset by his own jealousy and embarrassment to go back to the table. Behind him he could clearly hear Theo say, "I don't know what on earth has got into him!"

But after finding a quiet corner to sulk in, Ian began to feel a sense of shame and, even worse, foolishness for having stormed off like a petulant child. Still, he was too embarrassed to return, so instead, he dashed back up the stairs, turned into his room, and threw himself across the covers. He lay there for a long while, trying to sort through his feelings, and he thought about Theo's words and had to admit that he didn't know what had got into him either. He'd never been jealous of anyone in his life, but suddenly, he couldn't stand it that Carl seemed to be commanding everyone's attention.

After a long while, Ian rolled over and stared at the ceiling. With a heavy sigh he got up and moved to make his bed. It had been ingrained in him to do this every morning at the keep. Just as he was pulling the bedspread over the pillow, there was a knock at the door. "Come in," he said over his shoulder.

Ian suspected that it must be Theo coming to check on him, but when he turned to face the door, he was surprised to see Océanne standing there with a tray loaded with a plate of eggs and toast and a cup of steaming tea. "I've brought you some breakfast," she said kindly.

Ian's knees felt wobbly and he could sense a blush hitting his cheeks again. "Thank you," he said, his eyes quickly finding the floor.

When Océanne did not reply, Ian looked up again and noticed that she seemed to be struggling to find a place to put the tray. "I'll take that," he said quickly, crossing the floor to relieve her of her burden. She gave it to him and added a smile and Ian felt his blush deepen. She was so pretty, and her eyes so beautiful, that he thought he couldn't stand to look at her for very long, but neither did he want to look away.

After yet another awkward silence, Océanne finally said, "Well, then, enjoy your breakfast." And she turned to leave.

"Océanne?" Ian called to her, and she turned back to him just as he realized he had no idea what to say next.

"Yes?" she asked.

"Er . . . ," he said as sweat broke out along his brow. His eyes darted back to the floor while he searched for something smart to say to her. Some compliment to pay her. "Um . . . your jumper *is* very pretty." His eyes lifted and he was rewarded with the girl's brilliant smile. Ian smiled in return and he felt his heart soar, so he added without really looking down, "And your shoes are also quite nice."

But to his horror, this additional compliment only inspired Océanne to quickly look down at her stocking feet before covering her mouth with her hand, while attempting to stifle another laugh. She wasn't quite able to, and it appeared that the harder she tried, the more difficult the task, until she finally broke down into a fit of giggles.

Ian felt the humiliation right down to his toes. "Er . . . , I meant your stockings."

"Thank you, Ian," she said when she'd recovered herself, and he was almost sure he heard mockery in her voice. "Just leave the dishes outside the room when you've finished and one of our staff will collect them."

171

Ian nodded, looking anywhere but at Océanne, and to his relief, she left him then and shut the door.

He stood there for several moments longer, staring without seeing the tray of food in his hands. Finally, he moved to the bed, sat down, and pushed the eggs on his plate around with his fork. He attempted a small bite of the toast, but he found that this time, he really had lost his appetite.

A bit later he set the tray outside his door and moved quietly out of the room. He was relieved to see no one about and made his way downstairs, where he heard cheerful voices coming from somewhere nearby.

Peeking round a corner, he saw Carl and Océanne playing the card game that he and Theo had practiced on the train. Theo looked on and laughed as Océanne giggled infectiously and tried to guess the cards in Carl's hands. For his part, Carl seemed to be trying to help her along, tapping one of the cards repeatedly and laughing back at her when she didn't catch on right away.

Océanne finally laid her palm across the cards in Carl's hand and, turning to Theo, asked abruptly, "Theo, would you tell me my fortune?"

Theo appeared a bit taken aback by the request, but she smiled kindly. "Who told you I could predict the future?"

Carl coughed and got up quickly, as if the conversation was going in a direction that made him uncomfortable. "I think I'd like a glass of water. Would either of you care for one?"

Theo narrowed her eyes at him suspiciously. "No, thank you."

"Oh, yes please," said Océanne.

Carl nodded and wasted no time leaving the room, allowing the girls some privacy. Ian nearly pulled himself away, mindful that he was now prying into personal matters, but part of him really wondered what Theo would say to Océanne.

And in fact, Theo did oblige their hostess. "Very well, Océanne, now that Carl has given me away, I'll tell you what I see for you."

Océanne clapped her hands and inched closer to Theo, who had closed her eyes and appeared to be concentrating. "I see a romance," she said. Océanne gasped, but Theo ignored her and continued. "With a boy who lives in a foreign land. He is brave and handsome and charming, Océanne. And he would be most devoted to you if you would have him."

"Is it Carl?" Océanne asked excitedly, and Ian felt as if he'd been punched in the stomach.

He waited anxiously for Theo's reply, but to his chagrin, she opened her eyes and laughed before telling the girl, "Perhaps. I know he has blond hair, and that he's quite charming—which of course fits Carl."

Océanne laughed merrily and took hold of Theo's hands. "I like him very much, Theo," she admitted, and Ian felt that familiar knot of anger and jealousy wrap itself around his insides.

Theo glanced over her shoulder as if she expected Carl to come back into the room. "Yes," she agreed. "And I suspect he likes you too."

The girls then joined each other in a fit of giggles and Ian turned away, feeling such a pang of hurt and betrayal that he couldn't stand to listen to another word.

He spent all the rest of the day sulking outside, exploring the grounds and keeping well away from the house.

Theo found him in the late afternoon as he was sitting on a log overlooking a gentle brook. "Hello," she said cordially, taking a seat next to him.

"Hello," Ian replied, with no real warmth. "How'd you find me?" he asked. Theo held up the sundial and he frowned. "Ah," he said. "Yes, I'd forgotten about that."

Theo took Ian's hand and placed the dial in his palm. "This is yours," she said to him. "Laodamia meant it for you."

"The Guardian," he said with a sigh, and watched Theo frown.

"I don't want anything to happen to you, Ian," she said earnestly. He was about to reassure her when she added, "But I also know we *must* go through the portal to find the Healer when the time is right."

"That's likely to be a bit tricky, Theo, what with the earl forbidding us from going anywhere near the portal and that lock on the gate at the entrance."

Theo sighed. "I know. But Carl has a plan—"

She got no further than that, because Ian cut her off. "Carl!" he snapped, and spat into the dirt. He'd had all day to work up a good deal of resentment toward his friend and he was in no mood to hear about a new idea the younger boy had come up with. "I'm sure he's got a jolly *brilliant* idea to get us through the portal so that I can meet my end and he can have both you and Océanne all to himself!"

Ian hadn't meant for all that to come out, and was ashamed when Theo stared at him in stunned disbelief. "Me and Océanne? Have you gone completely *daft?*" she demanded, and Ian felt his cheeks flush when he realized she was asking seriously. "Ian Wigby," she continued when he said nothing to explain his outburst, but then her voice grew stern. "Carl Lawson is the *best* friend you'll ever have. And I know that because I've seen a glimpse of both of your futures and I know that his loyalty to you will never waver. Never.

"I've also seen a glimpse of Océanne's future, and I know that while her affections for Carl are quite real at the moment, they will shift dramatically in time. And her admirations will eventually point in a completely different direction, toward someone like . . . *you.* And once her affections have turned to you, Ian, they will not turn away again. Ever."

Ian, who had been looking shamefacedly at the ground, turned his eyes up to Theo, feeling hope bloom strong in his chest, but he was surprised when she returned his gaze with one of anger, glaring down at him with her hands on her hips. "But," she snapped, "might I add that what I see for you and Océanne is, at this very moment, in grave jeopardy of not turning out that way, because you are being so ridiculous and if you continue to make a fool of yourself, you'll not only lose any hope of winning Océanne's heart, but you'll lose your friendship with Carl too."

And then Theo stomped off without a backward glance.

Ian sat on the log for a very long time, thinking about what Theo had said. Several times he heard his name being called, but he did not answer. He knew that the others were gathering for dinner and he was being unforgivably rude by not making an appearance, but he couldn't bring himself to face them just yet. He felt unsettled by what Theo had told him—that she saw a point at which Océanne's attentions would turn to him—but for the moment, at least, Océanne was more taken with Carl, and he didn't know how to let go of the anger and jealousy he was feeling so as not to ruin his friendship with Carl.

He couldn't fathom why he felt so drawn to Océanne. The attraction to her was unlike anything he'd ever experienced. He'd never thought of girls as anything but mildly amusing and sometimes even annoying. Theo was the only girl he held much respect for at the orphanage, and not one of the other girls at the keep had ever commanded his attentions.

So what was it about *this* young lady that captivated him so completely? He had no idea, but he did know that he simply couldn't tolerate watching her affection for his best friend grow. And if he was to have any sort of future with her—as Theo had all but promised—then he needed to keep his distance from both her and Carl. At least until they could escape back to the keep, which he hoped would be soon now that the professor had finished translating the prophecy within Sir Barnaby's journal.

As the last rays of the sun were painting the sky beautiful shades of pink, lilac, and purple, Ian finally rose from his log and made his way back to the main house. He entered quietly through a side door and stopped short. Madame Lafitte was standing just inside the doorway, looking almost as surprised to see him as he was to see her. "Ian!" she greeted him with a smile. "We've been quite worried about you."

Ian cleared his throat and shuffled his feet. "I'm sorry, ma'am," he said. "I was down by the creek and I must have lost track of time."

"I see," she said, and Ian couldn't tell if she believed him. He was saved from further scrutiny when she ushered him into the kitchen and pointed to a small table. "Sit," she ordered, and hurried over to the icebox. "We've still got quite a bit of ham and leftover potatoes. Oh, and I believe one or two of the rolls may have survived Carl's appetite."

She said this with a wink and Ian couldn't help smiling, his spirits lifting just a bit. "He eats like that at home too," he told her.

"I've never seen such a thin lad eat so much!"

"I know," Ian agreed. "We're not sure where it all goes."

They made small talk while Madame Lafitte continued to fuss over him, giving him a plate loaded with ham, potatoes, and peas. Between bites he answered her many questions about the keep and Dover. "And the earl," said Madame Lafitte lightly. "He's happy in his castle at Dover?"

Ian thought that was a rather odd question. "Yes, ma'am," he said, wiping his mouth with his napkin. "He seems quite happy."

Madame Lafitte traced small circles with her finger on the table where they sat. "And does he have a female companion that he might be fond of?"

Ian blinked. "I'm sorry?"

Madame Lafitte laughed as if she was embarrassed to have asked. "Nothing," she said. "Of course you wouldn't know, now would you?"

"Are you asking me if the earl has a girlfriend?"

Madame Lafitte seemed to want to look anywhere but at Ian, and her finger stopped making circles on the tabletop and moved to pat her hair. "Why, no," she said. "That would be a most improper question to ask, of course!"

Ian squirmed in his chair. He wondered why his hostess was suddenly uncomfortable, and tried to reassure her by answering the question he thought she wanted to ask. "The earl doesn't have a girlfriend," he said. Madame Lafitte's eyes shot up to meet his. "At least, no one that I've ever seen, ma'am. He's always been a bit of a loner as far as I can tell, and he's more enthusiastic about hunting and his duties at parliament than trotting round with the ladies."

Ian couldn't be certain but he thought he saw a bit of relief in Madame Lafitte's eyes. And he thought she might ask him something else, but at that moment the earl himself walked right into the kitchen. "Ah," he said when he saw the two of them. "Ian, I've been looking for you."

"The lad's been out exploring the grounds, Hastings,"

178

said Madame Lafitte sweetly. "The poor dear missed dinner and I've just made him up a plate."

Ian was surprised at the earl's reaction. Without looking at her, the earl replied in a rather formal tone, "Yes, I heard from the professor that while I was out, Ian had gone wandering off. Theo assured me that you were fine and would be back soon, but as it's becoming dark, I thought I'd attempt to find you myself."

"You've been out looking for me, my lord?" Ian asked, guilt settling about his shoulders.

The earl nodded. "I needed to drive into town earlier to send a telegram and wait for a reply. There's some good news from the keep," he said. "Lizzy Newton, who, as you might recall, left our orphanage two years ago, has come back to collect her two siblings. She's just been married and her husband is welcoming her brother and sister into their home."

Ian felt his spirits rise even further. Lizzy Newton was a pretty, bright girl who'd been at the keep until she'd turned sixteen. Ian remembered that upon her release from the orphanage, the earl had worked diligently to find her employment and had finally convinced a duchess acquaintance of his to take Lizzy on as a personal secretary.

Since then, Ian had heard that Lizzy was getting on quite well at the duchess's, and that she'd even become engaged to a rather wealthy merchant. He was thrilled that her two much younger siblings, Jon and Emily, would be joining her and her new husband.

"That is excellent news, Hastings!" said Madame Lafitte

with a clap of her hands. "It's a marvelous thing when your children receive a happy ending."

The earl seemed to stiffen and Ian was confused by his reaction. Again he watched as the earl carefully avoided looking at Madame Lafitte and directed the conversation back to Ian. "It is excellent news," he agreed. "And the timing could not be more to my liking. I've two orphans in mind who might fit perfectly in with you all at the keep."

The earl spoke as if his words held a double meaning, but Ian was really more interested in hearing about how soon they might be able to escape back to England. "So we're setting off for the keep soon, my lord?" Ian asked hopefully.

"Tomorrow," said the earl. "I've just arranged for our passage, in fact. We leave promptly at noon."

With this new information, Ian felt the tension leave his shoulders. He relaxed for the first time in days, and as he shifted in his seat, his eyes caught Madame Lafitte's face. Strangely, even though she was smiling, Ian would have sworn that their hostess appeared disappointed.

"That's excellent, my lord," he told the earl. He quickly added for Madame Lafitte's benefit, "Although I've quite enjoyed my stay here, ma'am."

Her smile widened and she gave a gentle pat to his hand before rising. "Hastings, would you care for some dinner? We've plenty of ham and potatoes left if you're hungry."

The earl gave a tight smile, but still he did not look at her when he answered. "Thank you, Madame, but no. I was fortunate enough to have a meal in town. Now, if you will excuse me?" Without even waiting for a reply, he gave a small bow and hurried out of the kitchen.

Ian looked at Madame Lafitte as if to say, "That was odd," but he held his tongue when he saw the hurt look on her face. As quickly as it had appeared, however, it was gone and she'd forced a smile to her lips and asked, "And you, Ian? Are you up for more?"

Several hours later, Ian lay awake and restless after everyone else had gone to sleep. He finally sighed and sat up in bed. Enough moonlight filtered in from the window that he could just make out the figure of Carl sleeping soundly in the bed across from him. Seeing his friend brought back the shame he'd felt earlier about how he'd acted right after his dinner. On his way up to their room, he'd caught Carl and Océanne playing a game of checkers at a table in the front hallway. He'd wanted to leave his jealous feelings behind and had fully intended to approach the pair and be nice, but when he saw Océanne's head tilt back with a laugh as Carl said something funny about her last move, Ian found himself stomping off up the stairs.

He was positive that they had seen him. Especially when he passed Theo coming down the steps and she looked at him with such disappointment that he didn't think he could bear it any longer. He offered her a grumbled "Goodnight" and continued up to the room he shared with Carl, where he feigned sleep when the other boy came in a bit later.

Now, as he stared across the room at the other bed, Ian

regretted his awful behavior and quietly got up and padded out into the hallway.

On tiptoe he made his way along the corridor and down the stairs to a large sitting room with a lit fire and large plush chairs that looked so comfortable they practically begged for him to come sit for a time and ease his troubled mind.

He also noticed with delight that one of the walls in the room held shelf after shelf of books—just the thing he needed to take his mind off his worries. He walked to the bound volumes and squinted in the glow of the firelight at the titles, finally selecting one that had an interesting title. *The Hobbit* by some chap named Tolkien. Ian pulled the weighty novel off the shelf and opened it immediately. By the first paragraph he was already absorbed and sat down in the chair closest to the fire, pulling up his legs akimbo while he quickly lost himself in the land of Middle Earth.

He was ten pages into the story when he heard a soft chuckle nearby. "That must be some book."

Ian started and closed the novel quickly. "Oh!" he said. "My lord, I didn't see you sitting there."

The earl chuckled again from his seat on the chaise in the far corner of the room. "Yes, lad," he said. "I watched you enter the room and head straight to the bookshelf."

Ian had a moment's hesitation when he wondered if he might be in trouble for being up so far past his bedtime, so he quickly said, "I'm very sorry to be out of bed, my lord, but I couldn't sleep."

The earl got up and came over to occupy the twin chair

next to Ian, noting the title in Ian's hand. "I've heard of that book," he said cordially. "It's been quite the talk of London lately. You'll tell me if it's worth reading?"

Ian smiled in relief. "Yes, of course."

The earl sat back in his seat and sighed. "My own mind won't allow me to sleep either, Ian," he admitted, which caught the young man off guard.

"My lord?"

The earl regarded him thoughtfully. "You had a nice chat with Madame Lafitte?" he asked, and Ian instantly understood, so he nodded.

"She's quite nice. Monsieur Lafitte told us yesterday that you were the one who introduced them."

The earl's smile turned melancholy. "Yes," he agreed. "I did. The second-greatest mistake of my life, in fact." Ian was shocked that the earl would share such a secret with him. "That is why it pains me to come here. Of course, I would never admit such a thing to Leo."

Ian cocked his head. "Who?"

"Monsieur Lafitte," the earl explained. "We used to be quite close you know," he added. "Much like you and Carl, in fact. But the moment I discovered Jasmine had feelings for Leopold, I distanced myself from both of them, causing no small amount of hurt, I suspect."

Ian said nothing, deciding it best simply to allow the earl to speak. But the earl fell silent and Ian could sense that in the soft glow of the firelight, the earl's eyes were seeing things from the distant past.

Finally, Ian said, "My lord, you mentioned that introducing Monsieur and Madame Lafitte to each other was the second-greatest mistake you made. What was your first?"

The earl focused intently on Ian and it was a moment before he replied. "Allowing a young lady to come between me and my best friend, Ian. That is the biggest regret I have."

And Ian realized that the earl knew fully how he'd recently been treating Carl. Ashamed yet again, Ian ducked his chin. "Ah," he said. "Yes, that would be regretful."

The earl reached a hand over to Ian's head and ruffled his hair. "Read your book, lad," he said gently. "Then get some rest. We've a long journey ahead of us before we're back home again." And with that the earl got up and shuffled off to his own quarters.

Ian sat for a long time afterward, staring into the fire, *The Hobbit* resting in his lap, as he considered what the earl had said. And after a bit, he was finally able to firm up his resolve. The earl and Theo were right: no matter how he felt about Océanne, Carl was his best friend. Whatever it might personally cost him, he could never lose sight of that.

So he sat there until he could honestly promise himself that no girl would ever come between him and Carl again. Ever.

CONSEQUENCES

Dieter Van Schuft waited nervously in the salon of his opulent flat in Berlin. In the corner sat his beloved wife, Hylda, tapping her finger on the few pages of the journal she'd managed to recover.

He tried to send her a reassuring smile, but he could tell she was somewhat fearful of the coming meeting. "Tell him nothing of your encounter with the two boys," he warned for the hundredth time.

Hylda nodded vigorously. "As we discussed, Dieter, I will only mention the journal," she vowed.

Behind Dieter, over the large marble fireplace, the clock struck midnight. Above Dieter's head the floorboards creaked. Wolfie was out of bed . . . again. Hylda had clearly heard it too, because she tipped her chin upward and tsked. "*What* are we to do with that boy?" she whispered.

"Send him to boarding school," Dieter replied drolly.

The only thing he and Hylda ever disagreed on was the rearing of their young son. Dieter believed that his wife doted on the boy far too much. Dieter had wanted his son to attend boarding school in Vienna, but both Wofie and Hylda had made such a fuss that Dieter had reluctantly relented.

"He's too young, Dieter. The boy still needs his mother," Hylda argued now.

Dieter opened his mouth to reply but at that very moment the front door of their flat burst open and a thin haze of smoke wafted in. "He is here!" Dieter hissed.

Hylda nearly jumped out of her chair and came to stand next to her husband. With annoyance, he noticed she shivered slightly. "Steel yourself, *liebling*," he cautioned right before Magus the Black strode into the room, smudging their good carpets as he approached.

"Dieter," Magus said perfunctorily. "Hylda."

The Van Schufts bowed their chins. "Master," they said.

Dieter raised his head and did his best to secure a smile. "I have good news from General Walther von Brauchitsch. He sends his gratitude for your most generous donation, and he has agreed to appoint you civilian strategic advisor to his young nephew, Colonel Kaiser Gropp of the Eighth Armored Panzer Division."

Magus pursed his lips. "Where has Colonel Gropp been assigned?"

"To the Polish border, master. He is charged with crossing just south of the village you mentioned."

"Well done, Dieter. You will stay in Berlin while I am advising the colonel and ensure our interests are advanced." Magus next turned to address Hylda, his eyes as black as a cobra's.

186

"What have you brought me from your journey to Spain?"

Hylda cleared her throat and extended the hand holding the cover and very few pages from the journal she'd recovered in the streets of Madrid. "The English earl and his companions visited with a Señora Castillo, master. She possessed a journal once owned by her brother, Sir Donovan Barnaby. I did everything I could to recover the journal in its entirety, but I was betrayed by the man I'd hired, who threw the journal into traffic, where much of it was destroyed. As a consequence, I was only able to recover those pages for you."

Magus's expression was skeptical, and he took what remained of the journal and began to read the soiled, torn, and smudged pages.

Dieter held his breath, hoping that the contents were nothing his master would value. Dieter had read the pages himself and found them to be only the musings of an insipid fool who missed his sister and his homeland while he complained of the heat in Greece.

"Barnaby was the archeologist who first led me to Laodamia's prophecy," Magus muttered while he skimmed the pages. "I can see why the English would want to review it; they were likely looking for a clue as to where to find the treasure boxes. But nothing here looks relevant to our cause."

Beside him Dieter heard Hylda let go a relieved breath. "It is as I suspected, master," said Dieter.

Magus's head snapped up and he was about to hand the

pages back to Hylda when something caught his eye and he drew the pages to him again. At the top of every page, Barnaby had written the precise date and time he'd begun his journaling for that day. It appeared that he wrote in his journal at precisely the same time every night—just past six in the evening. Magus's finger lingered over the date and time written on one page before he let it move to the top right corner, where the edge had been singed by some sort of fire.

When Dieter realized what his master was focusing on, the hairs on the back of his neck raised in warning.

His fears were quickly confirmed as Magus looked up again, his face contorted in rage, and threw the pages to the floor. "You errant fool!" he shouted at Hylda. "Do you realize what you've lost?"

Dieter's wife clung to his arm, trembling in fear, and neither of them spoke, knowing it was better to remain silent, lest they make things worse.

Magus glared angrily at Hylda and shook his fist. "This comes from the journal that fool was keeping days before he discovered the scroll I killed him for! If he was writing in it the day he died, and it survived my fire, then there is obviously some clue about the prophecy on the pages *you* lost!"

Hylda's trembling intensified. "Ma-Ma-Master!" she stammered. "It was not my fault! I was betrayed! I was—" Hylda said not one more word. Instead, she collapsed to the floor, writhing in pain.

"Master!" Dieter pleaded, dropping to his knees to beg for his beloved wife's life. "*Please!* Spare her!"

Magus's lip curled in a snarl, and Dieter realized how

dangerous this course was. But he thought of his boy upstairs and he pleaded again. "We have a son!" he cried desperately. "And he is young! A boy needs his mother, Master!"

But there was no mercy in Magus the Black's eyes. He looked directly at the man on his knees and said, "If your son needs a mother, Dieter, you will need to find a replacement." And with the flick of his wrist, Hylda Van Schuft lay dead.

Dieter bent over his wife and pulled her limp body into his arms. Long after Magus left him, mournful cries of *"Liebling!"* could be heard echoing through the halls.

AN UNWELCOME VISITOR

Ian and the others made it safely back to Dover without incident, although Ian was quite weary after so little rest while they'd been away. The earl made only slight mention of what had happened to them in Spain, cautioning the children not to tell their headmistresses too much, lest it upset the two women.

The earl also gave strict orders to the headmistresses that for reasons of safety, Ian, Carl, Theo, and Jaaved should stay within the grounds of the keep, and the earl would increase the security staff around the orphanage until further notice. When he had an opportunity to address all the orphans at the keep, he cautioned them against venturing to the shore, which won him a sizable groan from the children, but Ian knew there was no other choice. No one was safe from Demogorgon's long reach.

Carl looked simply miserable after the earl's announcement, although he didn't complain to Ian about it. Instead, he moped off into the corner to stare moodily out the window of the keep's sitting room.

Ian felt a real pang of guilt. He'd been insufferable to his best friend and he knew it. All the way back from Toulouse, Ian had been polite but distant with Carl. And now, as he watched his friend sitting by the window, looking so forlorn, Ian decided it was time to put an end to the cold shoulder he'd been giving the lad.

"Oy," Ian said, gaining Carl's attention. "Fancy a game of cricket?"

Carl turned to stare at Ian, as if he couldn't believe that Ian was talking to him again. "That'd be brilliant!" Carl said, jumping up from his chair and dashing off to grab his wicket and bat.

Ian turned with a smile to follow him and caught Theo's eye. "It's about time," she said to him. Then she added, "Well done, Ian."

And Ian soon decided that it was indeed a good thing he and Carl were friends again, because the boys quickly grew bored keeping to the grounds of the orphanage.

By the end of the week following their return from France, Ian and Carl sat moodily up in the tower room, staring longingly from the window as a group of other children was ushered out of the keep's gates by two of the earl's men to enjoy the balmy summer day. Carl sighed wearily and turned away from the window. "Lucky gits," he complained.

Ian turned away from the window too. He was just as irritated as Carl at being cooped up and not allowed outside the orphanage grounds. "It's not as hard on Theo," he noted. "She's got Lady Arbuthnot coming over to keep her company." The earl's aunt was indeed below with Theo at that very moment, helping the girl to expand her intuitive abilities. Ian was convinced he wouldn't be nearly so bored if he had someone to visit him and challenge him mentally.

Carl kicked at a plank of wood. "There's nothing to do now that the fortress is finished," he moaned. The boys had finished the small wooden structure two days previously, and they'd played Viking invaders until they were well and sick of it.

Ian got up from his seat by the window and began to pace like a caged animal. There had to be something to do. Meanwhile, Carl moved over to the bench by the stairs. He stared at it for a bit before pulling up one of the slats. Setting it aside, he reached for another, then another.

"What're you up to?" Ian asked, eyeing Carl curiously.

"The earl didn't say anything about sticking close to the keep belowground, now did he?" Carl said before turning to look at Ian as if he were asking permission.

"That tunnel's blocked off, though, remember?" Ian said, even though he got up from his seat and walked over to Carl.

"Yeah," Carl agreed, turning back to pick up more of the slats. "But that doesn't mean we can't go down and inspect it from this side, does it?"

Ian smiled. "Right," he said, holding out his hand for one of the planks. "Let's have a look, shall we?"

The boys made their way down the ladder and went only a short distance before they found a large pile of rubble blocking the tunnel ahead of them. Ian frowned, all the enthusiasm leaving him. "Bugger," he grumbled. "It'd take us hours and hours to clear all that." Dejected, he turned to go back up the ladder.

But Carl stood there for a moment longer, kicking at the dirt of the tunnel floor. "Bloomin' waterspout," he growled before turning to follow Ian.

Just as the boys reached the top and were making their way out of the bench, they heard the door below open and quick footsteps come up the stairs.

Ian and Carl hurried to put the slats back into place before their visitor could see what they were up to. The boys still hadn't told a soul about the secret passageway.

Ian let out a relieved sigh when he saw Theo's blond head crest the stairs, yet one look at her face told him something was terribly wrong. "What's the matter?" he asked the moment their eyes met.

But Theo appeared unable to speak. Her lower lip trembled and tears poured down her face. She opened her mouth to talk, but the only sound she made was something of a mew. Ian reached out and pulled her into a hug. "There, there," he said, trying to soothe her. "It's all right, whatever it is."

But Theo shook her head into his chest and her sobbing carried on somewhat desperately. "What's happened to her?" Carl asked quietly.

"I don't know, mate," Ian said, still patting Theo's back gently. "Maybe you should go downstairs and see if anything's amiss."

Carl was about to go when Theo reached out and caught his arm. "Wait!" she said, visibly trying to collect herself. "I'll tell you."

Ian wiped the tears from Theo's cheeks and looked earnestly into her eyes, waiting for her to speak again. "It's all right, Theo. Whatever it is, we can fix it."

But that just seemed to upset Theo all over again and she resumed her crying. Carl made a face at Ian. "Nice going."

Ian resisted the urge to say something rude in reply. Instead, he hugged Theo again and gave her some more gentle pats on the back. "There, there," he said.

Finally, Theo pulled away, wiped her eyes, and announced, "There's a man!"

Ian gripped Theo's shoulders. "What man? Did he hurt you? Where is he now?" He asked one question right after another as he prepared to launch himself down the steps and chase after whomever had caused her such distress.

Theo shook her head and appeared frustrated. "Stop!" she said, holding up her hand as Ian continued to pepper her with questions. "He's just left."

"Who's just left?" Carl asked gently, looking pointedly at Ian, as if to instruct him in the art of talking to an upset girl.

Ian closed his eyes, thoroughly irritated with Carl, but before he could say anything more, Theo took a deep breath, let it out slowly, and explained, "While I was saying my goodbyes to Lady Arbuthnot, a man in uniform came to the door. He asked to speak to the headmistresses, so I fetched Madams Dimbleby and Scargill. There was something odd about the stranger, so I hid in your hiding place under the table at the top of the stairs and listened to what he had to say to them."

"What did he have to say?" asked Carl.

"I'm getting to that!" Theo said sharply, and Ian made sure to give Carl a rather smug look, as if to say, "See? It's not so easy, is it?"

"Sorry," Carl said. "You were saying?"

Theo exhaled wearily. "The man said his name was Major Fitzgerald and he had come to the keep in search of his daughter."

Ian's brow furrowed. He was having a difficult time understanding why this would upset Theo so, but he was determined to be patient, so he waited quietly while her voice caught and she attempted to swallow another sob.

"His daughter is here at the keep?" Carl asked when Theo seemed ready to continue.

Theo nodded. "That's what he believes. He said that twelve years ago he had made the acquaintance of a woman who had ended their relationship rather abruptly and then she disappeared. He said that his heart had been broken, because he'd fully intended to marry the lady, but believes now that his feelings were completely one-sided and that she had ended their affair because she did not return his affections.

"Then, one day a few months ago, a letter arrived from one of his fellow classmates, suggesting that the major's former love had in fact born a daughter nearly eleven years ago and that she had deposited the child here at the keep before vanishing from the countryside."

A very unsettling feeling began to creep into Ian's bones as Theo revealed the man's tale. There was something acutely familiar about it and his mind flashed back to a conversation he'd had almost a year ago with one Alfred Shillingham, who'd claimed to know Theo's mother from the university she attended.

"Who is the girl?" Carl asked.

"Theo," Ian whispered before he could catch himself.

Theo looked at him in shock. "Yes."

The three of them stood mutely for a full minute as they all absorbed this news. "He's lying," Carl finally said. "Of course, he's lying, Theo! The Van Schufts probably put him up to this!"

But Theo only bit her lip as more tears trickled down her cheeks. "The major says he has proof," she said softly. "He showed Madam Dimbleby several letters that my mother had written to him."

Ian looked sharply at her. "Were they signed?"

Theo nodded. "Yes. Madam Dimbleby read one of the shorter ones out loud. It was signed 'most affectionately, Jacinda.'"

Ian sat down heavily on the bench, his mind reeling. "That still doesn't prove he's your father!" he nearly shouted.

Theo's eyes filled again with tears. "The major . . . ," she said, her voice trailing off when her voice cracked again.

"The major what?" Carl coaxed.

Theo blinked and wiped her eyes with her sleeve. With trembling lips, she said, "Ian, I don't know, he seemed so earnest. He insists that he *is* my father, and he wants to take me home with him."

Ian stared up at her, his mouth open and his head shaking back and forth. He refused to believe it. "He can't take you away, Theo," he said softly but firmly.

Just below them on the stairs, they heard a gentle voice say, "Ah, but he can."

All three of them started. Ian had been so focused on their conversation that he hadn't heard anyone else on the steps, and it was clear that neither had Carl or Theo. When Madam Dimbleby came the rest of the way up to them, they fell abruptly silent. "I came to find you," their headmistress said to Theo, "to tell you the news, but it seems you've already heard."

Theo threw herself into Madam Dimbleby, hugging her fiercely. "Please!" she wailed pathetically. "Madam, please don't let him take me away!"

Ian looked hopefully at Madam Dimbleby and was stunned to see her eyes glistening with moisture. If he'd had any doubt about whether she believed the major's tale, the look on his headmistress's face told him everything. "I'm afraid, my dear," she said softly, "there is little I can do. If Major Fitzgerald is your father, as he claims to be, then I am powerless to stop him from taking legal custody."

"*No!*" Ian shouted, and even when Madam Dimbleby turned wide, astonished eyes at him for his outburst, he continued to rail at her. "You cannot allow it, ma'am! You cannot let her go! She doesn't belong with him! She belongs here!"

"Ian," Madam Dimbleby whispered, and reached out a hand to him, but Ian felt like he'd been struck hard in the stomach, and all he could think about was getting out of the tower.

He flinched to the side, out of her reach, and darted past her, running down the steps with balled fists and an anger and panic like he'd never felt before. He pushed through the door at the bottom of the stairs and raced through the hallway, down another set of stairs, and out onto the keep's grounds. He looked wildly about for a moment before dashing across the lawn toward the gates. The earl's warning to stay on the keep's property was all but forgotten as he sprinted down the drive and out to the road.

Ian had no destination in mind; he just knew he needed to get away. A terror and panic filled his heart when he thought about losing Theo. She was his to protect, to keep safe. Hadn't Laodamia ordained it when she'd named him the Guardian? How could they even consider allowing her to leave the keep's safety?

Ian knew that if this Major Fitzgerald was allowed to take Theo, she'd be left completely vulnerable. The Van Schufts or one of Demogorgon's brood would certainly hunt her down and kill her, and then what? They'd be facing the end of the world! No, that couldn't happen, Ian determined. The only one who could stop this charade was the earl. He had to get to the earl!

And to his surprise Ian discovered that he had already steered himself in the direction of Castle Dover, which loomed on the horizon like a safe haven. He knew that the earl was not in residence, but his staff would surely be able to reach him. Ian paused for a moment to catch his breath—he'd been running as fast as he could for several minutes—and that was when he heard fast-approaching footsteps. He turned defensively only to see Carl racing toward him.

"I'm not going back," Ian warned as his friend neared him. "I'm going to get a message to the earl."

Carl stopped short, huffing and puffing, cheeks red, and sweat soaking his forehead. "I know, mate," he said between breaths. "I came to tell you that Landis has already been sent to bring you back."

Ian looked over Carl's shoulder and in the distance he could see someone approaching on bicycle. "Come on," he said. "We can cut across the downs."

Ian and Carl dashed the rest of the way to the castle and quickly made their way to the front door, where Ian used the knocker a bit too exuberantly and the door was opened abruptly by the earl's head butler, Mr. Binsford. "I say!" he exclaimed when he took in the two sweaty boys on the front steps. "What *is* this about?"

"We're terribly sorry, sir," Ian said in a rush as he glanced over his shoulder for any sign of Landis. "But we have an urgent matter for the earl!"

"The earl is not in," Binsford said with a sniff, still looking put off by the racket Ian had made with the knocker.

"We know, sir," said Carl. "But it's a matter of life and death! Can't you send word to him and have him come back immediately?"

Binsford's expression suggested that not only had Carl

spoken out of turn, but what he was asking was highly inappropriate. "I'll do no such thing!" the butler said loudly. "Now off with you two before I alert your headmistresses that you are creating a disturbance!"

Ian's heart sank again and he was about to throw himself at Binsford's mercy when a voice from inside the great hallway asked, "Who is that, Mr. Binsford?"

The butler's face turned a shade of crimson. "No one, my lady. Just two lads from the orphanage."

"Oh! I've just come from there," said the earl's aunt. "Which two lads is it, then?"

"It's us, my lady!" Ian said loudly, ignoring Binsford's warning scowl. "Ian and Carl. If we might have a word with you? We've a very urgent matter to discuss. It involves Theo, my lady."

"Urgent matter involving Theo?" repeated the earl's aunt as she stepped to the door. "What's this about, Master Wigby?"

"Someone claiming to be Theo's father has come to the orphanage and he wants to take her away!" Ian cried, flinching when he heard his own voice crack.

Lady Arbuthnot's hand flew to her open mouth. "Oh, my," she gasped. "That *is* most distressing! Most distressing indeed!"

"Madam Dimbleby says she can't do anything to prevent the man from taking Theo away with him," added Carl. "That's why we need the earl. He's got to come back straightaway!"

Lady Arbuthnot looked keenly down at them. "Yes, I

quite agree," she said, and turned to the butler, who was quietly smoldering off to one side. "Binsford," she said, her voice full of authority. "Alert my nephew that he is to leave London and journey back to Castle Dover this very instant."

"We are expecting him the day after tomorrow, my lady," Binsford replied politely.

"That is not soon enough!" she snapped with an impatient hand gesture. "Send an urgent telegram. Insist that he come home at once! Tell him that I shall expect him no later than the morning, in fact."

Binsford looked from Lady Arbuthnot to the boys and back again. Knowing he'd been outmaneuvered, he bowed slightly. "As you wish, my lady."

Later that night Ian was back at the keep and sitting with Carl and Theo in his room. Below, the clank of utensils on china sounded, and Ian's stomach gave a small rumble. For leaving the keep's grounds, the boys had been sent to bed without supper and were ordered to their room until further notice.

In protest, Theo had also skipped her evening meal, and maybe because she'd done so voluntarily, she seemed to be in brighter spirits than the boys. "The earl will figure this whole affair out," she said for the fiftieth time. "He'll know what to do."

And also for the fiftieth time, Ian silently hoped she was right. He'd been fidgety and nervous since they'd returned to the keep, but was glad to learn that even though Madam Dimbleby had suggested that she would not be able to stop

Major Fitzgerald from taking Theo away if he could prove that she was his daughter, she had in fact told the major that for the sake of everyone involved, she would require more evidence than just the one letter from Jacinda Barthorpe to prove that he was indeed Theo's father.

This, she had told them as she escorted the boys to their room after Landis had brought them back to the keep, was in an effort to present the earl with as many facts as she could and allow him to make the final decision. Ian had immediately felt ashamed for not having had a little more faith in her.

"I wonder when the earl will arrive," Carl mused. He was faceup, lying on his bed, staring at the ceiling.

"Shortly," Theo answered immediately. "And someone's bringing us a gift," she added.

Ian was about to ask her what she meant by that when there was a soft knock on the door, and a moment later Jaaved entered with a rather satisfied smile on his face. "Hello," he greeted them, and quickly came inside and shut the door.

"Hello," the three of them replied.

"I've brought you something," Jaaved said, his grin growing bigger.

"We know," said Carl.

"You do?" Carl pointed at Theo and Jaaved nodded. "Oh," he said. "Yes, I forgot. There's no sense trying to surprise you lot with Theo around."

Theo giggled and Ian marveled at the way she could recover from such distressing news so quickly. He seemed to be having a harder time of it than she was, in fact. He'd hardly cracked a smile all the rest of the day.

Jaaved reached under his long shirt, which he insisted on wearing outside his trousers, and pulled out a napkin. Unfolding it, he handed over three dinner rolls and several slices of ham. "Jaaved!" Carl exclaimed as he eagerly took the food. "You're blooming brilliant, mate!"

Jaaved rocked happily back on his heels. "And it was all the more difficult because I was seated right next to Madam Scargill," he said proudly.

Ian took his share and forced a smile. "Thanks," he said, then wolfed his food down.

"Theo says the earl's going to be here soon," Carl said, licking his fingers after polishing off the meal.

Jaaved's eyebrows rose. "The headmistresses aren't expecting him until morning."

"You should go and tell them that he'll be along tonight," Theo insisted. "They don't like to be surprised."

Jaaved turned to the door as Theo added, "And tell them that he's bringing Lady Arbuthnot with him, and one other man."

"Who?" Ian asked her.

Theo's expression turned confused. "Why, I'm not sure. That last bit just popped out of my mouth, really." Jaaved smiled as if he understood, and left them to deliver the message.

"It's a good thing that the earl's bringing his aunt to discuss the matter, don't you think?" Carl said.

Ian smiled, feeling a sense of relief for the first time since that afternoon. "Yes," he agreed. "Lady Arbuthnot will surely be on our side. And the other gent could be a barrister, someone to help the earl with the legal matter of keeping you here, right, Theo?"

Theo stared pensively out the window, her hand fluttering up to the crystal about her neck. "I hope so," she whispered. "I sincerely hope so."

The earl and his aunt arrived at half past eight, when most of the children were already yawning and sleepy. Ian and Theo were both called downstairs by Madam Dimbleby for a meeting with the earl, and Ian was in high spirits until he looked to the bottom of the stairwell and realized that the man standing next to the earl was wearing a uniform.

As he and Theo walked down together, he noticed that the man turned anxious eyes to Theo, and his expression became delighted. Theo must have noticed too, because she reached out and gripped Ian's hand tightly.

Ian knew immediately that the man in their entryway was none other than Major Fitzgerald himself, and Ian had a difficult time controlling his anger toward the man claiming to be Theo's father.

Madam Scargill saw to ushering the rest of the orphans to bed while Madam Dimbleby led Lady Arbuthnot, the earl, Major Fitzgerald, Ian, and Theo into the headmistresses' private study for what was sure to be a most uncomfortable meeting.

Ian sat down on a small sofa right next to Theo and wrapped an arm about her shoulders. He noticed she refused to look up and meet the major's eyes. He also noticed that the major had a kind face, which saddened when she refused to look at him.

Once everyone was seated, the earl cleared his throat and addressed them. "Thank you all for agreeing to meet on this most urgent matter so late in the evening." Most of those in attendance smiled politely at the earl. Ian just stared hard at the major, willing him to leave them all alone. "I would like to begin by introducing our guest, Major Fitzgerald from Debbonshire."

"My lord Arbuthnot, you have my sincere gratitude for bringing all concerned parties together. I'm most anxious to settle this matter and take my daughter home."

Theo immediately began to cry. Ian scowled angrily at the major. Lady Arbuthnot tsked, as if she didn't approve, and the earl cleared his throat again. "Yes, Major, about that . . . ," he began. "My aunt the Lady Arbuthnot has informed me that you believe Theo to be your daughter, but as I explained to you on the telephone earlier this afternoon, Theo is a very precious member of my orphanage, and I shall not let her go without overwhelming evidence that you are, in fact, her father."

The major appeared taken aback. "Forgive me, my lord, but I've never heard of an orphanage requiring proof of lineage to remove a child and give her a permanent home."

The earl nodded, as if he thought that a perfectly reasonable statement. "Theo is not just any orphan, Major Fitzgerald. We have come to believe that she is a very special child, and we have also come to believe that because of

205

her natural talents and abilities, Theo's life would be in mortal danger should she leave the safety of my keep."

The major looked at the earl as if he were speaking in tongues. "I'm afraid I don't quite understand, my lord."

Lady Arbuthnot spoke then. "Theo is a very gifted young lady," she said. "She has demonstrated an extraordinary ability to predict the future, you see."

The major's eyes widened before he barked out a laugh. "You must be joking!" he said, slapping his knee. "Oh, Lady Arbuthnot, I had heard of your very clever wit, but I never expected you to pull such a lark at a time like this!"

Lady Arbuthnot's eyes narrowed. "I assure you, Major, I make no jest."

Major Fitzgerald stopped his chuckling immediately and stared at them each in turn, as if waiting for one of them to crack a smile and tell him this was all just a bit of fun. Madam Dimbleby wrung her hands as the awkward silence continued, and said, "Major, Theo *is* gifted with this extraordinary ability; we who have watched her grow up have witnessed it time and time again. And we also know that because of her abilities, there are those who would like to take Theo away and cause her harm."

The major's face showed concern. "Cause her harm?" he asked. "Who the devil would want to cause the young lass harm?"

The earl sighed heavily. "Terrible people," he said with sincerity. "Believe me, Major. We have been witness to their cruelty, and we do not make these statements lightly."

The major blinked at him, and Ian knew that the man

206

was having a hard time believing their claims. "I can protect her," he finally declared. "I'm a major in His Majesty's Armed Services and more than capable of protecting my own daughter, my lord."

The earl looked seriously at him. "I have no doubt that you would try, sir; however, the forces of which I speak are beyond any one man's abilities. Theo would be in grave danger should she leave this keep. Of that I am certain."

The major sat back in his chair and threw his hands into the air. "But she's my daughter!" he insisted.

"That has yet to be determined," the earl said firmly, and Ian felt a renewed sense of hope.

The major's brow lowered, his good humor all but gone. "I have given you my letters from Jacinda Barthorpe, who your headmistress has confirmed was the girl's mother. It is clear in those letters that Jacinda held a very special affection for me!"

The earl nodded. "Yes," he agreed. "I have read your letters, and they do indeed indicate that she carried an affection for you, but nowhere does she claim that you are Theo's father, Major. And until I am certain that she is of your bloodline, I'm afraid I will be compelled to keep Theo right here, where she is safe and protected."

Major Fitzgerald's face flushed crimson. "This is unacceptable!" he announced, getting to his feet. "I shall have no choice, my lord, but to involve the courts."

The earl's face remained calm but firm. "You will do as you must, Major. And I will not fault you for it."

For a moment no one spoke or moved. The major stood

in the center of the floor, staring at them as if they were all quite mad; then he donned his hat, gave the earl and Lady Arbuthnot a formal bow, and said, "You may expect to hear from my barrister in the morning. I shall see myself out." And with that, he walked angrily out of the study.

Madam Dimbleby got up from her chair. "I should see him to the door," she said before hurrying after him.

Once she'd gone, Ian felt his shoulders relax and he gave the earl his biggest smile. "Thank you, my lord!"

But the earl's eyes suggested that he was far more concerned about the way things had gone than he'd initially let on. "If he goes to the courts, we'll lose," he said softly.

Lady Arbuthnot agreed. "Yes," she said. "The letters and his classmate's testimony will surely get the court to side with him."

"But what about what you told the major?" Ian protested. "About Theo being in terrible danger outside these walls?"

Lady Arbuthnot looked at him with her kind eyes and Ian knew she held little hope for their cause. "Ian, no one would believe us if we told them the real reason Theo must stay with us. They would laugh us right out of the courtroom."

Ian's heart sank. He knew they'd hardly seen the last of Major Fitzgerald. The moment Theo had gone down those stairs, the man had seen not his daughter, but her mother, and Ian could tell that the major had dearly loved Jacinda Barthorpe. He knew that Major Fitzgerald would fight all the way to the high court to take Theo home with him, just

208

to have a close connection to the woman he'd obviously never stopped loving. "There must be something we can do!" Ian cried.

The earl wiped a hand over his face, looking far wearier than the hour called for. "I will stall as long as I can," he promised. "I will hire my best inspectors to investigate the relationship between Theo's mother and the major, and I shall insist upon unswerving proof before I hand the young miss over."

"He's not my father," Theo whispered, looking a bit desperate.

The earl's eyes flashed to her. "Lass," he said gently, "I must prepare you for the inevitable. It may not matter."

Ian, Carl, Theo, and Jaaved met in the tower room much later that evening. "What are we going to do?" Jaaved asked.

Ian stared at the floor, thoroughly dispirited. "I've no idea," he said.

"We could leave," Carl said softly. Ian raised his eyes to look at his friend. "I mean, why wait round here for the major to take Theo away when we've got plenty of money from the treasure we brought back from Morocco to take us someplace far away where no one would even think to look for her."

Jaaved shifted uncomfortably, and Ian knew that he didn't like the idea of leaving the keep. "You want to stay behind, don't you?" he asked the Moroccan boy.

Jaaved grimaced. "Yes," he admitted. "But I feel you'll

need me, especially if you plan to return to the portal. So I'll go where you go, Ian."

Ian smiled gratefully at him. "Excellent, Jaaved. That just leaves us with deciding where."

"We could go to America!" Jaaved suggested, his face suddenly lighting up with the idea of the adventure. "Or Australia!"

Carl pumped his head up and down enthusiastically. "We could!"

"But what about the prophecy?" Theo protested. "Have you all forgotten about our duty to Laodamia? We'll be called upon soon enough to go back through the portal and find the Healer."

"We could always return when the time is right, Theo," Ian said, liking Carl's idea more and more.

But Theo appeared unconvinced. "How are we to know when it's time if we're halfway round the world?"

Carl frowned. "She's got a point there."

Ian stood up from the wooden crate he'd been sitting on and began to pace the floor. "Don't you see that it doesn't matter, Theo? If we stay here and the major takes you away before we have a chance to find the Healer, none of what Laodamia planned for us will come true. Without you, the whole plan's off. If we leave now, at least we'd have a chance."

"He's got a good point," Carl said, and Ian gave him an impatient look. "What?" Carl said defensively. "You've both got good points is all I'm saying!"

Theo toyed with her crystal and turned to stare out at

the starlit sky. "Very well," she said after a bit. "We'll go." Ian beamed her a relieved smile. "But we'll not go far," she insisted. "We'll need to be close enough so that we can return to the portal quickly."

"America and Australia are out, then," said Jaaved.

"We could go back to France," Carl suggested. Ian flinched involuntarily. He knew what Carl was thinking— that their stay in Toulouse had been most pleasant for him—but for Ian it had been torture.

So he was greatly relieved when Theo said, "We can't go back and stay with the Lafittes, Carl."

"Why not?"

"Because they would surely contact the earl with our whereabouts."

"She's got a point there, mate," Ian said, adding a playful smile when Carl looked at him crossly.

"Yeah, yeah," Carl agreed. "Still, France or Normandy seem the best choice for us. They're just across the channel, and we could board passage from Dover."

"How will we sneak out?" Jaaved asked. "Someone's sure to see us leaving the grounds."

Ian tapped his chin thoughtfully. "We'll go at night," he said. "An hour before dawn. It'll be a bit dodgy, what with the earl's extra patrols, but we should be able to manage it without too much trouble. With any luck we can purchase our tickets and cross the channel on the morning ferry."

"I've seen the schedule posted down at the market," said Carl. "The first boat leaves at six in the morning."

"Perfect," Theo said. "What day shall we leave?"

"We'll need at least a week to gather supplies and such," Ian told her. "And we can use the knapsacks we brought back from Morocco. We'll collect our supplies, extra clothing, and our money and store them in the knapsacks at the bottom of the ladder under the bench."

Jaaved asked, "How much money should we bring along?"

"Enough for the tickets and a month's lodging, I suppose. How much do each of you have here at the keep?"

"I'm good for twenty quid," said Carl.

"I've got fifty," said Jaaved.

"I'm with Carl," Ian said. "I've got a twenty-pound note hidden under my mattress."

Everyone turned to Theo, who had an enormous grin on her face. "We'll have plenty of money, Ian. Not to worry."

"How much have you got?" Carl asked.

Theo swiped a blond curl from her eyes. "I've got five hundred pounds," she said proudly. They all gasped and Theo giggled. "Several weeks ago I had a feeling we'd be needing some extra money, so one day, while running errands with Lady Arbuthnot, I stopped at the Bank of Brittan and made a withdrawal."

"That's got to be enough for all of us to live on for at least a year or two," Carl said with a wide smile. "Good thinking, Theo!"

Ian could feel the tension of the past day leave his shoulders as their plans were finalized. "Smashing," he said with a clap of his hands. "We'll leave one week from tonight. Be discreet about gathering your supplies. Carl, don't forget to pack the torches, and some extra batteries. Jaaved, we may need to leave most of your crystals behind. I don't think there'll be room in the knapsacks for them. And, Theo, see what you can do about dropping hints to a few of the other orphans about how worried you are about going away with the major, and how you'd much prefer to go back to Toulouse."

"Why on earth would I say that?" Theo asked, and the other boys looked at Ian as if he'd gone daft.

"Toulouse makes sense," he explained. "When we come up missing, and the earl conducts a search for us, he'll begin by looking in the south of France. I'm sure he'll check with the port master to make certain we purchased tickets to Calais, which of course we'll do, but once we reach France, we'll turn right round and book passage to Dunkirk, then make our way to Amsterdam."

"We're going to Belgium?" Jaaved asked.

Ian smiled. Jaaved liked maps and geography just as much as he did, and the lad had learned quite a bit about the layout of Europe in the year he'd been at the keep. "We are," Ian told him. "I'll see about getting into the earl's library to pinch us an atlas for the journey."

With a plan in hand, everyone retired for the evening, both excited and nervous about the week ahead.

THE SERPENT

Two days after they'd made their plans, Ian was able to convince the headmistresses to allow Landis to escort him to Castle Dover on the pretense of finding a new book to read. Landis seemed more than pleased to take Ian to the earl's residence, and Ian suspected that this was due to the new laundry maid the earl had recently acquired.

Once a week some members of the castle's staff came to the keep to assist the headmistresses with laundry and food preparation, and Ian had seen Landis's eyes light up when he and the maid had been introduced.

And sure enough, the moment Ian arrived at the earl's library, Landis offered up an excuse about needing a bit of starch from the laundry room, and hurried away. Once Ian was alone in the large room, he began to scan the shelves for a suitable atlas. The earl had several, but Ian had his favorite. He knew just the one he wanted; it was a large leather-bound tome with fantastic detail and legible writing. He knew he wouldn't be able to take the entire atlas with

214

him on the escape five nights hence, and he'd already resigned himself to the necessity of tearing out the appropriate
page about Belgium and hoping that the earl didn't think to
search through his collection of atlases for a possible clue to
where they'd gone. He could only cross his fingers that the
earl would never notice, and if he ever found a similar atlas
on his travels, he would make sure to purchase it and send it
in replacement.

After looking in the usual spot for the text and not seeing it, he moved to a stack of books on a nearby desk and
spied it near the bottom of the pile. Smiling, he began to
move the books on top out of the way, and as he did so, he
set aside a newspaper that was hiding another book, which
appeared brand-new.

Ian's eyes widened when he took in the title. *The Hobbit*
was printed in black lettering across a gray-blue cover with
etchings of mountains and a menacing dragon. For a moment, Ian forgot his task and curiously opened the novel.
There, on the inside cover, was an inscription:

For Ian Wigby,
A lad of great courage and character, as the Earl of Kent
can testify

J. R. R. Tolkien

Ian's mouth fell open and he plopped down into a nearby
chair, stunned right down to his toes. He'd had to leave the
copy of *The Hobbit* he'd originally been reading back at the
Lafittes' after getting through only the first several chapters,

but he'd been so impressed by the novel that he'd talked it up quite a bit on the train ride back to Dover. He'd had no idea the earl would do such a generous and kind thing for him. His eyes moved guiltily to the atlas on the table and he felt a wave of shame wash over him. Not only was he about to desecrate the earl's property, but he was also about to betray his trust.

Ian closed the cover gently and smoothed his hands over it. He did not deserve such a gift, and he felt a terrible guilt for what he and the others had to do to keep Theo safe. With a sigh he moved the newspaper back over the earl's gift and stood up, ready to leave the atlas in place and untouched. He could purchase a map once they arrived in Amsterdam.

Ian was about to leave the library when he heard voices coming toward him in the hallway. One of them he was sure belonged to the earl, and Ian looked about quickly, then darted to the opposite end of the room, where he pretended to look thoughtfully up at the shelves.

A moment later the earl and his head butler pushed their way through the double doors. "They should be arriving on the evening train, Mr. Binsford. Please have my driver meet them at the station and take them to the keep," said the earl when he suddenly noticed Ian alone in the room. "Master Wigby!" the earl exclaimed. "Whatever are you doing away from the keep's grounds?"

Ian was quick to explain. "It's all right, my lord. Landis escorted me here to ensure my safety. I merely wanted a new book to read."

The earl's expression immediately turned to delight. "Well, my lad, I must say that you are looking in the wrong place! I have just the book for you, in fact." The earl strode over to the table with the atlas and moved aside the newspaper that Ian had just replaced. He pulled out the novel hidden underneath, walked back over to Ian, and gave it to him with an enormous smile. "Here you are, lad," he said kindly. "Happy early birthday!"

With a start Ian realized that the end of the month was his fourteenth birthday, and he could hardly believe that the earl had remembered. "My lord," he said, accepting the book and feeling guiltier than he could ever remember. "It's a copy of *The Hobbit*. You're far too generous."

The earl rocked back on his heels. "Not at all, my young man!" he said with enthusiasm. "Open up the cover, Ian. There's an inscription that I believe you'll quite enjoy."

Ian gulped. He opened the cover and read aloud the words written there, then closed the cover and held the novel tightly to his chest. "Thank you, my lord. I don't deserve such kindness."

The earl beamed happily down at him and gave him a pat on the back. "I had the great fortune of meeting Mr. Tolkien recently at a dinner party. Quite an agreeable chap, really."

Ian nodded dumbly. He found it difficult to meet the earl's eyes. Fortunately, he was saved from his patriarch's continued kindness when Mr. Binsford cleared his throat and asked from the doorway, "Will that be all, my lord?"

The earl turned around to regard his butler. "Oh, terribly

sorry, Binsford. I quite forgot you were standing there. Yes, that will be all, but tell Miss Carlyle that I shall be dining at the keep this evening. I'll want to be there to welcome the new orphans."

Binsford had barely bowed out of the room when Ian asked, "New orphans, my lord?"

The earl moved to a nearby love seat and sat down with a contented sigh. "Yes, lad, I've found the perfect replacements to fill those two empty beds at the keep, or rather, our talented schoolmasters have done the job for me."

"The ones you mentioned when we were in France?" Ian asked, still hugging the book.

The earl scratched his beard thoughtfully and explained. "Yes, lad. I know that you lot have been quite concerned about my order for you to remain at the keep and not venture through the portal, which is why, after receiving a particularly interesting telegram from your schoolmasters, I began to put forth a plan of my own.

"You see, Ian, I began to wonder if Laodamia might have foreseen certain obstacles getting in the way of the fulfillment of her prophecies, and took pains to ensure that we could work around them."

Ian furrowed his brow, confused. "I'm terribly sorry, my lord, but I'm not following you."

The earl laughed. "Right," he said, sitting forward to rest his elbows on his knees. "When we were in France, I received a telegram from Thatcher and Perry, detailing the progress being made at the orphanage in Cornwall where I'd sent them. Do you remember my assigning them to oversee the improvements I'd funded there?"

Ian nodded. "Yes."

"Well," continued the earl, "in their telegram to me, they spoke at length of the talents of a certain young lady who's recently been received at that orphanage. Her name is Vanessa. Her father, mother, and younger brother all perished from some terrible bout of the flu, or so I'm told. It appears this young lass is a most gifted child, and your schoolmasters claim that from the moment of her arrival, Vanessa has insisted upon spending most of her time in the orphanage's infirmary, assisting the headmistresses there with any ill or injured child. The Masters Goodwyn assure me Vanessa is quite adept at nursing these sick children back to health, and both Thatcher and Perry are most impressed with her."

The earl paused and seemed to be waiting for Ian to say something, but Ian was still confused about why the earl should be telling him this, so he attempted to be polite. "That's very nice, my lord. I'm glad to hear of such a kind young lady."

The earl sat up straight and exclaimed, "But it's more than that, Master Wigby! Don't you see the importance of this information?"

Ian shook his head. "No, I'm afraid I don't."

Again the earl leaned forward. "Vanessa is our Healer," he whispered. "She is the one that Laodamia spoke of, I'm convinced!"

Ian's jaw dropped. "She is?" He was wondering how the earl could arrive at such a conclusion.

"Yes," the earl insisted. "I rest my theory upon the final prophecy that was discovered by Sir Barnaby. I believe it was written sometime after Laodamia had scribed the other prophecies found in your silver treasure boxes, and I also believe—counter to the professor's theory—that you were indeed meant to hear it."

"But . . . ," Ian began before words failed. He couldn't imagine why the earl would be so convinced.

The earl, however, wasn't paying a bit of attention to Ian's outward expression of doubt. "Think of it, lad," he continued. "The greatest Oracle of all time must have known that after reading this latest prophecy, I would forbid you to go through the portal, and I believe she wrote it for that reason. She must have sensed that if you and Theo went through the portal in search of the Healer, you would both be killed. Therefore, she took great pains to warn you, and also provide us with the solution, by allowing me to bring the Healer directly to the keep!"

Ian scratched his head. "But," he said, trying again, "have the schoolmasters told you that Vanessa is actually able to *heal* these children she's attending to?"

The earl's pacing paused for a brief moment, and he turned to face Ian again. "Not in so many words, but their enthusiasm for her natural nurturing abilities and the comfort she brings to the sick orphans must not be overlooked. Hence, I have instructed them to bring Vanessa to the keep as quickly as possible. She will be arriving this evening with a young lad who she's been attending to and refuses to leave behind. She and the little boy—his name is William, I believe—will take up the two beds left by Jon and Emily."

Ian looked up at the earl with a mixture of thoughts and emotions. He knew that if the earl was correct, and Vanessa was in fact the Healer from Laodamia's prophecies, Theo would never agree to continue with their escape plan without her, and convincing a new orphan to run away with them was certainly a risky endeavor. What if Vanessa said no? What if she told the earl or the headmistresses of their plans?

Alternatively, staying at the keep almost certainly ensured that Theo would be sent away to live with Major Fitzgerald. And Ian thought that if that happened, he would surely go out of his mind with worry.

"Well, my lad?" asked the earl. "What do you think?"

Ian stared back down at his birthday present as yet another wave of guilt washed over him. "I think it's likely best to ask Theo what she thinks, my lord. I suspect we won't know if Vanessa is the Healer until Theo tells us so. And if Vanessa is not the Healer, then we'll know that we might still consider venturing through the portal again."

The earl eyed him thoughtfully for a moment. "Lad," he said, "did Theo immediately recognize Jaaved as the Seeker?"

Ian's breath caught. The earl had a point. Theo had not recognized Jaaved as the Seeker until he'd received a burn on his hand in the shape of a diamond, which had happened

221

several days *after* they'd met him. And this further complicated matters, because if Theo couldn't positively rule
Vanessa either in or out as the Healer, she might well *insist*
on remaining at the keep until she was certain. But Ian
could hardly express this concern to the earl, so he settled
for saying, "Of course you're right, my lord. Time will tell, I
suppose."

The earl gave him a broad smile. "Excellent!" he said.
"I'm glad that you see it my way. Now, I'll not keep you from
your adventures with Mr. Bilbo Baggins. Why don't you
fetch Landis and go on back to the keep? I believe I saw him
entering the laundry room earlier. . . ."

When Ian and Landis arrived back at the keep, Ian immediately alerted the headmistresses to the impending visit
from the earl, the schoolmasters, and two new orphans in
time for dinner.

He could well have saved his breath, because no sooner
had he finished telling them the news than Madam Dimbleby smiled and said, "Yes, Ian, Theo told us about
tonight's guests an hour ago."

Ian smiled ruefully. It was no fun having anything excit-
ing to share with Theo around.

He didn't have long to dwell on his spoiled surprise,
however, because not a moment later a motorcar arrived
from the earl's personal fleet with a small staff and enough
food for a feast.

Ian wanted to find Theo and tell her about the earl's
theory, but Madam Scargill ordered him to help with the

dinner preparations and he was quickly so busy that he lost track of time. Before he knew it, their guests were arriving, and Ian moved with the rest of the crowd outside to greet the visitors.

All of the keep's children turned out on the front steps when the earl's motorcar arrived. Carl and Jaaved sidled up to Ian as the earl, Thatcher, Perry, and the two new orphans got out of the car.

The young lady—Vanessa—was introduced first. Ian studied her closely, but she didn't seem at all special. Slight of frame, with large brown eyes and long dark hair, she appeared shy and waiflike.

The boy next to her was introduced as William, and he looked pale, sweaty, and sickly. Madam Scargill seemed to notice that the boy might be ill, because she bent down to him and felt his forehead, then whispered something to Madam Dimbleby and took the poor little lad by the hand, leading him quickly through the crowd back into the keep.

Ian overheard her mumbling something about a fever as she passed him, and then he remembered the earl's prediction that Vanessa was the Healer. He scanned the faces still gathered round their guests, looking for Theo, and he found her on the edge of the crowd, staring at Vanessa, her face stricken.

Alarmed, Ian began to edge his way closer to Theo to see why she appeared upset, but well before he could get to her, she turned and dashed back into the keep. Hampering his efforts further, at that moment the earl waved everyone indoors for the evening meal, and the eager and hungry children surrounding Ian blocked his entry for several moments. When he finally managed to get inside, Theo was nowhere to be found.

"What's the matter?" Carl asked from beside him as Ian turned his head this way and that.

"Did you see where Theo went?" Ian asked.

"I saw her run up the stairs a bit ago," Carl told him.

Ian felt a knot of anxiety form in the pit of his stomach. Theo wasn't often given to theatrics. Something must be terribly wrong. "I've got to find her."

"Why? Is something the matter?"

Ian sighed. "I believe so," he admitted. "But I've no idea what."

"Do you think she might be upset about that man claiming to be her father?"

Ian had almost forgotten about that awful business, and immediately his mind settled on it as the probable cause. "Perhaps," he said.

"Come along to the table, lads," said Madam Dimbleby from behind them. "We've quite a few mouths to feed this evening."

Ian turned to her and said, "Ma'am, I believe Theo might be upset again about that whole Major Fitzgerald business. Might I be allowed to find her and see that she's all right?"

Madam Dimbleby's mouth turned down as she frowned. "Oh, the poor lass," she said. "Yes, of course, Ian. Go, see to Theo. I'll save you both a plate of food and make your excuses at the table."

"Did you want me to go along?" Carl asked, and Ian had to give him credit for the offer, as Carl's eyes kept drifting toward the dinner table.

"Naw, mate. You go on. I'll be down with Theo in a bit."

With that Ian dashed up the stairs and looked first in his room. Then he knocked softly on the loo door, but no one answered. He looked back down the hallway and wondered where she could have gone when he got the smart idea to ask his sundial. Pulling it from his pocket, he said, "Sundial, show me where Theo is."

Immediately, Ian received his answer and he looked to his left at the door leading to the tower. Making haste up the stairs, he found Theo pacing the floor in quite a state of distress. The moment he crested the landing, she flew across the room and gripped his arms tightly. "Ian!" she gasped.

"What is it?" he replied, now very much alarmed.

"The serpent!" she whispered. "It's here!"

Ian wrapped an arm around Theo protectively, his eyes darting about the tower room as he expectantly looked for anything that slithered. "Where?" he demanded.

"That girl!" Theo told him. "It's the new girl!"

Ian blinked. He focused on Theo again and asked, "What? Theo, what do you mean it's the girl?"

Theo pulled away from him and returned to her pacing. "The new girl the earl brought here! She's the serpent!"

"You're talking about Vanessa?"

"Yes!"

For a long moment Ian simply stared wide-eyed at Theo,

wondering if all the stress she'd been under lately had finally caught up to her. "Theo," he began in a calm, even tone.

"I know what you think!" she snapped, looking at him with accusing eyes. "But she *is* the serpent!"

"She's a harmless girl!"

But Theo was not to be dissuaded, and she shook her head vehemently back and forth. "She's not! She's the serpent Laodamia warned us about!"

Again Ian was left speechless. How could he argue with such a ridiculous statement?

Theo's frantic pacing continued. "We must leave at once!" she announced. "Tonight, if we can! We're all in terrible danger if we stay!"

Ian ran a hand through his hair in frustration. "Theo," he said, trying again. "We cannot possibly leave tonight."

"Why not?" she demanded.

Ian sighed. She was being unreasonable. "Because it's Saturday! You know as well as I do that the ferries don't run on Sunday."

Theo stopped her pacing abruptly and her eyes misted over. "We're doomed," she whispered, and dissolved into a fit of tears.

Over the next half hour, Ian did his best to console her, but it was to no avail. Theo clung to him and cried and he began to wonder if she would ever stop. He was quite relieved when Carl found them after supper. "Is she all right?" he asked, cresting the landing, carrying two plates loaded with food.

Ian squeezed Theo tightly. "She's fine," he said, hoping that saying it aloud would make it true.

"Oh, Carl!" Theo wailed.

Carl set down the plates and moved quickly over to Theo, who shifted away from Ian to hug his friend fiercely and continue her wailing. Carl looked questioningly at Ian, but all Ian could do was shrug. How could he explain Theo's theory when he didn't even understand it himself?

Carl patted Theo's back and whispered, "The earl has requested a word with you, Ian."

"Now?"

"Yes. He's going back to London to meet with his barrister and he's leaving first thing in the morning. He's waiting for you downstairs right now, in fact."

"Will you . . . ?" Ian asked softly, pointing to Theo.

"Yes," Carl assured him. "I'll look after her."

Ian smiled gratefully and dashed down the steps. He found the earl standing in the foyer, addressing Thatcher. "You look a bit peaked, Master Goodwyn. Are you feeling all right?"

Thatcher put a hand to his head and attempted a smile. "I must admit, I've had a bit of a chill this evening, my lord. Nothing a good night's rest won't cure me of, I'm certain."

"Yes, well, we'll be off just as soon as I speak with Master Wigby." The earl spotted Ian on the stairs then and added, "Ah, there you are, lad! I've heard from Madam Dimbleby that Theo has had a bit of an upset this evening."

Ian nodded as he went the rest of the way down the stairs. "Yes, my lord. She's been most distressed."

"Ah, I should know better than to try to keep any recent

developments from her. She's always one step ahead, isn't she?"

Ian had no idea what the earl was talking about, and wondered if by some coincidence he knew about the serpent too. "Er . . . ," he said. "Yes, my lord. She's very adept at ferreting out the state of things."

The earl sighed and wrapped an arm around Ian's shoulders. "Well, I'm terribly sorry I couldn't have bargained you two a little more time," he said sadly. "But I'm afraid at the moment there is little I can do to halt these proceedings."

Ian's heart thumped loudly, a foreboding stealing over him. "My lord?" he asked. "I'm afraid I don't know exactly what you mean."

The earl looked taken aback. "Really? So Theo hasn't told you?"

"She's been a bit too upset to talk," Ian said.

The earl nodded, as if he understood completely. "My barrister sent word yesterday, but I did not receive the message until just before supper. It appears that our Major Fitzgerald has a most influential friend in the courts, and he has been awarded custody of Theo. He will be here tomorrow afternoon, in fact, to collect her and take her to his home in Debbonshire."

Ian felt as if all the blood rushed out of him at once. The world spun, and he was certain that if it were not for the earl's arm about his shoulders, he would fall down. Through a muddled haze he noticed that the earl was looking at him with such sympathy it only made him feel worse, and he knew he should say something, but words refused to form.

"I'm terribly sorry, Ian," the earl told him. "You have my word that I will do *everything* within my power to bring her back, but for now, I'm afraid we've no choice; we must comply with the court's directive."

Ian looked away. He felt almost faint, and he saw Madam Dimbleby across the room, her eyes red and watery. She knew too.

The earl gave a final squeeze to Ian's shoulder and released him. Ian heard him say something about needing to be off, and Thatcher and Perry followed him, but not before each of them gave Ian a soft pat on the back and looked at him with care as they departed.

For what felt like an eternity, Ian could only stand there, too stunned to move or speak. Eventually, Madam Dimbleby got up and took his hand, leading the way out of the room to avoid the prying eyes of the others. In her private study she hugged Ian fiercely as a wave of emotion overtook him.

Much later that night Ian met with Carl and Jaaved in the tower. "It's not right!" Carl said, his voice barely holding to the hushed tone Ian had insisted upon. Below, the rest of the keep was well asleep by then. "Isn't there anything the earl can do to stop the major from taking her away?"

Ian stared forlornly at the floor. He was having difficulty putting his thoughts in order, as the news from the earl had rattled him to the core. After he'd left the study, Ian had gone straight back upstairs to talk to Theo, but Carl had told him she'd been exhausted by her cry and had retired to her bed. "He promised to try," Ian whispered. "But for now, we've no choice but to let her go with the major."

"Then we should leave tonight!" Carl announced, getting up from his seat to pace the floor just like Theo had done.

"And go where?" Ian asked, a desperate note in his voice. "Tomorrow is Sunday, Carl. There's no way out of Dover on Sunday unless you've got a motorcar. Besides, we've barely collected half the things we'll need to leave. There's not enough time to make our escape."

Carl stopped in his tracks, dumbstruck. "Blast it!" he growled, and returned to his pacing.

Jaaved wiped his brow; Ian noticed he was sweating. "We could wait until we've gathered all our supplies, then retrieve her from Debbonshire," he offered.

And for the first time that evening, Ian had heard an idea that held a ray of hope. "Yes!" he exclaimed. "Jaaved, that's exactly what we'll do!"

Carl came back to sit down next to Ian. "We could have Theo write to us of her address, and when we get her letter, we'll strike out to rescue her and make our way to Amsterdam."

Ian smiled wisely and reached into his pocket, retrieving the sundial. "Waiting for a letter will take too long. If we simply follow the sundial once we take the train to Debbonshire, we'll find her soon enough."

"Oh, that's a much better plan!" Carl said.

"We'll go the moment we've got our supplies together. I

expect that should only take another day or two at the most," Ian said.

For the next few minutes the boys worked through the details of their plan, and when each knew his assignment, they stood and prepared to go back to bed. As they made their way down the stairs, Carl asked, "I suppose this business about the major taking her away was what Theo was so upset about?"

Ian paused on the stairs. "No," he said. "She didn't tell you?"

Carl shook his head. "She was too busy crying, mate. The most she said was something about the serpent and how Laodamia was right after all."

Ian grabbed Carl and Jaaved by the arms, halting their progress down the stairs. "You know what's strange?" he whispered.

"What?" they asked together.

"Theo didn't mention the major to me at all this evening. She gave no indication whatsoever that she was about to leave the keep for Debbonshire."

Carl's brow furrowed. "Then why was she upset?"

"She kept insisting that Vanessa was the serpent from Laodamia's prophecy."

"*Vanessa?*" Carl and Jaaved asked in unison.

"Yes," Ian insisted. "Odd, isn't it?"

"But she's harmless," Jaaved proclaimed. "I sat next to her at the table, and other than being a bit shy, she's really quite nice."

"Perhaps Theo has misinterpreted things," Carl said in that irritating way that suggested he thought Theo had gone off her nutty again.

"She's perfectly sane, Carl!" Ian snapped. He was feeling particularly protective of Theo right then.

"Of course she is." Carl was quick to reassure him. "But maybe this time she got it wrong."

Ian said nothing more; instead, he motioned for them to continue down to bed. Still, the fact that Theo had been far more concerned with Vanessa's arrival than her own departure troubled him deep into the night.

The next morning Ian and Carl were late to the breakfast table. Madam Dimbleby finally ushered them out of bed well past the time all the other orphans had been fed. "I've no time for your laziness this morning!" she snapped in irritation, which was highly unusual for Madam Dimbleby and caused Ian to quickly get up and promptly see to making his bed.

Madam Dimbleby fussed about the boys' room, picking up laundry and such, while the boys went through their morning rituals, and the whole time, their headmistress complained about the state of things that morning. "Gertrude has taken ill and I've sent her to bed, and several of the girls have come down with a fever. And that new boy, Will, is quite sick," she said. "I was so alarmed by his fever that I had to send Landis to fetch Dr. Lineberry, which has left only me to tend to everyone else!"

Ian paused in the making of his bed. "Did you say they're all sick?" he asked.

"Yes, Ian," Madam sighed, a note of exasperation in her voice. "There's obviously some sort of influenza infecting the keep, and I've no time to chase the likes of you two out of your beds!"

With that she turned in a huff and hurried out of the room. Ian and Carl were left to stare at each other. "Looks like we picked the wrong day to sleep in," Carl muttered.

"Come on," Ian said. "We'd best get downstairs and offer her some help. We'll also need to find Theo and tell her of our plans."

Ian and Carl dressed in their lightest clothing, as the summer day had already warmed to an uncomfortable degree. "Landis said we're in for a heat wave," Carl told Ian as they descended the stairs.

They found Madam Dimbleby straightaway and she told them to help ready those children feeling well enough for church. "I will have to skip the services today," she said. "I've just heard that Jaaved is also running a fever."

Ian stopped in his tracks as he remembered Jaaved's breaking into a sweat the evening before. At that moment, Theo entered the sitting room and their eyes met. He was about to motion her away so that he could speak to her privately when a series of urgent knocks sounded on the front door.

"Good heavens!" exclaimed Madam Dimbleby. "What now?"

Ian followed the headmistress to the front door, which she opened to reveal Dr. Lineberry, wearing a surgical mask, and beside him, the village constable, holding a large sign and a hammer.

"Oh, my!" Madam exclaimed. "Dr. Lineberry, I'm so glad you're here—"

Madam got no further than that. Dr. Lineberry held up his hand to silence her, and with the other he offered her a yellow telegram. "Madam," he said formally, "I'm afraid the keep and all of its occupants are now under legal quarantine."

Ian gasped, and now beside him, Carl and Theo did the same. Madam Dimbleby also appeared quite flustered and she hurried to read the telegram the doctor had given her. After a moment her hand moved to cover her mouth and she whispered, "Oh, my heavens! *No!*"

Ian leaned in to peer over her shoulder just as the doctor pushed past them on his way inside and the door was slammed in their face by the constable. Absently, Madam Dimbleby shoved the yellow telegram into Ian's hands and said in a voice hoarse with fear, "Stay with the children, Ian, while I assist the doctor." She then hurried after Dr. Lineberry.

From outside a loud tapping began to resonate through the wood door. "What's it say?" whispered Carl, motioning to the telegram.

Stunned, Ian stared down in disbelief at the words across the page. "It's from a doctor who's just attended several sick children at the Cornwall orphanage," Ian said as he skimmed the paper and his heart began to pound. "They've had an outbreak of polio. They believe they can trace it back to one girl named Vanessa, whose entire family recently perished from the disease. They believe she has spread it to several children there, and are most concerned about the welfare of anyone she has come into contact with."

All around him there were gasps, and Ian turned to look at the stunned faces of the children who had overheard him. Only one person did not look surprised—Theo. She stood nearby with a sobering expression, and he now fully understood that her predictions had been spot-on after all.

THE WITCH OF VERSAILLES

Caphiera the Cold and her sister Atroposa the Terrible walked through a darkened and deserted alley in the poorest and most dangerous section of Versailles. It was late enough in the evening that most people were in bed, but a few opportunists had been lurking about in the doorway of a pub that the sorceresses had passed before turning into the alley.

Litter along the cobblestone shuffled noisily down the passage, blown by the constant wind that surrounded Atroposa. The distraction of swirling debris annoyed Caphiera, who was wearing her sunglasses and having enough trouble navigating the darkened streets. Caphiera knew that her sister had no control over the constant wind that surrounded her, but it was still a bothersome thing that never failed to set the wintry sorceress's nerves on edge.

That was why she did not notice right away when two malcontents stepped into the alley just in front of them, blocking their way. "Look what we have here," said one with a laugh. "Two old hags out for a stroll."

"Got any gold on you, hags?" asked the other in a menacing voice.

Caphiera and her sister came to a stop and turned to each other. "Allow me," offered Caphiera, removing her sunglasses as the two men approached.

"By all means," moaned her sister.

"Allow you to what, hag?" snapped the first man. "Give over your gold?"

Caphiera smiled wickedly. She knew that the men couldn't clearly see her; the alley was far too dark. "Yes," she said coyly. "I've got your gold, but I'll need a bit of light to fetch it from inside my coat. Might one of you have a match?"

Instantly, one of the men produced a lighter and flicked it open. A small flame cast eerie shadows along the walls, but the men weren't close enough to illuminate Caphiera's face.

"Step closer," she said, encouraging them. But in that moment, the two mortals seemed to suspect something amiss.

"No tricks, hag," spat the second man. "Give us your gold or we'll have to hurt you."

"Tricks?" Caphiera said in her most wounded voice. "Why, I would never *think* of attempting such a thing. I'm an honest woman, after all. Look right into my eyes and you'll see I speak the truth."

The man holding the lighter lifted the flame and took

one cautious step forward. It was the last thing he ever did. Within seconds he had frozen solid. And he'd done it so quickly that the lighter remained stuck firmly in his hand. "Michele?" inquired his partner. "What's the matter?"

"Isn't it obvious?" Caphiera asked him. "He's so enchanted by my beauty that he's forgotten himself."

"He's *what?*" the other demanded, taking a step forward. Caphiera lowered her face a little closer to the light of the flame and opened her eyes wide. A moment later the man was crashing to the floor, frozen solid, just like his friend.

Caphiera sighed in satisfaction and stepped over the dead man. "Come along, Atroposa."

The two sorceresses continued through the alley to the last door on the right. Caphiera shielded her eyes with her thick glasses before giving the door three loud knocks. There were some shuffling noises from inside, and nearby a cat hissed at them before darting into a sewer grate. But soon enough the door was opened, and a middle-aged woman with pockmarked skin, deep-set eyes, and stringy gray hair looked up at them. "It is very late," she said irritably.

"And yet, witch, you will see us," said Atroposa, the howl in her voice echoing along the alley.

The woman scowled, but then she seemed to catch sight of the two unfortunate souls not far down the cobblestone street. The light from the doorway illuminated their tragic end, and the woman's face changed immediately. Her lips parted in a weak smile and she bowed low. "Of course, mistresses," she said. "Please enter and make yourselves comfortable."

The sorceresses swept into the tiny one-room flat. It was cluttered with all kinds of horrifying odds and ends stuffed into jars of various sizes. One seemed to contain an assortment of dried bat wings. In another were the pickled remains of a two-headed snake. A third was filled to the brim with pigs' eyes. And all about the small home was the cloying scent of incense.

Shutting the door behind the sorceresses, the witch waved them to two nearby chairs set in front of a tiny table, and hurried to take up her own seat opposite her guests. "How may I help you?" she asked, careful not to look directly at either.

Caphiera adjusted her sunglasses. She needed this woman's services and did not want to risk turning her into an icicle prematurely. "We have heard from our brother that you have quite the talent for forecast," she said.

The witch chuckled. "I am a very gifted seer," she assured them. "And is your brother the all-powerful Magus the Black, who did grace me with his presence some weeks past?"

"He is indeed," said Caphiera. "He has yet to find all of your predictions true, but we hear he was most encouraged by his visit with you."

"Excellent," said the witch, wrapping the woolen shawl about her shoulders more securely. The temperature in her flat had plummeted with the arrival of her guests.

"We also have need of your sight," moaned Atroposa, getting to the heart of the matter.

The witch reached behind her and brought to the table

a small crystal ball set on a bronze pedestal. "Ask me your question and I shall divine the answer," she instructed.

Caphiera said, "We seek an audience with the one called the Secret Keeper. We wish to know where to locate him."

Their host lit a candle and brought it close to the crystal. The flame was nearly extinguished by the swirling air that blustered about the apartment, so the witch cupped her hand around it and focused on the fractures within the crystal ball. "This man is of great importance," she said before glancing up to gauge the sorceresses' reactions. Caphiera nodded and the witch continued. "You are in luck, mistresses. The one you seek is not far away. He comes to France on a most urgent mission. One I feel you will be wise to thwart. He carries with him a treasure of sorts with roots that trace back to antiquity. He seeks to hide this relic and will go to great lengths to protect it until he does. I see a path where you are likely to intersect with him and capture the treasure for your own."

Caphiera smiled wickedly, exposing her ferocious teeth. The witch looked up again and started at the sight, which only made Caphiera's smile widen. "Where in France might we find him?"

The old woman lowered her head again, peering into the ball. "Paris," she said affirmatively. "Amidst great chaos he will be where others flee. But I warn you; there are more souls than you who seek him. And if they should get to your Keeper first, then your treasure will surely be lost."

Caphiera's smile vanished. She cursed and pounded the

240

tabletop, which was immediately coated with a sheet of solid ice. The witch gasped; her bronze pedestal was now stuck to the table, but she made no complaint . . . which was wise.

"When will the Keeper arrive in Paris?" asked Caphiera.

The witch attempted to collect herself before peering again into the crystal ball. "It will be in the summer," she said. "Nearly a year hence."

"Where is he now?" asked Atroposa.

The witch dipped her chin, her brow furrowed in confusion. "Lost," she said. "He is beyond my sight, mistresses. It is almost as if he has hidden himself from gifted seers like me."

Caphiera nodded. "He is a crafty one," she agreed. "He has eluded us all this time and has learned to conceal himself well." Getting up from the table, the sorceress called to her sister. "Come, Atroposa," she said. "We have much to do before next summer." She then laid a few gold pieces down on the tabletop, which the soothsayer greedily snapped up.

The sorceresses turned to the door but were stopped by the woman when she suddenly called, "Mistresses?"

Caphiera turned back warily. If the old hag asked for more gold, it would be the last request she ever made. "Yes?"

"Might you pass on a message to your brother?"

"That would depend on what it is, witch," said Caphiera.

The old woman tugged again at her shawl as the temperature dipped even lower. "Yes, of course," the woman agreed nervously. "You see, I've had another vision that he might find useful."

Caphiera was out of patience. "Out with it, then!" she snapped.

The witch jumped and her lip began to tremble. "If you please, tell him that I have seen the children he seeks moving beyond the reach of the fortress that protects them. I would be most grateful."

Caphiera and Atroposa exchanged a look. "This message interests us," Caphiera said, edging back to the table where the witch sat. "Where do you see them?"

The witch smiled, clearly relieved. "In my vision, they seem to be near a large hedge maze. They will be quite vulnerable, and I have no doubt they could easily be taken."

"When?"

"Within a day or two at the most, mistress. When the moon is at her zenith."

Caphiera smiled again and saw that the witch sat rigidly in her chair, clearly trying hard not to cower. "I shall pass the message on to my brother," Caphiera said before tossing one additional gold coin onto the slippery tabletop. "He shall be most pleased."

THE HEDGE MAZE

I an stood, covered in dirt and grime, at the top of the tower with Carl and Theo. "It's clear," he announced, feeling the weariness of hard work seep deep into his bones.

Throughout the past several nights—ever since the doors to the keep had been padlocked and a guard had been set outside to enforce the quarantine—he and Carl had been taking turns shoveling out the debris at the bottom of the escape tunnel.

"And I've got the last of our supplies," Carl said, holding up a knapsack. "The sundial pointed me to those extra batteries."

Theo looked out at the huge moon bathing the landscape in a soft silver glow. "We should leave immediately, then," she said.

Ian grimaced. With the quarantine in place, the threat of Theo's being taken away by the major had been delayed, but now they were all in fear of the polio virus, which was quickly wreaking havoc within the orphanage. Nearly a third of the children were deathly ill, and Jaaved's condition was most grave. Ian, Carl, and Theo had agreed to abandon their plans of escaping to Amsterdam and instead follow Laodamia's instructions to go through the portal and bring back the Healer; however, Ian still held quite a few reservations. "Are we quite certain this is what we should do, Theo?" he asked her for the tenth time.

She regarded him patiently. "We've no choice. You know that with each passing moment, Jaaved grows weaker. The boy Will has already died, Ian! Even Thatcher remains in peril, not to mention we've heard nothing of the earl. For all we know he could also be stricken in his apartment in London! Carl and I *must* go in search of the Healer before one more life is lost."

Ian turned away to face the window. She'd said the words that still cut through him. Only Theo and Carl were going. He'd been outvoted on that one, as they'd both pointed out that if Ian ventured with them through the portal, Lachestia would surely kill him.

Instead, he would see them safely to the portal and await their return, and if they had not come back by dawn, he would hurry back to the keep and make excuses for them. He thought it shouldn't be too difficult to hide their whereabouts for at least a day amid the chaos of the polio outbreak.

Carl rubbed his eyes tiredly. "There's one thing we still need to get past," he reminded them. "We've no idea how to open that lock on the gate leading to the portal."

Ian turned back around. "I may have worked out how to locate the key."

"How?" Theo and Carl asked together.

Ian reached into his trouser pocket and pulled out the sundial. "Dial," he said as he held it up to the light, "point the way to the key that unlocks the gate to the portal."

An instant later a shadow emerged across the dial's surface. It pointed directly to Castle Dover.

"That's bloomin' brilliant!" Carl exclaimed. "Good thinking, mate!"

Ian smiled, rather proud of himself, but he quickly sobered, because he had another matter to discuss with them. "When you find the Healer, I don't think the two of you should return to the keep."

Carl and Theo exchanged a look. "What do you mean?" Theo asked. "Of course we're coming back. You'll need help, and we'll still be under quarantine."

Ian shook his head. "I'll manage," he insisted. "And the Healer can cure you two if you are carrying the virus. You won't need to return here, because you won't be sick."

"But where will we go?" Carl asked.

Theo's mouth had fallen open and she grabbed Carl's arm. "To Amsterdam!" she said quickly.

Ian sighed in relief, glad she seemed enthusiastic about his idea. "It's the only way to avoid the major," he explained, recalling the scene several days earlier, when the major's motor car had pulled up to the keep, only to be turned away by the guard and the quarantine sign. Ian knew that as soon as the quarantine was lifted, the major would be back to claim Theo. "You two can go on to Amsterdam ahead of us, and after Jaaved is better, I'll sneak him and the Healer out of the keep through the tunnel and we'll join you within a day."

"But how will you know where to find us?" Theo asked.

Ian smiled at her and held up the sundial. "I'll find you."

Carl looked unsure and he turned to Theo to see if she agreed with the idea. "Yes," she said, nodding vigorously. "It's a good plan, Ian. As soon as Jaaved is well and the quarantine here is lifted, you'll come join us."

Carl shrugged. "All right," he said. "After we bring back the Healer, you and I will go to Calais, then Dunkirk, and make our way by train to Amsterdam."

Ian regarded his friend soberly. "Take care of her, Carl."

"You can count on me, mate," Carl assured him.

Ian truly hoped he could.

It took only another hour to make sure they had everything for their journey and creep their way down the ladder to the tunnel. At the bottom, Ian picked up one of the knapsacks, which he'd tucked away earlier. Inside were most of their money and food supplies. He withdrew the bulk of the funds and gave the pound notes to Carl, along with half the food. "There's enough here to see you safely to Amsterdam," he said. "When you arrive, inquire about renting us a nice flat somewhere close to the port so it will be easier for us to find you."

Carl took the money and the food. "A flat near the port, got it."

Ian then climbed onto the large standing stone that still barricaded the tunnel, and helped Theo along as she followed him through the hole he and Carl had managed to clear. When they were on the other side, Ian pointed his torch down the dark corridor of rock headed to the fork. At the fork, he turned to the right, which he remembered led them directly to the gardener's shack at Castle Dover.

It took them nearly half an hour to reach the ladder at the shack, but they made it through without incident.

When they emerged from the trapdoor in the shack, Ian again consulted the dial. "Sundial," he commanded, "show us where to find the key that unlocks the portal gate, but give us a route that ensures we won't be seen by anyone." Immediately, a shadow formed across the dial's surface, yet it seemed to be pointing behind him. Ian looked over his shoulder. There was nothing there but the trapdoor. Curiously, he turned the sundial in that direction, and the shadow thickened. "It's saying it wants us to go back down into the tunnel," he announced.

"The key's in the tunnel?" Carl asked.

Ian shrugged. "There's only one way to find out."

The three of them climbed back down the ladder and Ian pointed the ray of his torch onto the surface of the dial. "This way," he said, retracing his steps back the way they'd come. He'd gone about twenty meters when the shadow, which had pointed straight ahead at the twelve o'clock position, shifted abruptly to three o'clock. Ian halted and looked to his right. There was a very narrow alcove cut into the rock right next to him. "Why have we stopped?" asked Theo from behind.

"The shadow's pointing into the alcove," Ian said, showing her the dial. He wondered if he'd perhaps confused the dial by asking it the wrong question.

"But this can't be the way in," said Carl. "It doesn't lead anywhere."

Ian moved his beam away from the stone and shone it on the surface of the dial. "The sundial says it does."

"Well, that's rubbish," Carl said flatly. "Ian, there's nothing in there but some dusty old cobwebs."

But Theo had already ventured forward a few paces to inspect the alcove herself. "Maybe not," she said to them as she swiped at the webs and moved to the end of the tight space.

She then lifted her hand and knocked on the rock. It made a hollow sound like she'd rapped on wood. "Blimey!" gasped Carl.

Ian quickly moved forward and stood just behind Theo, as the alcove didn't allow them to stand side by side. He reached over her head to run his fingers across the surface of what appeared to be solid rock, and was both thrilled and surprised to discover that he was actually touching wood painted to resemble stone. " 'Blimey' is right!" he agreed.

"There's a handle," Theo whispered, motioning to the left about a foot under where Ian's fingers were feeling the paneling.

Quickly Ian moved his hand down and felt around, and almost immediately he found a small metal handle covered in dust. It had blended in perfectly with the color of the stone. He was able to turn it just like a doorknob. There was a click and a loud creak and the painted panel swung inward, revealing a set of stone stairs. Theo moved forward first and Ian and Carl followed close behind up one flight to another door. Theo turned the knob, and with another loud creak, it opened.

The three of them stood there for a moment, stunned into silence, and Ian felt Carl move up behind him to take a peek over his shoulder. "Best to get on with it, then," he whispered after they'd stared long enough at the dark interior.

Theo moved ahead first, followed by Ian and then Carl. Ian was amazed when he entered a dark room and discovered it filled with the mounted heads of dozens of exotic animals. With some relief, he realized immediately where they were.

"Gaw, would you look at *that*?" Carl whispered excitedly while he bounced the beam of his torch all about the enormous room.

"Where are we?" Theo wondered.

"The earl's study," Ian said. "I was here last year for a meeting with the earl and our schoolmasters."

"Meeting?" she asked.

"Yes," he said. "It was right after your first visions of the Fury, do you remember?"

Theo made a face. "Yes, but that's one vision I'd prefer to forget, thank you."

"Where does the dial say the key is?" Carl whispered, reminding them of their mission.

"Oh, right," Ian said, pulling up the bronze relic to shine his torch on the surface again. "I believe it's pointing over there." He swung his torch in the direction the shadow had indicated, across the room to a small table with a lamp.

Ian quickly traversed the room and began searching the table for the key. The table had one drawer, which he pulled open, but there was nothing inside, so he felt underneath, thinking perhaps the earl had hidden it there.

When his hand found nothing but the underside of the drawer, he pulled the table carefully away from the wall and searched behind it, but there was no key anywhere.

"It's not here," he said impatiently.

Theo held out her hand for the sundial, and while she inspected it, Ian looked at Carl and shrugged.

"It's not pointing at the table, Ian," she said after a moment, and he realized that she was tilting the sundial slightly. "It's pointing up the wall."

"Up the wall?" he said. "Theo, how could it be pointing up the wall?"

"Look for yourself," she insisted, showing him the dial. To his surprise he saw that when Theo tilted the dial toward the ceiling, the shadow lengthened and began to pulse, but when she tilted the dial down toward the table, the shadow all but disappeared.

Ian again looked up at the wall in front of them. "But there's nothing there," he said, frustrated. "I mean, other than the head of that antelope."

Carl and Theo both gasped as if they'd just discovered something. "What?" he asked.

"Behind the antelope's head!" Carl whispered excitedly. "Here, Ian, climb on this chair and see if you can have a look behind it."

Ian eagerly mounted the chair. Very carefully, he lifted the bottom of the earl's hunting trophy just enough to shine his torch behind it.

He had thought to find the key dangling on a nail, so it was with no small amount of surprise when he gasped and said, "There's a safe here!"

"Safe?" Carl and Theo said together.

Ian put his torch into his pocket and firmly lifted the antelope head off its nail. It was much lighter than he'd expected, and he handed it to Carl. Ian then pulled his torch back out to closely inspect the safe. It had a combination lock, and when he pulled on the handle, it was stuck fast. "We'll never get in," he said, disappointed. "Who knows what combination the earl's chosen for the lock?"

"Maybe he's written it down somewhere nearby?" Carl suggested.

"Where?" Ian asked him.

"Dunno, mate," Carl said with a small grin. "Ask the dial."

Ian held the dial up and asked, "If the earl has written down the combination to the safe, show us where we might locate it."

The dial formed a shadow, which pointed across the room. Ian looked up and saw the earl's huge mahogany desk

251

directly in line with the shadow. "It says it's in his desk," Ian told them. Carl and Theo dashed across the room and began to pull open drawers and search through the earl's papers. Ian got down off his chair and moved to help them. When he got close, he held the dial right in front of the desk, hoping it would point to a drawer, but instead it pointed directly at the surface. "It's somewhere in that clutter," Ian said, motioning to the pile of papers littering the top.

"Oh!" said Theo. "It will take us hours to sort through all this!"

Carl gave up rooting through the drawer he'd pulled open and suggested, "Why don't you go back to the safe, Ian, and when we find a set of numbers that look like they may be a combination, we'll call them out for you to try."

Ian nodded and hurried back to the safe. He waited several minutes while Theo and Carl sifted through the various letters, bits of scrap paper, and newspapers that were heaped on the earl's desk. "Nothing here looks to me like a combination," Theo said. Moving a pile of papers to the floor, she squinted at the earl's calendar blotter. "Maybe he's written it on here," she mused.

Growing impatient, Ian turned back to the safe and muttered, "What could the combination be?" After thinking on it, he came up with a small hunch. He tried the earl's birthday, which he knew because the date was celebrated every year at the orphanage. "Thirty-first, March, 1902," he said as he spun the dial to thirty-one, then three, then two. Crossing his fingers, he gently pulled on the handle. Nothing happened. "Blast it!" he muttered. He then tried several combinations of the earl's birthday, but to no avail. The safe remained sealed tight.

With a sigh he resigned himself to waiting for Theo or Carl to suggest something when he happened to glance at the sundial. The thinnest of shadows was flashing rapidly on the half-past mark. "Huh?" Ian said, squinting down at the dial, and then, as if an idea blossomed in his mind, he turned the combination to the number thirty. Immediately, the shadow disappeared, then reappeared eight notches down from the twelve o'clock position. Ian quickly turned the lock back to the number eight. Glancing down for a third time at the dial's surface, he was delighted when the shadow disappeared, then reappeared at the twenty-fifth notch. "Twenty-five," he sang, and spun the dial of the lock forward to that number. There was a click from inside the safe and Ian gasped. "Oy!" he whispered excitedly to his friends. "I've done it! I've cracked the combination!"

Theo and Carl hurried over. "You have?" Carl asked. "How'd you do it?"

Ian showed them the sundial proudly. "The dial pointed me to the numbers," he explained. "Thirty, eight, twenty-five!"

"Ian!" Theo gasped. "That's your birthday! Thirtieth of August, 1925. Oh! And now I know why it said it was written on the earl's desk! He's got your birthday marked on his calendar."

He blinked at her in shock. He was quite surprised that

not only had the earl marked his birthday, but he'd chosen it to hide his most valuable treasures. Ian didn't know what to make of that.

"Well, open it, Ian!" Carl said encouragingly.

Ian smiled and got back to the task of retrieving the key. Carefully he pulled up on the handle, which turned easily, and the door to the safe popped opened. Then he moved the beam of his torch to the interior, illuminating an enormous stack of English pound notes, glimmering gems, and various gold watches and other jewelry. "Blimey!" he gasped at the sight.

"Do you see the key?" whispered Theo urgently.

In the face of so much treasure, Ian had almost forgotten about the key. "Yeah," he said, spying it toward the back of the safe. "It's right here—" But as he reached for the key, something awful happened. A series of alarms sounded so loudly that he jerked back and fell off the chair. He toppled to the ground with a tremendous crash and Carl had to help him back to his feet. "Run for it!" his friend shouted as he tugged on Ian's arm.

"The key!" yelled Theo, stepping in front of them. "Get the key first!"

The sirens continued to wail and all about them they could feel the thunder of running feet as the castle came instantly to life and the earl's staff hurried to find the intruder. Ian was shaking from head to toe while he worked the chair back against the wall and climbed up to reach inside the safe again. He'd dropped his torch in his fall and had to feel around for the key, but finally, he had it in hand, and at that moment he leapt from the chair and dashed to the door leading to the yard.

"Where're you going?" demanded Carl. "We should go back through the tunnel!"

"From this side of the castle, the portal's just through the garden gate!" yelled Ian as he pulled open the door and waved at them to come along. "We can get there faster from here, and we've got to reach the gate before they realize we've got the key! If they know we have it, they'll send someone to intercept us!"

"Ian's right!" shouted Theo above the wailing siren. "Hurry!" she called, and dashed through the opening.

Ian held the door open for Carl, who had the foresight to retrieve the knapsack and torch from the floor before he followed Theo.

Ian was just hurrying out after Carl when the door to the study burst open and an explosion shattered the glass of the French door he was stepping through. Ian ducked low and made a sharp zigzag to his left as another loud explosion rocketed behind him and a clump of grass shot up just off to his right. *They're shooting at us!* he heard Carl shriek from up ahead.

"Get to the portal!" Ian commanded, making sure to weave his way across the lawn as several additional explosions sounded behind them and more grass flew up in huge clumps from all sides.

"It's too far!" cried Theo. "We'll never make it!"

And as if that weren't enough to deal with, somewhere nearby, rising above the wail of the sirens, a bone-chilling howl sounded in the night and nearly caused Ian to stumble. To make matters worse, that lone howl was immediately picked up by another, equally horrible, and the two haunting choruses reverberated across the land.

Ian's heart thundered. He couldn't decide whether it was safer to go back toward the people who were shooting at them or continue their mad dash across the lawn—which would lead them straight into the jaws of the beasts.

"They're coming up over the wall!" Carl screamed, his voice ragged with fear as he pointed straight ahead.

Ian nearly stumbled again when he caught sight of the enormous black shadow, which leapt easily over the gate they were racing toward. At that instant another explosion sounded from behind him just before a clump of dirt and grass whipped hard into Ian's thigh.

Making a split-second decision, he grabbed hold of Theo's arm and pulled her to the right. "This way!" he called, changing course and running sharply toward a large row of hedges on the west side of the lawn.

"Where are you going?" Carl yelled as he came up alongside them.

"To the maze!" Ian said. "We can hide in there until the earl's men deal with the beasts!"

Behind them it appeared that was already happening. Calls and shouts of "The beasts! The beasts!" were echoing about the lawn, and Ian was at once relieved that no more gunfire was being aimed directly at them, but also terrified that the earl's men had to contend with *two* of the ugly brutes. And he was sure there were two, because when he chanced a look over his shoulder, he could see a second black shadow clear the castle wall. With a gulp, Ian sincerely hoped the earl's men had more guns.

However, he had to focus on reaching the maze and hope that the beasts were far enough away that he could get the three of them safely hidden until they could figure out what to do next.

He realized belatedly that it had been a dreadful mistake to take the garden path instead of the tunnel, but there was no going back now. What was done was done.

With a small dose of relief, Ian reached the garden maze with the others and rushed inside. Theo led the way, which was a good thing, because Ian had not been there for many years. He knew that in recent months, Theo and Jaaved had often visited the maze, sometimes playing there for hours.

He followed her dutifully to the first right turn, then along the hedge for a bit to a left, then another quick left, and finally to an open spot, which had both a right and left exit. In the background was the now nearly constant barrage of gunfire, growling, howling, and commotion. He crossed his fingers that the beasts would be shot dead, but as they made yet another left turn, the gunfire ended, and Ian heard someone say, "I've run out of ammunition! Someone fetch me some bullets or find me another gun!" Ian bit his lip. There was a terrified scream then, and the sound of breaking glass. Theo nearly tripped in front of him and he managed to catch her before she fell.

"The beasts are attacking the castle!" Carl said from behind him. And sure enough, there was another roar and several more screams, followed by the sound of overturned furniture and splintering wood.

"We have to get as deep into the maze as we can!" Ian warned.

The hedge maze at Castle Dover was hundreds of years old. It had been built by the seventh Duke of Kent for his bride, and in all that time, the ancient hedges had grown thick and nearly impenetrable. They would not be able to stop a bullet, but they might hold back a monster made of flesh and bone—at least for a little while.

Theo ran on, twisting and turning with each new choice. Ian had no idea how she managed to keep track of such a complicated course, but finally she came to an abrupt stop, panting hard with her hand on her chest. "This . . . is . . . it," she wheezed with a sweep of her hand. "This . . . is . . . the center . . . of the maze."

The boys tumbled to the ground and lay there side by side, breathing heavily. Ian closed his eyes while his heart thumped loudly in his ears, but not loudly enough to drown out the chaos all about the lawn.

There was still a terrible ruckus happening near the earl's study, but suddenly a new series of explosions resonated from the northeast section of the lawn, followed by the deafening screech of a wounded animal. Ian's eyes flew open and Carl exclaimed, "They've shot one!"

Ian sat up, straining his ears for any indication that at least one of the beasts was dead. He could hear men shouting, and now a horde of dogs were baying and barking as the earl's hounds were released into the hunt.

A furious cascade of growls, howls, and baying all but obliterated the sound of the men, but soon more gunfire resounded in the night. Ian, Carl, and Theo held perfectly still while they listened intently, and soon the noise drifted off to somewhere well northeast of their position. "I think they're all moving toward the village," Ian whispered.

As if to confirm that, a howl pierced the din of dogs and humans, and it did seem to be coming from the direction of the center of Dover. "Oh, my," whispered Theo. "I hope they kill those awful creatures before they hurt anyone!"

Ian wiped the sweat from his brow. The sirens coming from inside the castle had stopped abruptly, and now they could clearly hear the voices of the members of the earl's staff who had not joined the hunt. A discussion was taking place somewhere nearby on the lawn.

"I shall alert the earl immediately," said a voice that sounded like Binsford's. "I just thank heavens that no one was hurt, although you may want to comfort Miss Baker. She had a frightful scare before we pulled her through the door away from that beast."

"What about the intruders?" asked a woman, and Ian suspected that it was Miss Carlyle, another of the earl's staff. "Was anything taken?"

"No," said Binsford. "I believe the alarm startled the intruders and they left before they could get their grubby hands on any of the valuables. I've looked through the safe myself, and the inventory seems intact."

"How did they find their way in?" asked Miss Carlyle.

"I'm quite certain they broke the glass on one of the

French doors and unlocked it," Binsford replied. "I managed to get several rounds off at them but I'm afraid I blew apart the door in the process."

"Did you get a good look at them at least?"

"Only one," Binsford confessed. "A wiry-looking fellow just shy of my own height, I'd wager." Ian's brows shot up in surprise. That was exactly how tall he was.

"I don't expect they'll be back tonight," said Miss Carlyle.

"No," Binsford agreed. "I suspect they'll take this opportunity to flee Kent, in fact—that is, *if* they manage to escape the beasts and our men on foot."

"You say that one of the beasts is dead?"

"Yes," Binsford confirmed. "It was shot by Robert the hounds man. A bloody good marksman he is. Shot the brute right through the heart."

Ian felt relief. If one of the beasts was dead, and the other was being chased off by the earl's men, then he, Theo, and Carl should be safe enough to leave the maze and make their way down to the portal without being seen. Ian was quite certain that every available man was in hot pursuit of the remaining beast.

"Well, we best get back inside and clean up the mess," said Miss Carlyle, and with that she and Binsford moved out of hearing range.

"We should go while no one's about and that beast is off at the village," Carl advised.

"Right," Ian agreed. Turning to Theo, he asked, "Can you show us the way out of here?"

"Yes," she said, but Ian noticed that she was shivering and still appeared quite frightened.

"You all right?" he asked.

She gripped her crystal and gave him a vigorous nod "Fine," she said, but Ian knew she was lying.

He got up, brushed the grass from his trousers, and moved over to her. "It's all right, Theo," he said gently. "The beast has moved off well away from us."

But Theo's eyes remained large and somewhat haunted, and her body looked stiff as it was wracked with shivers. Ian dug around in the knapsack and brought out her sweater, even though the evening was warm and balmy. "Here," he said, handing it to her.

She took it gratefully and waited until Carl had gained his feet before waving at them to follow her. They fell into step behind Theo while she walked them through the maze, and before long Ian was thoroughly lost. "Wait," he whispered, setting a hand on her shoulder. "Didn't we already pass this way?"

"No."

"Are you sure, Theo?" Carl whispered. "Because I could have sworn we crossed that fork ahead of us just a few moments ago."

Theo looked over her shoulder at them, and Ian could tell she knew exactly where they were and didn't appreciate their doubtful commentary. "That's done on purpose, Carl," she replied. "You're supposed to think you're going about in circles, because it's a *maze*, remember?"

Ian was about to defend Carl; he was, after all, only asking

261

a question, and Theo didn't need to be rude about it. But then a light breeze brought the whiff of something all too familiar to his nostrils.

Ian tilted his head and sniffed the air. "You smell that?"

"Smell what?" Carl asked.

Theo tilted her chin and took in a few whiffs. She then whirled around, a horrified expression on her face, and grabbed at Ian's shirt. "The beast!" she said in a tiny petrified voice.

Carl was also sniffing at the air, and the scent only grew stronger and more pungent. "Oh, no," he mouthed.

Then, as if the smell of the awful brute weren't enough to alert them to its presence, from the outside of the hedge came a low, rumbling growl more menacing than any noise Ian could think of.

He pulled Theo close to him and held her stiff and shivering body, hoping she didn't let go the scream he knew was building up inside her. To his relief, she made not a sound, but buried her head in his shirt and trembled in fear. Ian stared at Carl, whose alarmed expression confirmed that he also thought the beast was only a few meters away.

They could all hear the low *whuffs* as the beast sniffed along the hedge, and those massive paws thumped the ground with every step. Ian's heart pounded and he closed his eyes for a moment, attempting to gather his courage. Taking two deep breaths, he opened his eyes again and motioned to Carl to move ahead of them.

Carl shook his head and cupped his ear. "It will hear us!" he mouthed.

But Ian knew that if they didn't move, the beast would most certainly catch their scent and charge through the hedge. They'd be cut down before they even had a chance to run. Bending low, Ian whispered into Theo's ear, "We've got to keep moving. Can you lead us away from this section? Maybe to the opposite side of the maze?"

For a moment Theo showed no sign that she'd even heard him, but after a bit she gave an almost imperceptible nod, and still clutching his shirtsleeve, she began to tiptoe forward.

Ian grabbed Carl's arm and pulled him with them. They'd gone only a few paces when another low growl rumbled through the hedge, causing them all to stop. In the light from their torch, Ian could see that Theo was quietly crying and she was shaking so much now that the torch's beam was vibrating all about the ground. Ian lifted it from her hand and gave her an encouraging nod.

Theo eyed the hedge, where more *whuffs* could be heard, but started off again, this time leading them through a series of right turns. Soon the scent of the beast faded just enough to let Ian know they were definitely moving away from it, and after another set of confusing twists and turns, they came into a surprisingly open space with a gurgling fountain and a series of animal-shaped hedges. There was also a bench by the fountain and Ian took Theo by the hand and moved her over to it; he was concerned that she was so frightened she might faint. "Easy there, Theo," he whispered, noting that she was breathing far too rapidly for her own good, and even in the dim light he could see how pale she was.

"What are we going to do?" Carl asked softly.

"Dunno," Ian said, rubbing Theo's hands, which were frightfully cold. "Guess we'll have to stay here a bit and hope the hunting party comes back this way."

"But what if the beast comes into the maze? What if it follows our scent?"

Ian sighed. Carl was only making things worse with his what-ifs. "I suppose we'll have to hope that doesn't happen, won't we?"

"Ian," whispered Theo, suddenly clutching at her pendant.

"Yes?"

"Carl's guessed at it. The beast is here!"

Ian stared down at her and for the first time he noticed through a small gap in her fingers that the crystal she wore was glowing a soft red. He gasped when he remembered Jaaved's grandfather warning them that her pendant would glow like that when danger was near.

It was then that they all caught the heavy, disgusting smell of sulfur as it seeped its way through the hedges that surrounded them. But because the breeze had picked up slightly, there was no way to tell which direction it was coming from.

Ian looked around the small clearing. There were four exits out of the section and he had no idea which path the beast might be following to reach them.

"We should go!" whispered Carl.

"No!" Theo mouthed. "Stay!"

Both of them looked at Ian for the answer and his eyes kept creeping back to Theo's necklace, which was becoming so red it was beginning to resemble a ruby. Thinking fast, he pulled out his sundial and clicked on the torch. "Sundial," he said softly, "point to the path out of the maze that takes us away from the beast!"

Immediately, a shadow appeared on the face of the sundial and it directed them to the eastern exit. Ian turned the relic to show Carl and Theo, who nodded at him, and the group set off at a run, with Ian keeping the sundial out in front of him while holding the torch close to the surface.

From somewhere behind they heard a low rumble, and Ian knew that Theo had been right: the beast had caught their scent and was trailing after them. "Hurry!" Carl whispered. "I think it's gaining on us!"

But it was very difficult to acquire any speed in the maze, because every time Ian went more than a few steps, the dial would point in a new direction and he'd have to turn sharply. Once, he passed a left turn and the shadow he was following vanished for a moment before indicating that he needed to double back. "Blast it!" he exclaimed when he bumped into Theo and Carl as he whipped around.

"S'all right!" Carl said. "Just keep your eye on the dial!"

Ian found the passage and dashed ahead only to nearly stumble when the low, grumbling snarl of the beast turned into a terrible thrashing of hedges. Apparently, the beast was no longer content to follow their scent along the route and had decided to approach them more directly.

"It's coming through the hedges!" Carl cried.

As soon as he said that, the dial went blank again and changed direction, telling Ian to go back along the way he'd just come. He stopped only long enough to curse under his breath before motioning to Theo and Carl to follow.

More thrashing of hedges sounded somewhere nearby and Ian's nerves almost caused him to drop the dial. "It's going to break through to us!" Carl hissed as a hedge right next to them shook and nearly fell over on top of them.

Theo screamed when several branches brushed against her, and Ian grabbed her by the shoulder, pulling her out of the way just as a huge paw with giant daggerlike nails swiped at her head. "This way!" he shouted to Carl when he saw that the dial wanted them to change direction yet again.

Carl was right at Ian's heels while they ran in short quick bursts, trying to get as far away from the thrashing beast as they could. It seemed the creature was tearing apart the maze all around them, and its constant low, guttural growl reverberated through the hedges.

Ian held tightly to Theo's hand as he cut sharply to his right and came out into a long passageway, at the end of which he saw wide-open lawn. He ran the length of the path as fast as he could with Theo in tow, hoping they could yet elude the beast.

"Sundial!" he called to the bronze relic. "Show us the fastest way to the garden gate!"

But the dial's shadow never wavered. It continued to

point straight ahead, and it wasn't until they cleared the maze that he understood. The magical instrument had led them directly where they'd needed to go.

Behind him the beast continued to thrash and tear about inside the maze. Ian dared not look back, because he knew that at any moment the giant brute would clear the hedges, and he also knew from past experience that he could not outrun the hellhound. "To the gate!" he called to Carl and Theo.

Ian hoped that if they all reached the gate before the beast cleared the maze, they would trick the beast into thinking they were still hidden within the hedges. And it seemed that luck was on their side, because they did reach the gate before the beast was out of the maze. Ian gave Theo's hand to Carl while he unhitched the metal latch and went through first to hold the gate open for them. The moment they were through, Ian slammed it, but not before he saw the giant head of the hellhound emerge from the wreckage of the maze. His heart fell to his toes, but he managed at least to secure the latch, knowing that would do little to stop the beast, but at that point all he could hope for was to slow it down a bit.

"To the portal!" he shouted, and hurried down the path to the patch of woods just ahead. He hardly needed to direct his friends, because Carl zipped past him in two strides, holding tightly to Theo's wrist as he all but yanked her along.

Ian followed, looking constantly over his shoulder, and they managed to reach the woods without seeing any sign of the beast. Carl led the way to the familiar path but they had to slow their pace, because the woods were fairly dense and they couldn't risk tripping and twisting an ankle. "There!" Ian said when he could just make out the huge stones that covered the stairway leading down to the portal. "We've made it!"

But his relief was short lived, as a tremendous crash sounded somewhere behind them and Ian knew that the beast had either torn through or gone straight over the garden's gate. "*Hurry!*" screamed Theo, and she dashed down the steps.

"Do you have the key?" Carl asked when they began to descend the stairs together.

Ian paused and moved the sundial to his left hand, tucked his torch under his arm, and fished around in his trouser pocket, where he'd shoved the key. His fingers were shaking so badly that when he brought it out, he dropped it. They heard it clink somewhere below them. "Blast it!" Ian yelled.

"Where is it?" Carl shrieked, his voice high pitched and terrified.

Ian pointed his torch at the first two steps but couldn't spot it. "Where is it, where is it, *where is it?*" he chanted.

"What's the matter?" Theo asked from the bottom of the stairwell, by the locked gate.

"Ian's dropped the key!" Carl said.

Behind them a horrible howl erupted from the edge of the wood. "Well, find it!" Theo shouted.

Ian was now shaking from head to toe. The beast was

nearly on top of them and he still had to find the key and unlock the gate. Even if he managed that, he wasn't sure that the portal was open and ready to allow Theo and Carl through. And what if the beast was able to breach the iron gate? Would it hold against the beast's brute strength?

Ian's mind raced with all these panicky thoughts, which did nothing to aid his efforts to find the key.

"There!" Carl said at last, grabbing the torch in Ian's hand and pointing to the fourth step down before dashing below to retrieve it. Ian followed, and they'd made it only a few more steps when they heard the beast tearing through the forest at lightning speed, headed straight for them.

It was all the boys needed to leap the rest of the way to the gate, which barred their entrance to the tunnel leading to the portal. Ian struggled to hold on to his torch so that Carl could insert the key.

"Give it to me!" Theo demanded when she saw Carl fumbling clumsily at the lock. In her panic and haste, she wrenched it out of Carl's hand. Ian's own fingers reached instinctively to help her but she managed to insert the large key into the lock on the very first try.

And no sooner had she twisted the clasp open than a tree fell somewhere near the top of the stairs and a horrible growl echoed off the stone walls, alerting them that the beast had arrived. Theo and Carl both worked the lock free from the gate's metal bars and dropped it onto the ground. Ian reached forward and yanked on the heavy door, pulling it open with a tremendous creak, which was drowned out by a howl so loud and so horrible that Ian had to cover his ears.

He looked up just as the dim light at the top of the stairwell was all but blocked out, and in the darkness two glowing red eyes stared down at them.

"Get through and into the tunnel!" Ian shouted to Theo and Carl.

The next several seconds were a blur. His mind was focused on those murderous eyes at the top of the stairs, and for a long sweaty moment, he was so transfixed that he couldn't move. In the next instant, however, two things happened at once: Carl yanked him by the collar through the opening of the gate and the beast launched itself down the steps.

Ian lost his balance when Carl pulled him inside the tunnel, and he tripped over his own two feet, crashing to the ground and feeling the sundial pierce his palm. He let out a yelp of fear and pain and rolled to the side as he heard a loud crash right behind him.

Theo screamed and Carl shrieked and the beast howled and growled in fury. Ian scrambled to his feet; tucking his injured hand under his other arm, he tried to take in what was happening.

The beast had hurled itself against the iron gate and was biting at the bars, trying to get to them. Wide-eyed and terrified, Carl and Theo had scrambled away down the tunnel.

Ian moved back as well when the stench of the awful brute filled the tunnel, causing him to gag. "We've got to get you two through the portal!" he shouted, turning to his companions.

"It's not open!" Carl replied, twisting around and shining his torch toward the end of the cavern.

Ian could see he was right. The familiar stone wall holding the grisly remains of a skeleton barred them from any escape.

"Look out!" Theo cried, and Ian ducked as the beast attempted to swipe at him through the bars. He scooted a little farther away and he was again nearly frozen in terror as the massive creature bit and snarled and swiped at him. It seemed to be doing everything in its power to come through the gate, but the bars held firm. Ian couldn't be sure how long they would hold, however. He was immensely grateful that the door swung outward. If it had swung in, the beast would have had them. As of yet, the brute hadn't figured out that by throwing its weight against the door, it was keeping it securely closed, but Ian was well aware of the intelligence of the hateful cur, and he knew they likely had precious little time before things became perilous.

Turning to Theo, he asked, "Why isn't the portal open?"

"I don't have any idea!" she yelled above the sounds from the beast.

"What are we going to do?" Carl wailed. "Those bars won't hold it back forever!"

And even as he said that, the beast caught one of the iron rods in its teeth and pulled. The door creaked open a foot. "Uh-oh," Ian whispered as the snarling suddenly stopped and the beast stepped back for a moment in surprise, as if already working out how to open the gate and get to its prey.

With little thought for his own safety, Ian leapt forward and pulled on the bars. He managed to yank the gate shut again and dive out of the way just as the beast lunged toward him. One of its paws did put a mean slice in his upper arm, but it was worth it if it bought them a bit more time.

"We've got to do something!" Carl cried. "Theo, that creature will work out how to open that gate soon enough. You've got to open the portal now!"

"What do you mean *I've* got to open it?" she snapped. "I don't have the faintest notion how to *do* that, Carl!"

"How did you open it last time?" he asked.

Theo looked at him blankly for a moment, so Ian suggested, "Didn't you simply ask it to open, Theo?"

Theo blinked her wild, frightened eyes and she turned to the wall at the end of the passage and said, "Portal, please open!"

The three of them stared hard at the stone, waiting for the wall to disappear and reveal another world, but nothing happened.

Behind them the beast continued to snarl and spit and bite at the bars, and suddenly, the door gave another creak and Ian whirled around to see the beast with the gate in its jaws, pulling awkwardly back on it. It was a difficult maneuver for the horrid creature, because it had to grip the gate at an odd angle as it backed itself up the stairs.

"It's figured out how to get the gate open!" Carl shouted.

Ian pulled at the knapsack on Carl's shoulders, freeing it before he raced forward. Carrying it by the straps, he used it to club the beast through the bars just as the opening became large enough for the beast to wiggle through. The

ghastly creature was startled enough by the knapsack strik-
ing its nose that it let go and Ian gripped the gate and
heaved it closed again.

But this time the beast was far too quick for him, and it
lunged forward, biting his arm. Ian screamed as the vicious
fangs broke the skin and clenched straight through to the
bone. Carl was by his side in a moment, pummeling the
beast on the nose with his torch. "Back!" he shouted, and
he struck again and again.

The beast released Ian's arm and made to snap at Carl,
but the boy was quick and darted out of the way. Grabbing
Ian by his good arm, he pulled him away from the gate and
farther into the tunnel.

Ian was in so much pain that he could barely keep track
of what was happening around him. His fingers had gone
numb and blood dripped down his wrist and covered his
hand, and he realized that Theo had rushed to him to inspect his wound. "Oh, Carl!" he heard her wail. "He's got a
vicious bite!"

Ian was quickly becoming light-headed. As he struggled
to stay upright, he heard Carl say, "Do what you can for him,
Theo! I've got to secure the gate or we're all finished!"

Ian's head felt heavier and heavier and he let his chin
fall onto his chest. He was aware that Theo was talking
to him, but it was hard to hear over the commotion by
the gate. He managed to take a deep breath and turn his
head toward Carl. He could see that his friend was holding
in one hand the lock that had once secured the iron bars,

while he attempted to get the beast's attention with his other hand.

Carl was sticking his fingers through the bars and waving them dangerously close to the creature. "Here, stinky!" he yelled. "Come have a chomp on my fingers, won't you?"

The beast lunged at Carl's hand, and Carl managed to loop the lock around the latch with his other hand while snatching back his first. The beast narrowly missed taking off most of Carl's fingers.

But the hellhound was far too clever for the ruse. It immediately saw that Carl was attempting to lock the gate, and before he could secure the door, the beast lunged toward Carl's other hand, causing him to back up and drop the lock.

"Carl!" Ian shouted, struggling to get to his feet.

"Ian, sit still!" Theo warned. "I've got to stop the bleeding!"

But Ian was having none of it. He knew that Carl would never be able to distract the beast long enough to secure the gate. "He can't do it alone," he said to her, and half stumbled, half ran back down the tunnel.

"Oy!" Ian shouted when he was within a meter. "You like drawing blood, beasty?" he asked, and for emphasis he shoved his injured arm forward, just out of reach of the brute's snout. For a moment the mangy cur abandoned Carl and lunged again toward Ian. "Get to the lock!" Ian shouted, keeping his eyes on the beast even though he sensed he was very close to fainting. "I'll distract it while you secure the gate!"

Carl didn't need to be told twice. He dove for the lock,

snatching it and rolling away as the beast caught on to their plan and lunged again toward Carl. Ian leaned in and wiped his bloody hand on the bars as a searing pain shot up his arm. "Smell that, you hateful brute?" he shouted, and instantly the beast was back to his side of the gate, the scent of Ian's blood driving it to froth at the mouth and roll its red eyes up. Spittle and drool flew from its lips as it bit and snarled and licked at the iron bars where Ian had smeared his hand.

Ian was panting hard and he swayed in front of the beast, his knees weak and the air all about him filled with the cloying, suffocating stench of the hellhound. "Carl," he tried to yell, but all that came out was a pitiful cry. "I think I'm . . ." He could say no more. The world about him spun and he had the sensation of sinking into a deep pond, right before he felt something hard slam into his knees and then his side. He wanted to cry out in pain, but he found that he couldn't utter a sound. The last thing he heard was Theo's mournful scream.

CHESS MOVES

Magus the Black stood in the fading light of dusk, staring down the hill at the lush patch of forest that marked the border between Germany and Poland. Behind him, scattered about the lee side of the hill, was the German Eighth Armored Panzer Division. Eighteen tanks and well over a thousand infantrymen huddled in small groups, most of them bored and hoping for the orders that would finally allow them to invade Poland.

But at the moment, Magus was less interested in the invasion, and more interested in that cursed forest. His sister lay trapped somewhere in that dense thicket of trees; he could feel the dangerous undertones of her energy from there, and the scout he'd sent in had reported enough to confirm the sorcerer's suspicions.

But Magus dared not enter the forest himself, lest he also become trapped. A powerful old crone guarded the wood and held his sister fast. Lachestia's captor was a dangerous one, someone clearly not to be underestimated. And Magus understood that the only way to kill the crone was to free Lachestia, which made his sister's release all the more problematic.

Since the sorcerer could not enter the forest himself, he would need to rely on some other way to pummel and weaken the crone's defenses. He would need a force strong enough to overwhelm the stone prison where Lachestia had been held captive for over three millennia. And the German Eighth Army Panzer Division was just the firepower he needed.

All that was left to fulfill this plan was to convince the commander to go through the forest, instead of around it as Berlin had directed. "Magus!" shouted someone behind him.

The sorcerer narrowed his eyes, smiled evilly, and turned around. "Colonel," he said cordially, moving toward the ugly little man, noting with satisfaction that the colonel carried the chess set. "Have you received my request for a rematch?"

Two evenings previously, when Magus had arrived at his new post as strategic advisor to Colonel Gropp, he'd allowed the pompous twit to win a game of chess, and the sorcerer had offered the priceless chess pieces as a prize to the colonel.

"I have," said Gropp, his speech clipped and impatient. "But I fully intend to win another game off you. And since I already have the chess set, what will you offer me when you lose?"

Magus's eyes smoldered slightly at the petulant tone this

insufferable mortal was showing him. A flicker of smoke wafted out his nostrils and he forced himself to resist the urge to kill the colonel. Instead, he reached into the folds of his cloak and brought out a small velvet bag whose contents jingled temptingly.

The colonel craned his neck forward, showing great interest in the sorcerer's new prize. "What have you there, Herr Black?" he demanded.

"Gold, Colonel." For emphasis, Magus loosened the drawstrings and pulled out one gold bullion, which glinted beautifully in the late-afternoon sun.

The colonel smiled widely—an unusual expression for him—and accepted the terms. "Ah," he said smoothly. "I see now how you have gained such favor among the party elite in Berlin!"

Magus chuckled merrily. Gold bullion had been a factor in many of the influential connections he'd made recently. "I contribute where I can, Colonel."

Gropp tipped his hat appreciatively before barking orders at two nearby soldiers, and within moments a table was set for the players, and snifters of brandy were brought over for them to enjoy while they played their match.

Magus eyed the colonel with amusement as the man laid out his chessboard with efficiency. Such arrogance. Such confidence. Magus would enjoy shattering both. Yet he cautioned himself against winning the game too quickly. He had to secure the colonel's agreement to his plan first.

"Silver or gold?" asked the colonel.

"Gold," said Magus, knowing that on this chessboard, silver always went first.

His choice seemed agreeable to the colonel, who was quick to move his pawn.

They played for a time in silence, Colonel Gropp focusing intently on the game. Magus found that he quite enjoyed toying with the man across from him. He lured him into several false traps and kept the colonel on the defensive.

And when Gropp boldly moved his bishop to a vulnerable position, Magus nearly tsked. It left Gropp's queen exposed. But Magus wasn't quite ready to end the game, so he moved his knight aggressively toward the other man's bishop. Gropp would need to play defensively for a move or two, which would buy Magus a little time. He had to convince the colonel to disobey a direct order.

"Have you given any further consideration to my suggestion of moving your division through the forest?" Magus asked casually.

Gropp clenched his fists while he studied the chess pieces in front of him. "Yes," he said curtly. "But it cannot be accomplished."

"No?" Magus asked. "Why not, Colonel?"

"Because Deadman's Forest is too thick. The tanks would be unable to make it through and the prize on the other side is only a small village. Hardly worth the trouble. Besides," he added with a grin, "have you not heard? The forest is cursed, Magus."

Magus forced himself to laugh. "Yes, these Polish scum will think of anything to keep us from learning their secrets."

The colonel eyed Magus sharply. "What secrets?"

Magus pretended to appear surprised. "Have you not heard the truth behind these rumors of curses?" he asked. When the colonel shook his head, Magus explained, "The forest is riddled with spies, Colonel. They use the trees as a cover to watch over their border and report back to Warsaw."

Gropp—who had just moved his knight to cover his bishop—looked angrily at the forest, then back at his opponent. "Is this *true?*"

Magus offered him a crafty smile, exposing his jagged, frightful teeth. "It is quite true. The village of Lubieszyn is a breeding ground for Polish spies. Think of its placement, my friend. The village itself is tucked just on the other side of the border and is neatly hidden in the cove of those thick trees, which cover it from three sides. My sources tell me that the villagers have been spying on the motherland for some time now. They've been reporting on your movements for many days, in fact."

Gropp's eyes narrowed, and his face contorted into a snarl. *"Peasant scum!"* he spat. "You tell me there are spies just beyond those trees?" And for emphasis the colonel stood up and pointed down the large hill.

Magus nodded soberly. "Yes, Colonel, I'm afraid so."

The colonel sat back down in his seat heavily and drummed his fingers on the board in irritation. "We must destroy this village and all who live there," he said at last, and Magus's smile grew. "When we receive the order, I shall dispatch my men to go around the woods and attack them from the front."

Magus tapped his lips thoughtfully. "Good thinking," he said with a nod of approval. "However, as the village obviously has such a crafty network of spies on the lookout, it would seem they would be able to mobilize themselves quite efficiently and escape your revenge before you've even rounded the trees."

The colonel frowned. "We will hunt them down," he promised. "Every last one of those Polish rats!"

Magus stroked his chin thoughtfully. "Of course you will," he said smoothly. "However, that would take time away from reaching your goal. Your uncle would not be so happy to hear of your delay in reaching Warsaw, now, would he?"

"Then what am I to do?" snapped the colonel, his patience clearly at an end.

"Go *through* the trees, my friend. Strike the village from behind the cover of their own camouflage! There is a path that cuts through the very center of the forest, and the pathway is just large enough for your panzers."

"How do you know of this?" asked the German commander suspiciously.

"I have conducted my own reconnaissance," Magus replied calmly. "I have sent my own spies into the forest. They found the path. The way is perfectly clear except for a few large stones in the middle."

"Stones?"

Magus waved his hand as if shooing away a fly. "A crude barricade created to thwart your tanks. But these peasants have underestimated your power, Colonel. These stones are not so large as to withstand a blast from *your* panzers. And what a show of strength it would be to blow the stones to pieces! Think of the confidence it would give your men to know such an obstacle could be so easily dealt with."

"We cannot go around the stones?" asked the colonel.

"The way is not wide enough to maneuver the tanks," said Magus. "But there are only a few large megaliths to bar your path, I assure you. And you've more than enough fire-power to deal with them."

The colonel still appeared unsure. "You are positive in this, Magus?"

Magus understood that the man across the chessboard was weighing the pros and cons of the risky maneuver. "The village and the forest are polluted with spies," he repeated. "You would be doing the Führer a great favor by annihilating them. And the best way to reach them before they can escape is by going directly through the forest. The only thing standing in your way to glory, Colonel, are a few pesky stones."

The colonel considered this for a very long moment. "Very well, Magus, when Berlin sends the orders to invade, we will go through your forest," Gropp agreed; then he frowned as he looked again at the chessboard and realized the sorcerer had just taken his king.

"You played a very good game, Colonel," Magus said with delight. "But this evening, luck was on my side."

Gropp's ratty face became purple with anger and he stood up abruptly before storming away. Magus watched with immense satisfaction as the colonel slapped a nearby soldier who did not get out of his way fast enough.

Magus then carefully tucked the pieces of his chess set back into the case and wondered if his beasts had yet been successful back in Dover. He'd dispatched the three hellhounds to watch over Castle Dover after hearing from his sisters that the witch had discovered the children's vulnerability. He sincerely hoped that the little ones had indeed come out to play.

DEADMAN'S FOREST

Ian awoke to a searing pain in his right arm and shoulder that grew more and more unbearable with every passing second. His body was shuddering with involuntary spasms, and he found that he was having great difficulty breathing. "This is very bad," said a soft female voice. "We must take him to my grandmother's house immediately!"

"Can't we bring your grandmother here?" he heard Theo reply. "I'm afraid to move him."

"No," said the girl bluntly. "He must come with us to the house."

"I can carry him," Carl said. Ian gave another shudder. He didn't want anyone to touch him. He just wanted to lie as still as possible and fight the pain coursing through him from his shoulder down his side and across his chest. It felt like a thousand hot daggers were stabbing their way through the right side of his body.

"No," said the girl curtly. "I have a wheelbarrow just beyond those trees. We'll use it to carry him to the house."

"Don't . . . ," Ian muttered through gritted teeth, unable to say more.

"He's awake!" Theo gasped, and he felt her warm hand lie across his forehead. "He's freezing cold," she whispered, and Ian could tell she was desperately worried.

"He's been poisoned," said the girl. "Do you see that black ring around his wound? If it spreads to his heart, I'm afraid he'll die."

"Can your grandmother help him?" Carl asked, and his voice sounded desperate.

"Maybe," replied the girl. "But her services are not free."

"We have money!" Theo said, and Ian heard her rummaging around in the knapsack. "Here!" she said. "Take some!"

Ian pried one of his eyelids open as he continued to shiver and shake. He saw Theo and Carl sitting beside him, and all around was a dense forest. Next to them was a girl about his age with dark brown hair and beautiful amber eyes. She had pale unmarred skin and a small nose. He might have thought her very pretty if he weren't fighting so hard not to pass out again.

She took the bills from Theo and regarded them skeptically. "English pound notes?"

Theo and Carl exchanged a look. "It's all we've got," Carl told her.

The girl continued to regard them curiously for a moment. "Where did you come from, exactly?"

"England," Carl told her, but offered nothing more.

"But you speak Polish," replied the girl, "with no hint of an accent."

Theo reached out and took hold of the girl's hand. She looked imploringly at her and promised, "We'll explain everything to you if you'll just help our friend."

The girl considered Theo for a moment before her gaze swiveled back to Ian. She looked at him as if wondering if he was worth the trouble; then her eyes moved back to the money Theo had given her. "Very well," she said. "We will help him. But while you are at our home, you must obey *every* order I give you. Is that clear?"

Both Theo and Carl nodded vigorously. "We'll do exactly as you say," said Carl. "Just tend to him, all right?"

The girl got up and walked away several paces before disappearing around an enormous tree. She returned a moment later with a crude wooden wheelbarrow, already half full with green plants and various flowers. "Help me load him into here," she instructed.

Carl bent down on Ian's left side and whispered, "I know it hurts, mate, but you've got to work with me. I'm going to get you to your feet and move you to the barrow. On three."

Ian was making short little gasping sounds as the pain in his chest and side continued to spread. He wanted very much to cooperate with Carl, but the searing heat was too intense for him to manage anything more than gripping his friend's shoulder. "One," Carl whispered, moving his arms carefully under Ian's neck and lower back. "Two . . ." Ian braced himself. "Three."

Carl lifted Ian and the shock of the movement sent a

wave of pain through him that was so intense it completely overwhelmed him. Ian let out a scream of agony and faded into darkness.

Sometime later Ian came out of the black, blurry world he'd been floating in. He was still in a significant amount of pain, but his breathing was a fraction easier. He heard voices again hovering over him. The girl from the woods, he recognized: "Will he survive?"

Another voice, this one dry, old, and brittle, said, "I have cured him enough to keep him alive for now. He still carries a bit of the venom in his veins, which will weaken him over time, but for now his condition should improve, at least for another day or two, before the venom takes hold again and he will begin to decline. I will heal him fully when you have satisfied the price. And know that I have forestalled his death in advance of payment only as a favor to you, Eva, because you and your grandmother have served me well these many years."

"Thank you, wise one," said the girl.

Ian wanted to open his eyes and see who was talking, but the shudders and spasms running through him prevented him from doing anything other than gritting his teeth.

"What was the source of the venom?" the girl suddenly asked.

"The others would not tell you?"

"No. They're being very secretive. They've only told me that they come from England."

The old one snorted. "It does not surprise me that they don't wish to reveal their past, given that this one was bitten by a hellhound."

"A *what?*" gasped the girl.

"A beast of legend," the old one said. "Which means these children have obviously been exploring places they don't belong. Hellhounds rarely venture into populated areas. And the hellhound's bite is nearly always fatal. This boy was lucky to have entered my forest."

"Do you think the hound is still nearby?" the girl asked, her voice filled with fear.

Ian heard someone sniff loudly. "No," said the old voice. "It is nowhere nearby, which is curious, because I doubt the lad could have traveled far with a wound like that."

There was a long silence after that, and Ian suspected that the girl still looked worried, because the old one chuckled and said, "No need for concern, Eva. If any beast from the underworld were to set one filthy paw in *my* forest, I would know of it, and it would be the last move the creature ever made. Now, about my fee . . ."

"They gave me money," the girl said quickly. "English pound notes. They are very valuable and you may purchase your heart's desire with them."

There was a pause, and Ian had the distinct impression that the girl had said something offensive. "You know I have no interest in money," the older one snapped. "I desire *things*, Eva. Bring me a trinket to amuse me and the debt will be paid. Then I will heal the lad the rest of the way."

"I'll need some time," Eva said.

"I will give you a few days, but do not test my patience, girl, or your grandmother and this boy may suffer. Remember, the venom still courses through him. He will not be completely healed until you have paid the price."

"I will do my best to purchase something wonderful with the money they've given me."

"Do not disappoint me, girl," the voice warned.

"I promise!" Eva whispered earnestly.

"And the three of them are to stay here with you until the debt has been paid. I shall not look kindly upon them running amuck in my forest and disturbing the balance I have created here."

"On my word, I will keep them here," the girl swore.

Ian heard these last words and found that the darkness wanted to envelop him again. He tried to stay awake and hear more but was far too weak to fight, and a moment later he was back in the deep black void.

Ian became aware of the orange hue across his eyelids about the same time he became mindful of the terrible dryness in the back of his throat. He tried to swallow but couldn't manage even a bit of moisture. He took a deep breath and realized he was able to breathe more easily now. With effort, he opened his eyes a tiny fraction. His vision was blurred and he blinked to clear it. Theo's relieved face came into focus. "Hello there," she whispered with a smile. "We've missed you."

"Is he awake?" Ian heard Carl say. A shuffling of feet brought Carl next to Theo. His friend grinned broadly down at him, his complexion slightly flushed—as if he'd been running. "You gave us quite a scare there, mate."

"Water," Ian croaked.

Theo reached to the small table next to him for a cup. She gently eased a hand underneath his head and lifted it off the pillow so that he could take a drink. Ian slurped the water greedily. He downed the entire contents. "More?"

Carl took the cup from Theo and rushed away from the bed. He was back a moment later and gave the cup back to Theo, who again helped Ian drink. Afterward, Ian sighed. "Thank you," he said as the prickly feeling in the back of his throat subsided.

"How are you feeling?" Theo asked him.

Ian inhaled as deeply as he could and was relieved to find his lungs cooperating fully. "Better," he said. "But my arm and shoulder are still a bit sore."

"Can you feel your fingers?" Theo asked him, looking worried again.

Ian tilted his head, wanting to know why she'd asked him that. He glanced toward his right hand and realized with a start that the whole of it and most of his fingers were hugely swollen and the skin was bruised black and blue. Just above his wrist, where the beast had bitten him, was a thick bandage, and a green salve oozed out from the edges. "Blimey!" he gasped, fear racing up his spine. "What's happened to my hand?"

"Try to wiggle one finger," Theo said coaxingly. Ian looked at her and gulped. He laid his head back on the pillow and closed his eyes before very carefully wiggling the fingers on his right hand. Searing heat shot straight up his arm and he hissed through his teeth. But when he opened his eyes, Theo was smiling down at him in relief. "Well done," she assured him.

"Where are we?" he asked, looking about the room he was in.

"We were fortunate to find a very nice girl named Eva in the forest when we came through the portal," Theo explained. "She helped us bring you here to her grandmother's cottage, and she has been kind enough to offer us food, drink, and a place to sleep while you get better."

Ian nodded tiredly. "That's very good of her," he said.

"Yes," Theo agreed. "She's tended to your wound and has assured us that you'll get better, but she's also advised that we have you move your fingers as soon as possible. The beast's bite was quite poisonous, but Eva managed to draw most of it out with that salve. She said that it might take a few days, but she promised us that you would feel better very soon."

Ian waited for the heat surging along his nerves to subside before he asked softly, "Do you believe Eva is the Healer?"

Theo's face clouded. "I'm afraid I don't know," she said, glancing warily over her shoulder. "She certainly seems capable of treating you, but I'm afraid that when she was fussing over you, Carl and I could barely keep our eyes open long enough to observe exactly how she made you better.

"This morning we both woke up to see her smoothing some sort of salve over your wound, which she's been reapplying every few hours, and you certainly appear to be doing much better. But there's something not quite right about her or this place." Theo's hands closed over her crystal and the worried look returned to her eyes.

Ian then remembered the voices he'd heard earlier. From what he could recall of the conversation, someone else had been responsible for healing him. But he was unable to dwell on that at the moment. Another worry had entered his mind. "You brought me through the portal."

Theo smoothed the hair along his brow, her face a mask of guilt. "We'd no choice," she admitted. "A moment after you collapsed, the portal opened, and you were in such a terrible state, Ian. We couldn't leave you there—you would have died without help. Either the beast would have found its way through the gate, or the venom would have taken you."

Ian worked his good hand up to cover hers. "It's all right, Theo," he assured her. "I would have done the same if it were one of you."

"I made sure to note where the portal is," Carl told him. "And I rescued the sundial from where you dropped it." Carl dug into his pocket and pulled out the bronze relic. When his friend offered it to him, Ian shook his head. "You keep it for now," he said. Carl nodded grimly and tucked the sundial back into his trousers while he continued to reassure Ian. "We came out this side of the portal to a small cave not far from here. The first sign of Lachestia and we'll shuttle you back through, Ian. Don't you worry."

Ian nodded and closed his eyes. He'd concern himself with being on this side of the portal after he'd had a chance to rest. "I'm so tired."

Theo squeezed his good hand. "Eva told us you'd be very weak at first. You should sleep, Ian. We'll be nearby."

"Get some rest," Carl added. "We'll talk later."

In the next instant, Ian was fast asleep.

Sometime later Ian awoke to something cool and soothing being applied to his arm. He still felt weak and exhausted, so he waited to open his eyes. The dim light coming through his eyelids suggested that it was nighttime, and the familiar sound of Carl snoring in the background told him it must be quite late. "How is the lad?" asked a withered voice from across the room. Ian noticed that although the owner sounded old, the cadence and pitch of her speech seemed different from the woman who'd given him aid earlier.

"He's coming along quite well. His hand has lost much of the swelling and he seems to be healing nicely, Grandmother," said the girl. Ian nearly smiled when he heard the word "grandmother." For a moment, he heard it as the girl had actually said it: *"Babcia."*

"And the others?"

"Asleep."

"Careful not to give them so much tea," said the old

woman. "They'll start to suspect when they can't shake their grogginess."

"I had to give them a bit extra," the girl said. "I'm off to the village in the morning, and they must remain asleep until I return."

"The crone and her payments." The old woman tsked. "She's taken every heirloom we have. And now you've bargained to bring her another trinket?"

"I had little choice," Eva said. "The boy would have died without her help."

The old woman harrumphed. "I'm running low on elixir," she said after a bit.

"I'll get some more from the crone when I take her the payment," promised the girl. Ian felt her finish with the salve, and rewrap his arm very gently with a bandage. "There," she whispered to him. "That should help ease the sting in your arm and let you rest peacefully through the night."

Ian thought it best to pretend he was still asleep. "How long will they stay?" asked the old woman.

"Only a little while longer," said Eva. Ian heard her move away from his bedside. "At least until the crone accepts what I've brought her for payment and she heals the boy completely. Either way, they cannot leave without her permission."

The old woman harrumphed again. "We're all her prisoners," she croaked.

"Shhh!" Eva said quickly. "Don't say such things! You know her forest has ears!"

"Yes," her grandmother agreed irritably. "I'm well aware that this is *her* forest, Eva. I've lived here all my life, after all, bound by the crone and her potions. I should have left years ago. Before you or your mother were ever born."

"Nonsense," Eva insisted. "You would have died many times over were it not for her help, Babi."

The old woman sighed. "I've lived quite long enough, Eva. And I will not have you be a slave any longer than you have to for my sake. Promise me that the moment I die, you will leave this forest and never look back."

"Hush," her granddaughter said gently. "You're not dying and I'm certainly not going anywhere without you. Now drink your sleeping medicine and rest, Babi. It's quite late."

Ian struggled then to open his eyes. He saw the pretty girl from the forest leaning over a bed across the room, where a withered and frail-looking old woman sat propped up by many pillows and covered in blankets. Eva held a green bottle, from which she carefully dispensed a spoonful of liquid. She fed it to her grandmother, who took it willingly. The girl then set the green bottle down, replaced the cork top, and smoothed a hand over her grandmother's white unruly hair.

"Promise me," repeated the old woman, her eyes stern and unwavering.

"Hush," Eva repeated soothingly.

But the old woman was stubborn. She grabbed Eva's hand and held it to her heart. "Promise me!" she begged.

Eva appeared startled and unsettled by the urgency in

her grandmother's request. "All right," she said after a moment. "But you're not dying, Babi. So such promises are quite ridiculous."

But the old woman appeared satisfied now that she had Eva's word, and she sank back into her pillows and closed her lids. Ian found that he too was unable to keep his eyes open, and with a small sigh he fell into a comfortable but exhausted sleep.

Ian was shaken gently awake sometime the next morning. "Ian!" Carl was whispering to him urgently. "Come on, mate! You've got to wake up!"

Ian's eyes flew open and he stared up at the pale face of his friend, who seemed frantic and worried. "What's the matter?"

"It's Theo!" Carl whispered, looking warily at the other side of the room, where Eva's grandmother still rested.

"What are you two going on about?" she demanded.

"Nothing, ma'am," Carl assured her before closing his eyes and saying, "Tickety-boo, tickety-boo, tickety-boo."

Ian's brow furrowed. "Carl, have you gone daft?"

Carl snapped his eyes open and smiled. "Naw, mate, I've just got to make sure we're speaking the king's English, so I think of a word that doesn't translate to any other language, like 'tickety-boo,' and we pop from Polish to English just like that. The old woman can't understand a word I'm saying thereafter."

Ian eased up to his elbows, wincing only slightly when he put weight on his sore arm. Absently he noted that his hand had lost most of the swelling, although it still looked quite bruised. "Why don't you simply take off the pouch with the Star in it?"

"Because I need to understand what *they're* saying, Ian," Carl explained, as if Ian were the one who'd gone daft.

"Where's Theo?" Ian asked, wanting to change the subject and suddenly aware that neither she nor Eva was in the small cabin.

"Gone," Carl said. "Which is why I need you to get up. We've got to look for her."

Ian struggled to sit all the way up. "What do you mean she's gone?" he demanded.

"Eva left a bit ago. She said she was going to ask one of the villagers for a ride to the train station. She said she needed to travel into the city—something about needing to purchase a gift for an old friend. She tried to get us to drink that tea she keeps making for us, but Theo and I know she's put some sort of sleeping potion in it, so we only pretended to drink it. The minute she left, Theo got up and checked our supplies, and Ian—Eva's taken *all* our money!"

"I'll not ask you again!" said the old woman from across the room. "I demand to know what you're saying!"

Carl tore his eyes away from Ian and smiled at Eva's grandmother. "Just telling my friend here what a marvelous hostess your granddaughter is, ma'am."

The old woman appeared skeptical and pouted at them but said nothing more.

"Tickety-boo," Ian whispered after a moment, and Carl smiled. "So what happened to Theo?" he asked quietly.

"I'm running a fever," his friend admitted. Ian's eyes

widened. Carl did appear quite pale and his brow was slick with sweat, and now that Ian thought about it, Carl's breathing also appeared labored. "Theo thinks I've caught the virus and she's gone in search of the Healer."

Ian's jaw fell open. *"She's what?"*

Carl held up his hands in surrender. "She mentioned the idea right after she felt my forehead this morning, said I needed to stay here and rest while she went off to search the forest for the Healer. I told her absolutely not and she promised she wouldn't go without us, but then when I came back from the loo just now, she was gone!"

Ian wasted no time pulling back the covers and easing himself out of bed. "We've got to find her," he said, his heart racing as he struggled to get to his feet on wobbly legs.

"Can you walk?" Carl asked, coming round to support Ian under his shoulder.

"Yes," he assured him, even though he felt quite unstable. "With some help, at least."

"Get back into bed!" Eva's grandmother yelled at him. "You're not supposed to be walking around! And where is the girl? She isn't supposed to leave the cottage!"

"She's just outside," Carl said quickly. "Enjoying some fresh air. And I'm helping Ian to the loo. We'll be right back."

Carl made Ian sit on the side of the bed for just a moment while he helped him ease into his shoes, and then he got Ian to his feet again and snuck the knapsack between them, and they shuffled outdoors.

"Which way do you think she went?" Ian asked, looking

298

around. The cottage was situated in a sparse yard at the edge of a thick and ominous wood. The only other structure Ian could see was an outhouse.

"Dunno," Carl admitted, but then he seemed to get an idea and he reached into his trouser pocket and pulled out the sundial. "Perhaps this might come in handy," he said, holding it up to Ian.

Ian felt a bit of relief. They'd find Theo quickly with the aid of the sundial. "Brilliant, mate," he said to him as he lifted it from Carl's palm.

Ian glanced over his shoulder and saw that Eva's grandmother had herself struggled out of bed and was moving to the door, probably to see where everyone had gone. He remembered snatches of conversation he'd overheard, during which she'd warned Eva to keep them all trapped in the cottage, and Ian said, "Come on, let's get to the woods quickly before we have to explain ourselves to the old woman."

The boys moved to the closest path in the forest surrounding the yard. It was much darker under the shade of so many trees—especially given that the morning held dark gray clouds that clearly threatened rain. Ian made sure they were both out of sight of the old woman in the cottage, and feeling secure, he asked, "Sundial, please point the way to Theo."

A feeble shadow formed across the surface of the relic. Ian squinted—it was hard to see in the dim light—but he could just make out that the dial was pointing directly behind him. "She took the path on the other side of the cottage," he told Carl.

Carl opened his mouth to say something, but a coughing fit overtook him and racked his body for several moments. Ian stared worriedly at his friend, and terrible fear gripped him while he stood by helplessly and watched Carl struggle to take a clear breath. He remembered the others coughing at the keep, and felt dread at seeing the same symptoms appear in his friend. When Carl at last was able to breathe without coughing, Ian asked him, "Would you like to stay here? I can use the sundial to find Theo by myself."

Carl stared at him as if he'd said something offensive. "Are you joking?" he wheezed. "Lachestia's probably prowling these very woods, Ian! I can't let you go off on your own. Especially not in your condition."

Ian had to smile at the irony. Just a few moments before, he'd needed Carl's help to make it out of bed, and right then, Carl was the one who looked like he needed some support. "All right," he agreed. "We'll lean on each other."

Carl put on a brave face, reached into the knapsack, and pulled out an apple and some cheese. "Here," he said. "You've had nothing to eat since we came through the portal. Eat this while we look for Theo."

Ian took the food gratefully. "Good old Carl," he said, remembering Theo's words from the Lafittes' garden, reminding him that Carl was the best mate he'd ever have.

Carl smiled and started to cough again, and Ian felt foreboding go straight through him. When Carl could speak again, he said hoarsely, "Let's be off, then."

* * *

The boys spent much of the morning making little progress through the dense forest. Ian couldn't tell if there just wasn't enough light to read the sundial, or if Theo was moving so erratically that the shadow continually changed. After he'd eaten, Ian felt much better. He was still a bit weak, and his arm throbbed terribly, but it was Carl who was struggling to keep up.

Periodically the boys had to stop altogether while Carl worked through another fit of coughs, and to make matters worse, the gray clouds eventually let go of the rain they'd been holding. It wasn't long before both Carl and Ian were wet, miserable, and shaking with cold.

"I can't read the dial," Ian finally admitted. "It's too dark in these woods. There's not enough light to form a shadow."

Carl tugged the knapsack off his shoulders and fished around inside. He pulled out a torch and handed it to Ian. "Best to keep it dry if you can," he told him.

Ian used his body to shield the torch and directed it toward the dial. Relieved, he saw the dark shadow across the surface, pointing straight ahead. "This way," he said, moving forward.

"Didn't we just come from there?" Carl asked.

Ian stopped and looked about. The forest surrounding them was a very unsettling place, and Ian had tried to pretend not to notice the presence of something dark and sinister he'd felt shadowing them from the moment they'd set foot onto the path. But now, as he gazed into the trees, the ominous presence felt all the more oppressive. And then a slow rumbling came to his ears.

His eyes darted to Carl, who seemed to hear it too. "What's that?" Carl whispered.

"Thunder?" Ian asked, hoping it was only the weather.

Carl listened for a moment before commenting. "No," he said softly. "That's not thunder."

A rustling in the foliage called their attention and they both ducked low. "What's *that?*" Carl whispered as they crouched down.

Ian shrugged. "Dunno. But I don't think we should sit around here and find out. Come on."

Ian darted sideways, keeping low to the ground as he went. Carl was close on his heels and the boys made their way to a large tree and scooted around behind it, away from the rustling foliage.

But the distant rumbling was getting louder. "We can't stay here," Carl insisted, and to Ian's dismay he began to cough again, but this time the attack went on and on. Carl's pale face turned red with effort and he struggled to breathe. Ian could only watch and pat him on the back. Finally, Carl was able to take a few shaky breaths, and he nodded when Ian asked him if he was well enough to set off again.

Ian squinted out from behind the tree and spied something large and gray looming in the distance. Through the drizzle he could see that it was a sizable stone, and he hoped they could both find some cover behind it. "Follow me," he instructed before dashing out from behind the tree.

The boys were nearly to the stone when a figure stepped out in front of them, blocking their path. Ian stopped so abruptly that Carl crashed into him and the boys both went sprawling to the ground.

Ian managed to regain his feet faster than Carl, and when he stood up, he saw that it was only Eva, planted firmly in their path, looking wet and furious. "*What* do you think you're doing?" she demanded.

Ian helped Carl to his feet. "What do *you* care?" he snapped, irritated that she'd caused them both a tumble.

"You cannot be here!" she yelled back.

"I thought you went to the city," he said, noticing her formal—albeit rain-soaked—attire.

She narrowed her eyes at him. "My grandmother came to fetch me to tell me that you had left, and don't change the subject! You weren't supposed to leave the cottage!"

Ian glared hard at her in return. "What's it to you what we do?" he snapped, all the fear and anger and anxiety over Carl's illness and Theo's disappearance catching up with him. When she didn't answer him, Ian added, "I must say that although I am grateful for your care and attention, we are *not* your prisoners! We may come and go as we like!"

"Where is your sister?" Eva demanded as the slow drizzle suddenly turned into a downpour.

"What do you *care?*" Ian asked again in exasperation just as Carl began another coughing fit, which forced him to reach out for the support of a nearby tree. "You've helped yourself to *all* our money and we've left you in peace! What does it matter to you if we stay or go?"

Eva's face flushed crimson, but she continued to rail at

Ian. "My grandmother is old and feeble, Ian! You don't have permission to be in this forest, and when you left, you forced her out of bed to walk all the way to the village to fetch me!"

Ian shook his head, utterly furious at her accusations. "Your grandmother chose to get out of her bed, Eva. I certainly never forced her to do anything! And I've no idea what rubbish you're talking about when you suggest we don't have permission to be here. You can't possibly *own* this entire forest! We may walk about it as we see fit!" Ian made a move to step around Eva, but she jumped in front of him, blocking his path.

"No!" she said, her eyes panicked. "Ian, you don't understand! This forest is cursed. It doesn't allow trespassers, and I promised the crone that I would keep you within the confines of our yard until the payment has been made!"

Ian's head swam with too much information. He had no idea what Eva was going on about, and he found that he didn't really care. He needed to find Theo, and quickly. And he also needed to find the Healer in time to help Carl, who was coughing so consistently and with such effort that Ian knew he wouldn't stay on his feet much longer. He hated to think what he would do if Carl collapsed, because in his own weakened condition, he would be no help to him. "I don't care who or what you promised," he snapped. "Now step aside, Eva. This no longer concerns you." Ian turned to help Carl, who was still hunched over and gasping for breath, when there was a sharp crash right behind them.

Ian whirled around only to come face to face with the grille of a motorcar. He pulled Carl out of the way just as the automobile came to a rather abrupt stop. Ian struggled to comprehend what a motorcar was doing slogging through the forest, but he barely had time to digest its appearance before several uniformed and heavily armed men jumped out and pointed their guns directly at him, Carl, and Eva.

"What do we have here?" asked one mean-looking man with a rat-shaped face.

Neither Eva nor Ian replied—both of them were too stunned under the threat of the guns being pointed at them to respond—and poor Carl was doubled over, still coughing and fighting for air.

The rat-faced man stepped up to Eva and eyed her up and down suspiciously. "What are you doing out in the forest, you little Polish scum?" he snarled.

Eva gasped, and she shook her head. "I don't understand you, sir," she said in a quivering voice. "I only speak Polish."

The man slapped her so hard across the face that Eva spun in a circle before collapsing to the ground. "Stop!" Ian shouted at the soldier while he attempted to go to Eva's aid, but before he could move more than a foot, the nose of a gun was placed right against his temple. Ian froze and closed his eyes, not even daring to breathe.

He heard the squish of leather boots in the mud and opened his eyes again to look directly into the narrowed eyes of the rat-faced man. "Are you from the village?" the soldier asked him.

Ian believed that at that point, it might be prudent to lie. "Yes, sir," he said. "I live in the village."

The man rocked back on his heels, a triumphant look in

his eyes. "And you speak German!" he said. Ian couldn't help noticing the accusing tone his words held. "Herr Black was right! These woods are full of Polish spies!"

"Colonel," said another soldier, hovering near Eva, who was now struggling to her feet, "look at what has come out of the girl's pockets."

The colonel moved away from Ian, who was still held fast by the nose of the gun next to his head. He watched with wide eyes as the colonel bent and picked something up off the ground. Ian knew immediately what had dropped out of Eva's pocket, and he also knew that it would be their undoing. "An English pound note?" the colonel inquired, holding the bit of paper up to his eyes, which then moved back to Eva. "Is that who is paying you to spy on us?" he spat, his face turning red with anger.

Eva was shaking her head as she shivered in fear. Her left cheek was scarlet from the slap the colonel had given her. "Yes!" she told him. "Take my money! Take all of it!" And with that, she emptied her pockets of all the pound notes she carried; Ian knew quite well it was a small fortune.

The colonel glowered at her in disgust. "You see that?" he said to one of his men standing nearby. "She confesses."

Ian searched for anything he could say to the colonel, any explanation he might offer that would get them out of their situation, but before he could even form the words, the colonel had pulled out his pistol, held it up to Eva's chest, and fired.

The poor girl was flung backward by the force of

the point-blank shot, and as she fell, a scream echoed through the trees just behind Ian. He had no time to react, no time even to take in what was happening, but somewhere in the back of his mind, he knew who that scream belonged to.

"Ah," said the colonel, looking just past Ian. "Even more come out of the forest hoping for mercy. We will show them none." Turning to the man holding the gun at Ian's temple, the colonel said, "Sergeant, shoot these Polish scum. I am off to see if our friend Magus Black is correct and this path is wide enough for my panzers. We must make haste if we are to meet up with the rest of the divisions on their way to take Warsaw!"

Ian gasped at both the mention of Magus's name and what else the colonel had just revealed, but he barely had time to register that the vile sorcerer was working with the German army to invade Poland when his eyes swiveled to lock with those of the man the colonel had given their death orders to. He noted that the sergeant appeared uncertain.

"Colonel," the sergeant said quietly, and the nose of the gun came away slightly from Ian's temple. "They are just children. Are you certain it is necessary to shoot them?"

The colonel stepped up to the sergeant and pointed his own pistol directly at him. For a long tense moment, Ian was convinced the rat-faced man would shoot his own soldier. "Are you questioning a direct order?" the colonel asked in a dangerously soft tone.

The sergeant was quick to shake his head. "No, of course not, Colonel Gropp," he said. "I shall shoot these Polish scum, just as you so wisely commanded."

Gropp lowered his pistol and waved to the other soldiers to get into the motorcar. "You will meet up with us later," he told the sergeant, making a point of staring up at the rain coming down in a steady flow. "Perhaps a little time spent in this miserable downpour will reinforce how comfortable my car was." With that he got into his automobile and shut the door, but the car did not drive off. Ian suspected that the colonel wanted to watch his sergeant and make sure he did as he was told.

"You there!" the soldier shouted to someone just behind Ian. "Come out here at once!"

Ian heard the sound of soft footsteps and he felt a wave of despair. A moment later Theo stepped up next to him and took his hand. "I'm so sorry," she said to him, tears rolling down her wet face to mix with the rain.

Ian turned his eyes back up to the soldier aiming his gun at them. "Please spare her!" he begged. "She's just a little girl, sir! Innocent! She's done nothing wrong!"

"Silence!" the soldier commanded, his eyes showing no mercy. "Turn around and march over there!"

Ian glanced sideways at Carl, whose eyes were wide with fright. "Is he *really* going to shoot us?" Carl said, as if he could hardly believe it.

"*Now!*" shouted the soldier, and the three of them quickly turned around and walked to where the soldier had pointed. Behind them Ian could hear the man's heavy foot-steps and he braced himself, unsure when the sergeant would pull the trigger. They walked just a few meters down an incline to the edge of a steep ravine before the sergeant commanded them to stop. "On your knees," he ordered, "with your hands behind your head!"

Ian's mind was racing to find a way to escape their situation. Should they run? Should he tackle the soldier, hoping it would give Theo time to get away? *"Down on your knees!"* their guard shouted impatiently.

Ian sank to his knees, so terrified that he was unable to form a plan. All he could do was numbly follow the orders being given to him and pray for a miracle. He saw the car's wheels and underbelly up the hill. They obscured the view of the terrible man inside who'd just condemned them to death. "Hands behind your heads!" the sergeant shouted again.

Ian placed his hands behind his head and swallowed hard as he stared defiantly up at the man ordered to shoot him. He vowed to force himself not to look away. Suddenly, he felt the full weight of Theo as she ignored the soldier's or-ders and crawled over to hug him fiercely while she buried her face in his drenched shirt. Something flickered in the soldier's eyes as he looked down at Ian and Theo, and for a moment he hesitated, but then he demanded that Ian force Theo to let him go and place her hands behind her head.

But Ian had no intention of complying, and he suddenly didn't care if it angered the man with the gun. His dying breath would be spent trying to comfort the one person in all the world who meant the most to him. Ignoring the soldier, he wrapped his own arms around Theo, feeling dreadful shame for not having lived up to Laodamia's command to guard and protect the One. Lowering his head, he whispered in her ear, "Don't cry, Theo. It will be very quick, I promise you. Just a bee sting really, and it will all be over. Hold on to me as tightly as you can, and you'll hardly feel a—"

Ian's words were cut short by the explosive sound of a gunshot. Next to him, Carl grunted and fell backward. Ian squeezed his eyes tightly shut and held on to Theo for all he was worth, waiting with a hammering heart for his turn. The smell of gunpowder clung to his nostrils and the sound of rain pattered on the leaves all around him, and for a moment there was no other noise. Ian began to wonder what was taking so long when two more rapid shots deafened his ears. He startled at the noise and felt an immediate punch to his left side, which sent him sprawling head over heels. He landed hard at the bottom of the ravine, still clinging to Theo, whose lifeless body lay in his arms. After that, all Ian could do was wait for the world to go dark.

SHELTER IN THE TREES

For a very long time, Ian lay still, his breathing shallow while the pain in his side throbbed on and on. He listened to the squish of the soldier's boots when he walked away from them, the roar of the colonel's engine as it moved off deeper into the woods, and the soft but constant *thwap* of raindrops hitting the foliage all around him.

He focused with all his might on these sounds, because what had just happened to his whole world threatened to make him insane. He couldn't face the reality of it, so he listened to the rain and hoped his own death would come soon.

But then, with suddenness, a new sound added itself to the mix, and it took Ian a bit of time to comprehend it, because the noise was impossible.

Carl was coughing.

And if his best mate was coughing, then he was still alive. But Theo . . .

Ian resisted the urge to open his eyes and held her close.

She still felt warm. He swallowed hard; the reality he'd been fighting was starting to seep into him, like the venom from the hellhound, poisonous and bleak.

And then . . . a miracle. Theo moved.

Ian snapped his eyes open and pulled his chin down so that he could see the top of her head. She stirred again, and behind him, Carl's coughing intensified. Ian sucked in a breath and carefully sat up. Theo pushed against his chest and grunted. "Ian!" she complained softly. "You're holding me too tight."

Belatedly, he relaxed his arms, and Theo tilted her face to him and asked, "You all right?"

He was so stunned that all he could do was nod.

"He shot just over our heads," Theo said, pointing to a tree jutting out on the other side of the ravine. Ian could see that the trunk was missing three chunks of bark. "I thought for certain he was going to kill us, but when I saw that he marched us over to the edge of the ravine and shot above Carl's head before kicking him down the slope, I knew he was saving us instead."

Ian looked down at his left side and pulled up his shirt to reveal a red mark about the size of the toe of a man's boot. "He kicked us to get us to fall over?" he asked.

"Yes," Theo said. "I saw him kick Carl. . . ." Theo's voice trailed off as she looked past Ian to where Carl lay on the wet ground. She got to her feet, hurried over to him, and helped him sit up. Carl's cough had subsided just enough to allow him to look about in a daze.

"Are we dead?" he asked.

Ian shook his head. "Not yet, mate."

A loud agonized moan sounded from up the hill, and all three of them immediately looked in that direction. "Eva!" Ian said, scrambling to his feet and clambering up the ravine to her.

She lay on her back, staring at the sky in terror and pain. "It hurts," she mouthed while tears leaked down her cheeks. Theo and Carl joined him then and knelt down next to Eva. Ian gently eased the flap of her coat away from her right shoulder to reveal a gaping and bloody wound that went clear through the poor girl. The ground behind Eva was red with blood and her skin was starkly pale.

"We've got to help her," Theo said.

Ian looked about and saw the knapsack not far away. He retrieved it, then rummaged through the contents, coming up with a knife and one of Carl's extra shirts. He cut off several long strips and wadded up two of them, then placed those on the entrance and exit wounds and bound the wounds awkwardly with the other strips. He knew that the makeshift bandage wasn't likely to hold long, but it was the best he could do.

"We'll take her back to her grandmother's," he told them.

But Theo shook her head. "It's too far."

"We have to try, Theo," Ian told her firmly. "We can't very well leave her here."

Theo laid a gentle hand on his arm and looked over her shoulder. "There is somewhere we can take her that is much closer and will give her some shelter from the rain," she said to him, pointing. "I'd just discovered it when I heard you and Eva arguing."

Ian's gaze followed Theo's finger and he saw the large gray rock that he and Carl had discussed earlier. "But that's not much shelter," he told her.

Theo merely said, "There's more there than meets the eye, Ian. Come along. You take Eva's front and I'll take her legs."

But Ian shook his head. "That'll put too much strain on her wound."

"It's not far," Theo insisted.

Ian shook his head again and got his left arm under Eva's legs while moving his right under her torso. Counting to three in his head, he lifted her off the ground as gently as he could, but the strain on his own wound was enough to cause his eyes to water.

Theo looked at him worriedly for a moment but said nothing as she got up and led them slowly through the woods toward the rock.

They'd gone only a few meters when Ian had to stop. He sank to his knees, panting heavily, with Eva still cradled in his arms. "I can carry her," Carl suggested, but immediately he started to cough again, doubling over as great rattling hacks shook his body.

Ian waited until his friend had caught his breath again before saying, "That's all right, Carl. I can manage." Ian used all his strength and willpower to stand up again. Eva moaned in his arms. He knew she was in pain, and he focused on getting to the rock as quickly as he could so that he wouldn't have to keep moving her up and down.

With supreme effort they made it to the huge monolith, and Ian leaned against it, panting for air while his legs trembled underneath him and his arm screamed with fiery pain. "Over there," Theo said.

Ian turned his head dully and saw something remarkable. He blinked in the downpour and realized that he was looking at several planks nailed to a nearby tree, forming a makeshift ladder that led straight to a wooden bridge of sorts directly overhead.

The bridge linked a vast circle of trees together, and the trees seemed to mark the edge of a circle made of enormous stones just like the one he was standing next to. Within the circle of stones, nothing grew, and the rain was harsher there, because there was no foliage to stem the flow of the downpour.

Ian's eyes drifted back up to the bridge and he was even more startled to realize that there were structures within the branches of the trees. He counted four, in fact, and each looked like a small house. "You want us to take Eva up *there?*" he asked Theo.

She nodded at him. "She'll be safe and out of this rain," she told him. "We'll all be safe up there. If the soldiers return, they'll never think to look for us so high up in the trees."

"But, Theo," he protested, "what if someone already lives there?"

"Then we'll implore them to help Carl and Eva," Theo told him, and her voice indicated that there was no room for further argument.

Ian continued to breathe hard from the strain of carrying Eva, but eventually he nodded. "Very well, but I don't believe I can manage to carry her up that ladder, Theo. I don't have the strength."

Theo moved to the tree and he watched as she unhooked a rope from the other side and stepped out of the way as a wicker basket came down out of the branches. It was large enough to hold Eva.

Ian took a deep breath and pushed away from the rock to wobble awkwardly over to the basket. As gently as he could, he placed Eva inside, but the poor girl gasped when he removed his arm from around her and she fell against the back of the basket.

Ian also winced; his arm was now throbbing fiercely. "How do we get the basket up to the bridge?" he asked Theo.

Theo tilted her chin skyward and pointed to something at the top of the rope. "There's a hoist," she told him smartly.

Ian moved to the ladder, and that was when he spotted Carl still standing by the rock, not looking well at all. "Carl!" he called, but his friend barely seemed to hear him. Ian moved away from the tree and over to him. "We have to climb the ladder." For emphasis, Ian pointed to the nearby tree.

Carl blinked tiredly in the direction Ian was pointing. "I don't think I can manage it, Ian," he confessed just as his knees gave out.

Ian caught him and draped Carl's arm around his neck.

"Come on, mate," he said, surprised at the intense heat rising from Carl's skin. "Let's get you somewhere warm and dry."

Ian helped Carl to the ladder and stared straight up. He didn't think that Carl would be able to manage it either, and Ian wondered if he had the strength to hoist both Carl and Eva up to the platform. "Get Eva up first," Theo told him. "I'll tend to Carl and work him into the basket after you send it down again. And then I'll come up to help you hoist him the rest of the way."

Ian smiled gratefully at her and set Carl down next to the tree with instructions to get into the basket as soon as Theo asked him to. Carl blinked dully at him and coughed into his hand.

Ian hoped he remained conscious long enough to oblige. He went to the wooden ladder and began to climb.

Had he not been weakened by the hellhound's bite, navigating the ladder would have been child's play. But with all the overexertion he'd endured recently, the climb proved challenging. Eventually, he made it to the bridge, panting again for some time before he felt able to crawl to the hoist. It was a fairly simple design, and he found that by using his body weight, he was able to move Eva in slow jerky tugs up to the bridge.

When at last she reached the platform, Ian tipped the basket gently onto its side and eased the girl out of the wicker container. He paused when he realized she was no longer conscious, and bent to feel her pulse. Fortunately, she was still alive, although he knew she was in a most desperate condition. Ian released the basket, calling down to Theo to let her know it was on its way, and tried to get Eva some protection from the rain by moving her under a thick set of branches.

Once the Polish girl was resting peacefully under the leaves of the tree, he peered over the side of the bridge and saw that Theo was struggling with Carl, trying to coax him into the basket. Ian debated going down the ladder to help her, but that would require another arduous climb up, and he knew he didn't posses the strength. He settled for watching anxiously while Theo patiently half helped, half persuaded Carl into the wicker basket. The moment he was inside, Ian got to the hoist and began to pull and push on the crank.

The progress was painfully slow, even slower than it had been with Eva, and Ian quickly ran out of strength. Luckily, the hoist locked itself on the upward rotation, so after several turns, he was able to stop and lean over the crank to catch his wind. He felt a hand on his back as he was ready to try again, and he jumped only to realize that Theo had come up the ladder and was now standing next to him. "Might I lend a hand?"

Ian gave her a small smile. "Of course." Together they eased Carl up to the top, and Ian tipped the basket the way he had with Eva. Carl managed to crawl out of the cramped space on his own, and he stared up at them with such sadness that Theo kneeled down and asked him what was wrong.

"I'm not going to make it," he told her.

318

Ian stared at him, his heart sinking as he took in Carl's desperately pale complexion. "Don't talk like that," he said firmly.

But Carl shook his head. "I'm really sick, Ian," he said, shivering in the cold, wet rain, his blue lips quivering against his chattering teeth. "I don't think I'm likely to last through the night, mate."

Theo looked gravely at Ian, and he noticed with a pang that her hand was wrapped tightly around her crystal. "Let's get you to some shelter," she said to Carl, fighting back her tears. "We'll need to see to Eva as well."

While Theo helped Carl along the bridge, Ian struggled to carry Eva's limp form. It had been easier when she was still conscious and somewhat rigid. He found that he had to stop every other step just to prevent her from falling through his arms.

They eventually reached the first small house, built right into the cradle of branches, which supported it and that section of the bridge. Ian set Eva down gently and knocked on the door. There was no response, so he tried the handle. It turned easily and the door opened with a loud creak. "Hello?" he called into the dark interior.

No one replied.

"Let's go in," Theo said, trying her best to support Carl's weight. Ian wriggled the knapsack off his back and fished around for his torch. He clicked it on and shone the beam around the interior.

The small tree house was one room, much like the cottage where Eva and her grandmother lived, but the interior

319

was chock-full of so much clutter that it was hard to gauge its actual living space. Theo sighed impatiently behind Ian, and without waiting for his permission, she pushed forward, half dragging, half carrying Carl inside. She found a space on the floor and set him down, then looked up expectantly at Ian. "You coming in?" she asked.

Ian couldn't explain his trepidation; there was obviously no one home, if anyone lived there at all. All the things piled within the interior had clearly been there for quite some time, as they were coated with dust, and the place had that old, musty odor of being shut up for a long while without any fresh air. Still, he found that he was unsettled by the idea of trespassing. Then again, all he had to do was look down at Eva and he knew he had little choice.

He bent low and lifted her one last time, then carried her into the dry room and set her down next to Carl. Theo was already on her feet and moving about, inspecting their environment as she rummaged through a pile of odds and ends. "What are you doing?" he asked her in alarm. "Theo, what if the owners come back and see you going through their things?"

Theo pulled out a large quilt with a look of triumph. "We'll simply explain that our friends were in desperate need of their hospitality." She then brought the quilt over to drape it across Carl and Eva and grabbed the torch out of Ian's hand when something else caught her eye. After sifting through another pile, she retrieved an ancient-looking oil lamp which, by some miracle, still appeared to contain some oil. "Do you have any matches?"

Ian went to his knapsack, brought it inside, and handed over a box of matches from one of the interior pockets. Theo lit the lamp and the whole room was illuminated. The pair of them stared about in wonderment.

From floor to ceiling, and all around them, trinkets, toys, and knickknacks gleamed in the lamplight. Ian had never seen such an assortment and was at a loss as to why anyone would posses so much clutter.

"Have you ever seen anything like it?" he asked her.

"Only the professor's house can compare," she replied, and Ian remembered what a pack rat Professor Nutley was. Yet even his hoard couldn't match the assortment crowding the room.

A tremendous thunderclap rattled the contents of the house and sent tremors along the walls. "The storm is getting worse," Theo whispered nervously.

Ian looked at Eva and Carl. They might be out of the rain, but they certainly weren't out of danger. "We need to find them some help," he said. "Perhaps I can go fetch Eva's grandmother."

As if in answer, the dark atmosphere outside lit up for a split second and a terrible boom resounded off all four walls. The wind had picked up, and the floor swayed and creaked. It felt like being within the hull of a ship crossing a rocky sea. "You can't go out in this," Theo advised. "And we'll never get Eva's frail grandmother all the way through the woods and up here."

"Then what should we do?" Ian asked, exasperated by the many obstacles and few options.

"We must find the Healer."

Ian's eyebrows rose. "The Healer?" he repeated. "How are we ever going to locate the Healer in all this muck?"

"She's close by, Ian," Theo said, and her eyes held that faraway look that told him she could sense the Healer's presence.

There was another flash, and a horrendously loud clap of thunder drowned out all noise for several seconds. When it cleared, he said, "Yes, but how are we going to discover where the Healer is exactly, Theo?"

"Leave it to me," Theo told him. "I can sense that the Healer is near, so I know I could bring her back if I had to."

Ian wanted to laugh. If Theo thought he was going to let her out of his sight again, she was sorely mistaken. "You'll do no such thing!" he yelled over yet another boom from the sky. "What if the Germans came back and found you again? They'd kill you for certain."

"We can't just stay here and do nothing, Ian!" Theo yelled in return. "If we don't get help for Eva and Carl, they'll die! And we can't both go. One of us has to stay here and watch over them, and since I'm the only one with the means to find the Healer, I should go!"

Ian ground his teeth in frustration. And then he had an idea. He quickly pulled out the sundial, which he'd tucked into his trouser pocket, and held it up to the lamp. "Sundial," he said, his voice quivering with excitement, "point the way to the one who can heal our friends—the Healer from Laodamia's prophecy."

For two heartbeats nothing happened, but then a dark

shadow formed along the face of the sundial, and in another heartbeat, a second, more opaque shadow formed as well.

Theo peered down at the face of the relic. "*Two* Healers?" she gasped.

Ian stared down in surprise. "I suppose there are," he said. "One seems to be close by," he added, indicating the thicker, darker shadow, which was pointing directly behind him. The fainter one pointed off to the side. Ian looked up, his eyes passing over Carl and Eva to the far wall. "The other Healer must be located beyond the forest."

"But which one is correct?" Theo asked, clearly troubled.

"Both," Ian said simply. "Or either."

Theo stared down at the surface of the sundial, her hand toying with the crystal about her neck. "Very well," she sighed reluctantly. "You go in search of the Healer while I stay with Carl and Eva. But at least wait a bit to see if the storm clears, all right?"

Ian agreed, reasoning that he couldn't very well see the shadow on the dial in this gloom, and the rain was coming down so hard that if he attempted to use the torch, it would surely get wet and quickly become useless. "With a little luck, this tempest will sort itself out in a bit," he assured her.

As it happened, luck was not at all on their side. The terrible rainstorm that had soaked them to the skin continued to rage for hours. Heavy droplets pelted their small shelter, and the tree that it was held in was whipped by the wind so hard that both Ian and Theo found themselves shielding

Carl and Eva from clutter shaken loose from the piles all around them.

They managed to clean and re-dress Eva's wounds with fresh bandages and rainwater that Ian collected in a tin pot he found in the house, but Carl's fever continued to rage and soon he was hallucinating. When thunder reverberated across the sky, Carl shouted at Ian, "You have to get to safety! They're bombing us!"

Ian laid a wet cloth across his friend's forehead and attempted to calm him, but Carl was convinced they were under attack. Clutching Ian's shirt, he begged him to see Theo to safety. "I'm trapped," he said to Ian. "There's a boulder on my legs, mate! I'm stuck here, but you and Theo can still get away! Save yourselves!"

Ian couldn't help glancing down at Carl's legs, which were rigid, his knees locked. Curiously, Ian tapped on Carl's shin. "Do you feel that, Carl?" he asked. Carl lay on the ground and shook his head. "There's no pain," he said. "The boulder's cut off my circulation. Save yourself, Ian! *Save yourself!*"

Ian's eyes met Theo's, which he noticed were filled with tears. "He can't feel them," she whispered.

To make matters worse, Carl began to cough again, the sound deep and wet, and it wasn't long before he stopped his ranting and his breathing became a continuous gurgle. Ian could clearly hear the moisture rattling about in Carl's chest.

Finally, several hours into their vigil, when the owner of the tree house had not come back and Carl's breathing had become more and more challenged, Ian knew he had to go. "I've got to find help," Ian said. "He might not last much longer if I don't."

The patter of rain still sounded against the roof of their shelter, but Ian went to the door and opened it. Night had fallen. He'd lost track of time long before. Outside, the tempest still raged, and wind heaved the small house to and fro, and still there was no sign of the owner. Ian wondered if perhaps whoever had built the structure had done so only for recreation, or to provide extra storage space for their many collectables. Perhaps no one lived in the house up in the trees but only visited every now and again. He decided that if that was the case, they certainly wouldn't come round in this kind of a storm.

Ian pointed the beam of his torch at the bridge just outside. It bucked and swayed in the storm and he found it rather miraculous that it still held together. Tentatively, he stepped onto the wooden platform, and no sooner had he done that than a gust of wind sent him sprawling. In a panic, Ian grabbed for something to hold on to, felt the rough bark of a branch in his fingers, and gripped it tightly. But in the next second, there was a snap, and he was sent sprawling again.

His chest hit the wooden planks and the wind was knocked right out of him. He struggled to find something to grip, and the torch he was holding flew out of his hands and was lost. At the same time he felt his legs tumble over the side of the bridge, and knew he was about to fall to the earth some twenty feet below.

In that instant a hand gripped his shoulder so roughly that he yelped in pain, but he was pulled back before he slipped away over the side and then the hand holding him let go. Rain pelted him from all angles and the wind howled mightily. From inside the tree house, Theo called his name, and while he scrambled back to the center of the platform, he couldn't for the life of him figure out who had prevented his fall. It didn't look like anyone was on the bridge aside from him.

He wasted no time pondering it, however, as he gripped the wooden planks until he'd caught his breath, then scuttled on hands and knees back into the house.

"What happened out there?" Theo asked him. "I heard you cry out."

"The wind knocked me nearly over the edge," he admitted, wiping the rain from his brow. "And I lost my torch."

Theo looked terribly worried. "We've no choice, then," she said softly. "We'll have to wait until morning to look for the Healer."

The storm broke an hour before dawn. Ian and Theo took turns watching over Carl and Eva, and to their great dismay, both patients appeared to be getting worse.

Carl's breathing was labored and wet, and he was no longer conscious. His fever continued to rage even though he shivered underneath the quilt they'd covered him with.

Eva became paler by the hour, and when Ian felt her pulse, he could tell it was growing fainter. They had to continually change her bandage, and the wound was beginning to appear mean and infected.

To make matters worse, the pain in Ian's arm had not subsided even though he was taking care to rest it. In fact, it was beginning to worsen, and he could see that a fair amount of swelling had returned to his hand.

He remembered the voice from the first night he'd spent in Eva's cottage saying that the venom still coursed through him and would come back with a vengeance within a day or two.

Impatient to get them all the help they desperately needed, Ian got up and went to the door. Pulling it open, he looked outside. "It'll be light soon," he said. "And I'll be able to look for the Healer then. She'll fix them. You'll see, Theo. She'll help us."

Theo sat and stroked Eva's hair but said nothing, which Ian found most distressing of all.

Finally, the first gray threads of dawn broke through the darkness. Ian stepped carefully onto the platform, noting that the rain had finally subsided, although the morning was still gloomy and overcast. Holding the sundial up, he was dismayed to find it still too dark to see the shadow, and cursed himself for his folly in losing the torch.

"What have you there?" asked a craggy, weathered voice right next to him.

Ian jerked with a cry of surprise. He whirled around and stared into a face so ancient and wrinkled that it was hard to detect if he was looking at someone human.

"Who are you?" he gasped when he found his voice again.

The ancient one's cheeks seemed to move a bit and a hoarse-sounding laugh gurgled out of her. "Has no one taught you simple manners, lad?"

Ian blinked, realizing he had just been quite rude. "I'm terribly sorry," he said quickly. "It's just . . . you startled me."

The old crone nodded, and then she peered down at the sundial in his hand. "What trinket have you brought to me?"

Ian stared down at his palm and quickly closed his hand over the dial. "Sorry," he said again. "This isn't for you."

The old crone's eyes moved back up to stare quizzically at Ian. "No?" she said, and he shook his head. "Ah, but I thought you had come here looking for a Healer."

Ian's jaw fell open. "*You're* the Healer?" he whispered. And then snatches of memory came back to him. He remembered the first night he'd spent at Eva's cottage and the weathered old voice that had hovered over him as its owner made him better.

"I am," she confirmed. "But I heal no one without payment, lad."

Ian realized she wanted the dial, but he wasn't sure he could part with it. "My friends are very sick," he explained. "We had money, but the Germans took it from us. I know how to get more, though," he added. "And if you'll just come back with us to the keep where I live, we can pay you a handsome reward!"

The crone tilted her chin and laughed merrily. "What use have I for paper money?" she asked him. "No, paper is paper. It holds no value to me. I delight in things, objects, trinkets and such. Pay me in that and we shall see to your healing."

Ian looked back at the sundial in his hand. He considered what else he had to offer the crone, and he knew there were very few choices and only one other thing she might accept. Finally, he decided that he had no choice. He had to get medical attention to Carl and Eva or they would die. It was an easy decision in the end.

Ian opened his palm and offered up the sundial, noticing that there was now just enough light to see the two shadows on its surface, and one indeed was pointing straight at the ancient crone. "This is a magical dial," he told her. "It works much like a compass. If you ask it to find something you're looking for, it will point the way."

The crone reached out with greedy fingers to take the relic, but Ian closed his hand around it before she could claim it. "Will you take this dial as payment for your services?" he asked carefully.

She nodded eagerly. "Yes, yes," she said. "I will consider the debt paid in full."

Ian opened his fingers and stared down one last time at Laodamia's gift. He felt a wave of sadness at having to part with something so special and useful, but he reasoned that he would much rather have Carl well again than a thousand magical objects.

He handed over the relic and the crone snatched it quickly out of his palm; then she did something quite curious. She reached forward and placed her other hand on his injured arm, and Ian was so caught off guard that he simply stood there for a moment, wondering if she might be trying to steady herself. But in the next instant, a cooling sensation traveled from her hand all the way down to his throbbing fingertips. And what was more, the fatigue and weakness he'd been struggling against seemed to flow right out of him. He closed his eyes as these feelings intensified, and he relished in the rejuvenation coursing through him. Ian felt light as a feather and electrified with energy.

He couldn't explain it, but he felt almost as if he'd lived his whole life with only half the vigor and energy that he had now. He wanted the feeling to go on, and on, but too soon the hand on his arm let go and he was left dazed but still pulsing with energy.

Ian opened his eyes and stared down at his hand. The blue tinge that had colored his forearm down to his fingers was gone. Eagerly, he pulled away the dirty bandage that still covered the bite on his arm and saw that save for a mean-looking scar, the injury was completely healed.

"Thank you," he said breathlessly when he met the old crone's eyes again.

"We had a bargain," she told him with a wink.

Ian smiled gratefully before he realized what the crone had actually said. "Wait a moment," he protested as a wave of panic washed over him. "I didn't mean for you to heal *me*. I wanted you to heal my friends. They're in a terrible state, ma'am, and they need your assistance immediately."

The old crone nodded as if she understood perfectly, and moved past him to the door of the tree house. Ian sighed in relief and quickly followed. Theo looked up from her vigil next to Eva and Carl when they entered. "You've found her!" she exclaimed excitedly, and she got up from the floor and hurried over to the crone. "Our friends need your help," she began. "Eva's been shot and her wound is infected. She's lost a great deal of blood and I don't know how much longer she can bear it.

"And Carl has been running a terrible fever for the past two days. Yesterday he was out in the rain and his cough has grown much worse." She paused then and they could all hear the labored, wet breathing coming from the frail lad under the quilt.

The crone moved to Eva and Carl, then lifted the coverlet and inspected Eva's wound before feeling Carl's forehead. "They are both quite close to death," she announced.

Theo took Ian's hand and squeezed it. "Can you help them?"

"Of course I can," she said simply. "But we must first strike a bargain. What trinket do you have to offer me?"

Ian's panic returned, and he knew that somehow, he'd made a horrible mistake. "Ma'am," he began, "I'm terribly sorry, but outside I meant to offer you the sundial in return for healing my friends here. I didn't mean for you to give me any kind of assistance."

Theo looked sharply at Ian. "You gave her the dial?" she whispered. Ian nodded grudgingly. To his great shame, he felt Theo's eyes go to his right arm, and saw her look for the outline of his wound.

But his attention returned to the crone when she came back to stand in front of them. "Our bargain was not struck outside, lad," she told him. "It originated when Eva brought me to you some three nights ago, and I began the process of healing you there. Once I had received my payment, I only needed to complete the transaction."

"But what about our friends?" Theo begged. "Won't you please take the sundial as payment for all three?"

The crone shook her head sadly. "Only one offering per customer," she said. "That is the rule I have honored all these long years. To receive my gift you must offer me a gift in return, something I do not already possess."

Ian's eyes roved over the piles and piles of odds and ends stuffed into the tree house. He realized abruptly that there was exactly one of each item there—no multiples anywhere. "But they'll die without your help!" he said desperately.

The crone nodded. "Yes. They most definitely will, lad."

Ian ran to his knapsack and frantically began to empty its contents in search of anything the crone might accept as payment. Other than a few apples, cheese, and extra batteries for the lost torch, there was not much to offer her. "Does any of this interest you?" he asked, praying that maybe the old crone would take a battery or two.

She shuffled over to him and peered down to inspect his belongings. "No," she said softly. "I have no need for your food, and I've already received one of those." She tapped her foot near one of the batteries.

Ian looked at Theo desperately, hoping she had an idea. She seemed deep in thought, her hand clenched tightly about her crystal, and that gave Ian the answer. Quickly, he pulled at the cord around his neck and lifted the pouch containing the small piece of the Star of Lixus. With shaking fingers, he struggled to open the top and tipped the pouch over, allowing the opal to fall into his palm. "Here!" he said, offering it to her desperately. "Take it!"

The crone bent to inspect the contents of his palm. In answer she reached into the folds of her dark cloak and pulled out a fistful of gemstones. Ian could clearly see a large opal among the collection. "I'm afraid I already have one of those," she told him.

"Wait!" he said, getting to his feet, still attempting to offer her the Star. "You don't understand. This is a magical opal. The wearer is able to understand any language while wearing it."

To his dismay, the crone simply turned away with a chuckle. "I speak every language that has ever been known to man, lad. What need have I to carry such a trinket when I already have one that is far larger and more beautiful?"

Ian let his hand drop to his side. He had nothing left to offer, nothing in his meager belongings that the old crone might be interested in. He knew that she would not heal Carl and Eva, no matter how desperate their situation, without something of value.

A heavy silence fell over the small house, broken only by the terrible rasping of Carl's labored breathing. The crone made a small tsking when neither he nor Theo offered her anything further, and began to move toward the door.

"A moment, if you please!" called Theo.

The crone paused. "Yes?"

"I have something, ma'am. Something of great value. Something I'm certain you don't already have."

The crone turned back to her, clearly interested. "Show me."

Tears streamed down Theo's cheeks and she swallowed hard before reaching behind her neck and unclasping her crystal. She held the beautiful soft pink gem, rimmed in gold, up to the old woman. "This is called the Eye of Zeus. It is the most precious gemstone known to man. It can aid in the development of the seer sense and allow the wearer to know of things that have yet to happen."

The crone's expression was unreadable. She stared, transfixed, as Theo held the crystal aloft and the light from the lantern sparkled off the polished stone. Finally, the crone asked, "Where did you get such a treasure, lass?"

Theo wiped her eyes and inhaled deeply. "My mother gave it to me," she said.

The crone seemed to search Theo's face, as if trying to determine if she spoke the truth. "Your mother?" she asked. Theo nodded. "What is the name of your mother?"

"Jacinda Barthorpe, ma'am."

Again the crone studied Theo, and Ian could tell she was becoming uncomfortable under the peering eyes. "And where is your mother now?"

Theo's eyes flickered to Ian and he cautioned her with a subtle head shake not to reveal too much. "She's . . . ," Theo began. "Back in England, ma'am."

"Alive?" the crone asked, and Ian thought that an odd question.

Theo swallowed and squared her shoulders. "Of course," she replied simply.

It was hard to tell but Ian could swear the crone appeared disappointed. "Ah," she said, holding out her hand for the jewel. Theo placed it gently into the old woman's palm and the crone poked at it for a moment. "I once had a nearly identical crystal that I felt compelled to give away to a wise and beautiful lady, who would eventually see it to its rightful owner. It was the only trinket I have ever given to anyone, in fact, and this is even more surprising considering how much I valued it." With that the crone curled her fingers around Theo's necklace and held it to her chest, as if she treasured it.

After a moment the old woman spoke again. "I have lived longer than any mortal. I have been touched by the greatest good and the darkest evil, and their touch invested in me a great power. The power to heal even the most desperately ill of souls. But this power has come at a terrible price to me personally, and so I have exacted a price for my healing touch. All I have asked throughout the ages was for a trinket, a token, a show of good faith. Those who could or would pay the price received my gift and were grateful. Those who did not . . . perished.

"And while my services have been offered in the most gracious of attitudes, still my restless soul has been tortured. The greatest love of my life has been my darkest enemy and has kept me bound to this forest throughout the ages. I have shouldered that burden all these years alone. And here you come, child, offering me this gift, and I will receive it, for that is the promise I made to myself so long ago."

The crone then placed the crystal within the folds of her cloak, and Ian saw Theo's lips tremble. She looked like she was fighting hard not to cry again. "Which soul am I to heal?" the crone asked abruptly.

Ian's jaw fell open. "Both of them!" he said quickly. "The Eye of Zeus is priceless and should be valuable enough for both of them to be healed!"

The crone's dark eyes bore into his and Ian knew there would be no further argument when she reminded him, "One trinket for one healing. This price cannot be altered."

Ian felt his heart begin to race. They would be able to save only Carl or Eva. "Carl!" he said with a horrible guilty pang. "Save Carl."

The crone looked to Theo. "The girl is the one who offered the trinket," she said. "She should be the one to name who receives my healing."

Ian waited for Theo to say Carl's name, but as she stared at the two under the quilt, he realized she was unsure. He hurried to her side and whispered urgently, "Carl is our friend, Theo. You can't allow him to die!"

Theo stared straight ahead, her fingers near her throat where her pendant used to lie. "Eva was trying to save you," she replied softly. "That's why she took our money, Ian. She was going into the city in search of a trinket to offer the Healer who saved your life. And that's why she came after

336

you when she'd learned you'd left the cottage. She knew the Healer would expect payment, and she didn't believe you had it. She was shot trying to protect you."

Ian was shaking his head; he knew what she was saying. "No," he begged her. "Theo, *please*! Don't let Carl die!"

Theo closed her eyes; turning away from him, to the crone, she whispered, "The girl. Save Eva."

Ian sank to the floor, staring up at her in utter disbelief while the crone moved over to Eva and knelt down. But before she could do anything more, a terrible rumble began to echo through the trees. The three of them held perfectly still, listening as the sound got louder and louder . . . and then stopped.

For several long seconds nothing but the sounds of the birds singing merrily outside came to their ears, but then the quiet of the morning was shattered by a tremendous explosion. It sounded as if a thousand sticks of dynamite had been set off, and the explosion was followed immediately by a rain of debris, which crashed loudly against the surrounding trees, the bridge outside, and the roof over their heads. The crone stood more quickly than her age should have allowed. She ran to the door and threw it open. Ian was right behind her and what he saw was almost too astonishing to believe.

Below the bridge was an enormous tank, its gun aimed menacingly at the lower half of one of the giant stones circling the empty ground. The top half of the stone had already been blown to smithereens. The crone gasped and her hand flew to her heart just as the tank's massive cannon blew apart the lower portion of the stone.

Ian and the crone were thrown backward, and he covered his head with his hands as more debris rained down. When all came to rest again, they heard a familiar voice from outside barking orders and Theo gasped, "That's the colonel that shot Eva! The one who's working with Magus!"

The crone got to her feet and stared in surprise at Theo, as if seeing her for the first time. "What did you say?" she demanded.

"Eva was shot by a German colonel yesterday who said he was looking for a path through the forest."

The crone moved to Theo and gripped her by the shoulders. "What other name did you say, child?" she asked, her eyes wide with panic.

"Magus?" Theo asked timidly. The crone's jaw fell open and Theo was quick to explain. "You must believe me when I tell you that this Magus the Black is a vile and evil sorcerer working to bring about the end of the world!"

The crone released her and stepped back, her breathing rapid and fearful. "He has come," she said hoarsely. And then she focused on Theo and Ian. Slowly, something seemed to dawn on her. She reached into the folds of her cloak and pulled the sundial out. "Where did this come from?" she asked Ian.

Ian couldn't fathom why she needed to know that when outside a tank was blowing apart the crone's forest, but he told her the truth. "It was left to me by an ancient Oracle. A woman named—"

"Laodamia," finished the crone, a faraway look in her eyes.

"Yes," Ian replied, stunned that she knew.

The crone then turned to Theo and asked, "Do you really live with your mother, child?"

Theo's eyes cast down to the floor, and she said, "No, ma'am. I live in an orphange called Delphi Keep."

The crone sighed and lifted her steepled hands to her lips, as if thinking deeply.

Another explosion rocked the small wooden house and Ian had to brace himself against the wall merely to remain standing. When he looked up again, the crone was moving very quickly to Eva. Kneeling down, she lifted the girl into her arms and held her tightly, whispering and rocking her gently back and forth.

Ian's hopelessness returned when he clearly saw color return to the girl's cheeks while his best mate lay unconscious and dying right next to her. Ian felt so tormented by the scene that he moved to the doorway to distract himself by watching what was going on below. The tank had pulverized the first megalith in its path and was moving on to another.

And Ian observed something else that both startled and frightened him. The muddy clearing just below the circular bridge began to churn. He blinked to make sure he wasn't simply seeing things, but as the tank settled before another stone and aimed its turret in front of it, he knew it was all really happening.

He turned back into the house right before the tank fired for the third time, and when the hail of debris had finished, he saw to his amazement that Eva was sitting up, looking robustly healthy and quite surprised.

Behind her the crone was speaking intently to Theo, who was nodding and listening with rapt attention. The old woman then placed something in Theo's hands and folded the girl's fingers over the object. Ian could see a gold chain dangling and was shocked at the thought that perhaps the crone had reconsidered taking the crystal from Theo after all.

The Healer then moved swiftly over to Ian and cupped his face in her hands. "Ian Wigby," she said, and he wondered if Theo had told the old woman his name, "you must listen to me very carefully, because soon there will be no time for talk. You must flee this place; return to your fortress. You will take Eva with you, no matter how she fights you. You must not leave her behind." The crone paused to see if Ian understood, and he nodded.

"Magus the Black has come for my daughter," she said gravely. "Prophecy has ordained his success."

"Your daughter?" Ian asked. "Who is your daughter?"

The crone offered him a sad smile. "Lachestia the Wicked."

Had she not been holding Ian's face, his jaw might have dropped. "How . . . how . . . how is that possible?" he asked her. "*Who* are *you*?"

"My three sisters perished eons ago, but I survived the birth of my child. And the gods help me, I loved my daughter as much as any mother would love her babe, even though from the moment of her birth I knew her to be evil to the core.

"To protect her and others, I've held her here within this

forest for three thousand years. But today the prison I built for her will be destroyed."

As if to emphasize this, outside there was yet another explosion.

Ian's mind wanted to reject these claims. How could this be true? The professor had said that all the maidens who had given birth to Demogorgon's offspring had died. And that had been *well* over three thousand years before. How could any mortal live so long?

The crone regarded him thoughtfully, as if she were reading his mind. "As the years passed, the healing power within me that saved my life during that awful laborious night has grown stronger. It is how I have lived so long. It is why I can heal your friend. And it is also a power I am able to pass along."

"I don't understand," Ian said to her, but even as he said the words, he saw over the crone's shoulder that Eva had moved to Carl and was holding him exactly the way the crone had held her. "Take this," said the old woman, and she let go of Ian's face long enough to press something into his palm. "You will need it for the rest of your journey."

"But . . . ," Ian protested, looking down at his hand to see the sundial, with only one thick shadow on the surface now pointing directly to the left of the crone, where Eva crouched with Carl.

"There is a place that you must go," continued the crone, her speech quickening and her eyes pulling Ian back intently. "It is the place of my birth. It is the place where the Guardian and the One must eventually seek their own truths. Remember that, Ian. You must enter the mist and seek its wisdom. The choice of who goes first will be left to you, but I should think it wise for the Guardian to question the mist before the One."

Ian squinted at the crone. He had no idea what she was talking about.

She smiled sadly again and stroked his hair. "You will understand in time," she assured him. "Take faith that the questions you ask within the mist will be the right ones to ask in the end."

He nodded dully at her and the crone moved away to the door. There she paused to look soberly back at him. "I come from Ynys Môn, Ian. Enter the fog. Search for the answers to unlock your past and see your quest advanced." With that, the crone turned and moved onto the bridge as yet one more explosion rocked their world.

Ian stumbled and fell as the tree holding their house shook violently and a rain of debris pelted the wooden shack. When he looked up again, he had a clear view through the door. The crone stood on the edge of the platform, her arms raised and a strange tumble of words coming out of her mouth. Ian strained to hear what she was saying, but his ears were still ringing from the most recent explosion. With determination, he scrambled to his feet and hurried to the door.

He caught himself in the doorway as yet a fourth stone was blown to pieces. Forced to shield his head from raining debris, he attempted to call out to the crone, but the breath caught in his throat when he realized that below, the earth

342

was no longer simply churning; it was bubbling and roiling as if it were a cauldron of boiling liquid.

Above the ringing in his ears, he heard the sound of a thousand roots being ripped from the ground, and a great gap opened wide to reveal a monstrosity like none he could possibly have imagined.

A giant form lifted itself out of the ground, its skin pinkish gray and wrinkled, with dozens and dozens of roots shooting straight out at odd angles all along its arms, neck, and head. The creature's hair was made of long shanks of gnarled leafless branches, and its face was sharp and pointed, and it reminded Ian of a turnip.

Its black eyes were beady and cruel, and as it rose triumphantly from the ground, Ian realized with a sudden heart-pounding terror that he was looking directly into the eyes of Lachestia the Wicked!

Nearby, the crone stopped her chanting and looked back at him over her shoulder one last time. "I shall leave you one final gift, lad. May it be enough to see Theo to safety." And then the old woman fell forward in a graceful swan dive straight off the platform.

Ian gasped in horror as he attempted to reach out to stop the crone, but he was too late. He watched as she fell in perfect time to the rising of the evil sorceress. The pair met in midair, and Lachestia, wrapping her long spiny arms around the old woman, shouted in triumph when she clutched the crone, and snarled, "Hello, Mummy!"

The sorceress squeezed the crone like a python, crushing the very life right out of her. The old woman struggled in her daughter's arms, and Ian leaned over the lip of the bridge as he cried, "No!" but nothing could help the crone now.

The ancient one's head fell back limply, her mouth hanging open while she gasped for air. And all the while, Lachestia laughed and laughed and sank slowly back toward the earth.

Ian thought for certain that the old woman had already died when, suddenly, the crone raised both her fists high overhead. Something she held in each hand glinted in the morning light. Lachestia stopped laughing abruptly just as the crone brought her fists down sharply, using the last of her strength to plunge two small daggers into her daughter's eyes.

There was a scream so terrible that Ian fell to his knees and covered his ears, barely managing to crawl quickly back into the house. When the noise had mercifully faded away, he looked up into the stunned faces of Theo, Eva, and a very well-looking Carl and announced, "The crone is dead and Lachestia has risen. We must leave at once!"

CHECKMATE

Magus the Black stood still as a statue, lost in thought at the edge of Deadman's Forest. His eyes were closed while he focused on what was happening deep within the trees. There was one individual he was most concerned with, and as he stood there, he could sense her life force flutter out like the flame of a candle against a strong current of air.

Magus smiled evilly. His aunt the crone was dead. And as Lachestia was the only thing capable of killing the crone, that could only mean that the tanks he'd so ingeniously arranged to destroy his sister's prison had accomplished their task. The curse binding his sister had been lifted.

The sorcerer's smile spread even wider. He'd done it. He'd freed the sorceress of earth. And because it was prophesized that Lachestia would kill the Guardian and bring about the fall of the One, Magus's plans were all but complete.

So it was with great confidence that he stepped into the very woods he would not have set foot in even an hour before. The threat to him no longer existed. He had only to meet up with his wicked sister and convince her to find and destroy the Guardian and all would fall into place.

The sorcerer could hardly wait to tell his sire of his great success. And the only thing he looked forward to more was the look on Caphiera's face when she learned of her clever brother's deed. Surely Demogorgon would soon favor Magus above all his siblings.

Screams echoed out of the dark woods and gunfire erupted half a kilometer ahead. Magus's mood improved a fraction more. "Ah," he sighed contentedly as he made his way forward. "The perfect start to a perfect morning. Death, pain, and perhaps later, a bit of torture." And it was with these thoughts that he quickened his pace—not wanting to miss a moment of fun.

LOAM OF GROUND
NO LONGER TAMED

Ian launched himself across the room and lifted Theo off her knees. "We *must* leave here at once!" he repeated.

"What's happening?" Carl asked, his brow still wet but his eyes clear.

"No time to explain," Ian said, holding tightly to Theo's hand while he dashed back to the door. Looking over his shoulder at Carl and Eva, he asked, "Can you both run?"

Eva stood and nodded firmly. Carl wobbled as he got to his feet and nearly fell down again. Eva moved quickly to his side and pulled his arm around her neck. "I'll help him," she promised.

By Ian's side, Theo screamed. Ian whipped his head around to stare down at the ground, which was a churning mass of earth. Small clods of dirt shot into the air and pelted the tank attempting to back up out of the slippery mess. The roiling ground underneath prevented it from making any headway.

A German soldier opened the lid of the tank and they

could all see his wide, frightened eyes while he stared at the ground churning about his panzer. Suddenly, a gap directly underneath the tank opened and began to spread wider and wider, until the armored vehicle tipped onto its side and fell into the chasm with the soldier clinging desperately to it. In the next instant the ground closed up, and with a tremendous crunch, both the tank and its driver were no more.

Other soldiers on the ground dashed forward out of the woods to investigate, and as they drew close to the point where the tank had just been, small gaps in the earth opened underneath their very feet, and one by one, they began to disappear into their own early graves.

Ian and the others were too stunned by the scene below to move for several moments, especially when one soldier darted away from a hole only to be caught by a large spiny hand that erupted out of the earth and pulled him kicking and screaming underground.

"Gaw!" he heard Carl gasp. "That's frightful!"

It was all Ian needed to hear to pull him out of his own horrified stupor. "Come on!" he called, and moved out onto the platform, searching for the tree that held the ladder. But as they approached it, the earth beneath the trees that suspended the wooden bridge began to churn, causing the trees to pitch, as if the trees were being torn out by their very roots. And then the branches began to sag and dip inward, and the bridge that Ian and the others were on buckled and started to crumble.

"We can't go that way!" Theo shouted as the tree with

the ladder pitched forward and creaked in a slow fall down. "Run the other way!"

They turned as one and bolted for the opposite end. Behind them Ian heard a crash as branches snapped and limbs broke away from their trunks. The platform they were on started to break apart right underneath them, and Ian felt like he was running uphill. "Get to that tree!" he cried, pointing to one that supported a rope ladder.

He pulled Theo roughly along, willing himself to make it in time. They had mere meters to go when more crashing sounded and their platform pitched sideways, nearly dislodging all four of them.

Ian flattened himself against the wood and gripped the top edge tightly with one hand while holding on to Theo with the other. She screamed in terror and he prayed that he could hold on to her long enough to swing her back toward the platform. He saw Eva and Carl pitch forward and he cried out as they both swung over the top of the planks and disappeared from view.

"Carl!" he shouted. *"Carl!"*

"We're here!" he heard his friend call back from just below him.

Ian let out an anxious breath and concentrated on pulling Theo to safety. He swung her into his torso and said, "Use me to climb up!"

Theo clung to his shoulder and slowly worked her way to the top of the planks. Ian then pulled himself up and looked over the edge. Eva and Carl were dangling precariously on a nearby branch. "Can you make it to the ladder?" he asked them, pointing to the rope and wooden rungs, which were nearly within their reach.

Carl turned his head awkwardly, sweat glistening on his forehead as he swung himself up to straddle the branch before helping Eva up too. "I believe so," he said, motioning for Eva, who was in front of him, to go first. Ian saw that she was terrified, but she managed to move down the branch toward the rope. He hoped anxiously that she would get there before the tree they were in tumbled to the ground.

Below them, more and more soldiers were shouting in terror as they attempted to run away from the whirlpool of swirling earth. It seemed that every few seconds another of them was sucked down into the dirty depths.

Ian urged Eva to hurry. He knew they were running out of time. The brave girl scooted her way closer and closer, then stopped just feet away from the ladder, which was hanging at an odd angle away from the branch. "I can't!" she said, her voice hoarse. "I can't reach it!"

"Try!" Ian commanded. "Eva! You've got to try!"

The poor girl began to sob and she shook her head vigorously. "I'll miss it!"

Carl had moved right up behind her and he was doing his best to coax her along. "Just reach one arm out, Eva," he said calmly. "One hand to stretch to the ladder is all it will take. You won't fall. I'll hold on to you. I promise."

But Eva's panic was rising and she continued to cry and shake her head. "Carl!" Ian yelled, his heart racing as he felt their time running out. "*Make* her grab the rope!"

Carl ignored him and continued to speak softly to her. To Ian's immense relief, the method worked. Eva finally reached a tentative hand out, stretching for the rope, but just as her fingers were within reach of it, the platform gave another tremendous jolt and he and Theo were sent over the top again.

Theo lost her grip and fell. Ian reached frantically for her and just managed to catch her by the arm. She screamed and begged for him not to let go as she dangled twenty feet above the swirling ground.

But Ian's own grip on the platform was slipping, and he knew he could no longer hold both their weight. He looked about frantically for something nearby and saw that Carl had got Eva safely onto the rope ladder and was inching his way back down the branch toward him and Theo. "Hold on, mate!" Carl called. "I'm coming!"

But Ian didn't know if he *could* hold on. He closed his eyes and focused all his effort on gripping the platform. His fingers were numb and his arm throbbed with the strain. And then, by some miracle, Theo's weight was lifted from his grasp. He opened his eyes and saw Carl balancing atop the branch right under them as he brought her down to the safety of the branch.

Ian immediately reached up and grabbed the platform with his other hand, panting with the effort. "Ian!" Carl called, using his arms to balance on the branch. "I believe I can help you down as well! Just let go and I'll try and catch you, mate!"

Ian assessed the branch Carl was teetering on. Theo was

safely moving her way along the branch, but he worried that his weight would be too much for Carl to hold while keeping his balance on the branch, and they'd likely both fall off as a result. "No," he told him, straining to hold on to the platform. "Get Theo down, Carl! I'll find my own way!"

Carl gave him a worried frown, but he sat down to straddle the branch again and inch his way along to help Theo to the rope ladder.

Ian looked back up and tried to get his leg over the top of the platform, but it was too high and he was too tired. He hung there for a moment and tried to think about what to do, when to his immense relief, the platform began slowly to pitch sideways. Ian hauled himself onto the plank and waited for the movement to stop.

The bridge sank lower and lower, and he heard the supports snap one by one away from the trees that held it. His relief was short lived, because as the section he was perched atop sank several meters slowly at first, it quickly picked up momentum until it crashed to the ground.

Ian fell on top of the planks with a teeth-rattling thud, and the tree to his right tumbled to the earth beside him— a large branch nearly taking his head off. When the dust settled, he peeked warily about at his surroundings and froze.

Looming menacingly in front of him was the giant form of Lachestia, fully free from her earthen cradle, looking positively terrifying. The sorceress was even taller than she'd appeared to him earlier, at least eight feet tall, with elongated bony arms that stuck out from her wormy-looking torso as her grotesque head swiveled back and forth, as if searching for more victims.

Ian caught and held his breath as she hovered over him. He noted brown ooze dribbling down her cheeks, leaking out of her eye sockets. The sorceress's lips were pulled back in a tight grimace, exposing her sharp pointed teeth, and she was making loud heaving sounds as if in great pain.

Her mother had obviously blinded her—but Ian wondered if, in doing so, the crone had enraged the sorceress beyond all reason. He thought that in her current furious state, she was likely far more dangerous than she had been when she could see.

Ian held very, very still as he watched her, terrified that she would sense where he was standing and drag him under the earth like she had the soldiers. The sorceress appeared to be listening carefully for any sound that might indicate another victim was nearby.

Lachestia resorted next to sniffing the air, and with great dread, he realized she had likely picked up his scent. He made an attempt to crouch low, hoping the branches of the fallen tree would hide him if she decided to reach out with her hands and feel about.

The sorceress made a grumbling sound and then she did stretch out her hands. She sniffed again and patted the ground a meter to Ian's right. He considered running for it, but he knew she would hear his footfalls and swallow him up faster than he could get away.

He watched, wide-eyed and terrified, as she felt the

leaves of the tree, then the branches, then the planks of the wood nearby. Ian braced himself. She would find him at any moment, and his mind raced to come up with some way to distract her. Then, right in front of him, he spied a loose chunk of rock from one of the megaliths and carefully picked it up. The sorceress's hand made a clapping sound as it connected with the edge of his section of platform, and Ian took the opportunity to whip the rock over the sorceress's shoulder. It landed with a *whump* just behind her.

Faster than Ian would have thought possible, Lachestia whirled around and pounced on the rock. A hail of earth and debris exploded into the air as she disappeared with it underground. Ian wasted no more time watching her; he broke away from the platform and ran for all his life.

"Ian!" he heard voices calling. "Over here!"

Ian looked to his right and saw Theo, Carl, and Eva safe on the ground some twenty meters away, but before he could even react, there was a terrible rumbling behind him and the ground under his feet began to vibrate. It felt as if a train were approaching. Ian tried to lean into his stride to gain momentum, but the vibrations underfoot only intensified and his feet began to slip, slide, and sink.

He knew he was unlikely to make it to his friends, and even if he did, Lachestia would surely gobble all of them up. He had the macabre thought that this must be what Laodamia had been talking about in her last prophecy: how his end would come at Lachestia's hand. He also remembered that the Oracle had prophesized that if he was killed, then Theo would surely die, and Ian wasn't about to let that happen.

So he changed course and began running away from the three terrified faces watching him in horror. "Get Theo to the portal!" he yelled at Carl, and didn't wait for his friend's response. Instead, he dashed back to the ravine they'd been kicked into earlier, willing himself not to slip and fall before he got there.

Racing straight toward the drop-off point, he increased his speed in the last few strides and launched himself high into the air, landing on the far rocky side without room to spare. He hit the ground hard and rolled, tumbling over onto his side only to see the mighty sorceress burst straight out of the earth behind him and slam headfirst into a rock on his side of the ravine. The impact was so hard that it rattled and shook the earth where Ian was lying. The sorceress shrieked in pain and her nails clawed their way down the side of the ravine while she cursed and growled and snarled in anger. Finally, she landed at the bottom, sending a flurry of sticks and leaves and dirt high up into the air.

Ian watched her for a moment before he decided to waste no more time. Scrambling to his feet, he began moving again, searching for a place to hide. Ahead he saw a large boulder and clambered up on top of it; then he held perfectly still, trying to keep from breathing too loudly. He could hear the sorceress thrashing about in the ravine, her growls and snarls like a crazed wild animal's.

Then there were more digging sounds and Ian held his

breath. From the top of his boulder, he could see the earth all around swirl and ripple like water. He crouched down and waited with his heart thundering.

He knew that the evil sorceress was about to erupt out of the ground again; he just didn't know when or where. And then, to make a desperate situation even worse, a gunshot echoed from nearby at almost the exact moment something hot buzzed right past his neck. At first he was too stunned to move, but another pop and a chunk of rock from the boulder kicked up into his face made the situation crystal clear— someone was shooting at him!

Ian moved to the lee side of the boulder and lowered himself over the edge, hoping it was enough to give him cover. He knew he couldn't step on the ground without alerting Lachestia to his position, and he hated to think what she'd do to him when she sucked him into her earthly grave.

Another shot resounded across the forest and loud voices called back and forth to each other. Ian flattened himself as best he could against the far side of the boulder, but just behind him he heard a sucking sound. Glancing awkwardly over his shoulder, he saw to his immense horror that, smeared in mud and looking as frightful as anything Ian had ever seen, the sorceress was standing right beside him!

Terrified, Ian faced forward again, attempting to make himself as small as possible. He dared not breathe, but his heart was pounding so hard against his chest that he felt certain Lachestia would hear it.

He tried to calm himself, but his grip on the rock was

becoming more difficult to hold now that his palms were sweating. The sounds around him grew louder as more shouting echoed across the forest. The sorceress growled low in her throat, a noise that raised goose pimples along Ian's arms.

"There!" someone shouted. "Over there!"

"Shoot it!" someone else commanded.

A loud bang echoed from the other side of the wood, and a bullet whizzed past Ian a mere instant before he heard a soft, wet thwack.

Lachestia screamed and the noise brought tears of pain to Ian's eyes. It was so shrill and sharp he wanted desperately to cover his ears, but that would mean letting go of the boulder and he couldn't do that.

Eventually, the sorceress stopped her screech and Ian felt a whirl of air as she moved quickly back underground. "What is happening?" a stern voice from the forest demanded and Ian could swear he recognized it.

"I . . . I . . . don't know, Colonel. There is an entire battalion missing. Eighteen men and one tank came under attack somewhere across that ravine. One of the survivors claims that a creature rose up from underground and buried the men and the tank alive."

"Where is this survivor?"

"We sent him back across the border, Colonel."

"What are you shooting at?"

"There was someone over there by that boulder," said the soldier. "We assumed it was the enemy and opened fire."

There was a pause, then he replied, "I see no bodies,

Lieutenant." And with that, Ian heard the cracking of twigs and leaves as footsteps came through the underbrush. Ian felt his fingers slipping, and he tried to hold on, but he had to reach up and adjust his grip on the boulder. One of the men coming toward him must have seen it, because the footsteps halted and the German colonel shouted, "You there! Come out from behind that boulder with your hands up!"

Ian was shaking with both fatigue and fright. He knew that if he let go of the rock, the sorceress would pounce. He also knew that if he showed himself to the Germans, he would be shot. "Come out now or we will open fire!" added the colonel.

Ian closed his eyes. He was out of options. He would be either shot or sucked down into the ground by the sorceress. The only decision now was selecting which way to die.

After thinking for a brief moment, he considered that being shot might get the deed over with more quickly and perhaps even be less painful. So with great regret he pulled himself up on top of the boulder and stood with his arms raised.

Below him glowered the colonel with about twenty men, including the sergeant who had spared his life just the day before. The colonel seemed to realize this as well, because after taking one long look at Ian, he turned to the sergeant, raised his pistol, and shot his own man.

A hushed, stunned silence fell on the entire group as the soldier fell face-first to the ground with a loud *whump!*

The colonel swiveled, his gun still raised as he pointed it up at Ian. "This time, *I* shall make certain you die, spy!"

Ian closed his eyes, shaking from tip to toe atop the boulder, his arms still pitifully raised above his head. His heart continued to hammer away and he tried to think of something peaceful in his final moment before death, but nothing other than the angry rat face of the colonel filled his mind.

As Ian waited to die, he quickly became aware that the shot that was supposed to kill him had not yet come. He wondered what the German colonel was waiting for, so he risked opening one eye to take a peek.

But when he looked, he saw only a large hole in the earth where the colonel had been a moment before and the stunned pale faces of the soldiers standing nearby. And then pandemonium ensued.

Some men shouted and ran; others pointed their rifles at the ground, which Ian noticed was once again swirling; still more men trembled but otherwise did not move. And then, one by one, the soldiers began to disappear. Lachestia claimed the German soldiers who'd been standing closest to the colonel first, and moved her way outward, attacking each man in turn.

Ian stood on his rock, petrified, as the muffled cries of the victims filled the surrounding forest with panic and fear. He saw some soldiers throw their rifles down as they ran. Others shot directly into the earth but were still unable to get away; nearly the entire battalion was quickly and efficiently buried alive, save for the man shot by the colonel himself. Besides Ian, that soldier was the only body who remained aboveground.

With some guilt, Ian focused his attention on the prone figure lying just a few meters away from him. He couldn't tell if the soldier was still breathing, but he knew he had to find out. So when the earth rumbling around him moved off into the distant forest in search of two fleeing soldiers, Ian slid very carefully to the ground and crept forward on tiptoe to the soldier's side.

Kneeling down, he carefully rolled the man onto his back and found him conscious but clearly in pain. He'd suffered a gunshot to the left side of his abdomen, and Ian doubted he'd live more than an hour or two without medical attention. "I'm going to get help," he whispered to the man. "I know someone who might be able to heal you."

The soldier gripped his arm. "The curse is loose!" he gasped. "Leave me! Save yourself. Get out of this forest while you can!"

Ian, however, was not to be dissuaded. This soldier had risked his own life to save them, and he felt indebted to the man. "Stay here," he instructed. "I'll be back soon."

But the soldier would not let him go. "No!" he insisted. "The curse will kill you if you come back!"

"I've no choice," Ian told him. "You saved our lives. I'm not leaving you to die here alone."

The sergeant was hissing through his teeth, obviously in a great deal of pain. "Help me to my feet," he whispered.

Ian eyed him doubtfully, but the soldier pulled on Ian's

shoulder, determined to stand. The two of them got to their feet and, with the sergeant leaning heavily on Ian, made their way out of the small clearing.

Ian managed to pull the sundial from his pocket, and saw with some surprise that the dial still showed a shadow across the surface. "Sundial," he whispered, "show the way to Theo, Carl, and Eva." The shadow did not choose a new direction; instead, it thickened slightly and began to pulse. With careful, slow steps, Ian and the wounded German made their way closer to Ian's friends.

They walked as softly as they could, listening intently to the sounds of the forest. Periodically, there were short bursts of noise—gunfire, shouts, screams of terror. Ian knew that wherever these sounds were coming from, Lachestia was at their center, and he was grateful that for the moment, all of them seemed to be well away from where the dial was leading them.

After a time, Ian thought he began to recognize their surroundings, and as they emerged from behind a huge tree, he was certain that the small patch of gray and red in the distance was Eva's cottage.

"We're nearly there," he said encouragingly to the wounded man.

"I don't know how much farther I can go," confessed the soldier.

With his free arm, Ian pointed. "Do you see that? We just need to make it to that cottage and you'll be right as rain."

The soldier said nothing more as they moved stealthily

ever closer to the little house. But when they got to the yard, Ian stopped short. He heard someone wailing desperately from inside, and felt his heart plummet. "Oh, no!" he whispered, immediately worried that something had happened to Theo or Carl.

"What is it?" the soldier groaned, clutching his side in pain.

But Ian couldn't take time to explain. Instead, he lowered the soldier carefully to the ground, promising, "I'll be right back!" And then he dashed as fast as he could to the house, throwing open the door.

The inside presented a chaotic scene. It appeared that every stick of furniture had been damaged or destroyed. Clothing was torn and strewn about, and bits of china lay scattered all across the floor.

In the center of the mess sat Eva, cradling the prone figure of her grandmother and rocking back and forth while she wailed pitifully. Next to her sat Theo, trying her best to comfort the girl. In the corner sat Carl, teary eyed and looking terribly forlorn until he saw Ian, at which point he shouted and flew out of his chair, rushing over to his friend. "Ian! You're all right!"

Ian offered him a half smile and assured him that he was fine. No sooner had he done so than he felt Theo wrap her arms tightly about his waist. "Thank heavens," she said. "I was desperately worried!"

"I'm quite well," he insisted, his eyes never straying from Eva, who continued to cry inconsolably and hug her grandmother. Ian saw now how pale and lifeless the old woman was and he understood with a terrible certainty what must have happened.

"We came back and found her like that," Carl whispered. "Poor old thing—she never had a chance."

"Eva feels responsible," Theo whispered. "She believes that if she'd been here when the soldiers came that she could have saved her grandmother."

Ian shook his head. "She'd have been killed too," he told her, loudly enough for Eva to hear.

The poor Polish girl lifted her head, tears running down both cheeks, and she sobbed, "I'm too late! Too late!"

Ian gave Theo's shoulder a squeeze, moved over to Eva, and squatted down next to her. "It's not your fault," he said gently. "The soldiers would have killed you too if you'd been here."

Eva continued to sob and bowed her head, lost in her grief. Ian stood and addressed his friends quietly. "Lachestia is killing anything that moves out in the forest," he told them. "She very nearly had me, but a group of soldiers distracted her."

"What happened to the soldiers?" Carl asked.

"She killed them all," he said frankly. "Except the man who helped save our lives. He was shot by his own colonel and left to die."

"The sergeant who pretended to shoot us?" Theo asked in amazement.

Ian nodded. "I've brought him back here."

"You've brought him *here?*" Carl demanded. "Why would you do such a blooming foolish thing, mate?"

Ian shifted uncomfortably. "He saved our lives, Carl. We owe him as much."

"He's the *enemy*!" Carl shouted angrily. "And he or his mates did *that* to Eva's grandmother!" Carl pointed at the poor lifeless woman on the ground.

Ian sighed and turned to look at the yard. Through the door he could see the soldier still lying where he'd left him, struggling just to remain still while the wound in his abdomen caused him great pain. "We have to help him," Theo said, and Ian noticed that she too was peering outside.

Carl threw his hands up. "I'll have nothing to do with it!"

Ian looked at Eva, who had obviously overheard their conversation. Gently, she lowered the lifeless body of her grandmother, smoothed out her hair, and got up. "Where is he?" she asked softly.

Ian felt a rush of relief. "He's just inside the yard," he said quickly. "I know that you can heal him, Eva. The crone passed her gift on to you—"

Ian was cut short when Eva moved past him through the door. It was only then that he noticed she'd picked up a poker from near the fireplace and was walking with purpose toward the soldier.

"No!" shouted Theo. "Ian, stop her!"

Ian flew out of the cottage after Eva with Carl and Theo close on his heels. He reached the Polish girl quickly and grabbed for the poker, but Eva was stronger and more determined than he expected. She held on to her weapon firmly and pushed and shoved and kicked at Ian for all she was worth. "Stop it!" he yelled at her. "Stop it, Eva! He didn't do this! He's not the one who killed your grandmother!" With one final tug he managed to wrench the poker out of her hand, and he flung it away to land in the grass nearby.

Eva reacted by lunging at Ian, attacking him with her fists and her feet, pummeling, kicking, and beating him, all the while crying uncontrollably. He braced himself as best he could and took her blows without protest. He allowed her every kick, every punch until the poor girl was exhausted. And then he took her by the shoulders firmly but gently and forced her to look at him. "It won't bring her back."

Eva collapsed into his arms, clinging to him while she sobbed. He'd comforted Theo enough over the years to know how to pat Eva's back gently and tell her it was going to be all right.

But the moment was cut short when a hoarse and unsettling voice broke the stillness of the woods. "Well, well, well! What have we here?"

Ian immediately let go of Eva and turned defensively toward the voice that he knew all too well.

On the other side of the lawn stood the cloaked, smoky figure of Magus the Black. "How delightful to find such a prize within the forest!"

"Theo," Ian whispered urgently while still facing Magus, "take Eva. Get to the portal. Run as fast as you can, and do not look back."

"What about you?" she asked desperately.

"Don't worry about me," he told her firmly. "Now *go!*"

Theo took Eva by the hand and began to run. No sooner had they taken a few steps away than Ian raced to the nearby poker, picking it up to raise it above his head and run straight at the sorcerer. He had taken only three strides when he felt his insides begin to burn. He fought against the pain and forced himself to take two more steps. The heat increased and he doubled over, shaking as he struggled to hold on to the poker in his hand.

Behind him he heard a scream and smelled the oaky scent of burning leaves. Ian gulped for air and lifted his foot, wobbling as he pushed forward one additional step. Then another. Then another. He was within ten feet of the sorcerer, who smiled delightedly at him, exposing those horrible jagged teeth. "Well, well," said the sorcerer again as Ian raised his shaking hand, holding the poker. "It's not everyone who can ignore the pain of my heat, but then, no mortal has ever stood against the full power of my touch." With that, the sorcerer raised his arms. Ian focused hard through the increasing waves of pain radiating through him. He lifted his weapon higher and took one . . . more . . . step.

In the next instant, a mass of movement approached from the forest, and abruptly, the pain coursing through him vanished. The switch was so immediate that it left Ian frightfully dizzy, and he fell to the ground while the world about him swirled and chaos quickly followed.

THOSE YOU LEAVE
CANNOT BE SAVED

Ian lay on his back, gasping for air. As he stared upward, his vision began to close in around him, but he fought against the darkness. And then Carl was beside him, tugging on Ian's arm. "Get up!" he commanded. "Come on, mate! Get to your feet and run!"

Ian reached for Carl's hand and was yanked to his feet. He immediately became aware of dozens of men charging through the yard, running for their lives, shouting in terror. In the chaos, he realized that Magus the Black had been derailed from finishing him off by a cluster of men who had all barreled into him on their mad dash through the forest.

Ian decided not to wait around for the sorcerer to recover himself. Instead, he forced his feet to move as Carl continued to yank on his arm, hurrying in the direction he'd sent Theo and Eva. But then he remembered the poor wounded soldier and he turned to see the man also struggling to get up. He looked desperate and terrified and Ian knew he couldn't leave him behind.

He pulled away from Carl and darted over to the soldier. "We'll have to run," he said as he swung the soldier's arm about his neck. "But it's not far. And then we'll get you to a doctor as quickly as possible," he assured him.

The man groaned when they began to move. "The curse!" he said hoarsely. "It's coming!"

As if to confirm that statement, a loud rumble echoed from the forest and Ian heard screams as men were sucked under the earth by the terrible sorceress just below the surface. Ian risked looking back as the shouting and cries of panic intensified. The noise sounded as if it was coming closer, and to his astonishment, he saw Magus the Black free himself from the tangle of soldiers and swirling soil that had entered the yard. "Arise, my sister!" Magus commanded. "Arise and greet your brother, for I have come to fr—"

The sorcerer said no more. Instead, just like all the others, he was sucked unceremoniously belowground.

Ian wanted to laugh, and if he hadn't been so afraid of the approaching sorceress, he would have stopped to applaud. But he had to get everyone to the portal and the soldier was slowing him down. Just as Ian began to wonder if they'd reach it in time, Carl appeared and pulled the man up by the other shoulder. "It's that way!" Carl told Ian, pointing to an outcropping of rock with a small cave at its center, just visible through two massive tree trunks.

Ian squinted and saw the figures of Theo and Eva crouch and dart into the cave. He prayed that the portal would be open and that at the very least, the girls would reach safety.

He also hoped that the hellhound would be gone from the other side when they got through.

The rumbling behind them grew louder. "The soil!" Carl shouted, and Ian could feel it too. The dirt underneath their feet began to loosen and become slippery.

"Keep going!" Ian ordered. "We've got to make it to the portal!"

Ahead of them Theo appeared from the mouth of the cave. Spotting them, she shouted, "Run! Run for your lives! The portal is open!"

Ian gritted his teeth; the soldier was having a terrible time keeping up with the younger boys' strides. "Let me go!" the German panted. "Drop me and save yourselves!"

"We're almost there!" Carl shouted. "Come on, mate! We can make it!"

Fast footfalls approached. Someone was running up right behind them, but Ian dared not look back to see who it was, lest he lose some of the forward momentum they needed to reach the portal. The footsteps continued, coming closer and closer, until he was sure the stranger would run right into them, but at the last moment, there was a loud shriek and a gasp of pain and surprise, and then the footfalls were no more.

"She's right behind us!" Carl yelled.

"Run, run, *run*!" Theo begged.

And then the surging energy bubbling along behind them seemed to swell the ground underneath, and Ian, Carl, and the soldier were pushed upward with the earth before it moved forward and away. Ian could hardly believe their luck! Somehow the sorceress had missed the trio, but his relief was short lived, because in the next instant, a great explosion thrust dirt and fire high into the air and he and his companions were thrown sideways.

They landed in a tumble, and Ian, struggling to untangle his limbs from Carl and the soldier, sat up only to discover Magus the Black, smeared with dirt, his black cloak smoldering with hot embers, standing angrily not ten meters away.

He barely had time to take in the sight when Lachestia herself shot to the surface, spraying her brother with even more sticky wet clods.

"Enough!" Magus roared at her, and a flame shot out of his palm, scorching the sorceress's branchlike arm.

Lachestia hissed and buried her limb in the ground, dousing the flame. "Three *thousand* years, Magus?" she screeched, her voice sending a chill down Ian's spine. "You left me here for *three thousand years?*"

"I had not the means to free you, you fool!" he shouted back at her. "And if you had taken care to kill your *own* mother at birth like the rest of us, then you would never have been imprisoned from the start!"

Ian felt a tug on his shirt and tore his eyes away from the warring siblings now circling each other menacingly. "Let's go!" Carl whispered.

Ian reached for the soldier, who was still lying in the dirt. "Leave me!" he mouthed.

Ian shook his head firmly and he lifted the man's arm

over his head. "Now, come on," he whispered. "We've only a short way to go."

Carl took the other side and together they lifted the wounded man and the three set off, crouching low while giving Magus and Lachestia a wide berth.

The sorcerer was still trying to reason with his sister. "The time for our sire's uprising is at hand!" he said, darting away when the blind sorceress tried to tackle him.

"What do I care for Demogorgon's idle causes?" she spat.

"You will care when he is free from the underworld!" Magus argued, throwing another burst of flame just to the left of his sister when she got too near.

Ian's heart was racing. They were very close to the portal now, and it seemed that Magus and Lachestia were far too preoccupied with each other to notice them.

But just as they were taking their final steps, he heard Magus say, "And I have freed you to ensure you carry out your destiny, Lachestia. The Guardian is at hand! You have only to kill him and your place in our father's kingdom will be assured!"

A cold knot of fear formed in Ian's chest and it seemed a stillness had abruptly come over the forest all around them. "The Guardian?" Lachestia inquired. "The Guardian is in *my* forest?"

"Hurry!" Carl urged.

"To your right, my sister!" Magus called triumphantly. "Kill the Guardian and fulfill your destiny!"

Theo waved to them frantically from the opening to the portal. *"Quickly!"* she screamed, and Ian saw with dread that

371

she appeared to be looking just past them. "Lachestia is coming!"

Ian hoisted the soldier's arm higher onto his neck. "Hurry!" he shouted, and leaned into his stride to gain some speed.

But just as it looked as if they were going to reach the cave, the soldier did the most surprising thing: just before the opening, he lifted his arms and wrenched himself away from Ian and Carl. The boys were left to stumble the rest of the way, and it was only by sheer luck that they were able to maintain their footing. Ian twisted round while he struggled to stay upright, and looked back at the soldier. The German was no longer running. Instead, he was standing between them and the ever-increasing rush of moving earth that was rising behind them like a tidal wave.

He gave Ian a sad smile. "Save yourselves," he told them, and turned toward the great dark approaching menace. The soldier wavered on his feet but remained upright, and then he stomped his foot, as if trying to gain the sorceress's attention.

"Noooooooo!" Ian shouted, but Carl had hold of his arm and pulled him forcefully toward the mouth of the cave.

"It's too late!" Carl shouted as he struggled to pull Ian to safety. "Let him go, mate! It's too late!"

Ian staggered into the mouth of the cave, his attention remaining on the soldier now beyond his reach. He watched in horror as Lachestia the Wicked rose from her mass of dirt to hover high above the soldier, triumph playing on her terrible features.

The soldier bravely stomped his foot again, holding her attention. "My destiny!" the sorceress shouted, raising her arms high as she began her slow descent straight down on top of the figure at her feet.

In the next instant, a solid rock wall appeared right in front of Ian's nose and he stumbled back. The rest of the scene within the forest was lost to him, and Ian turned away while the verse from Laodamia's prophecy rang hauntingly through his mind.

> *Fly away, back to your cave*
> *Those you leave cannot be saved . . .*

YNYS MÔN

Ian, Theo, Carl, and Eva sat in stunned silence for long moments after the portal closed. Ian continued to stare blankly at the wall, silently cursing Demogorgon and his horrible offspring. Behind him, he could hear shuffling, and a moment later he felt Theo sit next to him and lay her head on his shoulder. After a bit she asked, "Are you all right?"

Ian swallowed hard. "Yes," he said hoarsely.

"The beast is gone," Carl told them. "At least, I think it's gone."

Ian sighed heavily. He then got to his feet, helping Theo up as well, and moved over to where Carl was standing, peering out between the bars at the morning mist gathering about the stairs. Ian strained his ears, listening for any sound of the predator beyond the bars.

He heard birds chirping happily as the first smoky tendrils of dawn brought a hint of light to the top of the steps. Ian had awakened before sunrise enough to know that it must be nearly five in the morning. He estimated that their

374

group had gone through the portal sometime near one a.m. Therefore, only four hours had passed—if this was still the same day they had left, of course. For all he knew, it could be days later, just like it was in Poland. Time was a strange thing when it came to the portal, so he was hardly sure.

"Carl," he said.

"Yes, mate?"

"Do you still have the key to the lock?"

Carl patted his trouser pockets and, after sorting through the contents, lifted the key up. "Here you are."

Ian took it and inserted it into the bulky lock. "We'll have to move as quietly as possible," he warned them.

"But what if the beast is still lurking about the castle grounds?" Theo asked, sounding worried.

"We'll avoid the grounds," Ian told her. "And it's too dangerous to risk running the kilometer back to the keep."

"Then where are we going?" Carl asked.

"To the schoolmasters' cottage," Ian told them. "Their house is just a short sprint across the downs. And Eva can help Thatcher when we arrive." His eyes swiveled to the shadowy figure of the Polish girl sitting with her back against the wall and her face buried in her knees, crying, "Oh, Babi! How could I have left you?"

Ian took pity on her and moved over to crouch down next to her. "I'm terribly sorry about your grandmother."

Eva lifted her face, and Ian could just make out the glint of tears running down her cheeks. "Thank you," she said, her voice cracking. Ian waited while she gathered herself and stood wiping her face and sniffling loudly. After a moment she asked, "Where are we?"

"We're in England," he told her. "Dover, England, to be exact."

Eva stared at him, openmouthed. "How?"

"I can explain everything to you later, Eva," he assured her. "Right now, I've several friends who dearly need your help. They're all very sick, you see, like Carl was before you made him well. Will you help us?"

Eva said nothing for several moments. Instead, she looked first at Ian, then at Theo, and finally at Carl. "Yes," she said wearily. "Take me to them, and I'll see what I can do."

Ian led the way out of the portal gate and up the stone stairs. He paused at the top, listening and smelling the air carefully for any hint of sulfur or unnatural movement.

Nothing unusual aroused his senses. "Come on," he whispered, and moved quickly but quietly through the small patch of wood and out into the open. There he and Carl paused to look this way and that, sniffing the air again. Finally, they nodded at each other, satisfied that it was safe.

With haste the foursome darted across the hilly terrain and steadily made their way to a quaint little cottage near the edge of the earl's property. All was dark inside and a very large sign was nailed to the front door. It read UNDER QUARANTINE. KEEP OUT!

Ian ignored the sign, approached the door, and knocked loudly. When no one answered, he pounded more earnestly until the door was yanked open and a very ruffled-looking schoolmaster stared down at him with a mixture of alarm and anger. "My word!" he gasped when he saw Ian and his companions at the front door. "Ian, you've broken your quarantine! I demand to know why you've done such a terribly foolish thing!"

"We've been through the portal, sir," Ian said quickly, "and we've brought back the Healer." He moved aside so that Perry could clearly see Eva, who was standing with a confused look on her face just behind him.

"You've . . . *what?*" Perry nearly shouted. "But the earl forbade you from going anywhere near there!"

Ian frowned. "I know, sir," he said. "But it couldn't be helped. We had to find the Healer and bring her back with us."

Perry rubbed his eyes, as if he wasn't quite sure if he was awake or still dreaming.

"How is your brother?" Theo asked.

Perry ran his hand through his hair anxiously. "He's in terrible shape," he admitted. "Simply terrible."

"Then won't you please let us come in and allow our Healer to tend to him?"

Perry seemed to realize he was still blocking the door. "Yes, yes," he said, stepping aside and waving them forward. "Come in before anyone sees that I've also broken the quarantine."

Ian, Carl, Theo, and Eva hurried inside, although Eva still looked quite out of sorts and awfully confused. Ian suspected that it might be due to their schoolmaster's appearance, but he found out the real reason when he overheard her ask Carl, "What is everyone saying?"

Carl smiled kindly and reached for the cord about his neck that held the pouch with the Star of Lixus in it. "Here," he said, taking it off and handing it to her. "Wear this and all will be clear."

"What language is Carl speaking?" Perry asked.

"Polish," Ian told him.

Perry gasped. *"Polish?"*

Theo took their astonished schoolmaster by the hand. "Come, sir, let's get you some tea, as we have much to share with you."

An hour later, after they'd told the tale of their adventure through the portal to their schoolmaster over some delicious breakfast tarts and tea, Perry sat pinching the bridge of his nose tightly between his fingers as if struggling with the sheer volume of all they had recently been through. "I do not know that you should share the full extent of your exploits through the portal with the earl."

"Why not, sir?" Ian asked, confused why his schoolmaster would want him to keep anything from the earl.

Perry leveled a look at him. "Because he's likely to murder you when he finds out how close and how often you lot came to getting yourselves killed."

Carl ducked his chin, attempting to muffle a snicker and failing. Theo scowled at him and argued, "But we *had* to bring back the Healer, Schoolmaster Goodwyn. All would have been lost without Eva."

Perry scratched his head thoughtfully. "Yes," he agreed. "But one thing still puzzles me, Miss Fields."

"Sir?"

"How did you know to choose Eva over Carl when the crone asked you which one you wished for her to heal in exchange for your crystal?"

Ian leaned forward. He'd almost forgotten about that, and he wanted to hear Theo's response. He still couldn't fathom why she would choose a relative stranger over one of her dearest friends.

"It was the sundial," Theo said plainly. "When Ian asked it to point the way to the Healer from Laodamia's prophecy, it formed two shadows. One was faint, while the other was much darker. I couldn't help but notice that in that moment the fainter shadow pointed directly to Eva.

"When the crone asked me to choose, the most unusual feeling crept over me. Even though I wasn't wearing my crystal, I simply *knew* that Eva was the Healer from Laodamia's prophecy. I can't really explain it more than to say it just suddenly burst into my mind that Eva *had* to live, and I hoped that if I was right and the crone could save her, Eva might come into her own power and help Carl, at least until we found another trinket for the crone. I never imagined that the ancient one was going to give Eva the full extent of her own gifts, but I knew in my bones that it would work out."

Carl looked a bit miffed even after Theo had explained herself. "Bit of a risk you took, eh, Theo?"

But Theo smiled kindly and gave his arm a gentle pat. "I knew you had a future, Carl. Don't you remember when I read your and Océanne's fortunes?" Ian bristled at the mention of

Océanne. He'd put their stay in France completely out of his mind.

"Océanne? What a lovely name. Who might it belong to?" a voice from the hallway asked, and a moment later Thatcher stepped into the small kitchen with Eva right behind.

"Thatcher!" Perry shouted, quite forgetting himself as he bounded up from the chair and rushed to pat his brother on the back. "You're looking rather dashing this morning!"

"We're identical twins, Perry," Thatcher said drolly. "You're only complimenting yourself when you say things like that."

Ian was amazed at the transformation. He'd gone upstairs with Perry to show Eva the way to Thatcher's room, and peeking in from the hallway, he'd seen the schoolmaster in a truly dire state. His skin had been so pale it was ashen, his brow slick with sweat, and one arm and leg were curled inward at awkward angles. "No, Master Goodwyn," Ian insisted. "Your brother is right. You look very well indeed!"

Thatcher flashed Ian a brilliant smile. "I feel jolly good too," he conceded. "My fever's gone and the feeling has returned to both my arm and leg."

"You're quite cured, sir," Eva announced with confidence.

"How can you be so certain?" Perry asked, worry clear in his voice as he eyed his brother from head to toe.

Eva shrugged. "It's a feeling," she told him. "I can only say that before I laid my hands on your brother, I simply knew there was a terrible sickness running through his veins, as if someone had fed him a bit of poison. And now that threat is completely gone."

Theo was beaming happily at her. "You've done a wonderful job, Eva. Now, may we convince you to come with us to our home at Delphi Keep and look in on a few others! We've a particularly good friend named Jaaved, who I fear is in desperate need of your gift."

"Of course," Eva said; then she dropped her chin and lifted her eyes shyly to Carl. "Are you coming?"

Ian's eyebrows rose and he and Carl exchanged a rather surprised look. "Er . . . ," Carl said. "Of course. My home is at the keep, after all."

Ian rolled his eyes. It was just like Carl to win the heart of a pretty girl. "Come along," Ian said. "We'd best not fanny around here. There are sick children to attend to."

"Yes," Perry agreed. "I shall take you over to the keep in the motorcar to ensure your safety. And then I must telegraph the earl immediately on these most urgent matters in Poland."

"What urgent matters?" Thatcher asked.

Perry clapped a hand on his brother's back. "I believe from what the children have shared about their journey through the portal that Germany is about to invade Poland."

Thatcher gaped at him. "How can you say such a thing? Do you know what would happen if that *actually* occurred, Perry?"

Perry nodded gravely. "We would be forced to declare war on Germany. Make no mistake, Thatcher, our fate is sealed. These four have brought us back grave tidings, and we must get word to the earl as quickly as possible."

Thatcher stared round the table with large astonished eyes. "Is this true?" he asked them. The group nodded as one.

"I'll explain what Ian, Carl, and Theo encountered later," Perry told him. "For now, you must go back to bed."

"But I feel perfectly well," Thatcher protested.

Perry narrowed his eyes at him. "Humor me," he said. "At least until Dr. Lineberry comes round to declare you well, all right?"

Grumbling, Thatcher agreed, but took a cup of tea and a whole handful of tarts with him back upstairs.

Once he had shuffled away, Perry clapped his hands. "Shall we be off, then?"

Much later that evening all the keep's children were gathered around the tables, eating their evening meal. Besides the orphans, in attendance were their headmistresses, the schoolmasters, and Dr. Lineberry, who was looking rather astonished at all the healthy, vibrant children who'd been so ill just hours before.

Ian was particularly grateful that Jaaved's health had been restored. Beaming at his friends from the other side of the table, the Moroccan boy appeared as healthy as he ever had.

The only one who seemed fatigued was Eva. She sat shyly at her place of honor at the head of the main table. Dr. Lineberry was seated to her right and was asking her all sorts of questions until Madam Dimbleby sniffed, "My good Dr. Lineberry, please allow the poor girl to eat something, won't you? She's exhausted herself this afternoon, giving so much attention to all our sickly residents."

Dr. Lineberry blushed, nodded, and patted Eva's hand. "Of course, of course," he said to her. "But tomorrow I should very much like you to come with me on my rounds, young lady. I have a few patients within the village who would surely benefit from your particular touch."

Ian looked at Eva closely. He could see she felt uncomfortable with the idea. And luckily, Madam Scargill didn't seem to approve either. "Now, now," she said, then tsked as usual. "There will be none of that, Doctor."

"None of what?" he asked innocently.

Madam Dimbleby explained for her cousin. "What Gertrude means, Alfred, is that if we send Eva outside of this keep to cure all the world's ills, we'd hardly be able to get her back. No, I think it best that Eva remain our little secret for now, especially in light of all the trouble the children have had these past few weeks. We don't want to invite any unwelcome guests to Delphi Keep, now do we? We have a duty to protect our special children, after all." Madam Dimbleby eyed Theo, Eva, and Jaaved meaningfully and the doctor seemed to understand.

With a sigh he said, "Very well, Maggie, I see your point. And to that end, I propose that we leave the quarantine sign up over the door for now—lest anyone in Dover wonder why the children weren't confined for the full thirty days."

There was a collective groan at the table, and the doctor

held up his hands to quiet them. "I think it best if you stay on the keep's grounds, but I won't confine you all to the indoors if you promise not to breathe a word of this to anyone outside the orphanage."

Thirty-odd heads nodded in agreement and the doctor lifted his water glass and toasted his decision.

Later, when most of the younger children had been put to bed and Dr. Lineberry had seen himself out, the schoolmasters sat with Ian, Carl, and Theo in the parlor and talked at length about the dramatic events that had unfolded through the portal.

"So you say that Germany will invade Poland at any moment?" Thatcher asked.

Ian nodded. "Yes, sir. We overheard the Germans talking about meeting up with the main force in Warsaw."

"This is very bad, Perry," Thatcher said. "Very bad indeed."

"I've sent a telegram to the earl," Perry told him.

"Is the earl well?" Ian asked. They'd heard nothing of the earl's health, other than he'd been confined by quarantine to his own flat in London.

Perry smiled. "He's quite well, lad," he said. "Carrying on his business as usual by telephone, letter, and telegram. Why, with this latest news I should expect he'll attempt to alert his friends in Parliament, but for now, I'm afraid there's little we can do."

Thatcher frowned into the cup of tea he was holding. "There is one missing piece to this adventure that has yet to be rectified," he said softly.

"What's that, sir?" Ian asked.

Thatcher looked up at him. "You brought the Healer back but not another silver box, lad."

Ian's eyes widened. He'd had no time even to consider searching for another box, but they all knew there was one for each Oracle they needed to gather. "Oh, no," Ian said, and looked round at Theo and Carl as it sank in that perhaps they'd failed in their mission after all. Without the next box in the sequence, there was no way to know how to find the next Oracle.

But Carl said, "There's still a bit of the prophecy we haven't encountered yet, Ian. Perhaps there's a clue or two there."

" 'Search for box within the mist,' " recited Theo. " 'Past comes forward with a twist.' "

"What mist?" Ian asked no one in particular. And then he remembered what the crone had said to him in the little tree house before sacrificing herself. "The crone," he told them. "She told me that it was important to our quest that the Guardian enter the fog and discover the answers there."

"But what fog?" Perry asked.

Ian was still recalling the crone's words to him. He closed his eyes to concentrate. "She said that the Guardian and the One must both eventually seek the wisdom of the mist, a place called Ynys Môn. The crone told me that the Guardian should look for the answers first, and that whatever questions I might wish to ask would be the right ones in the end."

"What questions was she referring to?" Thatcher wondered.

Ian opened his eyes and shrugged. "Perhaps I should ask it where the next box is hidden."

"What did you say was the name of the place she told you to go, again?" Thatcher asked.

"A place called Ynys Môn—at least, that's what I believe she called it."

"Do you think she and Laodamia were referring to the same place?" Perry said.

"Absolutely," Theo confirmed, her eyes staring far away. "Especially since the crone mentioned the One and the Guardian specifically. She must have meant for Ian or me to go to this place to discover the location of the next box."

Carl scratched his head. "But where *is* this place? I mean, I've never heard of Ynys Môn. Have you?" he asked the schoolmasters.

Perry and Thatcher exchanged a look. "No," they said in unison. "But perhaps Professor Nutley has," Perry added.

"How are we to ask him?" Theo wondered. "Dr. Lineberry may excuse your visit to us here at the keep, but I quite doubt he'll allow you all a trip to London."

"Leave it to us," said Perry, getting up from the sofa and waving for his brother to follow. "Come along, Thatcher. It's late and we mustn't keep these three up any longer than necessary."

Thatcher got stiffly to his feet, his limp slight but still evident. "Yes," he agreed. "Leave it to us. We'll bring the professor here soon enough."

* * *

But as it turned out, it was a full three weeks later before the professor was able to pay them a visit. As Theo had predicted, Dr. Lineberry was insistent on seeing that the rules for the quarantine remained intact so that no one from the village would suspect that it had been lifted early.

In the meantime, word managed to make its way to the keep that Germany had in fact invaded Poland, which had surrendered almost immediately. On hearing the news, Eva was all but inconsolable and spent many hours in her room crying on her bed.

Only Carl could comfort her, and Ian had to admit, grudgingly, that his friend definitely had a way with the ladies.

Two days after word arrived that Poland had fallen to the Germans came the terrible news that Great Britain and France were declaring war on Germany. Thatcher and Perry delivered this headline to the keep, and for the rest of the week, a sense of great fear and anxiousness permeated the orphanage. Ian noticed that even Madam Dimbleby, who was almost always chipper and optimistic, was much more pensive and subdued.

Theo spent much of her time up in the tower, staring at the churning waters of the channel, lost deep in thought. And try as he might, Ian wasn't able to pull her away even for a short period to play a game of cards.

A day after they found themselves at war, a telegram arrived from the earl. He'd been notified of their venture through the portal, and while he was clearly displeased, he realized that without the Healer, many of his children might have been lost to the virus.

He also indicated that Major Fitzgerald had notified him that a call to war meant the major would likely be deployed overseas. Still, Fitzgerald intended to have Theo stay with his sister until his return, and although her leaving the keep might be delayed a week or two while he sorted through his plans, he was still insisting that she leave Dover to join his family in Debbonshire.

This sent Theo into an unresponsive and weepy state, and Ian found himself staring at the ceiling of his bedroom long into the night, sorting through any possible way to hold on to his adopted sister.

He knew that their former plans to escape to Amsterdam were permanently lost; several German U-boats had been spotted in the channel and Dover was on high alert for German invaders. With the entire village scrutinizing every person who came to and went from the port, Ian was convinced they'd never make it to France without being questioned and directly reported.

He thought about writing a letter to the major and begging him to change his mind, or at least allow Ian to come along, but when he suggested such things to Theo, she simply regarded him sadly and said, "It's no use, Ian. He'll never change his mind."

All these events caused Ian great worry until Dr. Lineberry arrived and took down the quarantine sign, announcing that the keep's residents were now free to come and go as they pleased.

No sooner had the good doctor left than a familiar motorcar came rumbling down the drive. "The earl is here!" cried Carl, who'd been standing across from Ian as the boys kicked a football back and forth.

Ian swiveled happily to spy the earl's prized yellow Packard pulling to a stop near the front steps. Theo appeared in the doorway just as the earl got out of the car, and to Ian's surprise and delight, Professor Nutley and the schoolmasters also stepped out onto the drive. "Hello, children!" boomed the earl to a gathering crowd of excited young orphans. "I'm so very glad to find you all looking so robust and healthy!"

The earl then seemed to catch sight of Eva, who was standing shyly on the steps next to Vanessa, as the two girls had ironically formed a fast friendship. "And this must be our newest addition, Eva, is it?"

The girl fiddled with the pouch about her neck containing a small piece of the Star of Lixus. "Yes, my lord," she said with a curtsy. "It's very nice to meet you."

The earl approached her and took her hand fondly. "Thank you for the gift of your presence, young miss. I'm delighted to see you here, and am very grateful to you for saving my children, Master Goodwyn, and Madam Scargill."

Eva blushed down to her toes and curtsied again.

Next to her, Vanessa also flushed, and Ian could tell she felt a great deal of shame for having been identified as the source of the outbreak. Their kindly patriarch was not one to miss such things and he next took Vanessa's hand and said, "Not to worry, my dear. None of this was your fault. You meant no harm, after all."

Vanessa attempted a smile before she curtsied too and thanked the earl.

"Might we have a word with Theo and Ian?" the professor asked, looking impatiently from just behind the earl.

"Can I come along?" Carl asked.

"Of course," said the earl, who waved Ian, Theo, and Carl forward. "Let's have a word in the headmistresses' study, shall we?"

One by one, they filed into the study and took their seats. Ian hardly had time to wonder what this was all about, as the professor got right to the point. "Masters Goodwyn have informed me of everything that happened on the other side of the portal. And I was most intrigued to hear that the crone instructed you to venture to Ynys Môn."

Ian nodded. "Yes, but we don't know where or even what that is, Professor."

The professor leaned forward, looking thoroughly excited. "Why, lad," he said softly, "I'm sure you've heard of this place before. Ynys Môn is the old Welsh name for Avalon."

Ian's eyes widened. Carl said, "You mean, King Arthur's Avalon?"

The professor nodded and grinned. "That is exactly what I mean."

"So when Laodamia was referring to the mist, she really meant the Mists of Avalon?" Perry asked.

"I believe so," said the professor. He stood up then and began to pace back and forth. "Ynys Môn is the old Welsh name for the Isle of Anglesey, located just off the western coast of Wales. I'm quite familiar with it, because it is practically covered with standing stones and Druid ruins. And one additional detail that is worth noting here is that Anglesey's northernmost point is particularly boggy, filled with marshes and swamps. It's hardly habitable."

Theo sucked in a breath. "Laodamia's prophecy!" she exclaimed, looking pointedly at Ian.

He knew exactly which section she was referring to, and recited from memory, " 'Leave more questions to the fog, lest you sink within the bog.' "

"So, Professor, you believe the next box can be found somewhere on this Isle of Anglesey?" asked the earl.

The professor's eyes twinkled. "I do indeed, my lord," he said. "And according to the crone, it is up to Ian—our heroic Guardian—to enter the mist and seek the location of the box. Legend has it that the mists are bound to answer any question a traveler might ask, in fact, so if there is time, lad, ask anything else your heart desires."

Ian immediately thought of the two questions he'd always longed an answer to: who were his parents and where could he find them?

Theo interrupted his thoughts, however, when she asked, "You said if there is time, Professor. Do you mean Ian can stay as long as there is fog?"

The professor shook his head. "No, lass," he said. "The legend is very strict on this: a traveler may enter the mist to gain its wisdom, but absolutely no one is allowed to stay past the bells."

"Bells?" inquired the earl. "What sort of bells?"

The professor tugged at one bushy eyebrow. "According to legend, the mists will signal when they are ready to receive a visitor by ringing a bell. Once the visitor has stepped forward into the fog, a second bell will sound when the mist is ready to receive the visitor's inquiries. A third bell will sound when it is time for the visitor to leave."

"What happens if you don't leave after the third bell?" Carl asked.

The professor sighed. "No one really knows," he confessed. "And this might be because no one who has ever stayed past the third bell was ever seen again."

Ian gulped. "As long as I obey the rules, I'll return unharmed, is that it?"

"Yes," said the professor with confidence. "And because it appears we are not yet finished with Laodamia's second prophecy, I say we travel to Wales and discover what this mist has to share."

In the silence that followed, Ian felt butterflies fluttering about in his stomach. Until the year before, he'd spent his whole life trying very hard not to think about his parents, because if he thought about them, he would have to conclude that he was unwanted or that they had both died. Either thought always left him feeling sad.

But that was nothing compared with how he'd felt a year earlier when the earl had told him that on the other side of the portal, a gardener had discovered Ian's mother clutching her newborn child and that, for reasons unknown to anyone, his mother had insisted the gardener take Ian before she had disappeared behind the wall, shutting out any further knowledge of her forever.

Ian had been crushed by the revelation that he now knew all he would ever know about her. It was as if all hope of discovering who he really was and where he had come from was forever lost to him.

For months he'd looked for the gardener, who, upon arriving at the earl's home with a newborn babe and an improbable story, had been summarily dismissed. But Ian had found no record of the man after he'd left the earl's employ. The gardener was as lost to Ian as his own mother. Yet as Ian now stared at the earl, his schoolmasters, the professor, Theo, and Carl, hope bloomed wide within his chest, and he knew he would stop at nothing to gain the answers the mist might provide him. "When do we leave?" he asked.

The professor smiled broadly but left it to the earl to answer. "Tomorrow," the earl announced. "We shall leave tomorrow."

THE MIST

The seven members of the traveling party stood silently in the marshy fields at the bottom of a hill in the early morning hours. Dawn had barely broken on the Isle of Anglesey, and the landscape was shrouded in a fog so thick Ian couldn't even make out his own feet. It was as if the whole world were floating on a fluffy white blanket.

Beside him Carl yawned and rubbed his eyes. "I would've liked another hour in bed," he grumbled.

"You were welcome to stay there," Ian reminded him.

"What?" Carl said. "And miss all the fun? I don't bloomin' think so."

"Shhh!" Theo scolded. "We're supposed to be listening for the bells!"

Carl regarded her moodily. "We've been standing here for half an hour, Theo, and we haven't heard them yet."

Theo frowned. "We need to be patient," she insisted.

But Ian was beginning to have his doubts. He wondered if perhaps they'd chosen the wrong location.

When they'd arrived on the island, Professor Nutley had inquired with several local residents about the mists. Some had scoffed at him and told him not to bother with fairy stories. But a few had suggested that they fully believed in their magical isle, and that the mists could be found in one of four locations.

They had left it up to Theo to decide which one to visit and she had selected a particularly swampy section near a graveyard that had giant megaliths dotting the hillsides just behind it.

Ian quite approved of her choice, and that morning he'd been brimming with anticipation and confidence, but the longer they stood about waiting for something to happen, the more crestfallen he became. "What if they don't sound?" he whispered to Theo. "What if the bells never call me forward?"

She looked at him anxiously. "They will," she insisted. "Laodamia said as much, after all."

Ian inhaled deeply and attempted to calm his nerves. He'd practiced in his head several times how he would ask the mist to reveal the identity of his parents after he'd inquired about the treasure box. He hoped he asked correctly and he wondered what the mist would tell him.

The group waited yet another thirty minutes, with nothing but the calm quiet of the morning to reach their ears. More of their surroundings became illuminated as the sun rose a bit farther on the horizon. The gray cast to the landscape was now laced with patches of pinks and purples as the rays of the sun began to reflect off the dense fog. And still, no bells or ringing or anything out of the ordinary came to Ian's anxious ears.

He heard the professor sigh and caught the look that passed between the old man and the earl. "Perhaps we're in the wrong place?" the earl asked.

The schoolmasters nodded, as if they'd been thinking the very same thing. "There are three other locations we might try," said Perry. "Perhaps tomorrow will yield us a better result?"

"Smashing," said Carl, already turning to head up the hill. "I've a craving for some tea and toast. I think I'm chilled to the bone."

Ian watched reluctantly as everyone but Theo began to walk away from their vigil. "Come along," he said, bitterly disappointed. "Let's get something to eat."

"I'm sorry," Theo said. "I really thought I'd chosen the right spot."

"It's not your fault," Ian assured her. "There's always tomorrow."

He and Theo turned away and took a few steps, and that was when Ian heard one loud beautiful chord sing out across the fields. He and Theo both stopped dead in their tracks and stared wide-eyed at each other. "The bells!" they said in unison.

Carl looked over his shoulder. "What'd you say?" he asked as the earl also paused to look back.

"Didn't you hear that?" Theo asked.

"Hear what?"

"That bell!" Ian nearly shouted before turning his eyes

to the earl. "My lord, surely you heard it?" But the earl shook his head and looked back at him curiously.

"I heard nothing, Ian."

Thatcher, Perry, and the professor had also stopped on their way up the hill and were looking curiously back at them. "What did you hear, lad?" asked the professor.

"We both heard it!" Theo exclaimed, taking Ian's hand and turning back toward the thinning fog. "Ian, look!" she added, pointing to a small patch of mist that seemed to curl out of the terrain, snaking its way toward them.

"What?" asked the earl, hurrying down the hill to them. "Theo, what do you see?"

"You don't see that?" Ian gasped. "My lord, there's a thick patch of mist making its way to us!"

The professor, Carl, and the schoolmasters joined them and peered at the spot Ian was pointing to. "I don't see anything," Carl complained.

Ian looked at Theo. She nodded. "I see it too!" she told him.

The professor shrugged. "Well, then, by all means, lad, follow the mist. It is obviously beckoning you."

Ian felt a rush of excitement, but he was nervous too. He stepped forward several paces and waited for the curling fog to circle about him from the waist down, as if lassoing him. He glanced over his shoulder and saw that Theo was beaming with happiness. "Go," she told him. "Find your answers."

But Ian wondered suddenly if he was the only one the mist was beckoning. In a last-minute decision, he said, "Theo, come with me!"

Theo looked doubtful. "You don't need me," she told him. "You can find the way on your own."

But Ian thought differently. "I believe you're supposed to come, Theo," he said. "You heard the bell too. You can see the mist. And the crone did say that both of us would need to find our answers in the mist. Perhaps she wasn't suggesting that we'd do so at separate times, but now. Together."

Theo bit her lip while she considered him.

But Ian was afraid that if she didn't join him quickly, they'd both lose their chance. "Come on before it leaves again!" he implored her.

"I believe Ian might be right," said the professor kindly. "Why not go along at least and share the experience?"

Reluctantly, Theo stepped forward to join Ian, and the mist curled around both their middles, as if it wanted to tug them forward. Ian took hold of Theo's hand and together they walked into its center. "Remember not to stay past the third bell!" the professor called.

"I'll remember!" he promised eagerly, walking forward.

The pair made their way easily, following the fog still curled about them for at least a half kilometer. While they walked, Ian became aware that a white fluffy fog seemed to waft up out of the ground, forming an archway high above their heads—almost like a wide tunnel. Light permeated its misty walls so that Ian could still see Theo quite clearly, but much of the surrounding landscape was completely obscured.

When he chanced a quick glance behind him, he saw only white, and for the first time, he felt a tickle of fear when he realized he could no longer make out the rest of their party.

Theo, however, appeared captivated by her surroundings. Her eyes were wide with wonder, and a smile never left her face. "It's so beautiful," she whispered. "I've never seen a mist so pure and white."

Not long afterward, the smoky rope tethered about their middles faded away and Ian and Theo found themselves quite suddenly in the center of a huge four-walled room complete with thick white misty walls and a high ceiling. For several seconds, nothing happened, but then the eerie silence was broken by the sound of the second bell.

Ian waited breathlessly for something else to happen, but for several heartbeats nothing at all did.

"What happens now?" Theo whispered, squeezing his hand.

Ian shrugged. "Dunno," he said, a bit anxious about what he was supposed to do next.

"Welcome!" said a disembodied female voice that seemed to come at them from every direction. "We have awaited your arrival, Guardian, and glad are we that you have brought the One with you. Now ask us what you should desire and we will reveal all."

Ian felt a wave of nervous energy wash over him. Once the mist revealed where to locate the treasure box, he was free to learn everything about his parents! He looked at Theo, glad she was there to share it with him. She beamed him a brilliant smile, adding a nod of encouragement, and suddenly, he couldn't bear the thought of losing her in less than a week. He looked back at the white swirling walls and realized they might hold a truth even more important than the one he'd come here to seek. In the next moment he knew what he must do, and he decided to ask this most important question even before inquiring about the treasure box.

Still, he couldn't help regretting what he was giving up. He closed his eyes, lest he change his mind, and said, "There is a man who claims to be Theo's father. His name is Major Fitzgerald. I would like to know about Theo's mother, where she came from, and if the major is, in fact, her father."

Beside him he heard Theo gasp. "Ian, no!" Ian opened his eyes and saw her shaking her head vigorously. "Not me!" she insisted. "We needed to ask about the treasure box, and any question after that was supposed to be about *you!*"

But already the mist of the four walls was in motion and the disembodied voice said, "I have heard your request, and here is the answer you desire."

On the wall in front of them, shapes began to appear. At first the shapes were rough outlines of two people, but the more Ian stared at them, the more they seemed to materialize and increase in detail. Very quickly he realized he was staring at a young girl of about eight and an older woman of about twenty, wearing Grecian gowns. "Jacinda!" said the older woman. "What has happened?"

Theo gasped again. "That's my mother as a young girl!" she whispered.

"They've taken my father away, Adria!" the young Jacinda cried. Ian remembered immediately that Adria was the name of Laodamia's most faithful protégé. "My sisters are being held prisoner in our home," Jacinda continued, "but I stole away before they could discover me. I must find Mia and warn her! Her enemies will stop at nothing until they capture her and bring her before the council!"

The young lady named Adria hugged Jacinda fiercely. "The Oracle is aware of the danger, Jacinda," she said. "And she has hidden herself in our old meeting place."

"I must go to her!"

Adria let go of Jacinda and turned to reach for something within the fog. Her hand reappeared holding a small box with familiar etchings. "Laodamia told me you would come here. She insisted I give you this," she said. "She also advised me to send you to the cave where your brother's friend Calais was killed. The Oracle is hiding there. But here, take some food and water with you. Her condition is quite fragile, and I'm terribly worried about her."

"I know where the cave is," Jacinda said, taking the box and the supplies. "I'll go to her now!"

"Tell the Oracle that I'll come to her later this evening with more supplies. And please, Jacinda, tell her to rest. She must not overdo."

Jacinda nodded and dashed away into the mist.

The remaining figure of Adria dissolved and the mist swirled, re-forming itself into what looked like the opening of a cave. Jacinda was there, clutching the treasure box as she picked her way along the rocky floor. "Laodamia!" she called. "It's me! Jacinda! I must speak with you!" Ian watched, utterly spellbound, as the girl stepped forward across a familiar threshold, searching for the Oracle—who appeared to be nowhere in sight—and stopped when her foot kicked something on the ground.

Ian knew exactly what it was, and winced when Jacinda screamed as she realized she'd nearly stepped right onto a human skeleton. In her fear she darted forward, and then, quite suddenly, the way behind her was cut off. A wall appeared where none had been before.

The poor girl cried out again when she realized she could not go back, and she dashed out of the cavern as fast as she could, then dissolved altogether into a swirling of white mist. A moment later a new set of shapes formed. Jacinda reappeared looking a year or two older and much worse for wear. Her Grecian clothing was gone, replaced by more contemporary garb, but the girl was wafer thin, disheveled, and cowering in the corner of an alleyway while an elderly couple attempted to coax her out of the corner. "There, there," said the woman. "You poor thing! Out here on these streets, left to fend for yourself. Why, you can't be older than nine or ten years old!"

"You . . . no hurt!" Jacinda said with a rather pronounced accent as she shivered against the apparent cold and clutched a small satchel that Ian suspected held her very few belongings. Ian realized that since she'd stumbled through the portal from her home in ancient Greece, she'd become a poor urchin struggling to survive somewhere in England.

"Of course I won't hurt you, darling!" claimed the woman. "Why don't you come along with us and we'll make sure you get a good hot meal and some warm clothes?"

"Yes, little girl," said the gentleman. "We have a very large house and plenty of room. Come along with us and we'll take proper care of you, all right?"

Again the mist swirled and the figures dissolved. When they re-formed, Jacinda was at least eighteen, looking happy, healthy, and incredibly beautiful. Ian was quite surprised by her transformation, in fact. And the scene astonished him further when it revealed a familiar face. "Oh, Fitzy," she sang to a much younger version of Major Fitzgerald sitting next to her. "Whatever would I do here at school without such wonderful company as yourself?"

"I suspect you'd die of boredom, Cinda."

Jacinda laughed merrily and took his arm. "Now, tell me about this very handsome school chum of yours. What's his name again?"

The young Major Fitzgerald frowned. "Are you referring to Phillip?" he asked, and she nodded. "Oh, dear, Cinda, don't tell me you fancy *him*!"

Jacinda smiled coyly and laughed. "Of course I fancy him, Fitzy! Why do you think I insisted you invite him to the races on Saturday?"

The young Major Fitzgerald pouted. "The man's a lout," he warned. "He's not good enough for you."

But Jacinda seemed unperturbed. "He's adorable," she said wistfully. "And I believe I shall marry him one day."

It was difficult to discern in the fog, but Ian could swear that the major looked hurt. Before he had a chance to scrutinize it, however, their two figures dissolved again, only to re-form a moment later. This time the pair were standing in a parlor. Jacinda looked stricken and Fitzgerald held her hand, attempting to soothe her. "There was nothing anyone could have done, Cinda. We warned Phillip not to go out in those rough seas, but you know how much he loved to sail."

Jacinda's knees buckled, and Major Fitzgerald caught her before she collapsed to the floor. Carefully, he moved her to the sofa and set her down gently. "There, there," he said, patting her hand. "I'm so terribly sorry, my dear."

"Where will he be buried?" she asked after a bit, her voice pained.

"His family is having him shipped back to Switzerland. He'll be buried in the family cemetery."

Jacinda's lips trembled and she began to cry. "It's all ruined," she moaned, clutching her stomach. "Everything is ruined!"

Again the shapes dissolved and re-formed. This time Jacinda appeared holding a small bundle swaddled in blankets. She sat at a table across from Fitzgerald in what appeared to be a large teahouse. Her face was crestfallen, and her features pinched.

"I'm so sorry to hear about your parents," he said softly. Jacinda stared down at the table and hugged the baby in her arms. "When news of the accident reached me, I knew you would need your Fitzy."

Jacinda leaned over and gently placed her baby in a pram. Fitzgerald reached across the table to take her hand then, but Jacinda pulled it away. "Don't," she warned.

"Please," he begged. "Please come back to London,

Cinda. I know that your father's sister has claimed his estate, and that you've no money and no prospects."

Jacinda swallowed hard and glanced again at the baby in the stroller.

Fitzgerald continued. "We can be married. My family might not approve, but if I insist, they'll never stand in my way. And I'll even claim the babe if you like; just come back!"

Jacinda closed her eyes, as if to shut him out. When she opened them again, they were hard and firm. "No, Fitzy," she said. "I cannot."

There was a long silence as Fitzgerald sat stunned on the opposite side of the table. "But why?" he asked.

Her features seemed to soften then and she said, "Because as much as I adore you, I don't love you. And because this child is not yours; she's Phillip's. And while I must confess that I most appreciate your offer, marrying you would only put all of us in the gravest jeopardy. I could never forgive myself if anything happened to you, Fitzy. I simply couldn't."

"What kind of danger?" he asked earnestly. "Jacinda, what kind of trouble have you got yourself into?"

Jacinda shook her head. "It is nothing I can talk about," she said, and again her features were hard and firm.

Fitzgerald stared at her with a mixture of hurt and confusion on his face, but he did not press. "Where will you go?" he finally asked.

She sighed. "There is a place by the sea that I went to

405

many years ago," she said. "A quiet little village I remember from my childhood. I'd like to take my daughter there. Raise her and keep her safe. And someday, I shall tell her all of it. All of my story and the secrets of my past so that she might learn from my mistakes and be the stronger for it."

And then Jacinda did something that shocked Ian down to his socks. She reached to a familiar-looking necklace at her neck and gripped the thin crystal there, exactly as he'd seen Theo do a hundred times before.

"Will you send word to me and tell me how you are?" Fitzgerald asked.

Jacinda smiled sadly. "Yes, Fitzy," she said. "And in the meantime, I had hoped that you could hold on to something for me, to keep it safe?"

"Of course!"

Jacinda reached into the baby carriage and pulled out the small silver box with little balls for feet. "This is a priceless family heirloom that I've had since I was a young girl. I've held it all this time and kept it safe, but I worry that where I'm going, it might fall into the wrong hands. Will you keep it for me until I ask you for it again?"

Major Fitzgerald gently took the box from Theo's mother. "It would be my greatest honor," he promised, and his figure dissolved into nothing.

Ian blinked when he realized that the foggy figures of Jacinda and Fitzgerald were completely gone, and it took him a moment to understand that no further shapes would form. As he was about to ask the mist after his own parents, he heard the third and final bell.

Crestfallen, he had to swallow his disappointment quickly, because he knew they would have to leave. But when he looked beside him, he saw that Theo was openly sobbing. He felt terrible that he'd all but ignored her up to that moment, so he wrapped her in his arms and held her tightly. "Shhh," he said. "It's all right, Theo. There, there."

"She loved me," Theo cried. "My mother truly loved me!"

"Of course she did!" he assured her.

Theo lifted her chin and looked up at him desperately. "Then what happened to her? Why did she leave me out in the rain like that?"

Ian opened his mouth to say something, but words seemed to fail him. "I've no idea," he finally admitted. "But now we know that your mother actually knew Laodamia, and from what the mists showed us of her origins, she seemed to be in a bit of danger from her early childhood."

Theo sniffled loudly and wiped her tears. "Yes," she said. "Her father had been taken away, and others were searching for her." A thought then seemed to occur to Theo and she asked, "Do you think that whomever my mother was afraid of when she was younger could have come through the portal after her, Ian?"

Ian inhaled deeply while he considered that. "Given the magical properties of the portal, Theo, I believe anything is possible. And to answer your earlier question, I believe your mother would only have left you in that field on that stormy night if she was truly desperate, and perhaps she thought she was leading danger *away* from you."

407

Theo buried her face into his chest and sobbed anew. Ian wondered if it had been a good idea after all to ask the mist for Theo's history instead of his, and that was when he felt a wetness around his ankles and realized that while they'd been standing there, they'd also been sinking.

"Come on," he said, pulling away and grabbing Theo by the hand. "We've got to go. The third bell, remember?"

Theo sniffled and attempted to take a step. As she struggled to lift her foot, there was a great sucking sound. "Ian!" she said. "I'm stuck!"

Ian pitched himself forward, groaning while he leaned into the effort to free his own feet. After straining nearly all his leg muscles, he finally got one foot free, and then the other. He reached back, grabbed Theo's hand, and heaved, but their combined weight only pushed them both deeper into the bog. "We're sinking!" Theo cried.

Ian thrashed about, trying to keep them on top of the slippery, cold mud, but his efforts just made things worse. Before long he was panting heavily, and as he looked wildly around, he realized that the last threads of the mist were quickly disappearing, replaced by the bright glow of the sun.

"It's no use!" he said after straining forward a few more times. "Theo, I can't work us free!"

Theo held up one of her hands and begged him to stop moving. "I'm lighter," she told him. "If I can make it over there to that tree, I might be able to extend you a stick or a branch."

Ian turned to see where she was pointing. With a bit of relief, he noticed that just six feet away was an old gnarled tree. If Theo could somehow manage to make it there, they might have a chance.

He watched with amazement as she leveled out her body and made swimming motions. After a few strokes, she was to the tree, and after searching some of the lower branches, she pulled free a long stick and leaned out over the bog with it. "Reach for it!" she ordered.

Ian took a deep breath and leaned forward like he'd seen Theo do. He took two strokes and felt himself move forward. He took a few more and moved closer still. Finally, after eight more strokes, he managed to reach the stick, and with a groan, Theo pulled him to the tree.

He sat on its exposed roots for a bit, catching his breath. "Good work, Theo," he said when his chest finally stopped heaving.

"There are some downed logs behind the tree," Theo told him. "I believe there's enough of them to see us to firmer ground."

Ian leaned around the trunk and saw that the logs stuck out of the mud like stepping stones. After resting a bit longer, the pair made their way carefully, log by log, to the edge of the swamp and onto firm ground.

"There they are!" they heard Carl shout from nearby. A moment later the earl, Carl, and the schoolmasters were beside them, shrugging out of their coats to wrap round the shivering pair.

The professor puffed his way over a short time later. "Oh, my!" he said when he took in their muddied appearance. "You stayed past the third bell, didn't you?"

At the mention of the bells, Theo dissolved again into a puddle of tears. Ian wanted to tell them the story that had unfolded in the mist, but couldn't seem to form the words. Instead, he shrugged and shook his head. "It's Theo's story to tell," he said.

Everyone looked curiously first at him, then at Theo, until the earl wrapped his arms around her, lifting her up, and said, "Come, lass. Let's get you back to the inn for a warm bath and some clean clothes. And when you're ready, you can tell us what Avalon revealed."

THE TOMB

Magus the Black woke with a start. Surrounding him was complete darkness, which worried him for several reasons. First, when his sister Lachestia had killed the injured soldier instead of the young Guardian, Magus had lost his temper and had pelted her with bolts of fire.

He had not anticipated that his sister would defend herself so ferociously. They had fought for two terrible days, and at the end of it, Deadman's Forest was left a singed, smoking ruin, and whatever had remained of the Eighth Armored Panzer Division had also been annihilated—but no bodies would ever be recovered, as every man to the last had been buried.

Four times within those two days, his sister had sucked him under the earth—the only place Magus the Black truly feared—and he'd managed to claw and burn his way out. But when there was no more forest to offer him cover, Lachestia had cornered him within a semicircle of fallen stones.

Even cracked and broken, the megaliths held power, and

it was enough to sap his strength so that when she struck at him for the fifth time, Magus had been knocked unconscious.

Thus, his darkened surroundings were a mystery, except that at the moment, he was not being smothered by dirt. With a snap of his fingers, he created a flame to see by, and his brow pulled down into a grim frown as he stood and turned around in a circle.

It was worse than he'd imagined. Magus was entombed.

The flame at his fingertips flickered and dimmed, and he could have cried out in anger and frustration. On all four sides, overhead, and under his feet was rock, and not just any rock. He was encased in the magical stones of his mortal ancestors—and the lettering facing inward was slowly but efficiently extinguishing his power.

"Lachestia!" he screamed.

A slight rumble—a small tremor, really—reached his ears. His sister was somewhere nearby—keeping watch and exacting her revenge.

Magus sighed heavily and sat down on the hard ground to think. He was determined to get out of this makeshift tomb, and he vowed that when he did, he would make all his sisters pay.

ENDINGS AND BEGINNINGS

Several days after returning from the Isle of Anglesey, Ian sat with Theo and the earl in the earl's library, waiting on a visitor. Theo fidgeted nervously and several times she looked intensely up at the earl, as if seeking his reassurance.

He smiled back at her every time and even nodded once or twice, letting her know that he had complete confidence in the way the meeting would proceed. As the clock on the wall struck half past noon, there was a knock on the door, and when the earl called, "Come in," Binsford entered with a bow.

"Major Fitzgerald is here to see you, my lord."

"Please show him in, Binsford," instructed the earl.

Theo squirmed again, and Ian reached out to squeeze her hand. The earl had told them both to let him do all the talking, but still, Ian thought he might be just as nervous as Theo.

Major Fitzgerald swept into the room, his face confident and perhaps even triumphant. "Good afternoon, my lord," he said with a small bow of his own.

"Ah, Major," said the earl, getting to his feet and walking over to greet the man. "Thank you for agreeing to meet with us here at my home."

"I trust you have received the latest correspondence from my barrister?" the major inquired, taking the seat the earl directed him to.

"Yes, yes," said the earl, returning to his own chair. "Everything appears to be in order."

The major smiled broadly and stole a glance at Theo. "You're looking lovely today, miss," he said. "Are you ready to come home with me and my sister? We've prepared you a room that I think you'll find most accommodating while your daddy is off to fight the Germans."

Theo stared at him for a long moment without saying a word. Ian knew her well enough to read the mixture of emotions on her face, and wondered if the major would be quite so exuberant if he knew what Theo was thinking.

Before Theo could reply, however, the earl said, "About those arrangements, Major . . ."

"Yes? What about them?" Ian could clearly see the defensive posture the major adopted the moment the earl inquired into the man's plans.

The earl looked calmly at the major, holding his hands up in surrender. "I agree that the best place for Theo during these troubling times would be with the family of her father."

The major visibly relaxed. "I'm very glad to hear you're seeing things my way, my lord."

"Yes, my good man," the earl agreed, "but I might not be seeing them as much your way as I am the right way."

Major Fitzgerald blinked rapidly. "I'm afraid I don't quite understand."

The earl looked at Theo, who was still glaring hard at the major. "As I said, I believe you are right and that Theo belongs with the family of her father, as her mother's family is either unknown or deceased, am I correct?"

The major nodded hesitantly. "Jacinda's adoptive parents were killed in a motorcar accident and her father's sister never acknowledged the adoption. So, yes, my lord, you are quite right. There is no one left on Theo's mother's side to claim her."

The earl tugged thoughtfully on his beard. "Yes, which leaves her father's family."

"You mean *me*," said the major with feeling.

The earl's eyes narrowed as he looked at the major. "Oh, but I'm afraid we both know that's not true, Major, now don't we?"

Major Fitzgerald's face flushed and he squirmed uncomfortably in his chair. "While I admit that Jacinda and I were not married at the time, I can assure you, my lord, that I am the girl's father."

"No," said the earl.

Major Fitzgerald began blinking again. "No, *what*, my lord?"

"No, my good man, you are not Theo's father. I have it on very good authority that Theo's father was a man named Phillip Zinsli, who was in fact a devoted school chum of yours, was he not?"

The flush to the major's cheeks deepened to an even

rosier hue. And when he did not immediately answer, the earl continued. "My investigators have learned that Phillip drowned nearly twelve years ago in a rather tragic sailing accident. His father is a vice chancellor in Switzerland, if I am not mistaken."

"I—I—I . . . ," the major stammered.

"Yes," said the earl, as if he had not even noticed the major's reaction. The earl reached next to him and held up a piece of paper. "This, Major, is something that you might find interesting. You see, I've had my inspector conduct a thorough search of the public records, and he came across the most interesting bit of documentation. It seems that Jacinda Barthorpe and Phillip Zinsli were married almost exactly nine months before Theo's birth and the only witness to that private ceremony was a Sergeant Fitzgerald."

The earl paused for effect, and Ian nearly laughed at the incredulous look on the major's face when the earl handed him the marriage certificate.

"When I presented this news to Phillip's family, along with the birth certificate my inspector also discovered for Theo, noting her father's name to be Phillip Zinsli, well, their shock was to be expected." The earl also handed over a second piece of paper to the major. Ian presumed it was Theo's birth certificate.

"And while they were reluctant to claim a new heir to the family fortune—they are quite wealthy, you know—they did agree to allow Theo the use of the surname Zinsli as long as she made no future claims to her father's estate, which of course she readily agreed to."

The earl then picked up a third piece of paper and gave it to the major, who was clearly struggling to take it all in. "What is this?" he asked, skimming over the print.

"That is an award of guardianship for one Theo Zinsli to me, the Earl of Kent, signed by the girl's grandfather, Major. Theo is now my legal ward." The earl then sat back in his chair with a rather satisfied smirk.

The major reacted quite unexpectedly; he set all the papers aside and burried his face in his hands.

Theo took pity on him and moved off her chair to walk over to the major, where she took his hand and looked at him with the same sad compassion that her mother had so many years before. "I know that you loved her," she said to him when he looked up. "And I know that in her own way, my mother loved you too."

The major swallowed hard. "I did," he told her earnestly.

Theo nodded, as if she understood perfectly. "But my mother also considered it an unfair burden to force you to claim a daughter that wasn't yours," she told him in a voice that was wise beyond its years. "I know that she was grateful for your offer, but in the end, she could hardly accept. It would have ruined you, and she understood that."

The major continued to stare at her with wide eyes. "We would have been all right," he whispered. "I had my post in the military, after all."

Theo looked away and let the major's hand fall. "She

would have wanted you to be happy," Theo said. "And that, Major, is what I wish for you as well. I should also like to say that if I had actually been your daughter, I would have been most proud to bear your name."

A mixture of emotions washed across the major's face. Regret. Hurt. Sadness. And finally, acceptance. He stood then and offered them all a small bow. "I shall contact my barrister and withdraw my claim from the courts, my lord."

"Thank you, Major," said the earl.

The major then turned back to Theo with a look of chagrin. "And if there is anything you ever need, Theo, you consider asking your uncle Fitzy, all right?"

Theo smiled. "Actually," she told him, "there is one small favor only you could allow me, Major."

"Yes?"

"Do you remember the silver box my mother gave to you for safekeeping?"

Major Fitzgerald's mouth dropped open. "How could you know about that?"

"My investigators were quite thorough," the earl assured him.

The major smirked. "Ah," he said, then got back to Theo's question. "Yes, young miss, what about it?"

"Do you still have it?"

"I do."

"Might you see your way to returning it to me, my mother's rightful heir?"

The major squatted down in front of her and took her hand. "Yes, lass," he said earnestly. "Of course. I'll send it through the post the moment I reach my home, all right?"

Nearly a fortnight later Ian sat on the front steps of the keep, listening to the rest of the children playing out in the yard. Theo had told him that the box would arrive that day, and he'd taken up his vigil on the steps, waiting for the postman to come. He was rewarded a short time later by the sound of clopping horse hooves and the familiar carriage that brought the keep its daily mail.

Theo joined him just as Mr. Taggert, the postman, reached them. "I've a package for you, Theo, although your last name's misspelled," he said, swiveling in his seat to retrieve a small parcel wrapped in brown paper, along with a few letters, then passing them all off to her.

"Thank you, Mr. Taggert," she said, taking the delivery and showing Ian that it was addressed to Miss Theo Zinsli. "I've been expecting this."

The postman tipped his hat, then gave a flick to his reins, and his horse plodded back down the drive.

Theo and Ian sat in silence for a bit while they watched the carriage depart, and then Theo placed the parcel in Ian's hands. "Here," she said. "You open it."

Ian gave her a gentle nudge with his shoulder and tore off the wrapping and newspaper that the silver treasure box was packed in. Tossing aside the paper, Ian held up the box to inspect it. The relic was identical to all the others.

Turning it over, he began twisting the balled feet, and the top left foot turned. Quickly, he unscrewed the ball and held the tiny key at the end in triumph. "Shall we have a look inside?"

"Of course!" she said encouragingly.

Ian inserted the key, twisted the lock, and smiled when he heard the faint but familiar pop. Carefully, he opened the lid, and there inside were a small corked glass vial and the familiar-looking bound scroll. Ian extracted the vial and held it up to the sun. Although the glass was dark, he could clearly see a liquid inside. "I wonder what this is for," he said aloud.

"Maybe it's poison!" someone said with a laugh, and Ian and Theo looked up to see Carl standing before them, holding a football, with a curious glint in his eye. "I saw the postman," he told them before coming over to sit down next to Ian.

Ian shook his head with a smile and placed the glass vial back into the box before closing the lid and locking it again. "We'll let the professor take a look at the prophecy later and see if he can tell us what's inside the vial."

Beside him Theo giggled. "You'll have to tear him away from the attentions of Señora Castillo first."

Ian and Carl exchanged a curious look. "What do you mean?" Ian asked her.

Theo laughed again. "I overheard Thatcher telling Madam Dimbleby that Señora Castillo has finally come back to England. Apparently, she discovered Carmina nicking her silver and dismissed her outright. She then felt terrible about believing that one of us had taken her brother's diary, and has traveled here to apologize and reclaim it, but I understand that since her arrival, she and the professor have been on regular long walks together and sitting for tea every day."

Carl smiled. "You think the professor fancies Señora Castillo?"

Theo's eyes held a gleam. "Oh, I really do!" she exclaimed, and they all laughed.

After a bit Carl asked, "Was there any other mail?"

Ian eyed him quizzically. "Yes. As a matter of fact, there was."

Theo handed him the small stack that the postman had given her and Carl sorted through it quickly. He appeared to find what he was looking for and he held up the letter happily until he saw the quizzical look on Theo's and Ian's faces. He discreetly shoved the post into his pocket.

"Who's written to you, then?" Theo asked.

"No one," Carl said, his cheeks turning a brilliant shade of red.

Ian wanted to laugh, until it occurred to him who might be writing to Carl. "It's from Océanne, isn't it?" And even as he said it, he got a bitter taste in his mouth.

Carl looked away. "Maybe."

Theo laughed. "Oh, Carl," she scolded, "so many girls to choose from."

Carl blushed even more, and Ian furrowed his brow. He glanced at Theo, wondering what she was going on about. She motioned with her head toward the yard, and when he looked, he saw Eva playing tag with Vanessa and a few other children, though the Polish girl was clearly eyeing Carl every now and again.

Ian exhaled and stood up. "I'm off for a walk," he announced, moving away.

He'd taken no more than a few steps when he realized that someone was walking next to him. "I'd prefer to take this walk alone."

"I know," said Carl. "But I'd prefer to go with you."

Ian stopped to glare at him. "You're impossible!"

"I know that too," Carl replied, his face opening up with a huge grin. "Come on, mate, let's go find a new tunnel or something. Do you have your map on you?"

Ian reflexively felt his shirt pocket, where he'd tucked his trusted map. Several nights earlier he'd been about to mark the new tunnel under the keep when Theo had warned him not to, telling him only that she'd a strong feeling he shouldn't. He still desperately wanted to alter his map in some way, then have a look at the twin map still at the professor's to see if it mirrored the alteration, but for now all he could really focus on was the letter Océanne had written to Carl. He couldn't help it, and in the back of his mind, he wondered if anything would ever turn out in his favor again.

"What's the matter?" Carl asked. "And this time, I'm not settling for anything less than the truth, Ian. You've been a right sour chap ever since we got back from Anglesey."

Ian kicked at the dirt moodily. He'd never admit to Carl that he was jealous of his courtship with Océanne, so he only confessed part of his troubles. "I am glad that I gave the wisdoms of the mist over to Theo," he said, only when he was sure she was out of hearing range. "But a part of me wishes I'd taken the chance to find out about my own parents."

Carl nodded and the boys began walking again. "It's too bad we've never been able to find the gardener," he told Ian, almost as if he'd read his thoughts. "I'd wager there's even more to the story than he first told the earl."

Ian hung his head and kicked at the dirt again. "Yes," he agreed. "But we've asked everyone we can think of who might have known him and no one remembers where he might have gone."

Carl stopped abruptly, and when Ian looked back, Carl's face was alight with excitement. "Perhaps we aren't going about it the right way?" he said. "What I mean is, perhaps we shouldn't be asking a person."

Ian's brow furrowed again. "What?"

"Perhaps we should ask a *thing*, Ian!"

And just like that, Ian's mind flooded with understanding. He hastily thrust the box at Carl so that he could dig into both of his pockets, and with fingers shaking in exuberance, he pulled out the sundial, held it up to the sun, and said, "Sundial, point the way to the gardener who took me as a babe from my mother."

A moment later a small thin shadow formed on the dial's surface and both boys gave a triumphant shout. "Well then," said Carl, "shall we be off to find your gardener, then?"

Ian looked back at the keep and saw Theo still sitting on the front steps. She waved to him and nodded, as if she knew exactly what they were up to. "Yeah, mate," he said. "Let's have a go at it."

ACKNOWLEDGMENTS

Thirty years ago, my sixth-grade teacher, Mr. Lindstrom, practiced something quite unconventional for the time. Every morning from eight to eight-twenty, he would read to us from J. R. R. Tolkien's *The Hobbit*.

Even now I clearly recall Mr. Lindstrom in his starched white shirt, striped tie, and polyester pants standing at the front of the classroom, holding his book aloft, and delighting us with his many character voices. Those were the days when I would go to school even if I felt sick, because I couldn't wait to hear what would happen next.

And that was the moment I fell in love with fantasy. I'd never heard a story quite like *The Hobbit* before, and even my unsophisticated twelve-year-old mind understood that Tolkien was a true master.

So it is appropriate, I think, to begin these acknowledgments with a humble nod to both Mr. Lindstrom and Mr. Tolkien for delivering the marvelous Mr. Bilbo Baggins to my young, impressionable mind. It was love at first hobbit.

I would also like to thank my phenomenally talented editor, Krista Marino, who—I state without any hint of exaggeration—

is quite plainly the best children's editor in the business. (No kidding. She really is.)

Krista, thank you so much for your encouragement, your kind praise, and most of all, those tough questions you raise throughout the editing process. You really do pull the very best out of me, and I'm really, really grateful.

Of course, I must also give my profound thanks to the very best agent in the biz, one Mr. Jim McCarthy. Jim, there simply aren't words to describe how appreciative I am to you not only for giving me the best representation an author could ask for, but for being my good and faithful friend too. I adore you head to toe, sugar, and I thank you for always looking out for me.

Special thanks should also be given to my publicist, Kelly Galvin, who works tirelessly on my behalf. Kelly, this "nice" is for you!

And thank you also to my publisher, Beverly Horowitz, whose faith in this series has meant the world to me. I must also give praise to the marvelous artistic talents of my designer, Vikki Sheatsley, and cover artist Antonio Javier Caparo. Antonio, this latest cover knocked my socks off!

Personal thanks also go to my friends and family, but if I may single out just a few here who have graciously given their support or supplied some form of inspiration to this particular series, they would be Carl and Ruth Laurie; Mary Jane Humphreys; Elizabeth Laurie; Hilary Laurie; Betty and Pippa Stocking; Nora, Bob, and Mike Brosseau; Katie Coppedge; Dr. Jennifer Casey; Ingrid Brault; Thomas Robinson; and Karen Ditmars. I humbly and profusely thank you all.

ABOUT THE AUTHOR

When Victoria Laurie was eleven, her family moved from the United States to England for a year. She attended the American Community School at Cobham, and one day, while on a class field trip, she caught her first glimpse of the White Cliffs of Dover. Her trip to the cliffs, the year abroad, and her grandfather's stories of his childhood as an orphan left such an indelible impression on her that when she turned to a career as an author, she was compelled to write the Oracles of Delphi Keep series. *The Curse of Deadman's Forest* is the second book in this series. The first book, *Oracles of Delphi Keep*, is available from Delacorte Press.

You can visit Victoria at oraclesofdelphikeep.com.

Look for the next adventure
in the Oracles of Delphi Keep series,

QUEST FOR THE
SECRET KEEPER

YEARLING!

Looking for more great books to read?
Check these out!

- ❏ *All-of-a-Kind Family* by Sydney Taylor
- ❏ *Are You There God? It's Me, Margaret* by Judy Blume
- ❏ *Blubber* by Judy Blume
- ❏ *The City of Ember* by Jeanne DuPrau
- ❏ *Crash* by Jerry Spinelli
- ❏ *The Girl Who Threw Butterflies* by Mick Cochrane
- ❏ *The Gypsy Game* by Zilpha Keatley Snyder
- ❏ *Heart of a Shepherd* by Rosanne Parry
- ❏ *The King of Mulberry Street* by Donna Jo Napoli
- ❏ *The Mailbox* by Audrey Shafer

- ❏ *Me, Mop, and the Moondance Kid* by Walter Dean Myers
- ❏ *My One Hundred Adventures* by Polly Horvath
- ❏ *The Penderwicks* by Jeanne Birdsall
- ❏ *Skellig* by David Almond
- ❏ *Soft Rain* by Cornelia Cornelissen
- ❏ *Stealing Freedom* by Elisa Carbone
- ❏ *Toys Go Out* by Emily Jenkins
- ❏ *A Traitor Among the Boys* by Phyllis Reynolds Naylor
- ❏ *Two Hot Dogs with Everything* by Paul Haven
- ❏ *When My Name Was Keoko* by Linda Sue Park